D0629489

The Children of Hamelin

by
Norman Spinrad

Illustrated by Kent Bash

Tafford Publishing, Inc.
Houston

Tafford Publishing, Inc., P. O. Box 271804,
Houston, Texas 77277

ISBN 0-9623712-3-8
Library of Congress Catalog Card Number 90-71146

Printed in the United States of America
Printed on acid-free paper

Portions of this book were originally
serialized in slightly different forms
in *The Los Angeles Free Press* and *The Staff*.

The Children of Hamelin

1
Junk

Ted's broad, handsome face, across the kitchen table, seemed to blur in focus as he spoke, one of the few heroes of my youth seemed suddenly diminished, and I had to try very hard not to think of him as pathetic.

"Come on," I said, "two hundred dollars a month? Where you gonna get the bread? You'll have to give up eating."

Beside Ted, long-suffering Earth Mother Doris had a glazed intense look in her usually-soft-brown eyes that seemed way out of character. The two of them, snug in the kitchen of their messy East Side pad, suddenly reminded me of something I wanted to forget: those six months when Anne and I and smack were a cozy little threesome. *Two hundred dollars a month. Where you gonna get the bread? You'll have to give up eating. Memories—*

"Christ, that's trivial, man," Ted said with that old-time enthusiasm in his alive blue eyes. "Got my bike shop, gonna start painting again as soon as I can find the time, and Doris is making a hundred a week now. Fifty bucks a week between us is all it takes—look at it that way, Tom."

"Anyone shelling out fifty a week for therapy *really* should have his head examined," I said.

"Jeez, the Foundation isn't just *therapy*," Ted said, "it's a complete way of life. Harvey's really into something big."

"I'll bet he is. How many patients does he have?"

"*Members*, not patients. It's not that kind of thing."

"Whatever," I said. "How many?"

"Forty or fifty," Doris suddenly said in her soft sure voice. Yeah, it figured she would know. Looked like Ted was sucking her into this bag the way Anne had sucked me into the smack bag; she seemed to be at the point where she was about to stop doing it for him and was about to get hung up on the thing itself. Maybe she *wanted* to hear me put it down.

"Lessee," I said, "fifty suckers a month at a hundred a month per . . . is five thousand a month, sixty thousand a year. Yeah, I'd say old Harv is really into something big."

"Shit, you're thinking like a . . . " Ted caught himself short. Like a Great Dane puppy, Ted may have hurt a lot of people in the process of blindly doing his thing, but he never did it willingly, and there was guilt in his eyes for what he had been about to say. I smiled a genuine nonuptight smile because now I could afford it. That whole scene was over.

"Like a junkie," I said. "It doesn't uptight me—relax. Bet your ass I'm talking like a junkie—cause that's where *you're* at. This Harvey Brustein's got you hooked on his Foundation for Total Consciousness junk—and it seems like a pretty heavy habit, money-wise."

"Bull-*shit*, man! You're just putting it down because you're only half-conscious like everybody else. *That's* what Harvey's into. Total Psychotherapy isn't just something to make you not sick, it's the only way to wake up into Total Consciousness."

"I've heard that crap before," I said. "From various junkies. From Anne. Even from myself."

"Well sure! Junkies are looking for Total Consciousness too, just like everyone else deep inside. Difference is, heroin is the wrong place to look and the Foundation is the right place, is all."

I knew it was pointless to argue. Ted was sucked totally inside this latest bag, the way he had been sucked into Orgonomy, Macrobiotics, Scientology, Health Foods, Nudism, one total answer after another, always looking for the master key that would open all the doors. When I was nineteen and Ted was twenty-three, it mystified me. Ted had been everything that I wanted to be: tall, blond, built like a blacksmith when I was thin and wiry and medium-everything; had more chicks than he could handle (was even cheating on his second wife with his first); could write a little, paint a little, had a way with machinery, could play guitar and drums; was a center of the action in the circles we both moved in in the Village. So why should a cat who had everything going for him up front always be searching for some Cosmic All to give him what he had in the first place?

"Look, Tom," Doris said, "the Foundation is having an open party Friday night. Why don't you come with us and see for yourself?"

"A party in a looney-bin?"

"Christ, come on man, it's not just a *party*," Ted said. "Harvey's gonna give one of his lectures. It'll turn your life around. And there'll be chicks and beer and it's free."

Ted

Come on kid, I thought, the first one's on the house. It always is.
The first one is.

"Please," Doris said, and I thought I heard something plaintive in
it. Doris always had a funny thing for me I could never quite figure
out, not even sexual really, more like she sensed I felt a spectrum of
vibes Ted was blind to. Maybe she wanted to be saved, maybe she
wanted to see me put down this Harvey cat in the grand manner.
Maybe if I could turn her off it, she could wake Ted up. She'd done it
before . . . .

"Okay," I said. Maybe I *was* doing it for Doris. Maybe I was doing
it for Ted. Maybe I could pick up a chick there who was looking for
an answer and would find a better one in me than in Harvey Brustein—things were awfully dull lately.

Yeah, and maybe it was the challenge, too. I had been a strange
junkie when I was a junkie and I was a strange ex-junkie too—never
been so far into a bag that I pulled the hole in after me. When I finally
decided I had had it with smack, I just threw Anne out on her ass and
quit cold. A few days' agony and it was all over. I could do it because
I *knew* could do it. So maybe when this Foundation-junk was waved
under my nose, I had to dare a taste or wonder whether I was hung-
up in the ex-junkie bag—and heavy antismack is junk too, as you'll
know if you ever meet any Synanon types.

Or maybe I was looking for a different brand of junk, like Ted. It
comes in all shapes and sizes.

■　■　■　■　■　■　■　■　■　■　■

It was one of those stinking-cold New York November nights that
make you want to find a warm hole and crawl into it. Walking in the
dingy east Twenties with Ted and Doris, hunched forward in my toggle-coat, shivering, wanting only to get from point A to point B as
quickly as possible, was all too much like other nights, with Anne,
the whole slimy make-the-connection scene, shivers, damp, and all
the talk about the score to come. Always smack, smack, smack—we
ate it and slept it and talked about nothing else. Sometimes I think it
wasn't any real strength of character that finally made me chuck the
whole thing, but just the endless hassling and shivering and waiting
and the sheer stupid boredom—with Anne and pushers and junkies
with their endless junk-talk.

And now I was getting the same scam from Ted and only the

name of the junk was different: "Man, really into something . . . no phonies . . . you can feel it, how the people who've been around longer are really into it . . . really lay it on you . . . Total Consciousness . . . Harvey says . . . where it's really at . . . ."

Just a cold, shivering, going-to-meet-the-Man drag. Endless dank streets and endless junkie gibbering. Put me back in the last place in the world I wanted to be. Total Consciousness, ultimate reality— crap! Any junkie knows where all that ultimate reality shit is at: like death is the ultimate reality and when your nerves are scraped raw coming down off junk, you can't help remembering that and the only thing that'll let you forget it is more junk. And it comes in all shapes and sizes.

So it was really a relief when we stopped outside an old loft building with a small-but-fancy brass plate beside a plain metal door that said *Foundation for Total Consciousness*. Ted pressed a buzzer set into the doorframe, there was a hesitation, then the doorlock buzzed back and Ted pushed the door open. System designed to keep undesirable terminal junkies from flopping in the hallway, dig?

Up a long flight of stairs, getting warmer as we ascended, and party-noises drifting down the stairwell from the open door at the second floor landing, almost as if old Harv had planned it that way. Ted led us out of the cold and into the warm like a trapper stomping into the Malamute Saloon.

Into a long, narrow, dimly-lit hallway lined with closed doors, and way down at the far end, yellow light and the vibes of a big room filled with people.

Suddenly a woman emerged from behind one of the doors (sounds of plumbing in action, must've been the john); maybe forty or so, nothing figure in a schoolteacher dress, black hair in a bun, a face like your Aunt Clara.

"Ted!" she shouted, gave him a big hug, grabbed for his crotch— but so uptight you knew she would've fainted if Ted hadn't moved aside and made her hand close on air. But you knew Ted *would* step aside like the whole thing was choreographed.

"Ida, you dirty old nympho, you!" Ted made a grab for her ass, which, of course, also missed its mark.

Lo, how the mighty have fallen! I thought, looking sidewise at Doris who had stuck with Ted through endless *real* numbers like this which had ended up with Ted off somewhere balling the lady in question. Doris, though, was smiling like a smug female Buddha, sensing that this was just a walk-through, a castrated, let-hubby-have-his-little-fantasy scene. Doris was secure. I suppose it should have been groovy—but it was more like something had died.

"Ida, this is Tom Hollander," Ted said. "A friend of mine from way back."

"Welcome to the Foundation," Ida said. "If you're an old friend of Ted's, you can see what a difference the Foundation has made even better than we can. I hope you'll ... *dig the scene.*"

I choked back something nastier, said: "Main thing I figure I'll *dig* is the free beer."

Ida grimaced, scandalized. Ted gave me a vaguely dirty look. Doris seemed to be making an effort not to be amused.

"Harvey isn't here yet," Ida said, deciding to ignore the heathen. It figured. The Man is never on time.

■ ■ ■ ■ ■ ■ ■ ■ ■ ■ ■

I must admit that the big room at the far end of the hall was kind of cozy. Very floor-oriented: a scattering of folding chairs, a table at one end with a lot of beer cans and a bowl of potato chips on it, musty yellow light from a ceiling fixture, a low dais against the far wall with a single folding chair on it looking like an empty throne, the floor and the dais completely covered with dusty-beige institutional carpeting.

It was pretty crowded, people sprawled on the floor or standing around in clots, something over thirty altogether. An odd assortment of loser types: City College cats in clean Levis and skirts and peasant blouses; East Villagers in raunchier editions of the same suit; chicks in mumus; some middle-aged housefraus; one token Black in an Ivy League suit; seedy semi-Madison Avenue types; a hawk-faced biddy in a too-sexy black velvet dress; a red-nosed Irishman in a shiny blue suit with cuffs on the pants. Like that. An uptight, Subway kind of crowd.

Ted stomped into all this—in his red-checked lumberjack shirt, straight blond hair, black chinos and combat boots—a big smiling figure larger than life, drawing people into his wake like a whirlpool, thumping guys on the back, hugging chicks: a typical Ted Clayton party entrance. But there was something ... *off* about it. The kind of parties we used to make in the old days were open-house, bring-your-own-bottle-or-grass, drum-thumping unfoldings of the infinitely possible; this was a turned-inward, closed, almost family kind of scene and the back-slapping, girl-hugging, grinning stuff that used to come off as someone vital making a grand entrance seemed like the arrival of Good Old Uncle Charlie. Instant turn-off.

Then faces and names in a meaningless blur as Ted introduced me around—"Mike O'Brien" (the Irishman in the out of date suit), "Hilda Something-or-other" (the creature in the velvet dress), "George Blum" (an average professional student), "Myra" (a blond that might've been interesting if she sweated off about twenty pounds of blubber and did something about her acne)—and then Ted was off sitting on the floor near the dais engaged in some silly-ass conversation about somebody named Rhoda's penis-envy.

The beer seemed to be the only honest game in town, so I went over to the table, opened a can, found Doris standing next to me.

"You're really paranoid about the Foundation, aren't you?" she said.

"I'm not paranoid, it's just that everyone's out to get me."

Doris' full lips began a Buddha-smile. She caught herself, looked solemn, said: "What's that supposed to mean?"

"It means that paranoia is the only sane reaction to this scene," I said. "This is Losersville—one big bummer."

"Harvey says that hostility is the natural reaction of the average individual to an environment of increased consciousness," she said like a walking textbook (but something in her eyes gave me the feeling *she* knew how she sounded too).

"Aw, come off it, Doris, stop putting me on! You're not really swallowing all this crap. You got too much horsesense."

"It's . . . it's kept Ted out of other people's beds," she said softly.

"Horsesense or not, that makes wifesense."

"You mean old Harv lays on that Judeo-Christian ethic?"

"No . . . funny thing is, Harvey says it's natural for a man who isn't totally conscious to act out his fantasies. But since we've been coming here, Ted . . . hasn't gone near anyone else."

Maybe it was a touch of the old junkie cruelty, maybe just raw male reaction to the castrator's knife.

"And how much have *you* been getting off him lately?" I said.

Direct hit! But the twinge of anguish in her eyes was turned off before she spoke. "Harvey says . . . Harvey says it's a . . . necessary transitional state . . . a decrease in sexual energy while the choice of object is in the process of being transferred from fantasy to reality . . . "

"In other words, old Harv has messed up Ted's head to the point where he can't get it up."

"Tom . . . "

"Look, let's can the crap! I've been there, baby. Didn't make it with Anne for weeks at a time. Know why? Because I was a junkie, that's why. Crawled up my own navel and dragged my dick in after me. Junk cuts your balls off, and this Foundation *is* junk. It's a rotten, evil scene."

"Tom . . . you don't understand, you really don't. Wait till you hear Harvey." It was obviously the last word; she started looking around for an excuse to be elsewhere. She opened two cans of beer, said: "Ted wants some beer," and wandered away across the room.

I felt cruel and stupid and futile. I had told her the hardest thing any male can tell to any female, and all I had gotten was "Wait till you hear Harvey." I took a drink of beer—it was lukewarm, of course—and studied the crowd, trying to spot at least one chick worth talking to. Anything to kill time—which was where the whole scene was at. Waiting for the Man.

Over in a corner of the room, a girl in a green sack dress was sitting alone on the floor, seemingly just watching and waiting, detached from the whole scene the way I was—I hoped. Long brown hair, regular features, nice skin, a decent figure. Nothing spectacular, but the best action around at the moment.

■ ■ ■ ■ ■ ■ ■ ■ ■ ■ ■

So I crossed the room and sat down next to her. Big frightened doe-eyes and she nibbled her lower lip, trying to ignore me.

"Been a member here long?" I asked.

"I'm not a member yet," she said in a Bronx-intellectual voice just this side of being unpleasant. "I'm . . . just a guest." She sounded positively apologetic about it.

"Well, then meet a fellow tourist," I said. "Tom Hollander."

"Linda Kahn. Have you met Harvey Brustein yet?"

"I've been spared that dubious pleasure so far."

"Why are you so hostile?" she said belligerently.

"*Hey* . . . I'm just trying to be friendly."

"I mean about Harvey Brustein. Myra says he's a great human being, he's helped her more than any other therapist she's tried. Why are you putting down someone you've never met?"

Earth Mother Doris

"Why are you defending someone you've never met?"

She bit her lip again. "Haven't you ever wanted to believe in something? Haven't you ever *needed* to believe in something? I've tried just about every kind of therapy there is . . . "

"What's your problem?"

"What?"

"Why therapy in the first place?"

She stared at me as if I were crazy. "If I knew the answer to that, I'd be halfway there, now wouldn't I?" she said.

"Sounds to me like you *dig* therapy."

"I . . . " she paused, considering, then looked at me almost as if I were a human being. "I never thought of it that way before. But yes . . . it . . . gives me a sense of being human, you know, real contact with other human beings. That's important, isn't it?"

"Therapy is your idea of human contact? Telling stuff to some shrink that you should be telling to your lover?"

"I . . . I've never had what you'd call a lover. That's one of the reasons I'm in therapy."

"Or vice versa."

"I don't understand . . . "

"Look, if what you're looking for is real human contact, how about splitting with me right now? Forget therapy and pick up on a human being for a change."

"You're disgusting!" she said "Can't think about anything but sex, can you?"

"I said something about sex?"

"Didn't you?"

"You ever been on junk, baby?"

"Certainly not!"

I had had it. "That's what you think," I said. She stared at me for a long moment; furious but not quite sure what she was furious at.

Fortunately, at that point there was some kind of commotion at the doorway to the hall. A lot of people seemed to be clustering around someone I couldn't see. Ted was looking around the room. He spotted me, yelled: "Tom! Tom! Over here!" It was a convenient out. "Later," I grunted, getting up and walking toward the tumult.

Ted grabbed me by the arm, pulled me into the mystic circle at the center of which was a short, balding man of about fifty in a faded white tieless shirt and baggy gray pants with a soft, pallid pudding-face and watery mild eyes behind brown-rimmed glasses—just about the grayest cat you could ever hope to meet.

"Harvey," Ted said, "this is Tom Hollander, I told you about."

This was the great Harvey Brustein? The Black Villain or the Living Buddha, depending on which side you were on? This . . . *nothing?* This . . . this schmoo?

"Uh . . . yes . . ." Harvey said in a bland dentist's voice. "Pleased to meet you . . . uh . . . Tom . . ."

"Uh, yeah," I said. It was all wrong. A cat who looked like a scruffy accountant had all these people enthralled? How did he do it? How could Ted and Doris take this creep seriously?

"Well . . . uh . . ." Harvey said. "We . . . ah might as well get started."

He made his way to the dais, sat down on the folding chair. People began to settle themselves on the floor. I sat down on the floor near the back of the room with Ted and Doris. Good old Linda sat a good distance away. In a few minutes of shuffling around, the whole floor was covered with silent acolytes waiting eagerly for pearls of wisdom to fall from the mouth of the gray little guru in the folding chair.

■ ■ ■ ■ ■ ■ ■ ■ ■ ■ ■

Old Harv fished in a paper shopping bag under his chair, shuffled some papers, put them back. It got quieter and quieter. Harvey took off his glasses, rubbed the bridge of his nose, put them back. People hunkered forward. Ted's face was tense, his blue eyes strangely blank. Linda nibbled her lower lip. I began to take old Harv a little more seriously; he was doing that old Man number—make 'em wait—and he was doing it well.

Harvey opened his mouth. Everyone tensed. "Ashtray?" he said.

Almost an audible moan. He was really stretching it out, seconds into minutes, minutes into hours, making us wait, making the very corpuscles of our blood hunger for that dirty old surge. Old Harv knew his business, yes!

Someone handed him an ashtray. He put it down beside his chair. He took a pack of Winstons out of his shirt picket. It took him a full ten seconds to get one out and stick it in his mouth. Uptight! Uptight! What a pusher old Harv would've made! Everyone was twitching. Harvey reached into his shirt pocket for matches; they weren't there. Into the shopping bag. Shuffle, shuffle. Pack of matches. Pulled off a match. Struck it. Nothing happened. Jesus! Struck it again. Another match. This one lit. Sucked smoke. Exhaled. Sighed. Crossed legs.

"Why can't you all relax?" Harvey said in a soft, totally humorless voice.

Christ, was that whole number *planned?*

"Human beings consider themselves the most highly evolved form of life on Earth. A dog can relax. A cat can relax. Even a lizard can relax. All the way, thinking sweet no-thoughts. So why can't you do what a dog or a cat or a lizard can? Why can't you relax?"

Harvey took a long drag on his cigarette, drawing out the silence. A simple trick—uptight people, then tell them they're uptight. I tried to relax, just to show the bastard—but try *not* to think of a red-assed monkey. See the mind-game he was playing?

"You think too much, that's your problem," Harvey said. "You watch your own minds. An animal doesn't do that. An animal experiences its environment directly. It feels imperatives and it acts or feels no imperatives and relaxes. Animals can be frustrated, but if you eliminate the frustrating condition, the animal relaxes. Because animals have no time-sense, no worlds of memory. Animals experience no interface between inner and outer realities, no ego watching itself and remembering old frustrations, anticipating new ones. No hang-ups on things that have no present reality. Are you animals? Wouldn't you like to be animals?"

He paused again. I found myself drifting in a half-remembered dream . . . calm . . . blank . . . not caring . . . no hang-ups . . . like lying on the bed with Anne for hours, not moving . . . swathed in the soft sweet cotton batting of heroin . . . yes, there had been good times too that I had forgotten . . . when we were lush and torpid sunning ourselves like lizards on a rock in the timeless tropical sun . . . .

"Sure," Harvey said, "you're animals. But animals-plus. Plus that cerebral cortex that makes a man something more complex than an animal. What's in that lump of gray jelly? You are. The you that thinks of itself as `me'. Ego, memory, time-sense, fears, hopes, hang-ups. Total Psychotherapy concentrates on that cerebral cortex. It's all we have to worry about—the rest of us is pure animal, continuous with the environment."

He paused again, took another drag. I was beginning to understand why everyone around me was leaning forward, hanging on his words. Harvey was into something all right, something big. I found myself wanting to believe . . . in what? But I was also afraid . . . of what?

"Scary, isn't it?" Harvey said, as if reading my mind. "It's scary because it means that you're all unhappy, every one of you, simply because you're human beings. It's obvious. You all have memories. You've all experienced frustrations. Remember? Remember being a fetus floating in an environment designed for perfection . . . you were an animal then. And then you were ejected from paradise and everything since has been a downhill slide because it's less than the perfection we all remember. So in times of stress, we curl up into a fetal position, don't we? Don't we all love a good dreamless sleep? Because we're like animals then—no interface between external and internal realities, between desire and fulfillment, between the me and the it. No ego watching itself. The truth we all refuse to face is that the thing we love most—our `me-ness'—is the source of all unhappiness. The goal of the Foundation for Total Consciousness is first to face the truth and then to eliminate the interface, to become totally conscious not *of* the environment, but *in* the environment. Like an animal."

I felt as if I were alone in the room with Harvey, as if he were speaking directly to me, to a place inside me that was void. No longer did he seem gray or trivial. He was calling to something in me but somehow not of me. A blind something that yearned to throw itself into the arms of the infinite . . . the infinite *what?* There seemed to be something I should remember . . . had to remember, or be lost forever. And the feeling that *this had all happened before* . . . .

"Do you understand what I'm saying?" Harvey said. "Can you face it? What do we all fear the most? *Death.* But an animal doesn't fear death. Because it is the ego, that interface between the me and the it within us, which fears death—not the death of the body, but its own annihilation. Look at the promise of immortality upon which Christianity is based. The immortality not of the body but of the ego, the soul. *That* is the death we cannot face, the annihilation of the interface between external and internal realities. That's why you all need Total Psychotherapy, whether you've been told you're neurotic or not. Because the so-called normal personality is the disease itself. That artificial construct is the source of all unhappiness—and it defends itself with all the psychic resources at our command. So we must defeat our own innermost selves in order to be free. That's why only *Total* Psychotherapy can free us from the tyranny of our selves. You can't do it yourselves—because it is the *self* which must be defeated!"

And suddenly I understood. I understood it all. Harvey *was* pushing junk; he was pushing the very essence of junk, the void inside the needle, the end to pain and frustration and caring, the thing that makes so many terminal junkies finally give themselves the O.D., the last big surge, Dose Terminal.

Harvey was pushing the very soul of junk. And every junkie knows deep down that the soul of junk is death.

Oh yes, there was nothing trivial about what Harvey was offering. The straight, uncut stuff. And there were Ted and Doris, my friends beside me, and they were hooked, sucking at the teats of Kali, main-lining death.

A whole roomfull of terminal junkies, *really* terminal, and the bland pudding-face of the creature on the folding chair was a face I knew all too well: the Man, Anti-Life, the Sweet Destroyer, Prince of the Final Darkness.

Something human and screaming inside me moved my body and my mouth and I found myself on my feet shouting: "I know you, man, oh Jesus, I know you!"

A whole mood shattered. The people on the floor were looking at me as if I were crazy, I mean *conventionally* crazy. Linda Kahn's lips were curled in a grimace of disgust; Ted and Doris shook their heads at each other. And Harvey ... Harvey was just a gray little man, not ... not ....

"We'd like to hear your feelings," Harvey said in that other voice of his, the dentist's voice. And reality flipped over again for me: I looked at Harvey and saw the schmoo-mask. But behind it lurked the other reality: it *was* a mask, for wasn't I standing in a room full of people who were being sucked dry by what looked like a nonentity? Maybe he *was* just a dirty little quack, maybe it *was* just money to him—but that didn't matter, he was pushing death and they were buying. Some pushers are on the stuff and some wouldn't touch it. It doesn't matter to the clientele.

"Can't you see it?" I said "Are you all deaf? Didn't you hear the man? He's telling you to groove behind death ...."

Blank, vacant stares. Ted and Doris, my oldest, closest friends, and they didn't really hear a word I was saying—they were hooked like all the rest.

I was just making a public asshole out of myself. You can't argue with junkies, not about their junk you can't.

"You see?" Harvey said. "That's a very typical reaction. Your ego won't accept the necessity for its own annihilation. But your hostility

The Foundation

is actually a healthy sign—you've seen the truth and accepted it on a deep level and so you're afraid. That's the first step. Let me help you take the next one. Ask yourself: `Is my reaction that of a happy, tranquil man? Don't I want peace? Real peace . . . .'"

"Shut up! Shut up! I told you, I've seen you a thousand times in . . . ."

Christ, I thought, I'm starting to gibber! I've got to get out of here or . . . or . . . A terrible fear came over me: that knowing what Harvey was, knowing what lurked in his therapy sessions and mutual assassination groups, I would still be unable to turn my back on it; the fear of the ex-junkie that he can never really turn his back on junk.

I looked down at Ted, at Doris. Glazed junkie-eyes looked back.

"I'm getting out of here," I told them. "Now. Come with me."

"Tom . . . " Ted said, his voice full of genuine soothing concern, "take it easy man . . . ."

I looked around the room; empty eyes stared back with a loathsome pity. I looked at Linda Kahn; she looked away. I felt alone, terribly, finally alone. I turned, stepped over their bodies, making for the door and the long hallway back to reality. As I stepped into the relative darkness of the hallway, I heard Harvey's voice behind me: "Don't worry, Ted, it's a natural reaction. I think he'll be back . . . ."

Alone in the hallway, it was an effort not to break into a run.

■ ■ ■ ■ ■ ■ ■ ■ ■ ■ ■

Outside, it was cold and it was raining. I shivered. I felt the dank rain soaking my hair. I was cold and alone in the middle of the night.

And up there, in the warmth, were people who shared something I was not a part of, who had something to believe in—and who wanted me. I really believed that: they truly wanted me.

So had Anne.

Chilled to the bone, I began walking downtown in the rain, wondering what would happen if I met a pusher.

2
The Girl In The Rain

The roach-end of New York: Second Avenue between the beginnings of the classy East Side in the upper Thirties and the outskirts of the East Village at Fourteenth Street after twelve on a November night in the rain. Gray and lifeless as an IND Subway tunnel—an open air Subway-street, one-way downtown. With the staggered lights, the traffic in the gutter shoots past you in a blur like the A-Train Express and the sidewalks are almost as desolate as an empty Subway station—hulking gray tenements, silent lightless groceries and fruit stores, garbage decaying in puddles along the curb--and the few people you do see are super-uptight, because who's walking on a street like this except a mugger or a pervert or some kinda dope-fiend?

So why was I walking downtown in the rain with eleven bucks in my pocket on one of the easiest streets in town to get a cab on and with the Second Avenue bus running all the way to St. Mark's? Guess old Harv would call it a masochistic scene. Screw old Harv! What it really was was a playback of one of my old junkie numbers. (Junkies always feel they're doing everything for at least the second time and usually they're right.) How many times had I walked this street or a street like it (with or without Anne), having missed a connection for one reason or another with exactly the necessary $3.00 (usually in dimes and quarters) for a minimal bag in my pocket and afraid to blow a lousy 20 cents on the bus because I just *might* run into a dealer somehow in which case the difference between $3.00 and $2.80 would be all the difference in the world and you can never tell, I *might* run into a dealer, has been known to happen, better not take the chance.

So that was the place good old Harv had shoved my head back into. Because if I didn't play that mind-game, I would remember I had $11, would hail a cab, and once I got into it, would I be able to give the cabbie my home address or would I make it back to the Foundation where I knew I could score *something* to get me through the night? Old Harv expected me to come back, and I didn't want to find out he was right the easy way. Yeah, he had gotten to me with his mind-game: at least he had started me playing evil mind-games with myself again.

Therefore: walking home in the rain on Bummer Avenue. I remembered another mind-game. Once, when I hadn't been able to score any smack, I had gotten really bombed on some awful combination—Romilar and speed or something equally foul—and had to walk a bummer street to get from *here* to *there*, and I felt I just couldn't cut the trip between. So somehow (I mean I was *really* stoned) I had turned my mind off in one place, become a mindless walking robot for the duration of the trip, then woken my mind up again at my destination, thus cutting out the experience and the memory-track of the trip between. As far as my head was concerned, it was exactly as if I had teleported like some science fiction superman out of A. E. Van Vogt.

A handy trick, and I tried to make it work now. But I couldn't. I was all too straight, stuck on Second Avenue, in the cold, in the rain, on a bummer, thinking: "If this is reality, I'll take vanilla."

Pissed-off, too. At whatever was wrong with me or the scenes I made that I always ended up defining my sanity in negatives: didn't stay in the old parental looney-bin so I could finish college; didn't let myself end up as a terminal junkie with Anne, whatever gutter she was flopping in now; didn't let myself buy Harvey's sweet shit; didn't get into a cab which might've taken me back to the Foundation.

What *was* wrong with me? What if I had made the positive decisions? Stuck it out at home. Finished college. Never left that Flatbush never-never land. Never kicked Anne out. Stayed a junkie. Given myself to Harvey and his Total Consciousness. Where would I be now? Living on Long Island married to a plastic virgin from Vassar? O.D.ed in a doorway with Anne? Hooked on Harvey Brustein?

No, the hell of it was that every damned choice I had made had been the right one. And where had all those cagey right choices gotten me?

Soaked and cold walking alone down Second Avenue in the middle of the night.

Nearing Fourteenth Street: to my left, blocks of red brick housing project, a universe of beery Post Office Foremen and their big-assed housefraus and cherubic brats. Yeah, and I saw through that stage-set, too, the way I saw through my parents, saw through college, saw through junk, saw through my silly-ass job, saw through Ted and Doris and their little tin god, saw through every fucking thing, dammit! Just once, I'd like to look out through the eyeholes in my skull and have something greater and wiser and more beautiful than Tom Hollander look back.

Fourteenth Street—border zone. Below, the outskirts of the East Village. To the east, the street was the frontier between the housing project and some world's champion Puerto Rican slums on the south, all the way to the East River. To the west, Fourteenth Street was Puerto Rican Disneyland: Spanish movie houses, Army-Navy stores, a couple of slimy Chinese restaurants, pawn shops, *cuchifriterias*, cruddy Nedickses, an old movie house converted to a supermarket— "Hamburger 35 cents" sharing billing on the marquee with "Maxwell House Coffee 59 cents lb."

Standing on the northwest corner, waiting like a good little citizen for the light to change, I played another mind-game with myself: the choice game. I could turn east toward the project and the Road to Levittown, west toward El Bario and the Proletariat, north back to old Harv and Total Consciousness of the Total Void, or south into the East Village and what passed for home. Existential choice, dig?

Sure . . . .

Surprise, surprise, when the light turned green, I took destiny in my hands and opted for the East Village and home.

■ ■ ■ ■ ■ ■ ■ ■ ■ ■ ■

Still, the scene really *does* change when you cross Fourteenth Street. There are people who say they never go north of Fourteenth and they mean it. Even on a crummy night like this, Second Avenue starts to come alive between Fourteenth and St. Mark's. The weather kept the street scene down, but on those six blocks, you've got the Metro, a cheapo movie house, a library, two all-night candy stores, a brace of head shops, a late-night delicatessen, an Old Polacks' Home, and assorted floating Villagey shops.

At the corner of St. Mark's and Second, I felt almost like a human being again. South, the lights of Ratner's and the appetizing stores frequented by a weird mixture of ethnic old ladies and epicurean heads. To the east was home, and to the west the St. Mark's MacDougal Street East: head shops, funky little greasy spoons, marginal bookstores, button-and-poster shops, the Electric Circus, a flux of borderline discotheques and coffee houses, and a rash of tourist-trap boutiques. And quite a street scene on better nights than this.

■ ■ ■ ■ ■ ■ ■ ■ ■ ■ ■

I could go home, grab something at Rappaport's, see if Roy Ellern and that crowd of his were at the Dom, make the rounds, or even make it further east to the hard-core ethnic head scene and maybe cop some pot from Tash or something like that. But all those scenes, I suddenly realized, had been bringing me down for the past couple of months; my mind had started to drift through those crowds like a ghost, or vice versa. Still, I did sometimes make them and probably would again, so when I crossed Second Avenue and decided to call it a night, I had at least the illusion of free choice—which seemed to be my hang-up at the moment.

Ah, but all this is illusion, for on the other side of Second Avenue, standing in the doorway of a closed drugstore (somehow prophetic) I met The Girl in the Rain.

A set-piece, like something out of a Hollywood fake of a New Wave film: a slim chick in an old peacoat ten sizes too big and black plastic zippered boots. A patina of dew on her pale skin, overflow from her long, wild, rain-soaked black hair. No more than nineteen. No make-up. Huge, dark doe-eyes. And a smile that would've melted an Eighth Street fag turned on me like a spotlight, telling me in no uncertain terms that I was in her stage-center.

"Hello," she said, in a sweet little dirty-girl voice. "Don't you know who I am?"

Awkward pause; then she laughed, cooling my embarrassment, *just so.*

"Haven't you ever met a girl in the rain before?" she said.

I wanted to cry; I wanted so much to be wherever she was at but I couldn't find the words to cut in. It didn't seem to matter; her smile never wavered.

"That's who I am," she said. "Your Girl in the Rain." And she executed an incredible little bow.

But I mean, she made me *believe.* A number like that from a chick like that with even a hint of sarcasm for my paranoia to wedge into, and I would've been off into the galloping nasties. But whatever else this girl was, she radiated sincerity; she was offering herself and she made me believe it. And it was like slow pot suddenly hitting—I found myself going with the moment and to hell with the unreality. She made me believe I was a groovy cat who deserved to be sent a Girl in the Rain.

So I took her hand and instead of snuggling up to me or something else slightly off, she just took my other hand and we drank up each other's eyes at double arm's length. Every move was . . . *just so.* She had eyes you wanted to dive into and float around in forever. Magic! Yeah, magic on a bummer November night in the rain . . . .

■ ■ ■ ■ ■ ■ ■ ■ ■ ■ ■

I smiled like a kid on Christmas morning, finally managed to say: "What have I done to deserve this?"

"No one gets a Girl in the Rain because he deserves one," she said with a weird fragile solemnity. "A Girl in the Rain happens because you need her to happen."

"And how did you know I needed you?"

"I saw it in your eyes. Trust me. I trust you. Haven't you been waiting for a Girl in the Rain to happen to you?"

"I suppose I have," I said. "And you've been standing here all night just waiting for me?"

"No. I've been waiting here for the right someone to happen to. I just feel like happening to someone tonight. I'm the Girl in the Rain and you're my Man in the Rain, and if you ask any more questions, I'll turn back into a pumpkin."

I just smiled. "Tom," I said.

"Robin."

Unwillingly, I found myself remembering something Ted had once said: "Robin is a name girls give themselves." *Retro me, satanis!*

"Is there someplace we can go? Rain is beautiful for meeting, but not for making love."

"Two blocks down."

Suddenly she was ten years old. She bounced up and down. "Let's run!" she bubbled, and she yanked me forward into an all-out sprint. And we ran down St. Mark's, two kids laughing and panting hand in hand through the falling rain.

Although my apartment was on the fifth floor, it was still the best pad I had ever had, and I must admit I was kind of sneakily house-proud. The bathtub was in the bathroom and even had a shower; bedroom, living room and kitchen all had neat paint jobs and the furnishings were Salvation-Army-class.

So I gave thanks to the $100 a week I was knocking down at the good old Dirk Robinson Literary Agency as I raced Robin up the stairs, grateful that the magic of this moment was not about to be exorcised by the kind of seedy mess I used to inhabit in the Bad Old Days.

Panting, soaking and giggling, we reached the fifth floor landing. The pangs in my lungs, the wet clinging of my clothes to my body, the soggy tangle of hair over my forehead—as I led her to the door to my apartment, they made me hyper-aware of my flesh: the grace of my muscles under my skin, the blood moving down my thighs, the water dribbling down over my face. For the first time in many moons, I really noticed that my body was *alive*.

As we stood hand in hand at the threshold, I felt some conventional gesture was required. I started to draw her to me, but with the slightest widening of her eyes, a playful tensing of her palm in mine, a hint of irony in that overwhelming smile, she told me no, this was her show, and my timing was a little off, and just let it happen, baby.

So I unlocked the doorlock and the police-lock, swung the door open and the police-lock bar aside, and led her into the kitchen. The table and its clutter and the mess of dishes in the sink were barely visible in the light from the living room windows filtering past the bead curtain hanging in the doorway between kitchen and living room. Robin took one quick look around, seemed to grimace slightly, then wisely steered me through the bead curtain and into my own darkened living room.

I hit the wall switch and the orange-and-red-painted frosted globe I had put up over the bare ceiling fixture flooded the room with a fair imitation of firelight. I felt pretty smug about this room, having achieved true East Village Class here with a little of this and a little of that. The bamboo-matted floor and the plain white walls made the room look Japanese instead of just bare. Panels of colored cellophane glued to the windows hid the vista of fire escapes behind a stained-glass effect. Two old cots met at right angles in the corner furthest from the bedroom door and they were both covered with the same huge piece of black velvet I had copped somewhere, giving the effect of a giant sectional. In the center of the room and dominating it was a huge round red table (a Con Edison cable spool I had liberated and painted) with a pole-lamp growing up from the center hole like a brass tree. The stereo rig and record racks against the wall next to the

The Girl in the Rain

bedroom door were the only things in the room that were as expensive as they looked. The shelves of books beside them looked very intellectual, but were in fact mostly old science fiction paperbacks. And the warm orange light softened all the edges and hid the New York dust.

She took it all in without showing any surprise, which did little for my ego. But then she turned that smile on me, said simply: "Yes," took off my coat, tossed it to the floor with a grand gesture, gently pushed me to the section of couch by the windows, held finger to her lips, and with her peacoat still on, began rummaging through my records.

■ ■ ■ ■ ■ ■ ■ ■ ■ ■ ■

Let it happen, baby.

She finally came up with an early Ravi Shankar album, which seemed to fit the mood of the moment, and while I winced in agony for a minute, she put the record on the turntable, diddled with the controls, and sitar music set at very low volume barely textured the air.

She ruffled her soaked hair, then came across the room to me, moving with the music. Standing over me, she said, "Let's get comfortable," and unbuttoned the top button of her peacoat. She paused, seemed to change her mind about something.

And leaned over to me and unbuttoned my shirt. Then, putting her arms around my neck, she eased my arms out of the sleeves, and as she dropped the shirt to the floor, the tip of her tongue touched my ear briefly. Moving in a slow-motion dream, I started to take my undershirt off, but she shook her head, pulled my hands away, and kissed me very lightly on the lips as she took the undershirt off herself. And I finally got the strange, delicious message: *she* was going to undress *me*.

Let it happen, baby.

As she slid her hands down my naked chest, I felt turned on in a slow trance-like way I had never experienced before. I didn't have to make this chick, sell her anything, convince her to do anything, and there was nothing I had to prove. She wasn't going to let me have what I wanted; she was making me want what she wanted me to want, and then she would give it to me as a very special gift. And all I had to do was let it happen.

Took off my shoes. Socks. Tickled the soles of my bare feet. I could taste what was going to come but I had no reason to be in a hurry—a special sweetness I had never felt before.

Now she stood away from me and took off her boots; her legs were slim and naked beneath that silly peacoat she still had on. She undid the second button on the peacoat.

"Stand up," she said.

I stood up.

She undid my belt, slid my pants over my ankles, and I stood poised before her in underpants stretched taut before me like a sail before a full following wind. The moment hung . . . and once again, she did the perfect, delicious unexpected:

She sank to her knees. She toyed with the elastic of my shorts. And again the unexpected, more beautiful than even my best anticipating fantasy could be; instead of taking them off, her voice went through me like the touch of flesh: "Please, make yourself naked for me."

God! Her kneeling before me like that, eating me up with those eyes, and asking me to take off my pants for her as if it were a most special favor I could do for her . . . I never felt more wanted in my life.

Diving into her eyes, I took off the underpants. Her eyes never left mine as she ran her tongue slowly up my cock from root to tip like a little girl who had just unwrapped a Christmas lollypop; I felt man enough and big enough to fuck the universe!

But just that once—then, like a cat, she was on her feet, whirled around, leapt to the top of the table, and stood there, her hands on her hips, smiling down on me she began to unbutton the peacoat; beneath it was nothing but pale skin. Under the coat, she was completely naked. Where was I? Not in my own pad . . . This was a thing out of dreams.

She threw the coat to the floor and stood proudly nude before me—pale bruisable skin, wild black hair, small upright breasts with tiny nipples jauntily erect. I stood locked in stasis, afraid to shatter the magic of the dream.

Suddenly, incredibly, she leapt from the table like an uncoiling jungle cat and knocked me to the floor beneath her. At once tender and savage, she sunk tiny feral teeth into my shoulder and began caressing the insides of my thighs with a child's gentle hands.

I was gone: the thinking machine behind my eyes shorted out and my consciousness existed only at the interface where skin met skin.

Rolling and touching and biting, flesh melting into flesh, the taste of her, the taste of me, we seemed to merge in a tangled fusing of nerve-endings and moans . . . .

And my cock was thrust and sucked down a long warm tunnel of total pleasure that seemed to plunge on down forever into the secret roots of the universe . . . .

Motion enveloped me, mine and hers melding, we became the motion, cosmic motion of creation, slow-rolling breakers of an immense roiling sea . . . .

A wave of pure sensation devoured me, I was the wave beginning its rise at the soles of my feet, sweeping upward majestically, all the time in the world, building and building and building . . . .

And the cresting was a flash into timeless being, a merging with something infinite and oceanic, a thing beyond pleasure—for that flicker of eternity I think I really ceased to be.

And afterward, we went into the bedroom and cuddled together like innocent children. There was no need for marathons or fantastic feats. We had tasted an instant of perfection; the night was complete.

And there was nothing that had to be proved.

3

"Do Me Like You Did the Night Before ... "

Waking up on a cold New York morning is a massive bummer—because of the heat. Steam heat. If you turn the radiator off at night, you wake up in Siberia; if you leave it on, it's the Sahara: a choking, steam-seared stuffiness that glues your eyelids shut and fills your nose and throat with sawdust. Since I hate the cold worse than the heat, the first memory I have of Saturday morning is the feeling of being smothered in burning camel fur.

Pry one eyelid open. The other. A kind of green reptilian light leaking into the bedroom around the edges of the dark green shade pulled down over the single window. Lying on my back, my head on the pillow . . . a weight on my chest . . . ? A girl's head . . . ?

Click! Awake! Robin's body was half on top of me, her head face down on my chest so that all I could see was tangled black hair. She was breathing rhythmically, deep asleep. Warm, heavy, relaxed. I remembered the night before—but not the way you usually remember the night before: with the memory somehow becoming more important than the thing itself. The memory had no details (though there was no blank); I remembered that something beautiful had happened to me, remembered what it had been, but the reality of it was fuzzy, the way your memory of what you did when you were really stoned is somehow unconvincing.

But the weight of her against me, the warmth of her breath on my chest, that was convincing. There *was* a girl named Robin in bed with me. There *had* been something magic between us; certainly not love, but for the first time since Anne a place that had been dead inside of me was now alive. The place that believes in the core of the possible unfolding. Robin was an unknown, but an unknown filled with the infinite possible. And I was hungry to explore the limits of whatever was there.

But at the moment, all I was was a human pillow. That was okay while I was asleep, but at the moment it was a big drag. I wanted to meet her again. What to do? Wait it out till she woke up? What a drag! Wake her up? Gauche. Selfish. Would probably piss her off—if she woke up first and did it to me, *I* would not be amused.

Clearly, the situation demanded unfair, Machiavellian tactics. So: I closed my eyes, skewed by head at a crazy angle, began moaning gently in my "sleep." Then I abruptly rolled half over, tossing her head off my chest and onto the bed. I waited till I heard her mutter, sensed that she was awake.

Then I opened my eyes like an innocent babe. Her head was propped up on one hand. She was looking at me somewhat fuzzily, but not in anger. Mission accomplished.

"Hello," I said sexily.

"Uh . . . " she grunted. "Hi . . . uh . . . Tom?"

"Right . . . *Robin*. We do remember each other's names."

"Uh huh."

I stroked her hair. No effect. Her eyes were just a big as they had been the night before, but now they were just *eyes*. Something was missing.

She looked around the room, orienting herself, I guess. Just the bed, an old dresser, a closet and a night-table with a phone, a clock and some odds and ends on it. She didn't seem terribly impressed.

I moved to cup her face in my hands, but she kind of pulled away. She kissed my left nipple—a dry, mechanical gesture—then kicked off the covers, rolled away from me.

"I'm hungry, love," she said. "Haven't eaten since . . . whenever . . . ."

And she bolted out of bed, just like that, stood in the clear space at the foot of the bed, obviously looking for something. The same naked body—nice, slim legs, flat belly, sweet ass and all—but somehow it just didn't seem to add up to what it had the night before. Like *something* was gone.

"Uh . . . where are my clothes?" she asked. "In the other room?"

"All you had on was a coat and boots."

A blank look for a moment. Then an awful, flat "Oh WoW" that suddenly made her seem for an instant like a forty-year-old broad in a young girl's body.

I was really out of it. This just wasn't the same chick. I had so much to ask her and no way to begin.

So when she left the bedroom, I just got dressed in a bummer kind of daze and made for the bathroom, which was off the kitchen. She was standing there, between the plastic-topped metal table and the refrigerator, peering unhappily inside, still naked. She turned to me, and now she seemed like a pathetically shrewd sixteen-year-old war-waif.

"Nothing in here but frozen food and a little milk and some jelly and uh ... one egg ... " she said in a small voice. "And I'm so damn *hungry* . . . ."

"Yeah, well we'll go get some breakfast at Rappaport's."

"Uh ... I don't have any bread right now ... could you ... er . . . ?" In an awful kind of panhandling voice.

My turn to say "Oh WoW." I knew chivalry was dead, but this was too much!

"What the hell do you think I am?" I said. "Don't worry, I'll stuff you silly. Lox and eggs and—"

"Hey, you *are* a groovy cat!" she cried, throwing her arms around me, squeezing me briefly, then suddenly flitting past me into the bathroom, leaving me confused and touched and mildly pissed off all at once.

∎ ∎ ∎ ∎ ∎ ∎ ∎ ∎ ∎ ∎ ∎

Rappaport's is a little kosher dairy restaurant half a flight below street-level; only a block further up Second Avenue is Ratner's, a bigger, fancier place that serves exactly the same incomprehensible food. (Diary is supposed to mean no meat, but you can get fish, which I suppose they consider a vegetable or something.) So for decades, Rappaport's has had to survive on Ratner's drop-outs, and they've ended up as kind of the Viet Cong of the bagels and lox set. Once I went in there with three other dreadful-looking junkies to buy some pastries from the counter they have at the front of the place, and the old bird who waited on us refused to let us pay for them. As we left nibbling brownies, he was humming the *Internationale*. He thought we were the Downtrodden Proletariat, dig?

So I wasn't uptight about going in there with a girl dressed only in a coat and boots. The people who run the place are weirder than any of the customers.

The place was pretty empty, so we sat down at one of the tables along the left wall, with the whole width of the medium-sized room between us and the other customers who were all seated along the right wall by the mirror for some reason.

I forgot the confusion I had carried in with me as I recognized the balding waiter approaching us with two menus—ordering from *this* cat demanded total concentration.

"Never mind the menus," I said. "We know what we want."

"He knows what he wants!" the waiter sighed. "Listen, you maybe *think* you know what you want, but believe me, if you should make the mistake of ordering the herring today--"

"Eggs," I insisted loudly. "Two orders of scrambled eggs with lox. Two toasted bagels with cream cheese. Two coffees."

"With the eggs, you want in it onions, of course. And take it from me, today the bialys, the bagels this morning—feh!"

"No onions. It's too early in the morning."

He shook his head primly. "Twelve-thirty is by you too early in the morning for onions? Okay, okay, no onions. Toasted bialys."

With a Rappaport's waiter, you accept a negotiated settlement. I nodded, he nodded, and he split.

And I was alone with Robin who certainly was no Girl in the Rain. She stared across the table at me as if she were a female Dondi and I were the provider of the American Chocolate. It bugged the ass off me, made me feel like I was paying for it, made me feel old.

"Don't look at me like that!" I said.

"Like what?"

"Like buying you breakfast is some kind of pay-off."

"Isn't it?"

"Christ, no!" I snapped.

"Then why are you doing it?"

"Why last night? Did you go home with me so I'd buy you breakfast in the morning?"

A wounded "Of course not! I just grooved on you."

"All right," I said, making it with a warm smile, "So accept this in the same spirit I accepted that, dig?"

She smiled back. "I guess I just can't figure out where you're at," she said. "You don't seem all that, you know, straight, but I can't tell if you're . . . "

"A head?"

"Well . . . yeah . . . " she said nervously. The boxes people put themselves in!

"If it'll make you relax," I said, "I was a junkie for a year or so."

"I don't groove very well behind smack," she said, genuinely apologetic.

"Two points for you," I said. "*Was* a junkie—emphatically past-tense."

At that point the waiter arrived, set down plates of eggs and lox, buttered bialys, two cups of coffee. She began wolfing it down like there was no tomorrow. Maybe she knew something.

And then the question came, *the* question, in caps with tambourine bells on it: "Does this mean you're down on drugs?"

"I'm down on smack and speed and downers and anything else you can get really strung-out on. A steady habit is bad news—ask the man who owns one."

"But what about grass and hash and . . . you know . . . ?"

I smiled, gave her a "paisan" look. "It's a nice place to visit," I said.

I could tell that what was coming was going to be make or break for us as far as she was concerned, because she paused in her gobbling of lox and eggs and stared at me dead-on.

"Acid?" she asked, all too solemnly.

Well, I knew where *that* was at, what answer would turn her on and what would turn her off, but who wants to start a thing with a chick on the basis of an easily-exposed lie? So I opted for the third alternative: truth.

"I've never tried it," I said.

It was as if I had told her I was a virgin. She got *that* kind of gleam in her eyes.

"Really?" she said.

"Really."

"Are you afraid?"

I tried to let my true feelings speak for me: "I don't know. Seems like acid can turn a groovy situation into something beautiful and a mild bummer into a king-sized horror show. It's all in how you feel at the time deep inside. You've got no control. I've never had the opportunity to take it in a situation where I could be *sure* I wouldn't have a bummer."

"Was last night a bad trip?" she said.

"You mean . . . . ?"

"About 800 mikes worth."

Spasms boiled up my arms turning my hands to fists. I wanted to kill her. A fucking acid-head! *Literally* a fucking acid-head. The whole night had been a lie . . . all it had been for me . . . And what had I been for her? A goddamn zonk, a sexual kaleidoscope, an electric stereophonic dildo!

"You . . . you . . . " My throat was constricted with fury. "Last night . . . that wasn't even you . . . ."

"If it wasn't me, who was it?"

"You know damn well what I mean!"

"But do *you* know what you mean?" she said softly. "Was it good? Was it beautiful? Did it take you someplace you wanted to go?"

"But it wasn't real. It wasn't really you . . . it was the acid."

"Of course it was real; it happened, didn't it? The Girl in the Rain—that's me the way I *want* to be. That's more the real me than the me you're seeing now. So I use acid to make me more me . . . Be honest, which me do you prefer: me now, or the Girl in the Rain?"

She had me there. She had me cold, and we both knew it. Softening, I said: "Maybe I don't have all the answers. I guess I really don't know where you're at."

"Would you *really* like to dig my reality?" she said.

A cold chill foreshadowed what was coming next; still I said: "Yes."

She reached into her coat pocket, palmed two sugar cubes. "Take a trip with me," she said. "Let's get inside each other's heads. Let's make it all the way together. Trust me. Trust yourself. It won't be a bummer—you've got a good soul."

I felt myself paused at the brink of an abyss. Okay, I'll admit it, acid scared me. You get so high you don't know you're high, you've got no control. And all that ego-death stuff—that was Harvey's bag, and I knew where *that* was at. No thanks, baby, I was about to say.

But . . . there was something very much like love in her eyes as she held out the sugar cubes. And I suddenly realized that I was about to make another safe, cagey, negative decision. I was going to throw away a possibility. A berserker impulse came over me—for once, if I was going to have regrets, it would be over a chance I *had* taken.

If you want to walk through the fire, you've got to step into the flames.

I smiled, a kind of forced-bravado smile, took a cube, and without a further thought, swallowed it. I raised my cup, clinked it with hers, said: "Take me on a trip upon your magic swirling ship," and took a long warm swallow. And another.

And began eating lox and eggs again, waiting for it to hit, afraid of what I would see if I looked back.

4
"Take Me On A Trip Upon Your Magic Swirling Ship . . . "

"How much money do you have?" Robin said as we stood outside Rappaport's on what was turning out to be one of those rare warm New York November days.

I didn't like the question. "What do I need, a Dun and Bradstreet to qualify as a trip partner?"

"Come on, how much money do you have in your pocket, on you, right now?"

There I was, one o'clock in the pm standing outside Rappaport's with god-knows-how-much acid in me winding up for the pitch, and this chick was already hustling me for bread. Asshole that you are, I told myself, you're gonna get the bummer you so richly deserve for getting yourself into this.

"Come on, come on, I don't want your bread, just want to plan ahead, now, while we can."

I checked my wallet: a ten and three ones. In my pocket, a quarter, two nickels, a dime and a penny.

"Grand total of $13.46."

"Groovy," she said, doing some kind of calculations in her head. "Look, it should be hitting soon and we'll have maybe eight hours. Are you willing to blow ten dollars, I mean throw it around and don't look back, to have a super-trip?"

What the hell, ten bucks, I thought, about what Ted spends in one day on his therapy. And acid's going for about $5 a cap on the street, and I'm getting high free. Live a little!

"Girl," I said, "you are talking to the last of the big spenders. Ten bucks is a mere pittance. Consider the vast resources of my entire fortune of $13.46 at your command."

"Okay, man," she said, "let's ride the magic carpet." And she stepped out into the gutter, waved her hand, and hailed a cab like an uptown fashion model out slumming. Something about the authority with which she did it gave me a funny flash: one way or another, my Girl in the Rain was fully capable of taking me for a ride.

Five minutes and 75 cents including tip later, we were standing behind an iron fence overlooking the East River in the long, narrow strip of park that runs along the bank across the East River Drive from the big low-rent housing project that parallels the river along Avenue D. Uptown from us on the concrete path along the bank, a gang of kids from the project were doing their thing; we walked a few dozen yards further downtown and found an empty wooden bench facing the river in a section of the park that seemed deserted. It was well up into the fifties now—I felt it was a good omen—and warm enough to sit down on the bench, even though it was November.

"Feel anything yet?" Robin asked. She studied me with eyes that seemed to pick up a misty sheen from the gray water lapping at the stone embankment no more than a dozen feet in front of us.

Turning my attention inward, I seemed to discover a not-unpleasant vagueness in my stomach, a slight tension in my jaw muscles, maybe the hint of a light-headed buzz behind my eyes.

"I'm not sure . . . ."

She laughed, her face seemed to crinkle, said: "Don't worry, when it hits, you'll *know.*"

I stared out across the river where the smokestacks of Brooklyn were pouring gray smoke into the clear blue sky; digging the chugging factories far away across the flat graygreen water, and the two of us sitting alone on a bench in a thin strip of non-city without another human being in easy sight, I had the damndest feeling of being on the stern of a cruise ship slowly pulling out of the harbor, its bow pointed to the far horizon, slipping out to sea real peaceful and groovy.

"This is just about the grooviest place in the East Village to go up in," Robin said. "Of course if we were blowing heavier bread, we could've gone up to the Cloisters and gone up digging the Hudson . . . No, we'd never have made it up there in time, and going up in a cab can be a real bummer, especially if you get stuck with a cab driver who won't shut up . . . ."

I was beginning to see deeps in this girl: she knew what she was doing, she had an esthetic, and any chick who could get a cab to stop for her on Second Avenue wearing nothing but boots and an old peacoat had to have style.

"Did anyone every tell you you hail a cab with class?" I said.

A groovy little laugh like lips on my body. Her eyes were really starting to shine, huge and glowing. One of us was starting to feel something.

"It's all in the fingers and wrist," she said. She waved her right hand limply in the air. "Now who would stop for some dingy chick waving a dead fish?" She straightened her wrist and snapped her fingers once, imperiously. "Dig—*there's* a princess in a plastic hippy disguise!"

I took her hand, kissed it like a Transylvanian nobleman, ran my eyes slowly up her smooth white wrist disappearing into the floppy sleeve of her peacoat, along acres of midnight-blue felt parkland rippling and folded geologically over her hidden flesh like the frozen time of a Greek statue's concrete drapery, and met the cool black pools of her eyes phosphorescent surface sheen over wells of mysterious female darkness.

Time stopped. I swan-dived into the universe of her eyes, deep down, way down, all the way to a velvet-black grotto that seemed to go all the way through her, to open into an infinite void that was the same void behind my eyes too, where some essence of me mingled with the essence of her, and when I came bubbling up to the surface again, there seemed to be a tiny spark of her inside my head and from the now-hidden depths of her pupils, a piece of me seemed to look back.

"Hello," she said softly—a confirmation.

"Hello."

Silently, we looked out over the waters together, the rolling gray waters of the East River redolent with the wasted substance of New York, carrying its rich soup down to the ocean, there to nourish the amnion of the primal womb of all life. There the very shit and sewage of civilization would feed pure feral life; we were all part of the pattern of nature, down to our lowliest turd. We couldn't be anything but nature's own creatures on a planet that cherished our very foulness and loved the very ass-end of our dead residues back into life.

■ ■ ■ ■ ■ ■ ■ ■ ■ ■ ■

"Thank you," I said, not knowing if it was God or Robin or the universe I was thanking, seeing them all as one with myself in the rolling vastnesses of our mind.

"I told you, didn't I?" Robin said, ever young, ever old, preternaturally wise. "Acid is love."

Could she be right? Could acid be the universe's *aqua regia*, the

Universal Solvent of souls in whose deeps all merged into One? Had
I been given the Gift for which all life yearned?

Robin stood up, pulled me up with her. "Yes, this is a groovy
place to go up in," she said. "But now it's time for another magic carpet ride."

■ ■ ■ ■ ■ ■ ■ ■ ■ ■ ■

"Here?" I said when Robin told the cabbie to stop on the corner of
MacDougal and Houston. Clown Alley? The MacDougal Street freakshow? Honkie-tonk mockery of the best year of my life?

"Here," she said definitively. "You haven't seen what you think
you've seen till you see it with kaleidoscope eyes."

A squeeze of her hand said *trust me,* how could I argue with that?
My Magical Mystery Tour Guide hadn't made a wrong move yet. So
I paid the cabbie $1.40 and there we were on fabled MacDougal
Street, a block below Bleecker, where it was just a quiet brown little
Italian Village street sleeping in the soft shadows south of where the
Freakshow begins.

"Look, I don't mean to be an old man," I said, "but MacDougal
Street has worn some bumpy ruts in my mind."

And just thinking about it caused dopplering waves of memory to
whistle hollowly down the narrow brownstone canyon from the flash
and color of the MacDougal main drag I could dimly see a block
away.

That long golden summer when I had kissed Flatbush and college
goodbye and hadn't yet kissed Anne and smack hello, first and last
time of total freedom in my life, my Golden Age, when I knew every
face on The Street and Saturday afternoon was a walk down Mac-
Dougal from the Park to Ted's old loft on West Broadway and then a
choice of the best party of the night—

The ruins of the Golden Age: funky little coffee-houses turned into
rock joints, Art Kaiser's Jewelry Shop now a poster-and-button store
like the old Folklore Center and a dozen other remembered shops,
the ethnic little Italian sausage-and-pizza stands chromed and alu-
minized, the double line of parked cars that clogged the street and
made the sidewalks cozy now banished for efficiency's sake, making
the street seem twice as wide and half as warm, and all my friends
gone and the ruins overrun by teenybopper barbarians from the
northern wastelands—

Clown Alley

And in between these bookends of time, the Age of Decline, when MacDougal meant trying to scrounge together $3 in small change with Anne and whatever other junkies were freaking out in front of the Night Owl and frantic phone calls from the booths in the Village Drug Store to connections who never were there and the dirty old shakes at 3 in the am walking blearily down MacDougal to Bleecker and Snooky's, the junkie's terminal graveyard—

"MacDougal Street wears ruts in everyone's head," Robin said. "Dig it on acid and get a free roadmap."

"I don't know . . . some pretty heavy things . . . ."

"Fear is the mind-killer," she said, and, recognizing the line from a book I didn't believe we could've shared, I felt suddenly closer to her as she said: "Trust me, baby."

And she took my hand again and led me up MacDougal toward Bleecker past the solemn quiet tenements with their empty stoops, upstream against the waves of memory that seemed to fade into mist as I remembered what I had told myself when I dropped the acid a geological age ago: if you want to walk through the fire, you've got to step into the flames.

■ ■ ■ ■ ■ ■ ■ ■ ■ ■ ■

Time had dissolved into an illusion by the time we reached the Empanada stand tucked into a hole in the city wall between the Hip Bagel and the old Figaro just around the corner from Bleecker. Nothing had changed in this cosmic corner since the early Jurassic; same unobtrusive funeral parlor and tiny Italian coffee house across the street, same smell of the summer of the mind drifting down MacDougal: coffee and sausage and pot and human heat. Yes, Figaro's had existed in its own separate time-stream since the Dutchmen conned the Indians out of Manhattan; it was like the Eiffel Tower or St. Peter's Cathedral or Niagara Falls. The prototypical Village coffee house, the archetype; its existence was so bound up with people's memories and tourists' expectations that the image shaped the substance and preserved it in amber as it had been in the Golden Age as it was now as it would be when tourists from Jupiter would mingle unnoticed with tourists from the Bronx: a corner of picture-postcard Paris Left Bank bohemia plunked down in New York replete with weathered-brown sidewalk tables, glassed-in porch and entrance foyer, walls papered with old French newspapers, ornate espresso machine, and everything, including the clientele, aged in the wood to the color-texture of old bourbon.

Figaro's was the cornerstone of the Village in space and time: fronting on Bleecker and looking up MacDougal toward Washington Square Park, it was the southwest pivot of the street scene that boiled along MacDougal—the flow of motorcycle gangs, Jersey hoods in hot-rods, teenyboppers, locals, rubbernecking tourists, that promenaded down MacDougal to Bleecker, turned east at Figaro corner, then north up Sullivan back to West Fourth, meeting itself again at the West Fourth head of MacDougal and back into the cycle again. Existing as it did as the materialization of an image that belonged to no real Village era, Figaro stood outside all eras, timeless and unchanging, projecting into the nows of all Village time-loci but contained by none of them like the Rock of Eternity. Because it was always an anachronism, it would never be an anachronism.

And standing there in its nontemporal aura, all my MacDougals, past, present, and future, were one, existing in memory and anticipation, outside of time.

"This is the space-time navel of the Village," I told Robin, trying to explain the inexplicable.

She looked at me with warm but opaque eyes. "Oh yeah," she said.

Could she really understand what I meant that I had found a place to stand on this corner, some kind of common ground with the strangers in the street, with the kids from the Bronx and the tourists and the local Siciliani and even new generations of junkies yet unborn; that all this corner was a Hollywood Village set on which we were all extras. I could stand here forever and never get older like someone in a twenty-year-old stock shot of the Village reincarnated in a hundred B-movies . . . .

■ ■ ■ ■ ■ ■ ■ ■ ■ ■ ■

After a second or a century, I felt Robin tug at my hand. "Let's go to the circus," she said. She pulled me across Bleecker and back into the time-stream, the now of MacDougal Street that unfolded like a carnival midway before us as we seemed to float up the street on our private magic carpet past savory hero-and-pizza stands, poster shops, timeless Italian groceries, the Kettle of Fish, tiny candystores selling Zig-Zags and poisonous black Italian cigars, the Caricature, feedback whining and shrieking from hole-in-the-wall rock joints, a clot of skeletal speed freaks outside Rienzi's, Japanese sailors gawking at two sixteen-year-old chicks freezing their tight little asses off in out-of-season miniskirts, two old Eighth Street fags walking arm-in-arm, a bull dyke in a motorcycle jacket, a man in porkpie hat being walked by a shaggy brown Irish Wolfhound as big as a pony, an uptight Irish cop rousting three stoned heads off a tenement stoop, a Bowery bum bugging a bearded 1950's Village poet, four savage spades with port-reddened eyes: Villageland. The Disney version. Prop reconstructions of colorful old buildings.

A street scene in which at least half of the people weren't real. You could tell by their eyes, by the way they held themselves. They were part of the set, costumed extras: teen-age chicks in hippy costume courtesy of Fifth Avenue or girls whose faces reeked of uptown bread in last year's Levis and raincoats from Army-Navy stores; soulful CCNY students with long hair and beards down on weekend pass from the Bronx; Harlem spades carrying bottles of cheap wine in paper bags who had been told they could come here and fuck a lot of crazy white chicks; the aforementioned crazy white chicks who came from posh private high schools or had run away from Scarsdale for the weekend and had worms in their heads and Cuban Superman notions about black dick. The local color.

And digging these quaint natives in their accurately simulated natural habitat were the tourists: *gringas* from Moshulu Parkway and Flatbush with enormous asses; sailors from the Bolivian Navy; genteel retired ex-hookers; feed and grain salesmen from Council Bluffs; Herbert Hoover's third cousin; inebriated specimens of the Loyal Order of Moose; several Dirk Robinson fee-writers and the Vice Chairlady of the Society for the Prevention of Cruelty to Dope Fiends. Welcome to Disneyland East! See Teenybopperland, Junkieland, and the Needle Park of Tomorrow, folks! Watch the Fearsome Nigger make the Beautiful White Girl two pm every afternoon, extra performance on Sunday! Lookit all the creeps walking around STONED ON DRUGS!! The clientele.

Ah, but while these shadows were chasing each other up and down the street, you could see the *real* Villagers skulking around the fringes: a little clot of young kids with wasted pimply faces and rotten teeth fawning over an older cat sitting on a stoop who was obviously their connection; a good-looking hard young waitress from Figaro's who had just left her shift; a young longhair in Levi jacket and black chinos dragging his guitar and amplifier into the *Blue Goo;* The Old Dope Peddler Spreading Joy Wherever He Goes; Big Brown, world-famous pseudo poet; a real poet with a real beard; a bull dyke arguing with her fem; two tweedy old respectable faggots; Allan Block, the famous sandalmaker and fiddler; a cat smoking pot in a corncob pipe . . . .

And Robin and me standing on the corner of MacDougal and West Fourth looking back and digging it all stoned out of our minds on acid.

"Hea-*vy!*" I sighed.

"Yeah man, what a zonk!"

She didn't seem to get the point; how could she? She knew which scene was hers because she had known no other, but I had made it all three styles. I had first come to the Village as a CCNY student looking for Village Adventure and some of the fabled easy pussy and I had come out the other end of the long gold summer as an authentic Villager with a smack habit to prove it. And just now, today, hadn't I started down at the other end of Clown Alley like one of the weekend costume extras: the Superannuated Village Expatriot out for a sentimental visit to the old country on Dr. Timothy Leary's eight-hour round-trip excursion tour?

So where did that leave me now?

I could hardly become a tourist again after having been a native; could I really be a costumed extra after having paid junkie's dues to the scene?

Did that mean that once a real Villager, always a real Villager? Once a junkie, always a junkie? But I was off junk; had been for a long time and no urge to score. Yeah, but I was on acid, wasn't I? Didn't someone once say it came in all shapes and sizes? Wasn't that someone me? Was this place, this street, this freakshow, something that got inside you like a tapeworm you couldn't get rid of?

Did I really want to blot out my past? If I did, why did I let Robin drag me here?

Heavy, indeed! Like some Catholic spent his childhood in a Jesuit parochial school bummer, turned eighteen, got laid and gave the Church the back of his hand walking past St. John's and feeling he wants to go in, knowing what was done to him, but wanting to go in anyway, and wanting not to want to go in, and so finding out that he's got a need something outside him has put inside him that he's no longer dumb enough to feed, but the monkey's still there on his back whispering sweet nothings in his ear.

Sure, baby, that's what I needed, to see the Village with kaleidoscope eyes!

Robin was tugging at my hand. The light was green. She gave me a warm, concerned look, maybe picking up the vibes of my feelings but certainly not what was really inside my head, said: "Don't look back, baby." And steered me across the street and up the next block towards Washington Square Park like a tug guiding a wallowing liner in a storm.

Don't look back—something may be gaining on you.

Don't look forward—*you* may be gaining on *it.*

Don't look now—you may be there.

"And how many times can a man turn his head
And pretend that he just doesn't see . . . ?"

But where in the hell was that answer that was supposed to be blowin' in the wind? Not here in the dead calm of the Horse Latitudes. How about on the path between the leafless trees across the next street in the Park leading, like all Washington Square paths, to the fountain at the center—was the answer there? What was the question?

Staring up the path, gray concrete under a slating-over November sky, I clocked the contents of the benches under the bare spectral trees, got an awful flash: there they sat, young bodies in traditional Village garb—ponchos, old coats, war-surplus combat boots, faded Levis, brown chinos, sandals--young bodies with old faces, speed freaks with sunken cheeks and ruined eyes, skeletal young junkies, chicks not out of their teens who had already fucked themselves into old hookers' faces, the flotsam and jetsam of the Psychedelic Sargasso. And staring up the Desolation Row, I could see the puke-filled doorways, deadly bars and endless flophouse barracks of the Bowery and *these same faces* but now with bodies to match flopping in doorways with their flies open, lying maybe dead in the gutter unnoticed with the rest of the garbage, bumming quarters off each other, gibbering in the afternoon sun, pissing on parked cars, puking casually on stoops. Yeah, the same faces, the same clothes, and only the bodies aged an instant from today; their heads were already a million years old on Terminal Skid Row.

I knew I had shuffled a long way down that road once; had I gone so far that I could never get off the Bowery Inside?

And then we reached the big open space at the core of Washington

Square Park: the dry circular concrete-and-stone fountain and around it a wide asphalt-paved clearing with the pseudo-Arch-of-Triumph (over what?) at the north entrance to the Park—the hub on which the Park's radial paths converged.

Yes, this was the core of the Hip Stellar Phoenix, the heart of the Village fission-fusion-fission reactor that powered it all. Young kids fissioning off from the Bronx and Brooklyn and the Midwest grooving on the flash of freedom seated on the curved lip of the fountain rapping with each other and full of high-energy hope; lurking spades from Harlem radiating hot gamma rays of madness; uptight old Sicilians walking quickly past with glances of the Evil Eye; innocent holy refugees from Bible Belt mindlessness; the hot unstable elements of American's Periodic Table drifting into the imploding stellar heart of the Other America. Forming the rich nuclear soup of the Village in which a few dynamically stable elements—a tweedy couple tossing a frisbee back and forth, an old man with a neat white beard and cool calm eyes, a neat young Black and a sunny blond-haired chick pushing a baby carriage together—evolved and remained viable. But most of the human fuel finally ejected as radioactive waste-products, deadly, ashen, and leaden, spewed out of the central core through the sewer-pipe conduits to the Boweries of the mind.

The whole Village was a big pulsing pump that sucked in youth and spit out derelicts and let a few of the lucky ones bask in the sun at its heart, warming themselves in the glow of burnt-out youth force-drafted from the husks crowding its peripheral slag-heaps.

We crossed the open space headed northeast, and then up another path under more skeletal trees lined with still more burnt-out Village slag heaped on wooden benches.

I couldn't take the terrain inside my head much more; I tried to get outside by concentrating on the girl at the end of my arm who seemed off on some private head-trip of her own.

"Where are you at?" I asked.

"Just grooving," she said dreamily.

"*Grooving!* On what? This fucking garbage-heap? This sewer? This Bowery annex?"

Robin seemed to snap back from somewhere far away; her glassy, dreamy eyes were suddenly rodent-bright, turned on me like a camera zoomed in to close focus. "Hey man," she said earnestly, "what's bugging you?"

"I got one of those free roadmaps you promised me. I don't like the way the land lies."

"Old tracks," she said. "Don't let it freak you."

But it hurt; it hurt because she seemed to have seen all the way inside me and put my inner being down with two short words. And she was wrong, she had to be wrong! I had to make her understand to stop the hurting; if I couldn't make her understand, then may be she was right and I was old, old, old.

"Look at this place," I said. "It's the Sargasso Sea. Everything that's floating loose drifts down here and rots in the seaweed."

"It's the world, baby," she said with a softness older than anything inside me.

"What's the world, this freakshow?"

"No man, it's the world," she insisted.

"I don't understand . . . ."

"It's the world. Dig—I'll show you. Just keep walking and don't look back till I tell you."

■ ■ ■ ■ ■ ■ ■ ■ ■ ■ ■

We reached the northeast corner of the Park (don't look back), crossed the street, continued east, and suddenly reality became cool and dark and echoing as we crossed the frontier into a new country: a deep canyon of huge empty gray buildings, the gray silent monoliths of some moldering necropolis, the flesh-dwarfing Stalinist architecture of a black and white film of East Berlin and up the ghostly street, the only three people in sight, two blocks further east, seemed like primitive savages scuttling at the feet of the giant enigmatic tombstones of the Pharaohs. Canyons measureless to man. Endless acres of dead city, stone upon gray stone—was this the New York of "nice place to visit but I wouldn't want to live there," was this what the tourists saw, was the uptight cliche of New York of dead gray concrete canyons and frantic scuttling gray people the real thing after all? Was this concrete deathscape a map of our inner territory?

The drag of Robin's hand brought me to a slow stop like the chain of a sea-anchor. "Turn around and dig it now," she said.

I turned and stared down a long gray corridor of lifeless stone and my viewpoint seemed to flash down the cold canyon of buildings like a camera zoom-shot on Washington Square Park shimmering like an oasis beyond a desert of frozen gray sand. I was staring at a vision of the Village, an impressionist painting, all feeling and no detail, from the bottom of some horrible stone-walled pit, and now the Village-image shone like the dream of youth's awakening and I knew that no one ran away *to* the Village, you ran away *from* the gray void at the bottom of the city's pit, towards that shimmering vision of the Promised Land at the other end of the tunnel. Clawed your way up the rock walls, inch by inch if you had to, crawled along the desert sands towards the oasis . . . .

■ ■ ■ ■ ■ ■ ■ ■ ■ ■ ■

"It's the world," Robin said.

"Yes . . . ."

She knew, somehow, on some gut-level, she had known all along that the real choice wasn't between good and evil but between two different styles of reality and neither was Shangri-La. But down here, at the bottom of New York's Stalinist-gray bummer, I could see, could accept the fact, that the break from *this* to the Village had been a move towards freedom, a tropism towards light, a flight from a reality of walls to a place of the possible, where evil was ranker and good was more luxuriant, where "humanity festers rich as rotting fruit," life, is all.

I didn't like the game, but those were the cards, and it had been the only game in town. I had nothing to regret.

"Time for another magic carpet ride," Robin said.

■ ■ ■ ■ ■ ■ ■ ■ ■ ■ ■

We got out of the cab at Forty-Second Street and Fifth Avenue: the cabbie had been giving us the "dirty hippie treatment" all the way, so I handed him a single and two quarters for the $1.50 meter, paused just long enough to let him wind up for a curse, then handed him another single and said: "And that for you, my good man."

Walking up Fifth Avenue from the gaping cabbie, Robin said: "Why did you do that? That cat was bumming us all the way."

"Precisely," I said. Jesus, it had been the obvious move, hadn't it?

"Huh?"

"I did it to teach the bounder a lesson," I explained patiently.

"Man," she said respectfully but obviously uncomprehendingly, *"are you stoned!"*

Ah, the poor child, I thought with a sudden surge of well-being.

No sense of savoir-faire, no appreciation of true class, no instinct for the Grand Gesture. Jeez, it felt good to be walking up Fifth Avenue, posh gleaming banks, opulent shops, wide sidewalks, muted underplayed storefronts, great office buildings where the wheels of the world hummed, little touches of pure idiot elegance like the gilded lamp-posts and trash-baskets, all bathed in the Technicolor glow of a golden sunset.

"Dig it, dig it, dig it . . . " Robin mumbled.

"I dig, I dig," I assured her. This was the real New York where, as Dickie Lee says, the Big Game is played. Here the huge buildings weren't dead useless stone but great buzzing beehives, busy, busy, busy, fortunes won and lost, paper empires rising and falling, yeah, this is where the action is. That son of a bitch Dirk had pegged it right; he knew his own turf, had to give him that.

"Man, just so big, so big . . . " Robin said.

"Oh yeah, big all right!" Fifth Avenue on a sunset Saturday was empty but not deserted, expensive chicks in expensive shops, mysterious cats bustling around on mysterious day-off missions, tourists gawking; but still not the weekday mob jamming the sidewalks, moving at double-time. No, now Fifth Avenue was like some smoothly-oiled racing-engine taking it easy, idling, not much really happening, but man, dig the power in that lazy throb!

"Oh shit . . . wow . . . "

We were on the corner of Fifth and Forty-Fourth now; two blocks north was the second-string office building that housed the Dirk Robinson Literary Agency. A weird feeling, walking around outside the old boiler factory on a Saturday, with the building closed, stoned on acid! Wouldn't it blow old Dirk's mind to see me? Or would it? It wasn't blowing *my* mind; it was unblowing it. Fifth Avenue had a real reality, a sense of contact with the Great World Out There. Even my shitty job, stupid maybe, corrupt maybe, in that office on this street, put me in some kind of contact with the pathetic dreams of the losers and the Big Game of the winners; it was possible to sit behind my typewriter and sniff the goings-on in both realities of the office, to glide back and forth between the Big Game and the compost-heap of broken dreams . . . .

"Shit . . . shit . . . oh Christ . . . "

Hey, Robin was babbling! Her free hand was balled into a fist, her hand in mine digging into my flesh like a claw. I put my free hand on her shoulder, spun her around to face me. Her eyes were wild, unfocused; her mouth was trembling. She was off somewhere and it obviously wasn't somewhere good.

"Hey, what's the matter? Take it easy . . . ."

She seemed to come back from wherever she had been, but there was an awful look in her eyes, look of someone who has looked somewhere they shouldn't and now they know it.

"Dig it man," she said, "we're like ants. Dirty little ants crawling around their pantry. Nobody. Nothing. Dirty little ants. Oooh, shit!"

"Hey, take it easy, baby. Groove on the street. Dig it. Look at the golden garbage cans; isn't that a gas? *Golden garbage cans!*"

"Fucking gold garbage cans!" she shouted—and heads turned to sneer at the freaking hippie. I stroked her shoulder in a cool-it gesture. Softer, she hissed bitterly: "Yeah, those filthy cocksuckers with their gold garbage cans! What do they care? What do they know?"

Oh Christ, I thought, she's on some kind of paranoid trip!

"They just sit there in their office buildings ruling the world and all we are to them is dirty little ants in their cookie jars . . . ."

Oh wow, a hippie Proletariat workers of the world unite bummer!

"It's not like that," I said. "You've got to understand--it's the Big Game, is all."

"Game?"

"Yeah, it's all a big groovy game. It's their trip. They groove behind it, see?"

"We're only pawns in their game . . . ."

"Oh shit! You're getting paranoid. Nobody's out to get us." Why couldn't she understand?

"They're monsters! Playing games with our lives!"

Jesus, where did she pick up all this pseudo-Marxist shit? The Wolves of Wall Street, the Fagins of Fifth Avenue!

"Oh man, you don't understand, they control us all with wires in our heads and all they have to do is press a button and we jump and twitch and squirm . . . ."

Goddamn, there was no way to talk her out of it! She was freaking out and I had to *do* something, had to put her head in another place . . . yeah . . . *Yeah!*

I pulled her to the curb, waved my hand for a minute or so, finally got a cab (no real sweat on Fifth Avenue!), said "Magic carpet time, baby," and stuffed her into the back seat ahead of me.

■ ■ ■ ■ ■ ■ ■ ■ ■ ■ ■

The cab ride downtown started bringing me down like a slow dissolve. The more Robin gibbered about Them and how They controlled the world and how we were Dirty Little Ants, the more aware I became of the fact that she was having an acid bummer, which reminded me of the fact that she was on acid which reminded me that I was on acid which reminded me that the big light show that was going on outside the cab was an acid distortion which kind of put me in the position of still being high but now seeing myself as high and so I could see myself beginning to slowly and majestically sink back into the sea of reality. Whatever that was.

By the time the cab had dropped us off on Avenue D, outside the housing project near where the trip had started, Robin was quieting down, and I felt that I was half in one reality and half in another, and not quite knowing which one was really real, or even if there was such a thing as real.

"Hey man, where are we going?" Robin said in a pathetic scared little voice as I started to lead her through the admittedly-ominous giant red-brick buildings of the darkening, glowering project towards the pedestrian bridge over the East River Drive that led to the strip of park along the river. "Those big buildings with metal spiders in them . . . we're like ants . . . dirty little ants . . . ."

Some esthetic, some strange sense of symmetry, had given me the idea of taking her back to the same place we had gone up in. It had been peaceful and groovy there, and it seemed like the logical antidote to her bummer.

"Somewhere groovy," I told her as we puffed up the metal stairs of the pedestrian bridge. As we reached the arching span of the bridge over the snarling traffic of the East River Drive, I glanced down, winced as I imagined what it would do to her head now to see the cars shooting below us like crazed metal monsters.

"Dig," I told her, "close your eyes and hold tight to my hand, and when I tell you to open your eyes again, I promise everything will be groovy."

She looked at me with sick puppy-dog eyes, squeezed my hand, said: "I'm afraid . . . afraid of the dark inside my head . . . "

I put my arm around her waist, kissed her softly on the cheek. "Trust me," I said.

She nodded, screwed up her face, closed her eyes, and I led her across the bridge, haltingly down the stairs on the other side, through the width of the narrow empty park, and sat her down on a bench facing the river.

I tried to see the view through her eyes: the lights of Brooklyn sparkling smokily in the dusk across the black sheen of water, the sky deepening to navy; the red-and-green jewels of an airplane's running lights moving across the as-yet-starless sky.

I sat down beside her, put my arm around her shoulders, cradled her against me, said, "Open your eyes."

Her body shuddered once against me; she opened her eyes. Sighed. Didn't move for at least a minute that seemed to hang frozen in the air that was getting cold and dank.

Then she turned to me. She was smiling; her eyes were big and soft and calm. She kissed me gently on the mouth with soft-but-closed lips, held it for a long moment, then pulled away and lay her head on my shoulder, her cheek cool against mine.

"Thank you," she said.

"Full circle, baby. It was a beautiful place to go up in, so I figured . . . ."

"You're just a beautiful, groovy cat," she said. "I mean knowing how to bring me out of a bummer like that and you on your first acid trip . . . wow . . . "

"You're okay now?"

"Oh sure man," she said casually. "It was just a bad flash. It happens every once in a while. You get used to it."

A long moment of silence during which I wondered if a freakout like that was something I'd ever want to be able to get used to. Quite suddenly, I realized that I hadn't felt very high for . . . how long?

"I think we're coming down," I said.

"Yeah, it'll taper off for a few more hours maybe, but I don't feel very high anymore either. Not exactly the strongest acid I've ever had." She paused. "Ah . . . you don't know what time it is, do you?"

"Maybe five or six, I guess . . . ."

"Uh . . . look, would it uptight you if I split now?" she said. "I mean, I'll stay if you want, but I've got this thing I gotta do."

"How about if I came along?" I said, not really meaning it.

"Might bummer you."

Somehow, I didn't mind. It seemed fitting. I felt tired as hell, and maybe I had a thing to do too: collect the fragments of the trip and try to paste them in the scrapbook of memory.

"It's okay," I told her. "I could do with some aloneness now, I think."

She smiled, kissed me gently, go up. "You're a groovy cat," she said. "No goodbyes, okay? Just . . . later."

"When will I see you again?"

She laughed. "When you most want to and least expect to," she said. She started walking down the path, paused, blew me a kiss, and then was off like a wraith into the falling night.

I sat on the bench for a few minutes just staring into the water and thinking no-thoughts. My next real thought was that I was starting to get really cold and I was exhausted and thoroughly spaced-out.

So I got up and started walking home, looking forward to sleeping for about a thousand years, digesting the day's enormities like a torpid python ruminating on his weekly meal.

Acid was as heavy a trip as smack—heavier.

But I knew for dead-certain that I could never get really hooked on *this*.

5
The Big Game

In the hall on the tenth floor outside the agency, Dickie Lee said: "And what kind of weekend did *you* have, Tom old man?" And smiled that thick-lipped pleasantly shit-eating smile of his, raised his bushy black brows, rolled what he referred to as "my sensual brown eyes," did everything but drool. Good old Dickie.

"Kinda dull, Dickie," I told him. "Went to a party in a loony-bin, met the Devil, didn't like him, got picked up by a naked chick in a peacoat, balled her, she dropped LSD in my breakfast coffee, took me on a magic carpet ride, and I spent Sunday recuperating with the funnies. An off-week."

Dickie tsk-tsked. "I feel for you, m'boy," he said. "You lead such a mundane existence."

■ ■ ■ ■ ■ ■ ■ ■ ■ ■ ■

Dickie and I had a strange thing going: we pretended to believe each other's most outrageous bullshit while really not taking seriously a word the other said. Thus, I could tell Dickie the absolute truth about my lost weekend secure in the knowledge that he would accept it without blinking an eye as the usual Monday morning cock-and-bull story in our endless game of rank-counter-rank.

"I, on the other hand," Dickie said, opening the walnut-veneered door with *Dirk Robinson Literary Agency, Inc.* lettered in fading gilt on the upper toilet-door glass panel, "met an exiled Yugoslavian countess unfortunately afflicted with nymphomania and spent two solid days polluting my vital bodily fluids in a Park Avenue penthouse. I've got a charleyhorse in my dick."

Into the entrance foyer, paneled in walnut plywood, carpeted in black synthetic, lit by an atrocious monster of a chandelier, the walls festooned with a display of books the agency had had a hand (or even a pinky) in, and barricaded at the far end by an enormous desk behind which Maxine the receptionist-telephone-answerer-fee-writer-intimidator with the enormous tits should've been sitting in the usual tight blouse if she hadn't, as usual, been late.

"*La vida es sueña*," I commiserated with Dickie as he outflanked the desk and opened the door to the office itself by yanking on the giant brass doorknob.

"*Verdad,*" he said, as I followed him into the boiler room. The boiler room was another of Dirk Robinson's exercises in cut-rate image-mongering. From the entrance, you did not really notice that the room was painted a high-school-corridor gray and floored with the cheapest of beige plastic tiles because your vision was immediately channeled along the black strip of carpeting that ran from the door between two pairs of walnut desks that faced each other across it like an honor-guard before the big door in the walnut-paneled rear wall that bore a heavy bronze plaque proclaiming *Dirk Robinson, President.* The entrance foyer had been built along the right wall of the boiler room and if you looked to the left, you saw a smaller door in the rear wall that had *Richard Lee, Vice President* lettered directly on the wood in gold paint and backing the left-hand pair of pro desks, a business-like line of filing cabinets covering the entire left-hand wall. This was what the rare fee-writer who managed to penetrate the outer defenses saw.

But as Dickie trotted past the pro desks, where Phil and Bob, two of the three guys who handled the bona fide professional writers, had already arrived, I made a hard left turn, opened the gate in the waist-high railing and was in the sweat-shop area, hidden from the glance of the casual visitor by the inner wall of the entrance foyer partition: two parallel ranks of three-desk gray metal consoles facing the railing out of light-of-sight of the entrance. And don't think Dirk Robinson didn't plan it that way.

The front rank of desks belonged to Arlene, the bookkeeper and general top-level flunky who was already busy on her phone; Nancy, the bouncy little filing clerk who was busily sorting the Monday morning overload of manuscripts; and the probationary fee-reader of the moment, a nameless pimply youth who wasn't there and odds-on had been fired by Dickie on orders from Dirk last Friday.

I sat behind the middle desk in the back row, flanked on my left by Mannie Berkowitz, an aging, balding, promising young writer who was already moaning softly over a manuscript, and on my right by Bruce Day, a crypto-hippy in perfunctory Madison Avenue disguise (whom I copped some grass from now and then), and who was just sitting down as I planted my ass behind the old Royal electric typewriter.

"Another day, another ten points, another twenty dollars," Bruce

The Big Game

said, putting on his steel-rimmed glasses. (A subtle note of defiance he had adopted when the Man, through Dickie, had decreed that his beard had to go.) What Bruce was referring to was the Dirk Robinson fee-reader point-count system, otherwise referred to as the Track Record. Each incoming manuscript was assigned a point-value by Nancy according to its length: one point for short story, five points for the average novel, eight points for a long novel, ten points for some cretin's million-word life-work, and various intermediary point-counts for odd lengths. Each fee-reader had a weekly quota of fifty points and a base pay of $100. Therefore, each point was worth $2 to us. A real Stakhanovite could tear off as many as a hundred points in a week, especially if he had plenty of novels, and when one of us was hard up for bread, the general agreement was that he would get the bulk of that week's juicy five-and-eight pointers. What, one might ask, was each point worth to Dirk Robinson, Inc.? Well, the agency charged $10 for a one-pointer, $35 for a five-pointer, $55 for an eight-pointer and like that, so we figured (figuring in Nancy's salary, postage, stationery and etc.) that the Man made about $400 off an average week's mixed bag that netted one of us peons $100. Or something like $1,200 a week total, $5,000 a month, maybe $60,000 a year. Not bad at all.

Berkowitz moaned again, and dropped the manuscript he had been reading back on the untidy pile next to his typewriter. He fitted a letter-head sheet, a carbon, and an onion-skin second sheet (the Man did not miss a chance at saving a penny on the cheapest possible second sheets) into his typewriter and said: "The Mad Dentist promises us a novel by next week. I can't take him anymore. A nice easy five points, maybe eight. Do I have a taker?"

■ ■ ■ ■ ■ ■ ■ ■ ■ ■

Berkowitz must be cracking up, I thought. The Mad Dentist was a long-time fee-writer whose thesis was that fluoridated drinking water was a Communist plot to destroy the American economy by ruining the dental industry. He had exposed this hideous plot in about a dozen articles, half a dozen short stories, a nonfiction book and a science fiction novel. All of which we had of course rejected as "showing considerable talent but not quite meeting the current demands of the marketplace." I could tell what the new Dr. Owen F. Mannigan opus would be like without reading it; therefore it was an easy five-pointer; therefore Berkowitz had to be crazy for opting out.

"I volunteer," I therefore said.

"Sold to Thomas Hollander and may the Lord have mercy upon your soul!" Berkowitz said with a sigh of ill-concealed relief that I did not like one little bit.

"All right, Mannie," I said, "what's the kicker?"

Berkowitz's dark, perpetually-sour face lit up with a sadistic grin. "I quote from the latest letter from our beloved Mad Dentist," he said. He took a yellow sheet of legal stationery from his "In" and began reading:

> . . . since apparently the Bolshevik conspiracy to bankrupt the American dental industry has subverted the publishing industry as well, I have stolen a tactic from the handbook of the Communist Fluoridators and have cleverly disguised my latest expose of the Marxist-Leninist plot, titled, *SUCK IT TO 'EM!*, as what I believe is referred to in the publishing trade as a novel of sexual passion—

"Stop! Stop!" I screamed.

"Jesus Christ," Bruce said, "a sex novel!"

Shit! That bastard Berkowitz!

"Berkowitz," I said, "this is an atrocity. You have violated the Geneva Convention. I shall complain to the Red Cross."

But before I could get any further in what I knew was a lost cause, Nancy dropped the doubled-sized Monday load of muck on our collective desk and we fell to squabbling over the spoils.

> Dear Mrs. Clinestadt:
> Thank you very much for your most interesting short story, *A Mother's Love*. It is always a pleasure to encounter for the first time the work of a new writer with as much obvious talent as this piece clearly shows . . .

Ah yes, you old douche-bag, you clearly have an obvious talent for writing $10 checks. Stick with Dirk Robinson, baby, and we'll have you turning out five-pointers in no time.

> . . . and I especially admired your prose-style, which combines a sure sense of sentence structure with a wholly feminine ambience entirely appropriate to this touching tale of a mother's

unsuccessful efforts to save her son from the wiles of a wicked woman . . .

The technique of writing a Dirk Robinson fee letter is such a simple exercise in abnormal psychology that I just don't understand why so many fee readers bomb out after a few days. I suppose they just can't type fast enough or maybe they're stupid enough to read everything in the old compost-heap word for word.

. . . however I'm afraid that you, like so many other Dirk Robinson clients who later have gone on to fame and fortune in the literary arena, are not yet familiar with the elements that make a story salable on today's highly-competitive market . . .

Just follow the rules. Rule one: each short story gets a two-page (single-spaced) letter of criticism, four pages for a five-pointer, six for an eight-pointer, eight for a ten-pointer. (Which is why the five, eight, and ten pointers are valuable—less paper to cover with babble per point.) Therefore, write as inflated a prose as you can and use short paragraphs. (The double-space between paragraphs equals about fifteen words of letter.) Rule two: every writer is "talented"; bums we don't get at Dirk Robinson, Inc. *Never* criticize prose-style, that's sure to hurt the blown-up egos of the fee creeps, and a deflated ego means no more submissions and that makes the Man unhappy.

. . . therefore, I'm afraid that I'm going to have to return this story to you as unsuitable for the current literary marketplace. However, I feel certain that your undeniable talent, combined with diligence and regular production will soon place you within the ranks of our selling authors . . .

Rule three: hit them with the rejection quickly, cleanly, and before the end of page one and follow it *immediately* with praise for the old talent. Never tell them the story is a dog (remember, they're Great Writers); tell them it just happens to be unmarketable. And follow that with a sales pitch for more submissions.

. . . this is not to say that a salable story of this nature cannot be written, but due to the current state of the market, only a most unusually strong piece in this vein has a fighting chance . . .

Rule four: don't discourage nobody from writing nothing. Get those new submissions! Maybe this old bat can write only sniveling motherhood stories, the way the Mad Dentist can only write about the Communist Fluoridation Plot or Martin K. Beale about Aaron Burr. Let the creeps do their thing. Rule five: don't actually lie about the story. Tell them how great they are, then chop the story to pieces fast, and get out neat:

... I'm sorry that *A Mother's Love* could not be the story that breaks you into the ranks of our many selling authors, Mrs. Clinestadt, for your own sake as well as mine, since our modest reading fees merely cover our editorial costs in considering the work of new writers for the market. However, I feel confident that your next submission will be a giant step forward in your literary career. I'll be looking forward to seeing more of your work soon.
Sincerely,
DIRK ROBINSON

That's all there really is to it. Attach the letter to the manuscript and off it goes to the mailing room. And return bitches are the worry of Jack Miller, the fee-correspondence specialist. Dirk has it down to a science.

Even the moral angle, as the man would put it. Dirk unburdens his soul to Dickie (though it may be a plot) and Dickie tells Dirk Robinson stories to the rest of us, either out of genuine admiration or under orders, and probably both. But whether by accident or chance (fat chance!) we fee readers have been provided with an excellent moral rationalization (the only fringe benefit of the job) which I have no doubt Dirk thoroughly believes and which I may even believe too. The Gospel according to St. Robinson:

We are a legitimate literary agency with many successful authors in our stable. Therefore, when we tell the fee writers that we will evaluate their manuscripts for the market and sell them if possible, we are telling the truth. We are under no moral obligation, however, to inform them that we accept for marketing approximately one fee manuscript out of two hundred. We do not lie to them; they lie to themselves by assuming that their manuscript is worth the powder to blow it to hell. We are selling a service and a few professional writers have actually emerged from the depths of feedom. Therefore, we do good. Also, the fee operation pays for the entire overhead of the professional operation so that all commissions on sales are profits. Who can deny that *this* is a Good Thing?

Thus spake Dirk Robinson. I've even heard it from the man himself on occasion. It's true as far as it goes.

Of course, only a junkie, ex or otherwise, would pick up on the significance of the fact that Dirk is sometimes referred to in the boiler room as the Man.

Personally, I carry the justification a bit further:

Fee writers are shits. They are shits because, as Berkowitz, our resident Struggling Young Writer continually moans, they firmly believe that any prick with access to a typewriter is a Writer. Actually, fee creeps want to be Authors, not Writers. People who answer Dirk Robinson ads are the same people that answer Rosicrucian ads. They assume that they have Talent up front. They swallow the bullshit we dish out because we tell them what they want to hear. They are egojunkies. They are shits. They are asking for it, and we give it to them, is all. We fill a need, just like dealers in more concrete commodities like smack.

■ ■ ■ ■ ■ ■ ■ ■ ■ ■ ■

"I got one!" Bruce shouted, like a prospector who has just struck paydirt, at 3:22 P.M. (We're all clock-watchers, of course.)

I looked up from my letter to Theodore Q. Hurst, a regular fee writer who is a semiliterate cop in Pasadena, said: "Got what?"

"A nice little mystery story from a new freak. Worth a try, anyway." Bruce leaned forward and said to Nancy: "Fetch Dickie, wench."

We always love running across a submission that might be marketable. Because it gives us a sense of fulfillment? Not exactly. Because if Dickie accepts the thing for marketing, all that's required from us is a little note that says:

Dear Mrs. Carbunkle:
Thanks very much for your story, *Chickenfat Junction.* I found it entertaining, well-written, and I'm taking it right out to market. I hope I'll have good news on it for you soon.
Sincerely,
DIRK ROBINSON

Which sure as hell beats writing a two page single-spaced letter! These diamonds in the rough, however, put Dickie in a curious bind. The Man does not trust us lowly fee readers to unilaterally transfer a manuscript from fee country to the lofty heights of pro territory. Now Dickie had to read the thing and either drop it on the desk of one of the pro people for marketing or bounce it back to Bruce with a pained expression. Dickie, being Dickie, and therefore Dirk's prophet and a dedicated player of the Big Game, not only had to pretend that he was elated at the prospect of discovering a potential new pro client but had to psyche himself into believing it too.

"What? What?" Dickie said when he arrived with his usual air of having been interrupted in the middle of some Big Deal.

"This," said Bruce, handing him the manuscript.

"Which is?"

"A nice 3,500 worder for *Ellery Queen* or *Hitchcock.*"

Dickie tucked the manuscript into his armpit. "I'll take it under advisement," he said.

■ ■ ■ ■ ■ ■ ■ ■ ■ ■ ■

He started to go, then paused, leaned over the desk and drew us into a huddle like a quarterback who has just decided to change signals on a hunch—a sure sign that he was about to drop a carefully-calculated piece of gossip.

"Is there a pornographer in the house?" Dickie asked.

"Huh?"

"I've just gotten the Word," Dickie said. "*Slick* is looking for a new slush-pile reader. Dirk thinks he can get the job for one of his boys."

"It's not like Dirk to help promote one of his peons out of Dirk Robinson, Inc.," Berkowitz observed.

"What's his percentage?" I asked.

Dickie smiled beatifically. "Gentlemen," he said, "I ask you, who has more slush to drop in said pile than this worthy establishment?"

"Are you suggesting that said slush-pile reader would be expected to give special consideration to Dirk Robinson submissions?" Bruce asked.

"Would I suggest anything so unethical?" Dickie said archly. "*However*, Dirk in his childlike innocence assumes that he is not surrounded by ingrates. I say no more."

"Isn't *Slick* one of those LA stiffener magazines?" Berkowitz asked.

"Un-huh," Dickie said.

"Los Angeles?"

"You expect one of us to go to *Los Angeles?*"

"Feh."

Dickie shrugged. "Think it over," he said. "Fame and fortune awaits in the Golden West. Also, I am reliably informed, all the unretouched doity pictures you can eat." And with that, he hustled back to his inner sanctum.

"Something fishy," Bruce said.

"Isn't there always?"

"It just doesn't add up," Bruce insisted. "Big deal, Dirk gets an inside man as a slush-pile reader. So what? A slush-pile reader can't *buy* anything."

"You don't think Dirk is just being altruistic?" I said.

Bruce and Berkowitz rolled their eyes.

And, I suppose, that's why people stay on as fee readers at Dirk Robinson. None of us was about to involve ourselves in Dirk's machinations to the ridiculous extent of picking up and going to Los Angeles. But this was a taste of the Big Game, Dirk Robinson's exercise in paper empire building, and we *could* get into it any time we chose. In the very office we sat in, novels and stories were sold every day, foreign rights, coups pulled off, six-figure movie deals closed. Any day, I, me, Tom Hollander, *could* discover the Great American Novel in the shitpile. I *could* try for a pro desk. I *could* become a slush-pile reader at *Slick*. The Big Game swirled around me every day, and I could get into it any time I chose.

Of course I would do nothing of the kind—what a drag to actually *play* the Big Game. But it was a great spectator-sport and I had a front-row seat; I got the surge with no sweat involved. And all I had to do to keep my choice seat was traffic in the reading and writing of bullshit.

Sitting there, thinking about it, I remembered Robin and the acid trip and Harvey and his foundation. Remembered that both silly scenes had become just another bullshit story to tell to Dickie. My head had been turned inside out twice and sitting here digging the Big Game, it *was* just a joke. A fee manuscript from a lunatic ex-junkie.

Which I could laugh at in my present incarnation as a fee reader for the Dirk Robinson Bullshit Agency, Inc . . . .

Dear Mr. Hurst:
Thank you very much for your latest submission, *Black Pow-er—Or Red Power-Grab?* This hard-hitting expose of the Urban League is surely your strongest work so far. However, there are certain elements which . . .

As soon as I hung up the phone, I got the feeling that I should've brushed him off, but hell, I couldn't do that to Ted, could I? Ah, he just wants to come over and shoot the shit for a while on a quiet Wednesday night, he knows I've gotta go to work tomorrow, he can't be out to drag me to the Foundation or anything.

So I went back into the living room ready to make like a host. Ted lived only a few minutes away, but I figured I might have time to read one of the fee manuscripts I had taken home with me. I take a few home every once in a while, the real sickies which are good for a laugh; if I can get a little work done at odd moments I can go home early on Friday or rack up a few extra points and a few extra bucks.

I turned on one of the pole-lamp lights (you'd go blind trying to read in that orange light) and curled up to wait for Ted and Doris with:

The Little Blue Snake
(a fairy tale)
by Doris Wheeler Finche
Once many long years ago in a wee little country across the green ocean, there was a bosky dell in the deep dark woods. Under a cozy rock by the roots of a great oak tree there lived a cute little blue snake named Peter . . .

Hmmm . . . A little blue snake named Peter. *Peter!*

—Although he was the nicest little blue snake in the forest, Peter was not happy. He did not want to be a little blue snake. "Oh, why can't I be a big red snake and scare all the little girls who pick acorns around the roots of my tree?" he would sigh.

What? Jesus Christ! A little blue snake named Peter who wants to be big and red and scare the girls? Naw, this *has* to be a put-on! I turned a couple of pages, read at random:

. . . and so the evil magician waved his hand and Peter began to swell and swell and grow and grow and puff up red with pride. "Oh!" cried Peter. "Now I'll be just the biggest reddest fiercest snake in the whole forest and wait till those mean little girls . . .

Bleech! There are times when the fee desk at Dirk Robinson resembles the Black Hole of Calcutta. What a letter I'm going to have to write on this one!

Dear Miss Finche:
Thanks just ever so much for your fairy-tale. While it is clearly the sort of thing that would make Kraft-Ebbing puke, it does indeed display considerable literary talent . . .

Fortunately for my sanity, there was a tremendous thumping at the door that could only be Ted. I deposited Miss Finche's phallic fairy tale on the big red table near the central hole from which the pole lamp sprouted (dig *that* Miss Finche!) and went to the door.

In the hall stood Ted and Doris and an unknown girl in a green toggle-coat. Honey-blond hair, intense green eyes behind black-rimmed glasses, full lips *au natural*, pale smooth skin pink with the November chill, a flaring nose that was slightly but not unpleasantly Semitic, and giving off strange, somehow exciting, tense vibes. As Dickie would say, "A promising puss, old man."

"Well come on, man, invite us in," Ted said.

"Wel-cum to Cohumnist Chin-na," I said in a Charley Chan accent. Ted, Doris, and the slightly uptight blond stepped into the kitchen, out of which mess I led them at flank speed and into the living room. Ted took off his coat, tossed it on the big table and sat down on the wing of the couch under the windows, resting his combat boots on the table. Doris took off her coat and sat down next to him, but, typically, kept her feet on the ground. The girl in the green toggle-coat stood there like a girl in a green toggle-coat getting more and more uptight. In certain ways, Ted can be a prime shithead. Or was he setting it up for me?

"I must apologize for my neanderthaler friends here," I said to the girl in the toggle-coat. "However, I did notice that you came in with them and I assume you're not a gate-crasher, so if you'll take off your coat and sit down, maybe that creep who is digging holes in my table with his Wehrmacht surplus jackboots will condescend to introduce us."

A ghost of a smile I could not tell meant drop dead smartass or thank you; she took off the coat, handed it to me, I dropped it on the table over Doris's, she sat down on the empty wing of my jury-rigged sectional since Ted and Doris pretty well covered the other cot, and I sat down next to her. Neatly done. But by whom?

"Oh yeah," Ted finally said, "this is Arlene Cooper. Arlene, this is the world-famous Tom Hollander."

Strange vibes: Ted invites himself up, doesn't tell me he's bringing this chick, then makes it all so super-casual, but the chick is too up-tight for it to be all a spur-of-the-moment thing, more like she's meat for the monster and knows it.

"We met Arlene at the Foundation," Doris said. "She's a graduate student in English. Ted happened to mention that you worked in a literary agency and . . . "

Oh no!

"Actually, I'm in the school of Ed at City," Arlene Cooper said. "I mean, I guess I'll end up teaching English, I hope on a college level, but I've got to take my Masters in Ed because you have to be in the school of Ed for the grant I've got that pays the rent. You know . . . "

She shrugged a Gallic shrug and smiled a Jewish smile. Nice combination. Arlene Cooper was wearing a loose white blouse which revealed nice breasts (or maybe just a good bra) only when she shrugged and a shapeless black skirt that at least hinted at good legs and a nice ass.

"Arlene is a writer," Ted said, and shot me a look which seemed to say that her writing could be the key to her cunt. Meat for the monster, yes.

Arlene squirmed a little at this, gave me a little look that said she knew such a remark was gauche and pretentious, but what could you do. I gave her a little smile that told her I had read her look; she smiled back and so the seed of something was planted between us.

"I just . . . fool around a little," she said. "I mean, I haven't *sold* anything." Meaning of course that I was therefore a Figure of Significance. Meaning of course that if I played Literary Lion, I could ball her in about three simple moves. The prospect was exciting: something about her uptightness hinted at a really wild lay if I could uncork all that tension. And Ted had set her up for me with all of his old-time style.

"I don't know what Ted told you about my job . . . " I said, tentatively deciding: yes, I wanted to ball her, but no, I didn't want Dirk Robinson, Inc., pimping for me.

"He said you work for the Dirk Robinson agency. That's a big agency, isn't it?"

"Dirk claims it's the biggest," I said. Two points for first-naming Dirk.

I saw Ted smiling a go-get-her smile, Doris sitting back like a satisfied Jewish momma. Funny vibes.

"I read manuscripts, evaluate them, and write letters of criticism to authors," I lied truthfully.

Behind her glasses, Arlene Cooper's green eyes lit up. Her weight seemed to gravitate towards my body subliminally. Oh yes, this would be easy! Too easy—about as sporting as hunting rabbits with an elephant gun. I decided to give myself a handicap to make the game more interesting.

"Would you like to see the story I'm considering now?" I said with modest self-importance. Ted, who had heard plenty of Dirk Robinson stories, winced. Doris just looked confused at old Tom being self-destructive again.

Arlene nodded like a sweet little girl, which, behind the uptightness of being a would-be writer, an Ed major, and a Harvey Brustein sucker, just maybe she was.

I handed her Doris Wheeler Finche's little master(bation) piece; Ted rolled his eyes as she began to leaf through it. Doris looked pained. Ted, Doris, and I stared at each other peculiarly while Arlene skim-read (a natural fee-reader) *The Little Blue Snake*. After a couple of minutes, she tossed the manuscript back on the table as if it had leprosy.

"That's . . . why that's *pathological*," she said piously.

"Really?"

"I mean, it's an obviously phallic fantasy on an overt level. Who would publish a thing like that?"

"Nobody."

"Do you often see things as sick as that?"

"Oh, only about ten times a week."

"I don't understand," Arlene said innocently. "How can a literary agency handle writers like *that*?"

"They pay to have their stuff read," I said. "Ten bucks for a thing like that, for instance."

"You mean you'll consider *anyone's* work?"

"As long as the check doesn't bounce."

Poor Arlene looked as if she had fallen down a rabbit-hole. "But what can you *tell* someone like this woman? She obviously needs psychiatric help. Can you tell her that?"

"I tell her she's a great writer, but this story isn't quite suitable for the marketplace, that she should write another story and another ten dollar check and that the next one will probably make it."

"But the woman's *hopeless!*"

"It is the Dirk Robinson philosophy that no one is hopeless who can still write checks."

"But you're *lying* to her!"

"She doesn't think so. She *knows* she's a great writer who just needs a little minor help. We tell them exactly what they expect to hear."

"That's horrid."

"Indubitably," I said. So much for the handicap. Now the game should start to get interesting.

"You know," Arlene said, making some kind of dialectical leap from indignation to crusading, "you're really in a position to help people like this. Isn't there some way you could refer at least the ones in New York to the Foundation for Total Consciousness?"

Now *there's* an idea! "Y'know, you may just have something there . . . " I said thoughtfully. "Dirk just might go for it—if you think Harvey would give him a kickback."

"A *kickback!*"

"Oh, not a big one," I soothed. "Dirk would probably settle for something like 5% of the first year's take. He'd figure to make it up on the volume."

Ted couldn't take it any longer. "Cut it out, man," she said. "She thinks you're serious."

"But I *am* serious, Ted," I said with a big Dickie Lee shit-eating smile. "Dirk would go for it. Don't you think old Harv would?"

"Aw shit!" Ted said.

"And as a side-deal, Harv would get 5% of the fees from all the twitches he could refer to Dirk."

"Are you equating this disgusting swindle with *the Foundation for Total Consciousness?*" Arlene practically shrieked.

"Sure," I said blandly. "Fundamentally, it's the same con. Dirk and Harvey are both master bullshit artists. Same clientele, potentially. They're both peddling answers to a lot of empty people. They'd get along fine."

A long, long, grossed-out silence. Ted, Doris, and Arlene ex-changed shocked looks. Then the same kind of fever seemed to put a sheen on their six eyeballs: the intense rodent-mindlessness of a Sal-vation Army topkick in the presence of a sinner, the look of Dickie Lee about to persuade a neophyte fee-reader with delusions of con-science of the morality of the operation. Well, I couldn't say I hadn't asked for it.

"Look, Tom, I didn't really want to get into it," Ted said uncon-vincingly, "but you've really got a crazy paranoid thing going about Harvey. You should've seen yourself last week, man!"

I clocked Arlene; she was hunched forward like a rooting section. I was now damn sure there was more to this evening than met the eye. I was willing to bet the three of them had come here to play games with my mind. Okay, four can play that game too . . . .

"Will you admit one thing, Ted?" I said. "Will you admit that I should know a junkie's face when I see one?"

Another long awkward silence. Doris and Ted looked at each oth-er uneasily, probably wondering how to sweep the subject under the rug. Arlene just looked puzzled. I was back out ahead of them.

I looked straight into Arlene's big green eyes. "I was a junkie, you know," I said conversationally. "A pretty heavy habit." Her eyes got wider, then seemed to narrow, and a muscle in her jaw twitched.

"Yes, but he's been off it for a long time, right Tom?" Doris said quickly.

"Right," I said.

"How . . . how did you manage to stop?" Arlene said, suddenly the uptight square chick trying to make small talk with a Dope-Fiend. "Analysis . . . ? Lexington? Synanon?"

"Boredom," I told her. "It got to be a drag, so I gave it up for Lent."

"*Cold Turkey?*" she said. "Just like that?"

Oh WoW.

"Just like that."

"But wasn't it . . . ? I mean, I've heard that junkies almost never kick it by themselves. The withdrawal symptoms . . . "

"Are greatly exaggerated by bullshitartists who write about dope-fiends," I said. "And by junkies who use it as an excuse to take the next shot. I did a certain amount of puking and shivering and sweat-ing and screaming for a few days. Combine three consecutive days of the twenty-four hour virus with a migraine, malaria and a bad hang-over and you'll get the idea. Fun it ain't, but honest, you can live through it."

Muscles all over Arlene relaxed; her eyes got warmer; I almost got the feeling she was undressing me in her mind. She was impressed. And no wonder—here was a chick who was convinced she needed a shrink because of penis-envy or some other Freudian fairy tale face to face with a junkie who had locked himself in a room and beat 99 to 1 odds by going "Cold Turkey." Thanks to *The Man With the Golden Arm* & Co., I was now a bona fide existentialist hero in her eyes. God bless you, Otto Preminger.

"But you *couldn't* have been . . . the usual junkie," she said admiringly. "I mean, it *is* true that most of them can't stop." Now I was reasonably impressed. Also, she had handed me the straight-line I was angling for.

"Most of them don't want to stop," I said. "It's not the withdrawal bummer—that's just an easy cop-out. It's why they become junkies in the first place. Most junkies become junkies because they're junk-prone personalities. I became a junkie because I was living with a junkie and it was what came naturally. When I got good and tired of her bad scenes, I threw her out, and once she was gone, there was no reason for me to stay on smack. So I stopped. Because I'm not a junk-prone personality. You and Ted and Doris are."

"What???" More or less in chorus.

"Man, that's the Foundation! All of you sitting there and mainlining old Harv's Total Consciousness junk."

"Bull-*shit*, man!" Ted said. "You're just playing word-games and you know it."

But Arlene seemed to be even more fascinated than before. "What do you mean?" she said earnestly. Old Ted had said exactly the wrong thing; the would-be writer side of her had been turned on. She leaned a little closer. I could fee the warmth of her body beside me know.

I turned to her; Ted and Doris were strictly excess baggage now, whether they knew it or not.

"Why do you go to the Foundation?" I said.

"Why . . . ah . . . to achieve Total Consciousness . . . "

"What's Total Consciousness?"

"I don't know how to put it into words . . . "

"You want to be a writer and you can't put it into words?"

She frowned, smiled, then shrugged and said: "Well . . . ah, Harvey says it's . . . losing your ego hang-ups . . . being able to live totally in the immediacy of now . . . Kind of a Buddhist thing, the annihilation of the ego . . ."

"Ego-death?"

"Well . . . I suppose so, but I mean not as *negative* as it sounds . . ."

"Ego-death doesn't sound negative at all the way some people say it."

"You mean Timothy Leary and his acid cult?"

"Uh huh. You could say they're acid-junkies." Did I really believe that? Was Robin an acid-junkie? Well, what the hell, true or not, it was the right move in the game.

"But acid isn't like heroin," Arlene said. "Heroin isn't a psychedelic." Of course she was right; that *was* the difference: heroin turns you off, acid turns you on.

"Neither is the Foundation for Total Consciousness," I said.

Arlene and I stared at each other, me projecting, she receiving, I thought. I hoped. Win or lose, she was at least giving me a good game.

"Bull-*shit* it isn't!" Ted said. "Total Psychotherapy is the only real consciousness-expander."

I kept my eyes locked on Arlene's. "See?" I said, smiling at her, not bothering to answer Ted. "He admits it's a drug."

"But not like heroin . . ."

"Oh no?" I said. "It hooks you, doesn't it? It changes your head like junk."

"Acid changes your . . . head too, doesn't it?"

"Sure, but the idea is to come back—it's called an acid *trip*, right? But people who get hung-up on junk like the Foundation or heroin want their heads to *stay* changed."

"I think I see . . ." Arlene said slowly. "You're right about one thing anyway . . . the Foundation's thing is to make the change permanent . . ."

The lines of relationship in the room were on the verge of shifting. Ted, Doris and Arlene had come in together; I was the outsider. With a little nudge, Ted and Doris would become the outsiders, and Arlene and I . . . .

"Aw bullshit," said Ted.

Now I looked at him, but it was a posture I made strictly for Arlene's benefit. "You mean you *don't* want the Foundation to change your head?" I said.

"Well sure . . . but . . . "

"But there are good changes and bad changes," Doris said.

"Yeah," said Ted, "and the Foundation puts you through good changes."

"How do you know that till you've changed?" I said.

Silence.

"You don't," I said. "You know you don't know—you just hope. Question is, Arlene Cooper, why do you hate Arlene Cooper so much that you're willing to take the chance of letting some cat play with your mind when all you really know is that he'll change you, for better or worse, in sickness or in health, till death do you part?"

She stared at me as if I could be her next guru-candidate. Which, of course, was exactly the idea. "Sometimes . . . sometimes you've got to take that chance, I guess . . . " she finally said.

"But only with someone who's taking the same chance with himself on *you*," I said. Our eyes bored holes in each other.

"I . . . I suppose that's one of the things a man and a woman want out of a relationship," she said.

I nodded. "I'd be willing to take that chance with you . . . ."

Out of the corner of my eye, I could see Ted and Doris fidgeting, exchanging glances, realizing, I hoped, that it was time for a quick exit.

"I . . . I . . . might be willing to take that chance on you too," Arlene said. A jaw muscle twitched.

"But you're afraid." I smiled at her. "I'm a little afraid too," I said. "That's a good sign." I touched her hand lightly. She didn't pull it away.

"Maybe we . . . should . . . talk about it . . . " she said.

"Well, uh, look," Ted said loudly, "we gotta be going. Gotta make my private session with Harvey in about an hour. Coming, Arlene?"

"I don't have a session tonight," she said. Aha!

"It's still pretty early," I said. "Why don't you stick around and we can . . . ."

She smiled at me, squeezed by hand.

"All right," she said, with just enough uptightness coming back into her voice to let me know that she knew that I had a bit more in mind than discussing the ethical structure of the universe.

Check.

And mate?

6
Belly to Belly

I closed the door behind Ted and Doris, slid the policelock bar into place and walked back through the clutter of the kitchen to the doorway of the living room, where I stood quietly for a moment clocking Arlene Cooper.

She was sitting up very straight on the edge of the couch, staring at the bookcases against the far wall, or maybe just staring. Her medium-length blonde hair looked coppery and sensual in the orange light, but the line of her jaw was firmly set, her eyes seemed withdrawn behind those glasses, and her fingers were toying nervously with the folds of her black skirt. Standing there, I got a cold feeling in my stomach, fighting the warmth in my groin; digging her in a just-the-two-of-us-alone situation, I was pretty sure this was going to be a lot more complicated than I had thought.

Girding my equivocal loins, I entered the lion's den, sat down beside her, smiled, and was surely about to think of a brilliant lead-in, when she began to knead her hands together and said:

"Look, Tom, I don't want you to think . . . I mean that I usually . . . put myself in this . . . kind of situation at the spur of the moment . . . I mean . . . I'm not . . . "

Oh shit, I thought, honest baby. I'll just respect the ass off of you! "Not what?" I said, with all the deep, serious concern I could muster.

"Well . . . you know . . . I don't usually go . . . hopping into bed with guys I've just met . . . ." Smoothing the cloth of her skirt with her hands now.

"Why not?" I said.

"Why not! What do you think I am?"

"A girl," I said. "What do you think *I* am?"

Now at least she was puzzled instead of angry. She looked at me strangely, cocking her head to one side like a parrot.

I took her hand. It was cold and sweaty and rigid in mine, but she didn't pull it away.

"Let me tell you my terrible secret," I said. "Many times in the past, I've been perfectly willing to hop into bed with girls I've just met. In fact, I've done it on every occasion I could. Do you now consider me cheap? Am I just an easy lay? Will you now use me callously and then toss me aside?"

She laughed; the lines in her face relaxed and her hand softened in mine. But it went rigid again and the muscles in her jaw tightened as the laugh passed and she said: "But you're a *man*."

"Nice of you to notice."

"You know what I mean . . . ."

Oh WoW, did I know what she meant! I was getting the shitty end of Ye Olde Double Standard, only upside down and backwards.

"Yeah, I know what you mean," I said. "But do you really know what you mean?"

"I know how men think."

"Really? Are you on the Pill?" (Might as well kill two birds with one stone.)

"Of all the—" She pulled her hand away.

"Take it easy. I'm not trying to be gross," I said. "I'm just trying to show you something about yourself. Humor me for a minute. *Are* you on the Pill?"

"Well . . . yes . . . ."

"Okay. Now, it's logical to assume that you're on the Pill because you don't want to get pregnant, right?"

"Right."

"And unless you *really* have delusions of grandeur, there's only one way to get pregnant, right?"

"So?"

"So if you're on the Pill, you're walking around thinking it might happen at any time."

She cringed at the truth. I took both her hands. Her palms were stiff and sweaty.

"You really don't understand what I'm saying, do you?" I said. "Look, all I'm saying is *it's all right.* I'm thinking about making it with someone I just met. You know that for openers, you expect it. You'd be insulted if I *didn't* want to, wouldn't you? You don't think it makes me a shit, do you?"

"Just a man," she said.

"Okay. So why judge yourself harder than you judge me? Fucking is fun. We both know that, I hope. You don't put me down for wanting to enjoy your body. So why should you think I'd think any the less of you for wanting to do what I *want* you to want to do?"

She looked at me wide-eyed. I could sense that I had gotten to her mind, but there seemed to be a whole lot of weird garbage between

her head and her cunt. This was all really starting to bring me down.
I smiled a mock-coy smile. "Okay," I said, "so relax. I promise I
won't even make a pass at you. I dig you. We'll forget about sex until
we've come to a more complete understanding of the ethical structure of the universe."

"Very funny."

"No, I mean it," I said soberly. "You're a woman, but you're also a
human being. I'm not going to con you into doing something you
don't want to do. I'm perfectly willing to pass up a little fun to prove
that to you."

She looked at me long and hard. She frowned. She smiled. Her
lower lip trembled.

"I . . . I think we're starting to carry this intellectualizing a little too
far . . . " she said. Paused.

And leaned over and kissed me on the lips. My mouth was caught
closed. Her mouth was open. She opened my lips with hers and
jammed her tongue into my mouth, moved it around powerfully, almost athletically. Our tongues met for a moment, disputed the territory. Our lips parted. We looked into each other's eyes.

It had been a very clumsy kiss, but coming from this girl at this
time, in this situation, I appreciated it for the brave and magnificent
gesture it was, and in the brief moment when our lips parted, I loved
her for it.

"Arlene Cooper," I said, "there's a woman inside you."

She smiled a sweet little girl smile, took off her glasses, and placed
them on the table. Somehow, in context, it was a terrifically sexy
thing to do, turned me on better than a fullscale strip.

We reached for each other, our lips met, and again her tongue
forced itself into my mouth, huge and stiff and awkward. I forced it
back with my own; she resisted for a moment, then understood. All
at once, her mouth went nice and woman-soft, and her lips welcomed
my tongue in, and my arms were tight around her, and her hands
moved slightly over my back. I ran a hand over her breasts: full and
sighing but constricted by her brassiere. I caressed her tongue with
mine and stroked her outer thigh. She was wearing a girdle. She
moved liquidly against me, moaned softly into my mouth. I pulled
my lips slowly from hers and the kiss ended with the tips of our
tongues touching outside our mouths.

We faced each other inches apart. Her green eyes had gone soft. I
had gone hard. Electricity at last in the air between us. She smiled

shyly. I smiled back, squeezed her hands.

"We could go into the bedroom . . . " I suggested softly.

She looked down, squeezed my hands back and, without looking at me, nodded yes.

■ ■ ■ ■ ■ ■ ■ ■ ■ ■ ■

"I've got a ten o'clock class tomorrow," she said as we stood before the bed. "Could you set the alarm for 8:30 . . . ."

A mood-breaker, but necessary, I suppose. "I've got to be at work by nine," I said. "It's already set for eight, okay?"

She nodded, reached to turn out the light on the night table. I grabbed her hand before she could reach the switch. Our eyes met in argument. I won.

I pulled back the covers and sat down on the bed. She turned her back on me and kicked off her shoes. I took off my shoes and socks. Still with her back to me, she unbuttoned her blouse, took it off, and tossed it over her shoulder onto the night table. Her brassiere was white and faded and cut deep into the pale flesh of her back. I took off my shirt and undershirt and threw them over her blouse. She undid her skirt, stepped through it and put it on the night table. I took off my pants and sat on the bed in my shorts digging her as she detached the tops of here stockings from her girdle and rolled them off her legs functionally and unsensually. She unhooked her bra, took it off. I could see the red marks across her back. I took off my shorts and enjoyed my nakedness as she struggled out of her girdle. More red welts above her soft, full ass.

She paused, then turned, and I saw her nakedness for a moment: heavy full breasts with pale pink nipples, the slightest concavity to her belly, smooth firm thighs, whispy red pubic hair, an uptight smile as she looked at my body stretched out on the bed, a tremor in her lower lip as her eyes passed briefly across my hard-on.

Then she threw herself on top of me, flipped off the light, tangled my hair in her hands and whispered with a forced throatiness: "Let's fuck!"

In the darkness, I felt her body moving on mine in jerky, exaggerated rhythms. She kissed me, started to push her tongue inside my mouth—I clamped my arms around her, rolled her over and beneath me, pulled my mouth away from hers and flicked my tongue inside her ear. I felt her shudder.

Quickly, I began stroking the inside of her thighs with one hand, kissed her and began moving my tongue inside her mouth in slow pelvic rotations and she sighed soundlessly and began moving her hips to the touch of my hand in a softer, more deeply-felt rhythm.

I ran my other hand up and down between the cleft of her breasts and over her soft stomach, up, down, and around, up, down, and around, keeping time with the motions of my hand between her legs, my tongue in her mouth.

Our mouths parted softly around her moan; her belly under my hand began to tremble like a luffing sail—her legs clamped tight around my other hand and she began to buck her hips awkwardly. She reached down and grabbed the shaft of my cock in one hand and began milking it savagely. Dammit, we were fighting each other; she was breaking my slow and building rhythm with hard staccato frenzy and her pumping hand was bringing me along too fast! Too fast!

Still stroking her thighs with one hand, trying to get her to go with my rhythm, I reached down with my other hand and the two of us fumbled with my parts in silence, then with hers, then everything together. Feeling myself in danger of letting go, I finally got her hand away and got myself inside. She bucked me out. "Shit!" I cursed audibly, and bumbled my way inside again, planted myself firmly with a heavy thrust of my hips.

I began moving my hips slowly, slowly, slow it down, baby! She slowed down, trying to match my rhythm, but she wasn't making it, she wasn't grooving with my moves; now she was a half-beat ahead of me, now a half-beat behind. Damn!

She began to moan loudly, wordlessly. I felt myself moving towards the crest, but only from the waist down. I couldn't tell *where* she was at.

Then suddenly, she clamped her legs around my waist, hard. She started to squeeze my body with her thighs as if she were trying to get out the stuff at the bottom of a toothpaste tube—harder and harder, faster and faster, like an engine out of control.

All at once, with no warning, I came; soundlessly, hardly feeling it. And she was still moaning and squeezing me with her legs frantically. I felt myself starting to lose it . . . .

Goddamn, I would not let this chick do that to me! From somewhere deep inside, maybe from the pit of pure fury, I found the stuff to keep myself going. I began thrusting, harder and harder against her pounding rhythm, faster and faster, sheer brute force, knowing it was now or never, feeling myself starting to go soft, pounding ahead on memory alone. Bang! Bang! Bang!

Finally, she let loose a nasal scream, her body gave a tremendous heave, and it was over. Just as I felt myself leaving her.

Reflexively, I half-rolled off her, then paused, kissed her lightly on the cheek, perhaps more than half-sarcastically; then I did roll off and pulled the covers over our panting bodies. I reached for the light switch; her hands caught mine and pulled it back.

"Please . . . " she said softly.

I sighed, pulled my hand back under the covers, and we lay there for long moments, not speaking, not touching.

Jeez, what a bummer! I thought, remembering Robin, remembering just about every lay I could to avoid thinking about what had just happened. Like fucking some out of control milking machine . . . I felt used up, fucked out, spent and sticky . . . .

"Thank you," she finally said softly, breaking the ugly silence.

"For *what?*" I answered coldly.

"For . . . what you did . . . for helping me come after . . . after the way it was for you . . . ."

All the anger and frustration went out of me like air out of a balloon. Oh you poor kid . . . you poor lost sorry kid . . . .

"I'm . . . I'm not very good at it," she said. "I know I'm not very good at it . . . ."

I hated myself for it, but I dissolved into a sloppy mass of tenderness. What could I say? What could I do? I moved closer to her, letting her feel my skin against her. She was tense and rigid. What the hell could I say . . . ?

"You . . . you seem to like it . . . " I finally managed lamely.

"I . . . I do like it. I like the way it feels . . . But I can't . . . I can't . . . " I felt her choke back a sob. I put my arm around her and pulled her head down on my chest.

"I can't seem to . . . connect up," she said. "I can feel what happens to me but . . . I can't feel a man . . . .It's good for me, but I know . . . ."

She began to cry lightly. "I know I'm a terrible fuck," she said.

"Aw, you're not that bad," I said, stroking her hair.

"Don't lie to me!"

"All right, I won't."

"I know what my problem is," she said. "Harvey says I can't give myself to a man because I cling too tightly to my ego. I'm afraid of merging my consciousness with a man's. That's why I can't let go . . . ." Now she had stopped crying, drying her honest tears with the cruddy towel of textbook intellectualizing. Shit!

"Screw Harvey Brustein!" I snarled. "Shove his Total Consciousness up his anal-retentive syndrome!"

"Stop it! Harvey's helped me and no one else ever has. Before I came to the Foundation, I couldn't even come."

Do you believe it? I felt like a character in some idiotic Feiffer cartoon. For a hundred dollars a month, you too can learn to come . . . Just you and me and Harvey makes three. But if that filthy mother were *really* in bed with us, I'd tear off his right arm and beat him to death with it! Stinking son of a bitch!

"Stick with me, baby," I said, "and we'll have you seeing novas." Now why the hell did I say *that?* Was my manhood involved or what? Well maybe it was—if I couldn't do more for her with my dick than Harvey could with his gibbering, it was time to hang up!

"You mean . . . after . . . this . . . you still want to . . . to see me again?"

"After all, practice makes perfect," I heard myself say. What the fuck was I getting myself into?

She kissed me lightly on the lips, so grateful I wanted to cry, and all the hassle I saw coming suddenly seemed worth it.

"You know, you're the only man I could ever talk about it afterward with who even cared . . . ."

I hugged her to me, the poor sorry bitch. A bad fuck with a good heart. Shit! How did I get into these things? You should kiss this poor creature goodbye, I told myself. Swine if you do, I answered back. Conscience, yet!

"Tom," she said, "I'd like to ask you a big favor."

I felt the cold breath of still more trouble down the back of my neck. Nevertheless, I said: "Ask away."

"Come to my therapy group this Friday," she said.

"No dice. I'm not about to let Harvey and company waltz through my head."

"For me . . . please? It could be what I need for a real breakthrough, having someone in my group who understands first hand . . . who cares . . . "

Damn! Right in the old ego, not to mention the old conscience. Ooooh, that fucker Brustein! What this chick really needs is some Acapulco Gold and a solid weekend of getting her brains fucked out. Literally getting those damned Foundation-ridden brains of hers fucked out of her system.

Yeah . . . Well, why not? Okay, go to the damn therapy group and show it up for what it is and then take her home for the weekend and fuck some sense into her!

"Okay, baby." I said. "But I warn you, I go in there out for blood."

She kissed my forehead. "Tom Hollander," she said, "you're not half as tough as you come on. You're an old-fashioned gentleman, is what you are."

Do you believe that? How could I let a chick who said something like that to me go down for the third time? How could I let her throw her life away sucking up old Harvey's junk?

But as we drifted off to sleep in each other's arms, I seemed to remember that I had once thought I could win Anne away from smack . . . and how *that* ended up . . . .

But it wasn't really the same thing . . . no, not the same thing at all . . . .

7
Room 101

Somehow, it seemed appropriate that the room Arlene led me into had no windows. In fact, it had nothing but cheap gray fiberboard walls, a frosted-globe light fixture, institutional carpeting on the floor, and a semicircle of eight green metal folding chairs, each with a cheap ashtray beneath it.

Arlene and I were the first to arrive. "Welcome to Room 101," I said. I sat down on the chair at the left end of the semicircle. Arlene sat down two seats away.

"What's that for?" I said. "I used Ban this morning."

"One of the rules," Arlene said. "Two people who are . . . involved with each other can't sit together. If they did, they might give each other support."

"Wouldn't that be a disaster?" I said. Arlene seemed about twelve light-years away behind her glasses; seemed to be no human connection between us at all now. I was really starting to feel like an asshole for letting myself get sucked into this thing. *Starting?*

"What do the rules say about freebies?" I asked. "I hope I'm not expected to pay for this."

"You're allowed one free trial group session. Then you can have your first six weeks' groups and membership for only $50. That doesn't include private sessions, of course."

Old Harv sure had it down to a science. One free shot, a cut-rate ounce, and then when you're good and hooked, the price takes off for the stratosphere.

"Am I expected?" I asked.

"Of course."

Uh-huh.

At this point in walked Ida, the biddy who had faked the ass-grabbing game with Ted at last week's party, looking like a female version of Torquemada with her hatchet-face and her hair in a Mrs. Grundy bun. She sat down between Arlene and me and lit a cigarette (blindfold optional).

Followed closely by my lost love from last week, Linda Kahn, who gave me a you'll-get-yours look and sat down on the other side of Arlene. Then, just as I was beginning to wonder if this was Tom Hollander-versus-six-uptight-chicks night, two guys walked in: a thin, blond cat of about forty in a Madison avenue brown suit and image but with the slightly-mottled skin and rheumy eyes of an obvious rummy; and a kid in blue Levis and checked flannel shirt with medium-long straight black hair that just didn't fit with his thick Brooklyn-hood face.

The Mad Ave type walked over to me as the kid sat down on the far right-hand chair, held out his hand. I took it; it was soft and squishy.

"Charley Dees," he said, with a hollow three-martini-lunch smile.

"Tom Hollander."

Old Charley sat down next to the kid, who muttered "Rich Rossi" across the room at me. Just for kicks, I gave him the "V" sign. He didn't quite know how to take it.

And then bad, bad vibes walked into the room with Doris. Doris! I had the distinct feeling I had been set up for something.

"Welcome to old home week," I said sourly.

"Hello Tom," Doris said from behind some bullet-proof glass wall. She sat down next to good old Charley, leaving a central seat vacant for guess-who.

Not exactly a cozy group. I was sure that this thing was stacked against me—and even paranoids have enemies.

And then the Man entered the Star Chamber and closed the door behind him. Harvey was dressed in the same baggy gray pants and crummy tieless white shirt he had worn at the party. Or was he? I wouldn't put it past Harvey to have a whole closetful of baggy gray pants and dirty white shirts.

Harvey sat down on the empty folding chair, lit a cigarette, exhaled smoke, and said conversationally: "Are you still smoking pot, Rich?"

Rich squirmed, pouted. He looked more like a Brooklyn hood than ever.

"Come on, Rossi," Charley said crisply, "a simple yes or no answer."

"Are you still a lush?" Rich snarled.

"We're not talking about Charley," Arlene said.

"Are you still getting stoned every day?" Doris said.

"Ted fucked you lately?" Rich said.

Doris flushed. I think I flushed, too. What kind of crazy shit was this?

"Come on, Rossi," Charley said, "you ashamed of it?"

"Fuck you, dad. No, I'm not ashamed of it. I just don't dig listening to all you dumb assholes trying to make me ashamed of it." Well, well. Maybe Rich wasn't a complete prick after all.

"Then why do you come to group?" Ida said.

"Same reason I go to the zoo."

Two points for you, Rich baby.

"Baloney," Charley said. "You're hiding from reality."

"You wouldn't know reality if it bit you in the ass, creep."

"Don't you think you're reacting a bit hostilely?" Harvey said in his dentist's voice.

"So?"

"So you're being defensive," Linda uptight Kahn said.

"So I'm being defensive."

"So if you're being defensive about it, it means you're ashamed of it," Charley said.

"You're trying to make me paranoid!" Rich whined.

"You're afraid."

"Yeah, you're afraid you're hooked."

Oh WoW.

"Because he *is* hooked," Ida said. "He's been here four months and he's still turning onto pot. You're a pot-head, Rich. That's what you're afraid of. You can't stay off drugs."

"Dope fiend!"

"Junkie!"

The wolf-pack was howling. Ida and Linda and Charley seemed to be getting cheap, pious thrills off the game. Doris, thank God, was beyond that. Arlene—who knows? Rich was trying to stare them down, but his fat lower lip was starting to quiver. Have some balls, man! I telepathed.

"I . . ." The poor bastard was letting the cretins get to him. I had had just about enough. Rich might be a jerk, but he was on the right side.

"You are all full of shit," I said loudly.

Heads swiveled. Rich looked at me uncertainly, maybe remembering that "V" I had flashed him and wondering if maybe it *hadn't* been a put-down.

"You are all full of shit," I repeated. "Pot isn't addictive. Pot is just good clean fun. *You're* the paranoids. Nobody can get . . . *hooked* on grass."

Rich grinned at me and made a "V". "Sock it to 'em, baby!" he said. Oh WoW. A stoned jerk is still a jerk.

"You've been sitting here five minutes and you've already got all the answers," Linda Kahn snarled. "How did you get so smart so fast?"

"Clean living," I said.

"Tom's been a junkie . . . ." Doris blurted. Rich's eyes widened. Jesus, what kind of game was this that turned your friends into consciousless swine? Doris . . . what's been done to you, baby?

"Ex-junkie," I said, "and the little lady knows it."

"There's no such thing as an ex-junkie," Charley said.

"How would you know, wino?" I asked.

"Once a junkie, always a junkie," Ida chanted like a snotty little smart-ass brat.

"Once a virgin, always a virgin," I chanted back. Ida blanched, shot me a look of pure hate, and edged to the far side of her chair.

"Hey man," Rich said respectfully, "you were really a junkie? You really got off smack?"

"Scout's honor," I said.

"Junkies have no honor," Doris said. Jesus! Doris! What the hell's happening to you?

"That sounds pretty strange coming from you," I said.

"What's that supposed to mean?" Doris said, with genuine innocence.

"You're supposed to be my friend, remember? So what's with the dirty-junkie business, Doris?"

"But I *am* your friend, Tom. I remember what you were like then. I said it to help you."

"Horseshit!" I snarled. But the hell of it was I knew she actually believed it. What were we *doing* to each other here?

"Do you identify with Rich?" Arlene said.

"With every hung-up person in the whole wide universe," I told her.

"Don't you think you might have the same problem as Rich?" Harvey suggested.

"What problem? Neither of us has a problem. You jerks have a problem."

"Then what are you doing here?" Linda Kahn asked smugly.

I looked across Ida at Arlene. Her uptight eyes, her clenched jaw, her hands toying with the fabric of her skirt told me: no, please, no, don't say it. Well, what the hell, I could take it.

"Just slumming," I said.

"You've got a drug problem," Doris said quietly.

"Aw come off it, Doris, you know I haven't had any smack for a long, long time."

"But you still smoke pot, don't you?"

"Sure I do," I said. "In fact, I seem to remember blowing pot with you and Ted on occasion."

"Not since we've been members of the Foundation," Doris said righteously. "Pot gives you a phony feeling of increased consciousness which keeps you from *really* expanding your consciousness." Obviously, the Gospel according to St. Brustein.

"In other words," I said, "Harvey here is dealing a better grade of shit."

You could almost hear the room gasp. A grin from Rich. An Earth Mother shake of Doris' head. Linda, Charley and Ida pumping uptight adrenaline into the air. Arlene knowing how I felt but not expecting me to actually *say* it. All grossed-out in their own ways.

Except Harvey. Not a flicker of emotion on his gray pudgy face. "An interesting idea," he said smoothly. "Let's try going with it for a while, Tom. Let's see if I understand you—you're saying that the Foundation acts like a psychedelic drug because it expands—"

"Not so fast, man! Take your words out of my mouth. I'm saying that your Foundation suckers are like junkies because they're trying to get the same thing off the Foundation that junkies think they can get off junk. I'm not saying that *either* brand of junkie really gets anything."

"All right," Harvey said. "Let's go with your feeling. You were a junkie, tell us what you wanted from heroin."

I was about to fake them out by explaining that I had been an atypical junkie, that I had gotten hooked because of Anne. But no, that was the trap, a private thing that was none of their business, a way for them to get inside of me and scramble my brains. I had no intention of playing *that* game, so I decided to wing it—I sure had known enough hard-ass junkies to know where they were at.

"Heroin," I said, "is a religion and a lover and a way of life. A junkie is never bored—he's either high or running around like crazy trying to score or scrape together the bread to cop. A junkie has no identity problem—he's a junkie and that's his whole bag."

Ah yes, I was putting on a good show for the peanut gallery. Ida,

Linda, Charley (and Arlene?) fascinated at a glimpse into nitty-gritty street-reality, or so they thought, so fascinated they were almost forgetting to be uptight. And I was Rich's hero at the moment, Captain High. And Doris was giving me a maternal look, proud of me for supposedly baring the secrets of my soul. Dirty voyeurs!

"In other words," Harvey said, "a junkie is someone with an identity problem."

"No man, a junkie is someone who has *solved* his identity problem. The operation was a success but the patient died."

"But why do you feel that being a Foundation member is like being a junkie?"

"Are you putting me on? This is the Foundation for *Total* Consciousness and your thing is *Total* Psychotherapy, right? *Total*—that's the magic word. You're pushing a Total Answer. So is the smack dealer. So is the Pope. And all the lost nobodies scoffing up the first Total Dope they get a whiff of . . . "

Oh yes, I was in good form all right! Rich was totally confused, couldn't figure out if I was defending his thing or putting it down. Arlene seemed to be entranced at the intellectual structure I was putting together out of sheer bullshit—it figured. Doris was making an effort not to smile, caught between feeling that she should be pissed off at the way I was cutting up the little tin god, and knowing deep inside that I knew a few things about dope that Harvey didn't. The rest of 'em were just plain outraged.

But nothing could break through old Harv's cool. Just as bland as could be, he said: "So you think people look for the same thing in heroin that they look for in the Foundation—something to fill the void inside."

"You got it, baby."

"But the void exists?"

"Yeah, the void is alive and well in Argentina."

"And in you?"

What? Three words, and suddenly there was a cold empty feeling in the pit of my stomach—the void? Void that had led me to Anne to smack to—Aw bullshit! *My* bullshit. Yeah, that was it, old Harv was a mean man with an argument, turning my own bullshit against me, missing the point on purpose, yeah that empty feeling inside, the fear of something that didn't even exist, it was just a trick is all, trick of Harvey's trade. Well he's not gonna get away with pulling that crap on me!

"You're not listening to me, Harvey," I said, shaking my finger at him like a schoolteacher lecturing the class dunce. "I said I was an *ex-junkie*. Ex. Ex. *Habla inglés?* That means I do not use smack any more. I am off it. Cured. Finished."

Harvey smiled a warm, sympathetic, rice-pudding smile that made me want to put my fist through his face. "I believe you, Tom" he said. "I believe you're finished with heroin. But what about the need?"

"Look, I just told you, man, I don't—"

"I know," Harvey said, breaking in on me without raising his voice. He took a drag on his cigarette, exhaled, considered the smoke. "Take a look at what you've said," he finally continued. "You've told us that people turn to heroin out of a need to fill a void inside them, because they don't know who they are. You've told us that *you* were a junkie. Therefore, you've told us that you had this need. Now you're off heroin. And here you are at a Foundation group which you pretend to loathe but actually fear. And which you yourself have equated with heroin. Don't you see the obvious conclusion?"

"No, I don't see the obvious conclusion."

"Don't you think the need might still be there?" Harvey said.

Time seemed to stop. Something bubbled up from my gut leaving a humming hollow space where it had been and exploded in my head like . . . like the surge from a needle in my vein. The room's reality seemed to go dim and flicker. I was back on MacDougal Street with Robin crying for the lost golden summer of my past to which I could no longer belong standing outside the Village Drug Store with Anne trying to cop and remembering the cotton batting comfort of smack coursing along my arteries walking downtown in the cold rain knowing that Ted and Doris were back there in the warm feeling cold and hollow inside.

I remembered stories of acid "return-trips"; was this a residual acid-flash? Or something else? *Why* was I afraid of the Foundation? What was there to be afraid of unless . . . unless . . . unless there was something here I couldn't turn my back on . . . .The room was whirling around me. Huge eyes out of Keene paintings were staring at me out of seven faces . . . .

"Are you all right?" Arlene asked.

"Yeah . . . sure . . . "

"Are you *sure* you're okay?" Doris said. Her voice was gentle, concerned; she really cared.

"Yeah! Yeah! I *said* I'm okay."

"You felt something then, didn't you?" Arlene said. "A need, a longing, *something*, even if you don't know what that something is . . . ."

"Ah . . . I dunno . . . " Sure I felt something, but what would I let myself in for if I told them it was an acid-flash? And that was what it had been, sure, just an acid-bounceback-bummer. Or was it? Or was it really something empty and churning at the core of my being? Could I even trust my own feelings now?

"We understand," Charley said.

"We've all felt it," Ida said.

"All of us."

"You're not alone, man," Rich said.

Yeah sure, the words were there and maybe they even meant it. But I knew damn well Ida and Charley had never dropped acid, so how could they have *really* felt what I felt. Unless . . . unless acid had nothing to do with it . . . But . . .

"An important thing just happened to you, Tom," Harvey said. "You've started to face the fact that you're unhappy, that you've got an unfulfilled need. That's what unhappiness is—unfulfilled need. That's why no one can really be happy till he's achieved Total Consciousness; unhappiness is the unresolved tension between your ego's needs and the environment. Didn't you say you took heroin to fill a void inside? Isn't the void still there? Isn't the void your inability to fit in? We all have that void inside because we all want to merge with something greater than ourselves. Everyone who ever lived has shared that desire because some primal wisdom deeper than the ego knows that the sick separation between the internal and the external that we think of as the self is the enemy. The fear you feel when you confront that need is the sickness of the self fighting to preserve its warped existence."

"The self *is* loneliness," Arlene said.

I was scared; I admitted to myself that I was scared. Man, I just didn't know. I couldn't prove that Harvey wasn't right, and if he was, everything I believed in, everything I was, was wrong. But if he was wrong—and he couldn't prove he *wasn't* wrong—then his voice was the voice of smack, of darkness, of evil. And I just couldn't know. Harvey had shown me that there was a question at the core of my universe, not certainty. And I wasn't even sure what the question was. And even if Harvey knew how to ask the right question, that didn't mean he had the right answer. And, sick or not, my instincts retched at everything he said.

I felt drained, drained and uncertain of where I stood or what was real. But I damn well knew I didn't want to talk about it any more. What was there left to talk about? Need? Yeah, I felt a need—a need to kick things apart, get back to reality, clear all this metaphysical shit out of my head, let someone else suck up the void for a change.

So I said: "Why did you *really* drag me here, Arlene?"

It worked. I could see their eyes shifting from me to her. If it had been an acid return-trip, then I had come down; this was, after all, just a roomful of pretty screwed-up people rapping on each other.

"Drag you here?" she said. "That's not fair. I just thought you needed—"

"That's not what you told me in bed," I said. Arlene winced. Well, wasn't this what she had asked for? I could play by their rules too!

"Oh, so you've been making it with this guy," Charley said.

"How was he?" Ida said, trying to sound malicious, but coming on envious despite herself.

"How could I describe it to *you?*" Arlene said. Ida blanched. *Ug*-ly!

"That's not the question, now is it?" Doris said.

"Yeah," said Rich, "the question is, how was *she?* How about it man? What kind of a lay was she?"

What the hell had I started? You shit, you! I told myself. I tried to read Arlene's face; jaw clenched, eyes expressionless as two chips of green glass. I could tell she was thoroughly uptight, as she had a right to be, but at me? at them? at herself? I tried to tell her with my eyes that I wouldn't betray her.

"Come on," Linda Kahn said greedily, "tell us how she was."

"It's none of your business," I said.

"Oh yes it is," Ida said. "We're supposed to be totally honest in here. No holding back."

"So call me a party-pooper. I still say it's none of your business."

"He doesn't really have to tell us, does he, Arlene?"

"Yeah," said Charley. "You're wasting your time playing gentleman, Hollander. This sorry creature has been whining about what a lousy lay she is ever since she started coming here. You've gotten yourself involved with a real loser."

"Watch yourself, man," I said, getting up on the edge of my chair, "Or you'll find yourself spitting teeth."

"No violence," Harvey said, not raising his voice even now. "You don't understand the rules—no violence is one and complete freedom to say whatever comes into your mind is the other. Those are the only rules in here."

"Yeah, well shove your rules," I told him, "Because I've just made another: Charley watches his dirty mouth, or I kick his ass."

Arlene shot me a dirty look, a hurt look. "Please Tom," she said, "this isn't doing me any good. I know you mean well, but I don't *want* you protecting me."

How does anyone with the standard number of testicles react to *that?* What do you do with a chick that's so screwed up she defends the creeps you're trying to defend her from?

"You don't know her as well as we do, man," Rich said. "She *digs* telling us what a crummy fuck she is. It's her thing. Isn't it, Arlene?"

Arlene started kneading her hands together. Her body was stiff as a board. Fuck their stupid rules! There were higher rules—like the way human beings should treat each other. Stinking sadistic voyeurs!

"I . . . I . . . can't help it . . . " Arlene said. "I just can't let go . . . I can't feel . . . can't let a man . . . ." Her body started to shake, working up to a sob. She seemed to be blinking back tears. I felt a tremendous wave of tenderness for this poor lost chick; and at the same time a red flash of fury. By Jesus, I wouldn't let these shits do that to her, and I damn well wouldn't let her do it to herself!

"Take it easy, baby," I said. "Your only real problem in bed seems to be that you don't know how good you are."

Arlene stared at me; her eyes widened but they were cold as ice, maybe even angry. She knew I was lying, but she didn't appreciate it; she probably didn't even know why I was doing it. And that was the saddest thing of all. It thoroughly pissed me off. I would damn well be her Knight in White Armor whether she liked it or not!

"Oh wow," Rich said, "what've you been screwing lately, man, dead bodies?"

"What I told Charley goes in spades for you, creep," I told him.

"You just don't understand, Tom," Doris said patiently. "You're not doing Arlene any good. She's been telling us how bad she is in every session."

"Yeah, well did it ever occur to any of you that maybe *that's* her problem?" I looked around the room: Harvey didn't seem like the type to ball the clientele, and even if he did, he sure wouldn't admit it here; Charley was too old; Rich was too young. Seemed like a pretty safe bet.

"Any of you actually made it with Arlene?"

Silence.

"All right," I said. "Well I have and you haven't, so none of you can sit here and put her down as a bad lay and have any claim to know what the hell you're talking about. Only me—and I'm not complaining, dig?"

Arlene stared at me, saying no with her eyes. I stared back and her eyes seemed to change, go softer, widen, as if she were finally at least accepting what I was doing as an expression of, well, love. Jesus Christ, hadn't anyone ever stood up for this poor chick before?

"You're just not making it as the defender of feminine honor," Charley said. "You're not fooling anyone, Hollander."

I gave each of them the evil eye in turn, thought hardass images at them: Cagney, early Brando, Bogart; like that.

"I, Tom Hollander, am saying that Arlene Cooper is a good lay, dig?" I said evenly.

Arlene favored me with a grim little smile. Admiration, understanding of the feeling behind what I was doing, maybe even affection. But not the gratitude I deserved.

"Bullshit," Rich said.

"What did you say?" I whispered, making like Jack Palance.

"I said bullshit."

"Are you calling me a liar?"

"I—"

"Before you open your mouth again, friend," I interrupted, "You better understand that anyone who calls me a liar to my face had better be prepared to back up his mouth with his fists."

"The rules—" Harvey started to say.

"This room is your turf," I said. "But sooner or later, Mouth here is going to have to step outside, and then we play by my rules. That goes for everyone else in this room. I am a dangerous psychopathic ex-junkie and I will kick the living shit out of anyone who calls me a liar. Dig?"

"I noticed that you seemed excited at the prospect of a fight between two men, Ida," Harvey said smoothly.

That ended that. After a few riffs on Ida's ambivalence about her well-aged virginity, Linda's paranoia about men, Doris' all-too-justified jealousy over Ted's history of balling everything that moved, and an old Charley's booze and failure hang-ups, the session broke up.

∎ ∎ ∎ ∎ ∎ ∎ ∎ ∎ ∎ ∎ ∎

Outside in the hall, Doris came up to me grinning like a momma cat that just watched her kitten eat its first canary.

"You were very impressive in there," she said. "I never saw anyone open up that much in their first session."

"Yeah, well I thought *you* were pretty shitty in there, bringing up all that junk crap."

"It got you to where you had to go, didn't it?"

"Did it?"

Maybe I was asking myself the question too. I couldn't kid myself that *nothing* had happened, but couldn't that flash have been a standard reaction to Harvey's standard pitch? He was damn good at his own thing, whatever it was; had to give him that. So maybe he started with whatever handle he could find on every potential sucker and then worked it around to that "void inside" thing; you had to be some kind of psychic superman not to get *some* kind of bad flash off that, even without an acid return-trip to back it up. Yeah, no doubt about it, Harvey had a pretty good Big Question working for him.

But that didn't have to mean he had any Answer.

Rich passed us on the way to the john. He smiled at me. "You were real heavy in there, man," he said.

I goggled at him; I had been ready to mop the floor with this cat and here he was acting like we were old buddies.

He must've seen it on my face, because he shook his head and said: "Oh, that's not real in there, man. It's a separate world. You don't carry any hassles that go on in a group outside."

I was going to point out that if I had broken his jaw in there, he sure as hell would've carried *that* outside, but before I could get my mouth open, he was in the john.

But it really did seem to work that way for all of them. Ida and Linda, who had been at each other's throats toward the end of the session, walked towards the stairs yakking with each other like two Bronx housefraus over the fire-escape. Charley nodded to me as he split. I didn't know whether to be touched or disgusted—it would be unbelievable messy to continue the nastiness that went on in the group in the real world, but wasn't it sheer gutlessness not to?

"Well, what do you think?" Doris asked.

"About what?"

"The Foundation. Are you going to give it a try?"

Well, fifty bucks for six weeks was less than ten a week and I could sure afford that . . . I caught myself making the calculation and that brought me up short. I had to face the unpleasant fact that I *was* considering the six week bargain sale. Why? Just because Harvey had hit me with a question I couldn't answer? It didn't follow that I would find any more answer here than I had in smack.

But on the other hand, it didn't follow that I wouldn't . . . .

I looked up and down the narrow hallway. Except for our group, the place was empty on Friday night, but according to Doris, they had a party of one kind or another every Saturday night; that could be groovy, I suppose. Watch it! You're letting yourself get sucked into this thing!

Where the hell was Arlene? She was the reason I had come back here in the first place; idea was to get her out of here, have dinner and then try to make all the lies I had told in there come true. Anyway, it would help change the subject . . . .

"Hey, where is Arlene?" I asked Doris.

"I think she's in the office talking to Harvey."

"Where's that?"

Doris pointed up the hall away from the big Foundation living room. "Is there really something between you and Arlene?" she asked.

"You heard what went on in there."

"Aw come on, Tom," Doris said. "So you went to bed with her and told a few lies for her. How much does that really mean to you?"

"Who said I lied for her?"

Doris shook her head with that old knowing grin. "It's *me* you're talking to," she said. Yeah, that was the old Doris. For some reason, it made me feel sad.

"Why didn't you say that in there?"

Doris grinned at me in mock terror. "I was afraid you'd punch me," she said.

"Tsk, tsk. You mean you didn't play by the rules?" I pouted like the teacher's pet.

"You can carry the rules too far," she said, suddenly serious.

"Just between us chickens, Doris, how much of all this are you really taking seriously? Cross my heart, I won't tell."

"I don't really know, Tom. Ted takes it seriously, and I take Ted seriously . . . And Ted *has* been faithful to me for the first good long stretch since we were married. That's real. That's serious. The Foundation did that. But . . . but . . . "

"But you're not sure whether all this has changed Ted's head or just made him incapable . . . .

"Yeah . . . ." A tiny whisper.

"But what's it done to *you?*"

Doris forced a little smile, looked at me with her big sad eyes and shrugged. "Who me?" she said. "I'm just a stable Earth Mother type, right . . . ?"

I almost reached out and hugged her. I really wanted to; she was the best woman I had ever known, had to be to put up with Ted, and she deserved so much better than this bummer. Ah shit, Doris, if you weren't really in love with Ted and I--Thought-crime!

Fortunately, Arlene and Harvey emerged from the office at the end of the hall and the moment was gone before Doris could sense what I had been about to think.

"Well there they are," Doris said. "Are you going to try six weeks at the Foundation?"

Something in her voice seemed to say "please." And I thought I understood why: mind to mind, Doris and I were closer in a way than Doris and Ted or Ted and me. The thing between us had never really threatened to become sexual (although if I believed in that crap, I would've thought that Doris and I had been lovers a couple of incarnations ago); but we thought in the same style and Doris, being uncertain about the Foundation beneath all the bullshit, wanted to see how I'd react so she could sort out her own head. I was her place to stand, her alter-ego, her psychic litmus-paper. I suddenly realized that if I didn't give it the six weeks, I'd be letting her down in a weird way.

Which, I supposed, not really being able to kid myself all the way, was as good a rationalization as any.

"Okay Doris," I said. "We'll see what happens."

Doris smiled, and then diplomatically faded away down the hall as Harvey and Arlene came up to me.

"Ah . . . I don't know if you realize it," Harvey said, "but . . . uh . . . you did quite well for a newcomer today."

"So I've been told."

"Er . . . if you'd like to give the Foundation a try . . . ."

I drew out the suspense for Arlene's benefit. She had a hungry look in here eyes, as if she felt she would cut time off her stay in Purgatory if she brought a convert into the fold.

"Fifty bucks for the first six weeks?" I said.

"Ah . . . yes," Harvey said. "It's . . . uh . . . only fair to give you a chance to really see what it's like before you . . . uh . . . make a stronger commitment. We don't want anyone heavily committed to the Foundation until they're . . . ready for it."

Uh-huh.

"And just what does the fifty dollars get me?"

"Uh . . . one group a week, attendance at all parties and meetings, a vote on . . . ah . . . anything we vote on while you're a member . . . Plus a ten dollar a session discount on private therapy."

Knowing what I was going to say, I still took one good last deep breath, looked at Arlene running her tongue across her lower lip, at Harvey just standing there holding out the dope but not really pushing, not hard—ah, what the hell, price of ten acid trips, is all! An extra five points a week for the next six weeks'd more than cover it.

"Okay, why not?" I said.

Arlene exhaled, smiled, took my hand.

"Leave your phone number at the office and I'll get back to you next week with your group assignment," Harvey said. "Probably keep you in this Friday group . . . ." And up the hall he went, shrewdly leaving me alone with Arlene.

"Surprised?"

She smiled at me strangely, a nervous smile. What did she have to be uptight about *now?* "Not really," she said.

What the hell? A muscle was twitching in her jaw. Her hand in mine was cold and stiff. She seemed a million miles away. I don't know what I expected—maybe for her to leap into my arms—but I sure didn't expect *this*. After all, I was doing this for her, wasn't I? For Doris? For . . . ?

"Look, why don't we have something to eat and then . . . go down to my place?" I suggested.

Her hand went limp in mine; she studied the floor. "I don't think so," she said.

"Why not?"

She frowned, nibbled her lower lip, took her hand away from mine. "I just don't feel like it," she said.

"Not hungry . . . ?"

"Oh come on . . . it's not *that*. I just don't feel like . . . you know . . . I mean after talking about it like that . . . I just couldn't . . . ."

Jesus! After all she put me through! "We could . . . just have dinner and then . . . talk . . . or go to a movie . . . or . . . ."

She stared at me dead-on, her eyes at once knowing and a million miles away. "That's not what you want and we both know it."

"Yeah," I admitted. "Look, I don't understand . . . did I say something . . . ? I mean, does having talked about it mean that we can't . . . that it's finished between us . . . ?"

She kissed me briefly on the lips; her lips were cold and hard. "No, no, it's not like that," she said. "You've got to understand . . . it's not *you*. A group leaves me . . . drained, you know? Decreases my libido, I guess. I just can't stand being with someone I might want to have sex with after a session. If I refused you, I'd feel guilty. And if I didn't refuse you, it would be . . . *awful* . . . just awful for both of us. You *do* understand . . . ? Please understand!"

Yeah, I understood all right, and a lot better than she did. Anne and I had never made it when either of us was on smack or right after either of us had come down. Junk sucks you inside your own head and you don't want company and sex seems just . . . *ugly.* Yeah, that's where she's at now; she's right, it would be awful. And suddenly I also understood the real reason Ted wasn't making it with Doris—he was going to two groups, a private session with Harvey and a Foundation meeting every week. He was either waiting to go up on Foundation-junk, on it, or just coming down all of the time. Poor Doris!

Poor me if I got hung up on a chick making the same scene.

Poor Arlene . . . .

"Yeah, I understand," I told her. "When you want me, just whistle."

"Does that mean we're through?"

Poor bitch! I smiled at her, squeezed her hand. "Just whistle and see what happens," I said.

She smiled bravely, kissed me again, said: "Give me time. I'll make it up to you . . . I promise."

"Yeah, sure . . . "

Well, what the hell, I was committed to fifty bucks worth of Foundation shit; I could give her six weeks to get her head straight. After that, she would either split this scene with me, or I'd split alone.

And at least now I knew how I'd play those six weeks I let myself get talked into—*mano a mano* with Harvey, no holds barred.

"You're a good person, Tom," Arlene said.

"Yeah, baby. I'm the regular salt of the Earth. Regular saint, is all."

8
"Have a Whiff, Have a Whiff, Have a Whiff On Me . . . ."

Looks like a bummer Friday night, I thought, flopping down on the couch in my silent empty pad. I had tried to drown my sorrows in wonton soup and pork with szechuan hot cabbage at Sing Wu's, but the soup went down like dishwater and the pork and cabbage tasked like Nedick's leftovers and the whole thing sat in my guts, along with what had been shoved down my throat at the Foundation, in one indigestible lump.

Fact: I was out fifty bucks. Fact: I had bought six weeks' worth of Foundation. But what had I *really* bought? A shot at straightening out Arlene? Okay, she was a good-looking, intelligent chick with a good heart. But she was trouble in spades: not only was she a bad fuck, she wasn't even a *reliable* bad fuck. What was the point of being involved with a chick who would put me through changes every time I wanted to get her into bed and if and when I did, would throw me a lousy fuck?

Okay man, admit it, you're not being as cynical about Arlene as you know you should be. You're *involved*, the way you were with Anne, and logic has nothing to do with it. The chick deserves better of the world than she's got and you want to give it to her.

Or was *that* just a rationalization for getting myself hung up on the Foundation? Had getting involved with Anne been a rationalization for getting myself hung up on smack? What was love? Five feet of heaven in a pony-tail . . . ?

A neat little equation: Anne equals Arlene, smack equals the Foundation. I had thought I could save Anne from smack and ended up a junkie. I thought I could save Arlene from the Foundation, therefore . . . .

Ugh!

Or peel another layer off the onion of reality: was I getting involved in another save-the-damsel-from-the-dragon number?

Oh yes. Harvey was right about the void inside, at least. Or was he? Or was reality *really* like an onion: peel off all the layers and you end up with a handful of nothingness, thank you Jean-Paul Sartre?

I'll bet this is just the way old Harv's shell game works: start you doubting your motives, then doubting your doubts, trying to find out which shell the pea of your essential core was under. But what if there was no pea at all? Shit, if *that* was the con, you could get sucked into the Foundation and never come out. Wasn't that the way smack worked? Wasn't The Answer always just the next fix away?

Or was *that* just my cruddy ego's defense against groovy old Total Consciousness? Shit!

Maybe what I really needed to clear my head was just a half-bag of sma—Thought-crime! Man, *now* look where the bastard's putting your head at!

A knock at the door.

It sounded like a girl's knock. Had Arlene changed her mind . . . ?

I got up, trying not to hope too hard, went into the kitchen, undid the police-lock, and opened the door.

"Hi," said Robin.

She was wearing the peacoat and boots, but also a pair of tight blue Levis and therefore probably something north of her navel under the coat too.

"Hi yourself," I said. "Come on in."

As we went into the living room, it was a pleasure to realize how glad I was to see her. The knot in my gut seemed to dissolve: my mind shed its coating of belly-button lint as Robin brought me back into contact with a whole world out there where the onion of reality was just something that gave you heartburn and bad breath if you ate it raw.

I turned on the warm orange ceiling light and turned off the cold white pole-lamp light as Robin took off her coat, revealing a plain white man's shirt under it. As the light in the room flipped over and we sat down on the couch together, simple good vibes washed away all the uptight convoluted pseudo-Germanic bullshit: here I was in my own pad with a chick I had had a good acid-trip with, a chick who had been there to give me the fuck of my life when I had needed it most, a chick who could reasonably be expected to give me a good honest fuck again, without hang-ups, or navel-probing discussions. There was nothing but good vibes between us, and Christ it felt nice! I didn't feel uptight, or predatory, or even horny; I was ready for anything or nothing at all. Just sitting there digging a beautiful girl with wild black hair and huge dark eyes and already knowing her body, not a care or a scheme in the world.

"How's your head?" Robin asked.

"Seems to be attached to my body now."

"No after-effects?" she asked.

"No, my vital bodily fluids have never felt more unpolluted."

"You looked kind of funny when you came to the door," she said. There was simple non-Freudian concern in her eyes, nothing more. "Sometimes acid changes your head permanently, a little. Things look different and stay that way, even after you've come down."

I had no eyes to go into what had happened to me since last Saturday, none of which had anything to do with our acid trip, and I certainly didn't want to talk about Arlene. So:

"Things look any different to you?" I said.

"Yeah."

"What?"

She put one hand on my knee—a perfectly unself-conscious gesture. "You look different," she said.

"Oh?"

She smiled a nice warm smile. "It's not you that's changed," she said. "I'm just seeing you differently. I think I'm deeper into you."

Still keeping one hand on my knee she took hold of my hand with the other. "You know, that night I met you on the street, I was really stoned," she said.

"No shit?"

"Dig, what I was grooving behind was the idea of picking up a nice cat who was kind of square and really blowing his mind."

That stung a little. "So I'm your idea of square?" I said. But as I said it, I became more amused than hurt. I doubted whether this chick had paid the kind of dues I had and somehow her thinking I was unhip was kind of . . . well, touching. The notion that a young chick could see me as an innocent . . . .

"No, dig, what's what I *thought* you were. But man, you turned out to have the hardest mind to blow I've ever seen. You just grooved behind my Girl in the Rain number. I thought getting you to drop acid would be a big hassle, but it wasn't. I thought you'd have a paranoid thing about me hustling you with all those cab rides. I thought it'd be a heavy scene being your guide on your first acid trip, and what happens, a cat who had never dropped acid before ends up pulling *me* out of a bummer!"

She cocked her head, stared at me with a little knowing smile, said: "Man, *you* were putting *me* on, weren't you?"

"Who, me?"

"I mean, that wasn't *really* your first acid-trip, was it?"

"You got my acid cherry, baby," I said. "Scout's honor."

"Man, I guess I believe you, but . . . wow . . . "

"There are heavier trips than acid," I told her.

She kissed me lightly on the lips. "You're a beautiful cat," she said. "I can't figure out where you're at, but you sure can put my head through changes."

I smiled. "That's the name of the game," I said, feeling just great.

We stared into each other's eyes. Looking down into her unknown depths, I got a flash of what she must be feeling, what *I* had felt that Friday night: the sense of something beautifully alien, mysterious, unfathomable behind another human being's eyes. Ah, how sweet to be someone's Man of Mystery!

"Know what?" she finally whispered. "I think it'd be a gas to smoke some pot with you."

It sounded like a perfect idea, but I didn't have anything around, and I was certainly in no mood to run around trying to score.

"I don't have any grass around . . . " I said apologetically.

She laughed. "No sweat," she said. "I know a cat who's got some good stuff. He'll even deliver. Can I use your phone?"

I nodded. "In the bedroom," I said.

And off she went into the bedroom to do the thing. I just leaned back and relaxed. Ah, now this was more like it! This was the proper way for a chick to act: show up like Santa Claus when you're really feeling crummy, tell you what a gas you are and how groovy you make her feel, and then go fetch some pot for the Lord and Master. No hassles, no talking her into bed, no Foundation scenes. I Tarzan, you Jane, is all. Why did I mess up my head with a girl like Arlene when there were chicks like Robin in the world . . . ?

Robin came out of the bedroom, sat down on the couch beside me. "He'll be here in a little while," she said.

"Look . . . ah, I'm kind of low on bread," I told her. "I mean, I hope you didn't tell the guy I was going to buy an ounce . . . "

"Don't worry man, it's all cool," she said.

She put both of her hands on both of my knees; I covered them with my own. We dug each other's eyes.

"You know," she said, "he won't be here for maybe a half hour . . . .Know what I'd like to do while we wait . . . ?"

I looked at her looking at me looking at her, felt the warmth of her hands now slipping to the insides of my thighs.

I smiled. "I know what *I'd* like to do," I said.

I took my right hand and slid it up the rough denim onto the tightly-outlined V of her crotch.

She laughed, moved her hands up my thighs and openly fondled my thoroughly-ready cock. She gave me a great look of mock innocence and said: "What *would* you like to do?"

"Same thing you'd like to do," I said. We laughed—

And suddenly each of us clutched the quick of the other, hard, no more games—

We moaned deliciously into each other's face—

And I hugged her to me and she tangled both hands in my hair—

We kissed fiercely; I thrust my tongue deep down into her mouth till my jaw ached—

And we wrestled each other like bear-cubs—

Rolled each other off the couch and onto the floor, Robin atop me—

I rolled her over, unzipped the fly of her men's Levis, pulled them down to her knees, felt the curly hair directly beneath the denim as she undid my pants, gripped the root of me—

She thrust her hips up at me and I—

Plunged down into her, all the way in one long, smooth stroke like a dip in a roller coaster—

She screamed, instantly began rolling her hips in a circle, faster and faster and faster while—

I pumped up and down up and down up and down like a piston engine galloping towards redline, and—

We—

Screamed together squeezed together came together like two healthy young rabbits—

It had to have been the purest fuck I had ever shared. The Earth had not moved, love had had nothing to do with it, there had been nothing transcendental about it; it had been the pure animal pleasure of fucking strictly for fucking's sake. And what made a pure animal fuck such a groovy and complete experience in itself was knowing that we were also capable of the other thing together—we had already had the other thing together. Somehow, being able to simply fuck without it having to mean anything was the closest communion of all.

Afterward, we just lay there on the floor, side by side, only our hands touching, our pants still down by our knees, our shirts still on, panting hard, feeling the moment's total satisfaction, but neither of us really sated.

"Mmmm . . . ."

"Oh man . . . ."

Our eyes met. We just grinned at each other.

Robin looked down along my body, saw that the ball didn't have to be over. She touched a finger to the tip of me—an electric shock brought it the rest of the way up—she laughed, said: "Oh *yeah?*"

I laughed back, answered: "Oh yeah!"

And we started to roll together—

Knock-knock on the door.

"Just a minute!" I yelled as we grabbed for our respective pants. Still buckling my belt as I walked through the kitchen, I got a nice silly cheap thrill out of fumbling to the door in this state, kind of hoped Robin would still be tucking her shirt in when I let the guy in. Hmmm . . . if the Sexual Freedom League ever succeeds in making sex totally pure and clean and open, maybe the world will have lost something after all.

The guy standing in the doorway was not as tall as he looked because he was thin as a reed. He wore a black raincoat, shades and a satanic beard, had medium-length black hair and an A-head's pimply complexion. He really had a traditional dealer's image. "Uh . . . ?" he asked greasily.

"Yeah," I told him, "this is the place."

I led him through the kitchen and into the living room where Robin, her hair nicely mussed, was standing in front of the couch zipping up her fly. The dealer started to move towards her with his arms open to hug, paused, grunted "Oh yeah," and brought himself up short. Chalk up another nice cheap thrill.

I sat down on the couch and Robin sat down next to me. The dealer unbuttoned his coat but did not take it off and sat down on the edge of the table facing us.

"Terry, Tom Hollander," Robin said. "Tom, Terry Blackstone."

Terry Blackstone and I exchanged nods and grunts, all very supercool.

"Good shit," Terry Blackstone said in a constricted voice like someone speaking around a lungful of pot. Man, he was really doing that thing! I'd love to meet a dealer who admitted his grass was grown in an empty lot in Chicago and was cut fifty-fifty with catnip.

But I suppose even dealers have their ego-trips.

Terry Blackstone pulled two prerolled joints out of an inside coat pocket in the manner of a French postcard salesman. That struck me as awfully weird—it was the time-honored ploy of disreputable dealers unloading a bad ounce: the pot in the joints would be the Good Stuff but the stuff he was selling would have enough oregano in it to keep a pizza joint going for a month. I didn't really give a damn—all I wanted was a nickel bag and I wasn't exactly expecting Acapulco Gold—but why was he doing this silly number on a lousy nickel bag deal?

Terry Blackstone lit a joint with a monogrammed Zippo, took a drag, and passed it to me. I sucked on the joint—it was strong and hot and harsh, with a slightly bitter aftertaste and I had to fight my cough-reflex as I passed it to Robin. Not exactly subtle stuff.

By the time it came around to me again, it was more than half gone, and after I took another drag, Robin, with a truly heroic toke, reduced it to a roach. Terry Blackstone ate the roach—I hadn't seen *that* for years. A real traditionalist, old Terry.

The pot was harsh and foul-tasting and probably stale (because it burned so hot) but strong it was: by the time I exhaled my second lungful with a half-stifled cough, I was getting a definite buzz. My flesh felt warm and light and the smoke in the room seemed to roll and flow like liquid lava in the sunset-orange light.

"*Yeah,*" said Terry Blackstone. He lit the second joint, took a huge lungful in a long series of little puffs, and passed the joint to me. I dragged. Robin dragged. Terry dragged. I dragged. Robin dragged. Terry reduced the joint to a roach.

He handed me the roach; according to Emily Post, I was obliged to eat it. Suddenly the whole ritual seemed cosmically silly, I mean *eating the roach*. Origin of the custom was paranoid desire to dispose of the evidence in case the cops just happened to bust in the next five minutes. Which of course made no sense in the present cycle of the wheel of karma, since Terry was holding. Anyway, nobody who was anybody ate roaches any more—it went out with "a stick of tea." Poor old Terry—a closet-reactionary!

At the time-locus, it occurred to me that I was stoned—I mean, such significance hanging on the point of etiquette of to eat the roach or not to eat the roach, that is a question?

So I popped the roach into my mouth, made elaborate phony chewing motions, and said: "Winston tastes good like a cigarette should." Fun-*ny!*

Mmmm . . . Apparently not. All I got was a strange look from Robin. Terry Blackstone seemed to have discovered a fascinating picture on the inside surfaces of his shades.

"Good stuff," I said. The expected thing to say—but some day, in this situation, I'm gonna say: "Not bad for Lipton's tea," or something equally gross. I've never quite been able to work up to it—but then how many times have you seen someone in a fancy restaurant take that first trial sip from a bottle of wine and then tell the wine-steward: "Tastes like Chateau Horse-Piss, '53, my good man?"

But now I was on another sticky wicket. It was my pad, and Robin, at least at the moment, was my chick. Therefore, Emily Post (not to mention male ego) demanded that I transact the business. But this was Robin's connection; I didn't even know the cat and furthermore, I had no intention of buying more than a nickel bag. And something fishy was going on—who ever heard of a dealer dragging his ass over to a stranger's pad just to tell a lousy nickel bag, not to mention turning on nickel bag customers with *his own dope?* But Robin knew the cat and had told me I wouldn't be expected to buy more than a nickel. Did not add up to me. Hopefully, it did to Robin. Therefore, Emily Post and/or male ego notwithstanding, she should do the thing. But I couldn't tell her that in front of Terry Blackstone, now could I?

Fortunately, Terry Blackstone did not seem troubled by such subtleties of etiquette. "You got the bread?" he asked, brilliantly cutting through to the heart of the issue.

I started to reach for my wallet—then I realized that he was looking at Robin, not at me. And she was fumbling in her hip pocket.

"Hey, wait a minute—"

"Don't worry, baby," Robin said. "It's on me."

"Oh no it's not," I said. "What do you think I—"

Terry Blackstone viewed this domestic spat with cosmic disdain. He reached into one of those mysterious coat pockets of his and pulled out two baggies filled with pot. Each clear plastic bag held an ounce. Fifty bucks' worth, all together, at street prices. What the—?

"Take it easy, man," Robin said. "It's free." And she pulled a wad of bills out of her pocket. What the hell was going on . . . ?

Robin counted out eight five dollar bills, stuffed the last two fives back into her pocket, and handed the $40 to Terry Blackstone. Terry handed over the two baggies.

"What's going on here?"

Robin shot me a heavy cool-it look that made her seem ten years older. It finally penetrated my fucked-up brain that what was happening was a *deal*, you asshole! Robin was doing a connection number. In my pad, the dope-exchange was meeting. I didn't care for that, not one little bit.

But it also penetrated that I had been gibbering like a flaming red asshole for the past couple minutes, a *square* asshole with angular edges, and I liked *that* even less. What I wanted now was for Robin to get the thing over with and get Mr. Terry Blackstone's ass out of here so I could chew her head off in private.

Therefore I *did* cool it. Or at least shut up.

Instead, while Robin inspected the merchandise for twigs or bugs or something, I concentrated on projecting bad vibes at Terry Blackstone. I'm an ax-murderer! I telepathed. I'm a crazed junkie! I'm a narc in a clever plastic disguise! I'm J. Edgar Hoover in drag! Grrr!

Paranoia being the occupational disease of the professional dealer anyway, it did not take long for Terry Blackstone to get the message.

He stood up, shuffled his feet, bobbed back and forth, played with the buttons on his raincoat, pulled on his beard, finally wheezed: "Well . . . uh . . . look, Robin, it's okay isn't it? I . . . uh . . . gotta go see a man about maybe scoring a key . . . ."

"Show you the door," I offered genially—the perfect gentlemen, natch.

■ ■ ■ ■ ■ ■ ■ ■ ■ ■ ■

By the time I had conducted Mr. Terry Blackstone to the egress and secured the police-lock bar behind him (so that's why they call the thing a "police-lock": makes it impossible for the fuzz to kick in the door!), Robin had a stack of manila pay envelopes out on the table, had dumped one of the baggies out on a magazine, and had a joint hanging from her mouth like a nineteen-year-old female racetrack tout.

She handed the joint to me as I stood glowering over the pot. Reflexively, I took a drag.

"Uh . . . got any oregano around?" Robin asked.

"*Oregano!*" I screamed, blowing pot-smoke into the already-smoggy air like Puff the Magic Dragon.

"Hey, what's the matter, man?" she asked, in a little girl tone of voice pure as the driven snow. She began to roll another joint.

"What's the matter?" I roared in a fair imitation of Jehovah on a bummer. I pointed the finger of wrath at the pot and the nickel bag envelopes on my very own table. *"That's* what's the matter, is what's the matter!"

Robin licked the joint, lit it, took a deep drag, held it a moment savoring it, exhaled. "Come on man," she said innocently. "This stuff may not be Gold, but it's not *that* bad."

Something seemed to tell me I wasn't quite communicating. I took another toke from the joint in my hand. Yeah, this was nowhere near as strong as the stuff he had given to us to taste. Might be the same grass, but if it was, it had already been cut. The old burneroo!

"This stuff has already been cut," I said, sitting down next to Robin. "Old Terry has pulled a fast one."

Robin shrugged. "That's Terry," she said. Then more defensively: "I wasn't gonna put *much* oregano in it. No more than a nickel's worth in each ounce." She took another toke and began filling the pay envelopes by eye, not even bothering to ask for an honest shotglass. She exhaled. "The stuff is still strong enough to take it," she said.

I took another drag. Something important seemed to be escaping me—I had wanted to bitch about something when I came back from the door, and I *was* bitching about something, but I had this feeling that I was bitching about something other than what I had started bitching about. Of course, one could argue that bitching itself was really the essence of the thing . . .

I exhaled.

She inhaled, still filling nickel bags. "Look," I said, "whatsa deal here anyway? Where'd you get all the bread? Why do you want to cut this low-grade shit?" She exhaled. I inhaled.

"Dig," she said, "we've got two pretty light ounces here. That's maybe five good nickels an ounce or six light ones, right?"

I exhaled. "Right."

She inhaled, spoke in a wheeze around a lungful of pot: "Got fifty bucks. Ten nickel bag customers. Grass costs forty bucks."

She blew out the smoke. "So if I give them all a good count, that leaves me with ten dollars and us with no pot for ourselves. So if I throw in two nickels of oregano, I can take out two nickels of pot, everybody gets a good count and we can keep a dime, dig?"

I shook my head sadly, and took a long slow drag. By God, that was absolutely immoral, kind of thing that gives Dope a bad name.

Cut grass with oregano or catnip, cut smack with sugar or powdered milk. Oughta be a law. Pure Food and Drug Administration oughta keep drugs pure, right? Of course, the freaks in Congress could argue with a certain justification that the practice was merely a logical extension of the basic principle of our Sacred American Way of Life— quantity equals quality. I exhaled.

"Woman," I said, "lips that touch oregano will never touch mine."

"Huh?" She had already filled five envelopes, leaving about a nickel's worth still sitting on the magazine. She opened the second plastic bag and dumped the pot out on the magazine.

"Dig," I said, "you got five light nickels out of the ounce, plus one for the house, right?"

She filled another nickel bag. "Yeah," she said, "but I haven't sealed them yet. I'll buy some oregano and fill them out before I deliver them."

I took a final drag on my joint and roached it into the ashtray. Robin took a last drag too and roached her joint, keeping up nicely. Holding it in, I tried to organize the irrefutable logic of my argument. The room was reeling and it wasn't easy. I exhaled. Robin exhaled and started rolling another joint.

"Look," I said, "You wouldn't smoke a pure oregano joint, would you?"

She giggled. "I've never been *that* hard up," she said.

"All right. So no one can get high off oregano—if someone could, it'd be the Nobel Prize for sure. So if you stick some oregano in those light nickels, it doesn't *really* make the count any better, now does it?"

Robin lit the joint, took a drag, passed it to me. "But it. Looks like. Better count," she wheezed.

"Shit!" I said. "Are you dealing pot or making pizzas? It may look like a better count, but it *isn't*, girl." I took a drag. Robin was filling cheapo nickel bags again.

"Man," she said, "you are one righteous cat! What you're saying makes sense to me, but it won't make sense to these nickel bag freaks. They get awful uptight if the count looks short."

I passed her the joint. "Tell them the truth," I said.

"Huh?" she said around a lungful of smoke. She filled the last pay envelope. Now there were ten unsealed nickel bags on the table and about a dime's worth still on the magazine.

"Dig," I said, "what you do is buy one little box of oregano. Then, when you lay a nickel on a customer, you say: Here's your nickel, baby. It looks like a short count, but it's an uncut bag.' Then if he bitches, you whip out the box of oregano and tell him: `If you really want to smoke oregano, be my guest.'"

Robin goggled at me. "Wow," she said, "are you stoned! That's a weird idea . . . .You don't think it'd really work?"

I picked up a nickel bag, licked the flap, sealed it and tossed it back on the table with a flourish. "In certain limited circumstances," I said, "honesty is actually the best policy. Dig the advantages: not only do you get a reputation for honesty, but one box of oregano will last you forever."

I sealed another nickel bag to punctuate my sermon. Robin took another drag—perhaps to reinforce her moral fibre—shrugged, and then began sealing nickel bags herself.

When we had finished sealing up all the nickels, I had—aside from a gluey tongue—a fine feeling of moral accomplishment. I had shown a previously-disreputable connection the error of her ways and guided her firmly to the straight and narrow. I had saved ten poor innocents from the possibly-carcinogenic horrors of excessive oregano inhalation. And I had succeeded in asserting my authority in my own pad. Were I a Boy Scout, surely I would qualify for a dealing Merit Badge.

Still, something I couldn't put my finger on was still nagging at me: I remembered I had been pissed off at something besides the horrors of oregano before I got sidetracked and now I couldn't remember what. Ah, I was probably just so stoned I was imagining things. It would not do to give in to paranoia.

"Man," Robin said, "you are something else. The more I think about that oregano number the better it sounds. I mean, after all, over the years the cost of oregano *does* add up . . . ."

Jeez, the sheer classlessness of the chick! She was so classless that she was the essence of classlessness which gave her classlessness a class of its own—she was the archtypal street-urchin, the pure thing itself. Hmmm . . . that was probably why she was such a good fuck: no moral, ethical, or esthetic hang-ups at all.

"You ever been a dealer?" she asked.

Well now, anyone who's ever been a junkie has copped smack with other people's money, one way or another. Lots of times Anne and I had gotten together enough bread from other junkies to buy a few bags in one lump and shave enough off each one to keep a free bag for ourselves. But I had *never* gone out and bought smack with my own capital and then resold it. An all-important technical point: I had never been anything more than an occasional connection, never had become anything as loathsome as a pusher.

"Certainly not!" I told her indignantly.

"You'd sure be a good one," Robin said.

And how's *that* for a compliment? But she was looking straight at me and her eyes were huge and shining and the world was spinning around them like they were the twin navels of the universe and the fire of total sincerity burned behind them and all for me. *She really meant it.* And she really meant what she meant by it: I was *muy macho,* a hip and groovy cat in her book. I felt a surge of affection from my head down to my cock for this totally innocent, totally corrupt chick. Corrupt by conventional values, which maybe I hadn't quite blown out of my system; but totally innocent by her own standards. She had never sold herself out because from where she stood, there was no way to sell yourself out except by refusing to act out the feral impulse of the moment. Didn't I really envy her that? And at the same time dig her for it . . . ?

"That's the nicest thing anyone's said to me all week," I said, and meant it in a weird way.

She laughed, snuggled close to me on the couch and leaned her head on my shoulder, pressing her soft check against mine. I stroked her long silky hair. She touched me lightly on the thigh, and I put my arm around her. She lifted her face to me, parted her lips, and we kissed.

Feeling the clean hardness of her teeth against mine, the soft wet world-filling reality of our tongues touching, I felt a great weight lifting off my soul. I felt my mind, hang-ups, worries, fears, reservations, past, all that sorry bullshit, melting into the pure animal reality of tongues and teeth and spit and skin.

■ ■ ■ ■ ■ ■ ■ ■ ■ ■ ■

Short blond hair (long and black)—lighting the surge of a needle in my vein—open bag of smack on red Con Ed spool table—"You'd be a great dealer" she said. "Let's go down to Snooky's and collect some quarters"—streets are full of narcs—hit them with police-lock bar—three-to-five for this for sure—"Come on, you can't just stop"—"You're a beautiful cat"—living room full of pot-smack in all the sugar bowls—Tiger O.D.ed last night—cut with oregano—dirty spike—I

was awake. I was awake with Anne naked in the bed beside me dead
to the world.

No . . . no . . . I shook myself mentally. Robin, not Anne. Just a
dream. This is reality—now, Robin, pot, not smack.

Now I was wide awake, I realized that I was straight, and, realizing that, I realized how stoned I had been.

Ten nickel bags sitting on my living room table—reality.

Jesus, Robin had cut up two ounces of pot in my pad, and I had
been too stoned to even bitch about it; all I could think of was some
damn stupid thing about oregano!

Waves of paranoia washed over me—not bust paranoia, no I
didn't seriously believe that the cops were about to break in and find
those damn ten nickel bags all cut up and ready to peddle to high
school kids on street-corners. No, it was the existence of those ten
nickel bags in my pad and the dream of Anne melting into Robin pot
melting into smack me melting into . . . into something used
again . . . too much dope in the apartment . . . games being played
with my head . . . just a connection . . . never been a dealer technical-
ly . . . tell it to the judge . . .

Robin turned over in her sleep. Her face was relaxed and peaceful;
her lips pouted around a baby's smile.

Get ahold of yourself, man! You're getting paranoid over nothing;
a bad dream, is all. The chick digs you, is all. Don't blow it. Don't be
square. Don't get paranoid.

I let out a deep breath and closed my eyes. What, after all, was
there to be uptight about? I wasn't uptight about smoking pot with
her; why should those ten nickel bags put me on a bummer? Don't be
a hypocritical shit, man!

Yeah, sure I would be cool in the morning.

But I would damn well make sure she took the stuff with her tomorrow and didn't try to stash it here. I wouldn't blow what I had
going with her by getting righteous over her thing. But I wouldn't let
myself get eaten by it again, either.

Thing to do was maintain, man, maintain!

9
The Unmoved Mover

"Dear Mr. Casey:
Thanks very much for your hard-hitting article, "The Man Who Turned Off the World." With drugs so much in the news today, one would think that such an article on J. Harry Anslinger, the man most responsible for the prohibition of marijuana in the United States, would find a ready market. Indeed your piece has much to recommend it in the way of literary skill, exhaustive research, and particularly passion . . . ."

"You look like you're gonna puke, man," Bruce Day said. It was 2:30 Wednesday afternoon, the exact center of the Dirk Robinson work week, when five o'clock Friday is just as far away as nine o'clock Monday and the week seems like it has gone on forever and will probably never end.

I looked up from my letter to Mr. George Casey, waved the manuscript in Bruce's face and said: "It's things like this that make this job disgusting."

"Another sickie?" Bruce asked.

"I wish that's all it was," I said. "I'm getting that old *Miss Lonelyhearts* feeling again."

"And this, too, shall pass away, or so they tell me," Berkowitz grunted without bothering to look up from his typewriter.

I ignored him. "This thing," I told Bruce, "Is the Dirk Robinson cherry of one George Casey, a nineteen-year-old kid living on Avenue D. According to his letter, he's just finishing out a year's probation, having been busted for pot at the tender age of eighteen."

"*I Was a Teen-Age Pothead?*" Bruce asked.

"I wish it was," I sighed. "But what it is is a kind of ultimate poison-pen letter called 'The Man Who Turned Off the World.' A meticulously researched put-down of our beloved former Chief Narc J. Harry Anslinger. The kid seems to have read every word of Anslinger's that ever saw print and everything ever written about him. He takes little pieces out of context and strings them together with his own obsessions and paranoia and proves that Anslinger is responsible for every disaster in the past thirty years, possibly excluding the

Second World War."

"So what's your problem?" Bruce asked.

"I like it."

"In your heart, you know he's right, eh?"

I nodded. "But in my guts, I know he's nuts. The kid expects us to sell the thing to either *Life* or *The Reader's Digest.* You know— 'The Most Unforgettable Character I Never Met.'"

Bruce gave me a nasty, pious grin. "Why don't you pass it on to Dickie?" he said.

"Are you nuts? Dickie'd just bounce it and get pissed off at me in the bargain."

"True," said Bruce, "but the look on Dickie's face—"

"Day, you have no soul!"

"And then when Dickie bounces it, you can go over his head to the Man himself . . . the look on *Dirk's* face . . . ."

"As he boots Tom's ass out the door," Berkowitz observed without missing a beat on his typewriter.

"There is that," Bruce admitted. "But just what is your real problem with the damned thing? You *know* we're not going to market it . . . "

"Problem is," I said, "that I know no magazine would touch it with a fork. Not only is it a propaganda piece for the International Dope-Fiend Conspiracy, it's probably instant libel suit too. What do I tell the cat?"

"Man, I don't understand you," Bruce said. "You tell him what you just told me."

I look at Bruce, trying to *esp* it to him. Bruce was what you might call a "gentleman dealer": he liked pot but didn't like to pay for it, so he'd buy a key every few months and deal enough of it to get his bread back and keep the rest to smoke. Bruce would understand why I was identifying with this Casey twitch, why I was hung up over what to tell him, if I told him about last weekend's scene. But if I told Bruce, I'd also be telling Berkowitz, who I just didn't make for a connection for even a fellow-traveller of connections, and sooner or later it would get to Dickie. I had the feeling it would only make points for me in a weird way with Dickie—but Richard Lee, Vice President of Dirk Robinson Literary Agency, Inc., in his secret identity as a company fink would be honor bound to report to the Man. That might be interesting, but then again it might be *too* interesting: it might blow the one thing that kept Dirk from manipulating me the way he manipulated everyone in the office, the fact that I was totally opaque to him. If Dirk knew I was involved with dope, he might can me. Or worse, it might be some kind of key to my head for him, in which case I could easily end up as another pawn in the Big Game. Dirk had made it obliquely clear to me on several occasions that I could have a pro desk if I asked for it. That I knew this, and that he knew I knew, and that I had made no moves in that direction, kept me in the position of playing with his head, instead of vice versa. Which was the way I intended to keep it. Therefore, I had better not run off at the mouth.

"Thing is," I said, "that almost any underground newspaper *would* print it, and that would make the kid happy. But you know what Agency policy is on referring suckers to nonpaying markets . . . ."

"More to the point," Bruce said, "if the kid has a dope record and that thing sees print, it'll keep the fuzz crawling all over him till they find something to bust him for."

Yeah, Bruce was right. It was kindly old Uncle Tom's (ugly thought right there!) duty to tell the kid to cool it before he ends up on Dry Tortugas. And that was really what was bugging me: less than a week after Robin did her thing in my pad, here I was speaking *ex cathedra* telling some kid to cool it before he got himself busted.

"I guess it's my duty as a member of the New York Literary Establishment to tell him to shit-can it, I sighed.

"Now *there's* a thought!" Bruce said. "I'll cherish your image of fee-readers as members of the Establishment every time I get to thinking of us as the Wage Slaves of Fifth Avenue."

"I dunno," I muttered, "maybe I'm getting too involved. I keep telling myself 'fee-writers are shits' but sometimes I almost don't believe it."

"Any time you start feeling sorry for the cruds," Berkowitz said, "just contemplate the Mad Dentist and Company, Nathanael West, and have the innocent purity of your cynicism magically restored."

He had a point there; my attack of conscience was probably nothing more than the Wednesday afternoon blues. Thus purged of thought-crime, I returned to my letter to old George Casey:

"Frankly, Mr. Casey, the finest writer in the world could not do a piece like this in a manner that would render it salable to a national magazine. The obvious legal question of libel aside, no major magazine is as yet ready to publish an article which unequivocally advocates the use of marijuana as a positive good . . . ."

Was I getting through? Could he tell that I was telling him I was on his side? Shit, if only I could say what I wanted to say for once!

"There are so-called 'underground' publications which might publish the piece, but since they pay little or nothing for material and since 10% of nothing is very little indeed, no reputable literary agent can afford to deal with them."

A neat piece of double-talk: I had given him the Dirk Robinson party-line while really telling him where he *could* get the thing published. But I had to tell him what the consequences could be or I'd be nothing better than a pimp for the narcs . . . .

"Moreover, if I may, I'd like to warn you against submitting the piece to these markets on your own; in view of your conviction for a narcotics violation, publication of this article might very well serve to focus the attention of certain governmental agencies whose interest you might find less than desirable upon your person to your general detriment and to the detriment of your promising career as a writer . . . ."

A word to the wise, kiddo. I had done as much good deed for the week as I was going to; from here on in, it was strictly The Word according to St. Robinson:

" . . . Nevertheless, this article does demonstrate a powerful and well-controlled writing talent at work, and when you apply that talent to a less commercially-limited subject in your next submission—"

"The Man craves your presence in his inner sanctum."

Huh? I looked up: it was Dickie who had appeared in front of my desk in a puff of ectoplasm while I was hung-up with my conscience. A moment of idiot panic—had Dirk somehow picked up my brainwaves? Was he calling me on the carpet before I had even finished the offending letter? Talk about paranoia!

"Who me?" I said.

"None other."

"Into the Valley of the Shadow . . . " said Berkowitz.

"Ah, fuck off!" I rejoined brilliantly over my shoulder as I followed Dickie through the boiler room to his office. (The main entrance to Dirk's office was strictly for Big Name Writers and other VIPs; we peons entered the Holy of Holies through the airlock of Dickie's little private cubicle.)

"Who did I kill?" I asked Dickie when we were inside his office (a large closet containing a window, a door to Dirk's office, a shelf of books Dickie had had a hand in, and a desk overflowing with correspondence, books, manuscripts and used paper coffee-cups).

Dickie grinned at me as he opened the door to Dirk's office. "Fear not, Tom me lad," he said. "Fame and fortune await within." And in I went, and Dickie closed the door behind me with a doorman's flourish.

■ ■ ■ ■ ■ ■ ■ ■ ■ ■ ■

Dirk's office was set up as a movie set of Dirk Robinson's office. A monstrous, Danish-modern walnut desk faced the entrance across about an acre of black wool carpet. The wall behind the desk was festooned with white and gold drapery to hide the fact that the windows overlooked a magnificent view of the seedy office building next door. The wall facing me as I entered from Dickie's office was given over to bookcases displaying the published works of clients to denote worldly success; the wall behind me to bad paintings done by Dirk himself symbolizing artistic concern. Two uncomfortable modernistic armchairs faced the desk; between them was a large low table which was empty except for a small bronze bust of JFK.

The huge free-form desk itself was absolutely bare expect for a telephone and a bronze In-Out basket (unlike Dickie, Dirk had a clean desk fetish) but the typing-table joined to the desk at right angles held the latest IBM Selectric and Dirk, in his big clear-plastic swivel-chair, was working at it as I entered.

Dirk swiveled his chair to face the armchairs, said: "Sit down, Tom" in that soft, too-even voice of his. I sat down facing Dirk Robinson: a slightly overweight cat of about forty-five in shirtsleeves-and-tie, with a soft, flabby, easily forgettable face except for the small hawk-nose and the bright dark eyes that told anyone with a brain in his head not to be conned by Dirk's insurance-salesman appearance.

"How long have you been working here?" Dirk said, leaning forward across the desk at me. He knew how long more precisely than I did and we both knew it. His face was, as always, professionally un-readable. I started to sweat inside. What was going on behind those fox-eyes of his?

"A little less than a year," I said.

Dirk nodded like an emperor over all that gleaming walnut. "A lit-tle more than ten months," he said, scoring some kind of points in a game of his I couldn't fathom. "How do you like your job?"

What was he fishing for? Was he going to can me? Or try to ma-neuver me into asking for a pro desk again? Okay, Dirk baby, so let's play games.

"It's an education," I said.

Dirk leaned back in his chair, spread his arms to rest the fingers of each hand on the edge of the desk, smiled. "You don't want to be a writer," he said evenly. "We get three basic types on the fee-desks: would-be writers like Mannie Berkowitz, guys who see it as the first step up the ladder, and guys like Bruce Day who aren't thinking be-yond an easy hundred bucks a week. I *know* you're not a would-be writer. I get the feeling you're one of the easy-buck boys."

Was this the lead-in to a firing? What the hell else could he be get-ting at? Well, if he was going to fire me, I wouldn't make it easy for him.

"Could be," I said.

Dirk hunched forward suddenly, hands still on the edge of the desk; now he looked like a pudgy panther ready to spring. His ex-pression never changed, but his eyes seemed to be laughing at a pri-vate joke. "The easy-buck boys last longest at the fee-desk," he said. "Bruce could be here indefinitely, but I don't give Mannie Berkowitz another six months."

Now I understood the joke—he *wasn't* going to fire me, but he had known that was what I would think and he had played one of his mini-mind games. But what *was* he up to? I decided to relax and ride with it—Dirk had just given me a little reminder that it was pointless to try and think a step ahead of him.

Dirk subsided into his chair, suddenly an old Dutch Uncle. "The guys that interest me," he said, "are the ones who see the fee-desk as the first step on the ladder. I think you're selling yourself short, Tom."

"What do you mean by that?"

"In the ten months you've been here, you've sent about forty scripts on to Dickie for marketing. Dickie had to bounce only about a dozen. About twenty of the rest eventually sold. That's pretty impressive."

So that was it—now I was supposed to ask for a job handling pro writers and then he'd make me sweat a little before he gave it to me. Now I *was* a step ahead of Dirk: I knew where he was going and I had no intention of playing his game.

"To tell you the truth, I never thought about it," I said.

Dirk leaned forward slightly, nodded almost imperceptibly, frowned the frown of a man who had heard what he had expected to hear. I saw another unexpected curve-ball coming. "I know," Dirk said. "Your trouble is just that: you haven't learned to think far enough ahead. Right now, you're thinking I'm about to offer you a pro desk, right?"

"Right," I said, knowing a second before I said it that it had to be wrong.

Dirk seemed to know I knew: he smiled and fixed me with a bright rodent-stare that seemed to look into places in me where I didn't even know I had places. "Wrong," he said. "You'd be a pretty good pro man, but you'd be more trouble than you're worth. I don't want you for a pro desk for the same reason I wouldn't want *me* on a pro desk if I walked in the door: I'd be a fool to trust me and I'd be a fool to trust someone like you. A good pro man has to be a team-player like Dickie; he has to get a real charge out of contributing to Dirk Robinson Inc. and getting a private office with his name on the door. That sure wouldn't be *me*, if someone else was top dog. And it's not for you, either."

"That's some kind of compliment?" I asked.

"Wrong again. Neither of us is cut out to be a pawn in someone else's game. But that's as far as it goes. When I was your age I was well on my way to setting up this agency. You're going nowhere."

"They say money can't buy happiness," I said.

Dirk leaned back, seemed to suck his neck into his shirt like a turtle. "Bullshit," he said evenly. "I'm not talking about money and you know it. Money is just a convenient way of keeping score. I'm talking about who is Tom Hollander ten years from now. Picture yourself as a fee-reader pushing forty."

I stared at Dirk, staring at me. A cold empty feeling in my gut. *Forty.* Christ, forty! Forty living in a pad in the East Village knocking down an easy hundred a week balling Robin blowing pot—ugh! But what else was there? You stinking son of a bitch!

"To tell you the truth," I said softly, "I can't see myself pushing forty, period."

Dirk hunched forward and again rested his fingertips on the edge of the desk. "Of course you can't," he said. "You can't see yourself at forty the way you are now and you can't see yourself as a forty-year-old Dickie Lee with your own little office and your name on the door either."

Job or no job, I had had about enough of this crap. That lousy hundred bucks a week didn't buy Dirk the right to talk about me like my goddamn father!

"Come on Dirk," I said, "what the hell is all this about?"

Dirk rose up on his fingertips and ass. He gave me the coldest look I had ever seen. "I'm telling you the facts of life, Tom," he said. "You're the kind of guy who'll reach forty in only one of two conditions: with a game of your own or out in the gutter. You're just not a company man."

"So?" I snarled. Who the fuck did he think he was, reading me the dirty-hippy riot-act?

But I couldn't even get a rise out of him by acting antsy. He was still old, unflappable Dirk Robinson. Instead of getting uptight, he sank back in his chair and gave me his clever plastic imitation of a warm smile.

"So I'm going to give you a chance to get started playing your own game," he said. "Dickie's told you about *Slick*. They need a slush-pile reader, and confidentially, they'll take anyone I recommend. Say the word and the job is yours."

I've got to admit I was touched. Sure it was just a dumb job in LA and something I had no eyes for, but from where Dirk sat, he was really doing me a favor, saving me from myself, acting fatherly. Maybe he saw in me a young Dirk in danger of ending up someplace he had once feared he would end up. Who knows? But on his terms, he was doing me a real favor, and I would be a shit to treat it otherwise.

"How much does it pay?" I asked, feeling I had to at least make a show of considering it.

"A hundred a week."

"A hundred a week? That's what I'm getting here! Why the hell should I drag my ass to LA to make the same bread reading crud for a lousy stiffener that I'm making here?"

"Because LA *is* the boondocks in the publishing industry," Dirk said. "To be honest, magazines like *Slick* are staffed mostly by middle-aged editorial derelicts who couldn't make it in New York. Lushes. Queers. Unsuccessful crooks."

"You're a great salesman for the job, Dirk."

"You're missing the point," Dirk said. "There's a tremendous turnover in an outfit like that. A young guy with something on the ball could start as slush-pile reader and be editor of the magazine in a couple of years."

"I don't see myself as the forty-year-old editor of some crummy West Coast stiffener either."

Dirk smiled; his eyes seemed to sparkle; suddenly I saw this seemingly phony room for what it was: the lair of one hell of a predator. Dirk did his own thing, and did it all the way.

"You're starting to think the right way," Dirk said. "The editor of something like *Slick* is either an old has-been who really never was or a hungry young kid on the way up. Get the point?"

"On my way up to *what?*"

Dirk shrugged. "If you were the kind of guy who'd let me tell you that, I'd rather keep you on my team."

Which reminded me of what Dickie has said about the *Slick* job—the payoff Dirk would expect for the favor.

"As long as we're being so man-to-man, Dirk," I said, "just what's in it for you? I never made you for an altruist."

Dirk laughed a real laugh. "I've been called a lot of things," he said, "but never an altruist. Still, I *can* be an altruist when altruism is good business. I've been in this business for eighteen years. Hundreds of guys have passed through this office. A couple dozen have used it as a stepping stone to jobs at magazines or publishing houses. Most of them owe me for getting them started. Some are senior editors now. Some are personal friends. That's why this is the biggest agency around—I've got my people all over the publishing industry."

"You expect payoffs?"

Dirk leaned forward, gave me a little smile, seemed to be acknowledging that in a weird way, our minds worked on the same wavelengths. "Nothing as crude as all that," he said. "The whole thing runs on gratitude. Genuine gratitude. I don't ask for a thing—which is why I get more than I could possible get on a quid pro quo basis."

"What about ingrates?"

Dirk looked me straight in the eye; it was like looking into the eye of a camera or a one-way mirror: he saw everything. I saw a shiny glass surface. Dirk was a monomaniacal genius, I realized, a self-forged weapon; the Big Game *was* Dirk.

"I've come as far as I have," he said, "with only one basic talent: I know what people will do in given circumstances. Once you know that, all you have to do is create the particular circumstances that will make people do what you want them to do because *they* want to do it. I can smell out an ingrate a mile away. You're no team player, Tom, but you're no ingrate either. And for the same reason: your only loyalty is to your own sense of honor."

"*You* dig *honor?*" I blurted out, thinking of the whole slimy fee-operation.

Dirk seemed to choose his words with mathematical precision: "I understand how honor functions," he said. "Well, what about it?"

For some reason I found myself saying: "How long do I have to decide?" And as I said it, I understood why: Dirk and I had gone past some point of no return. If I didn't take the *Slick* job, my days as a fee-reader were numbered anyway. I mean, I had *no* intention of getting involved in Dirk's machinations, but the longer I could stretch it out, the more hundred dollar checks I could collect before the shit hit the fan.

Nevertheless, I had the unpleasant flash that Dirk understood all this and saw something behind it that I didn't see as he smiled with phony indifference, said: "It's a big move and a big decision. I can give you maybe a month. After that . . . ." He shrugged. I could read anything into that shrug that I wanted to. And of course Dirk knew that, too.

"I'll think it over," I lied.

Dirk swiveled his chair back to face his typewriter. That was it; I was dismissed. Back to the salt mines.

Shit, where *would* I be at forty? Even the question seemed totally unreal. And for some reason, it reminded me that I was supposed to go to some kind of Foundation meeting tonight.

And *that* put me even more uptight. Out of the mind-game frying pan into the mindfucker fire. Now there would be a contest! Harvey Brustein vs. Dirk Robinson for the Heavyweight Mindfucking Championship of the World.

Or would it? Naw, I'd have to put my money on Dirk. Harvey did his thing well enough with mental cripples and therapy-junkies, but Dirk's game was to take on the world. No contest.

Somehow that made me feel better. Dirk's head was as different from mine as mine was from Harvey's, but the thing was I *knew* Dirk would react to Harvey the same way I did. And could cut him to pieces without raising a sweat. And would expect anyone he respected to be able to do likewise. And Dirk respected me. Therefore . . . .

■ ■ ■ ■ ■ ■ ■ ■ ■ ■

Having made the twin mistakes of killing a couple of beers with Bruce after work and then eating at a nice little Japanese restaurant on 43rd Street, I blew the chance to change out of my one decent office suit before going downtown and so eight pm found me squatting on the dusty gray carpeting of the Foundation living room trying pretty unsuccessfully to keep the suit in a condition to wear to work the next day.

As a result, my legs were cramped, and so even before Harvey got there (late as usual by design, natch) I was in a reasonably poisonous mood. The big room was packed—the row of folding chairs against the rear wall had been filled up long before I arrived, and except for the little raised dais with Harvey's folding-chair throne on it, the entire floor area was covered with wall-to-wall Foundation creeps, sprawled out, squatting, hunkering, and generally milling about and lowing like cattle in the pens outside the slaughterhouse. At least forty people crowded together in the dimly-lit, hot, stuffy room and many of them definitely unwashed types. A lot like being on the D Train during rush-hour stuck between stations and waiting for the damned thing to move. To make the evening complete, Arlene—my only real reason for being there—had not shown up yet. Ted and Doris, sprawled on the floor to my right, were discussing Ted's last group in which he had admitted to homosexual fantasies or some such bibble. To my left, Rhoda-something-or-other, a middle-aged Park Avenue therapy-connoisseur drenched in perfume which smelled worse than the armpit-stench it was meant to hide, was smoking a cigarette and constantly blowing smoke in my eyes. In front of me, Bonnie Elbert, a Slum Goddess from Scarsdale, was brushing her long black hair. She had dandruff. Charming. Fuckin' *charming*.

"Just what are we sitting on this floor for?" I asked Ted, trying to find a better way of passing the time than digging all the uglies.

"Because there are no seats," Ted answered reasonably.

"Jerk," I said (in no mood for reason), "I mean just what are these meetings all about?"

Doris leaned across Ted, said: "Nothing in particular. If someone has something to say to start it off, they say it. Otherwise Harvey starts things going. Either way, we just let the meeting go where it seems to want to go."

Not bothering to tell them where I'd like the meeting to go, I asked: "Where the hell's Arlene?"

"I think she had a late class today," Ted said. "Don't worry man, the chick'll show up." He gave me one of those old Ted-smiles of his (or a plastic imitation of one). "How you doin' there?" He attempted a leer which didn't quite come off.

"Does Macy's tell Gimbel's?" I said. That sounded pretty hollow, too. In the old days, wife or no wife, my chick or not my chick, Ted had to be considered at least a possible rival for any decent-looking girl. It really pissed me off then—especially since Ted was more competition than I could handle and we both knew it—but now I was pissed off by Ted's essential harmlessness. You can get nostalgic for some pretty freaky things.

Suddenly I got a flash of Ted at forty—or rather I thought of a forty-year-old Ted. But there wasn't any image attached to the idea. I *couldn't* picture Ted at forty any more than I could picture *me* at forty. Or maybe deep down I *could* picture Ted at forty and it was just too ugly to look at. Dirk had really hit a nerve. Was this why Ted was always leaping from Answer to Answer? Was he afraid of finding himself out in the middle-aged cold with nothing but the ghosts of his youth to keep him warm?

Looking around the room, I was pretty sure that this was where a lot of Foundation-heads were at. Ida, the Ancient Virgin. George Blum, a CCNY undergraduate pushing thirty. Even the housefrau types like Rhoda-in-front-of-me, and Ida's friend Frieda. And a couple of the Village types: Tod Spain, a very old promising young actor and his chick; Rich Rossi. Yeah, and old Charles . . . People with their futures all behind them deluding themselves that they could change their presents by playing mind-games with their pasts. What the hell was *I* doing in this garbage-heap of broken dreamers? Playing that old Savior game again . . . or . . . had Dirk *really* hit me in the core of my being . . . ?"

Oh, yes, I was in a fine nasty mood indeed—

Then a commotion at the entrance, and in walked Harvey dressed in his usual grubby white shirt and baggy gray pants but this time also decked out in the most godawful Madras sports jacket this side of a Miami Beach skid row. Nodding to the faithful, Harvey threaded his way through their bodies like a man walking down the Bowery taking care not to step in the dogshit, vomit or bodies littering the sidewalk. Reaching the dais, he sat down on the folding chair, lit a cigarette, exhaled more smog into the already-carcinogenic air and said: "Did you ever really think about New York?"

He took another drag, exhaled more smoke. All the smoke in the air (a lot of tobacco-heads in the old Foundation) was starting to get to my throat, and so I *did* really think about New York, about how New York is a Winter Sinus-Cold Festival.

"Did you ever think about how living in New York affects your consciousness?" Harvey said. Did he have sinus trouble? Why else would he be on this kick? Old Harv did have a point: a sinus cold is definitely consciousness-contracting.

Harvey leaned forward. "After all, New York is a pretty over-whelming environment," he said. "So overwhelming that if you've grown up in it, you don't even notice how your mental style is molded by it. For instance, you'd think that something like the Foundation, which deals with internals, wouldn't be very much influenced by the external environment. But here we are sitting in a room in a converted industrial loft. Why? Because in New York, it's the only kind of place that's big enough for our purposes that's cheap enough to rent. In Los Angeles, we might have a whole house, but we certainly can't have anything like that in Manhattan. Now since most of you are New Yorkers, you're probably thinking: 'So what?' Well, look around . . . go ahead, look around."

Like the other jerks in the room, I looked around. I saw people sitting on the floor and on folding chairs, faded yellow walls, three windows at the far end of the room looking out on more loft buildings. So?

Harvey had taken a drag on his cigarette. He exhaled, smiled wanly, said: "I thought so. You don't see it. Because all your apartments are like this loft. You've lived this way all your lives, so you don't see that the significant thing is what you *don't* see: trees, grass, or even hills and valleys. New York has no natural geography; it's a totally synthetic environment. You don't have any consciousness of the natural world here. And because of that, all the offices and apartments that you live and work in are inward-oriented, designed to shut out the external world. You don't even notice it. But do you really think it doesn't affect your consciousness?"

"But you're just talking about living in *any* city," A familiar girl's voice said from the back of the room. I turned; yep, it was Arlene, looking pretty groovy in a green sheath dress, carrying a brown coat and a couple of books under one arm. The evening might not be a total loss after all. I waved to her through the smoke, caught her eye. I motioned for her to come and sit down beside me; she gestured at the solid clot of bodies on the floor blocking her way and shrugged. Oh well . . . .

"Oh bullshit! Bull-*shit!*" It was Ted, up on his haunches, eyes intense—I vaguely remembered that Ted used to make some kind of idiot technical point out of his having been born in Ohio and therefore not being a *native* New Yorker, even though his family had moved here when he was six.

"Dig, dig," Ted said, waving his arms wildly like . . . er..*like a New Yorker.* "New York's not like any other city . . . it's not even part of the United States . . . ."

"It's maybe in Russia?" Frieda Klein shouted in a heavy parody of a Bronx-mama voice. Giggle, giggle.

Harvey held up his hand a la Chief Shitting Bull. "I'd like to know what Ted means by that," he said. The natives subsided.

"Man," said Ted. "I've been all over the country (he had spent a few months bopping around on his bike once) and none of it is like New York. Compared to everywhere else, New Yorkers all seem like they're on amphetamine. Everybody running around all the time with their shoulders hunched, looking out for muggers. Rest of the country's scared shitless of New York. They're afraid to even come here."

"Then *they're* crazy," Arlene said, "paranoid about some place they've never even seen." *Ole!* I gave her the "V" sign. So old Arlene was a New York patriot . . . .

"No, no!" Ted shouted. "They're afraid of New York because they've seen New Yorkers. Lousy posture. Pimples. Uptight. Talking a mile a minute. Dig, if you met some Martians in Cleveland and they were all pimply and had nose colds and were out of their minds, y'know you might get the idea that Mars was an unhealthy place." All the while waving his arms like an Orchard Street peddler.

"Anti-Semite!" someone yelled.

"I notice you're still here, Ted," Arlene yelled. Two ears and the tail, baby!

"Yeah . . . well . . . I . . . "

"That's the whole point," said killjoy Harvey to the rescue. "Your environment gets inside you so when you leave it, new environments make you uncomfortable, even if they're better, because they start to get inside you too, and suddenly you feel strange because you're not in the environment you're used to. You feel the new environment starting to change your consciousness and it makes you twitchy because change, even change for the better, feels like a threat unless you know how to deal with it. As the saying goes: 'If you work in a stable long enough, you can end up missing the smell of horse-manure.'"

"Aw come on, Harvey," Rich Rossi said, "you saying New York is horseshit?"

Harvey smiled a 100% plastic smile. Something about the smile alerted something inside of me: it was a pale imitation of a Dirk Robinson smile, kind of smile Dirk gives you when he's maneuvering you into something and trying to show you he isn't maneuvering you. There was something *planned* behind all this rapping on New York . . . .

"I'm just saying that New York, like everywhere else, is unique. There *are* other cities in the United States where things are cleaner, less hectic, more in contact with nature . . . where people are therefore a little more open, a little healthier. Where you *might* feel happier and freer *if* you could get past the shock of change. Los Angeles, for—"

A great groan went up.

Harvey smiled that same plastic smile. "I'm not saying Los Angeles is any *better* than New York," he said, "just a different environment. So is Boston . . . New Orleans . . . San Francisco—"

"Yeah, San Francisco!" Ted shouted, up on his haunches again. "That's a groovy town."

"You've been to San Francisco, Ted?" Harvey said. "Yes, it is more relaxed and . . . But I think it's more interesting to see how it struck a New Yorker." The rank odor of fish suddenly filled the air. Harvey had pounced pretty quick on San Francisco. There was definitely some kind of mindgame being played here . . . .

"Well, it's the most beautiful city in the country," Ted said. "I mean, beautiful the way a city is beautiful, not a mess like LA. It's as much a city as New York, except it's smaller, cleaner and it's . . . you know, part of the land. All those great hills, and you can see the Bay from most parts of town if you climb the nearest hill. I dunno . . . it seems . . . slower, more relaxed, less uptight. Funky, y'know? The houses have *character*. And from what I saw, living is more . . . possible."

"What's that supposed to mean?" Rhoda-in-front-of-me (*Steiner*, yeah, that was her name) said.

"Just less hassle about everything," Ted said. "You don't have to put down a big deposit to get the gas and electric turned on, you don't have to pay some fucking agent a month's rent and a month's security to get a good cheap pad, and the apartments are better than what you'd get for the same bread here. Just less hassle."

Harvey took a puff on his cigarette. Behind the glasses, his eyes got dreamy (or was it an act?). He blew smoke out slowly and said: "Yes . . . I've lived there. You could rent a big house up on a hill, two floors at least, with a garden and a view, for what this loft costs here. An open kind of place where you can feel a part of the land . . . ."

"Yeah," said Ted, "living in San Francisco is just an opener, groovier feeling."

"So what're you doing back here?" Arlene said. Man, she just would not let go! She seemed to be taking all the put-downs of New York as if they were put-downs of her. I couldn't quite see why, but I *was* beginning to see how I could use it to score points with her . . . .

Ted sat back down. "I dunno . . . " he said. "Look, I'm here because I've got a consciousness problem, right? So *something* made me leave San Francisco, maybe something that New York did to me, like Harvey says. Maybe . . . maybe if I had something like the Foundation in San Francisco, it would've been different, I dunno . . . ."

"You think the Foundation would've helped you to adjust to living outside New York?" Harvey said.

His eyes seemed hooded for a moment; he had said that *awful* fast, had leaped to Ted's conclusion. No doubt about it now, he was playing Ted like a fish. There was nothing freeform about this meeting at all—Harvey was controlling it all the way. But he was doing it strictly with bank-shots, mainly off Ted. But what was he up to?

"Well . . . I guess so . . . " Ted said. He laughed nervously. "Shit, if the Foundation can do me good in a crazy place like New York, it really oughta work in a place like San Francisco, right?"

"You think that the Foundation would be better off in San Francisco," Harvey said, real supercool.

Click! Sure, that was it, that was the capper, *that was no question.* Harvey had maneuvered Ted right to that conclusion. That was what this meeting was all about. Harvey wanted the creeps to think that they had gotten the idea that the whole freakshow would be better off in San Francisco. But what was his percentage . . . ?

"Never really thought about it . . . " Ted said. "But . . . yeah, why not? We could sure have a better place for the Foundation . . . and I think the town might be better for our minds . . . ."

I studied faces around the room—here and there I could see the idea lighting up the empty space behind some eyes. Rich Rossi. Linda Kahn. Tod Spain and his chick Judy. Some kid named Johnny, looked like a reformed acid-head. Bill Nelson, boy Welfare Investigator. The younger ones, the ones with less to lose. But Doris had that look on her face that said: "Here goes Ted on one of his fantasy trips." And when I looked back at Arlene, her jaw was clenched, and she was really scowling, *very* uptight.

"Well, it's a thought anyway," Harvey muttered (was it an act?). "I don't know how I'd feel about going back to San Francisco, but—"

Ah-hah! "Hey Harvey," I yelled, cutting through the murmuring that had sprung up, "you just said something about going *back* to San Francisco. You've lived there?"

I could feel a certain tension in the room now; I had played the game Harvey had been playing all along: reached for control of the flow of things by seeming not to control, by asking a leading questions. Suddenly it was me and Harvey playing some kind of game *mano a mano*, and everyone else felt like an audience.

"I believe I said that," Harvey said evenly. Yeah, he sensed what was happening. "Now the point is—"

"How long did you live in San Francisco?" I said.

"I don't see what this has to do with—"

I smiled, playing to the bleachers. "We're supposed to just free-associate, right? Follow things where they want to go and not try to . . . *control* them, right? So let's see where I'm going, okay?"

I thought I could almost see anger in Harvey's eyes. *Almost.* But he didn't dare show emotion; he was trapped in his own chosen image of the Unmoved Mover.

"Yeah, come on Harvey," Blum said, "you keep putting down New York. What's your thing with San Francisco?"

"I was merely using San Francisco and New York as examples," Harvey said. "The interesting thing is some people's reactions. Have you noticed how some of you have been defending New York? As if you were defending you own sense of—"

"Come on, man!" I shouted. "Answer a simple question. How long did you live in San Francisco? *What are you afraid of?*"

I got a lot of funny looks. But Harvey was getting a few too, and more to the point, Arlene was eating me up with her eyes. Harvey puffed on his cigarette, sizing up the situation. The vibes I was getting told me that if he tried to get off the hook again, he would be in a little trouble: he was starting to show his own feelings, and that could blow his image.

But Harvey was too good to make that mistake. "As a matter of fact," he said with a cool I had to admire, "I'm a native San Franciscan. I lived there more often than not till I came to New York five years ago."

A moment of dead silence as that sunk in. A few people—Doris, O'Brien, Bill Nelson, Blum maybe—were getting the message. Arlene's eyes had narrowed: like a handful of the others, she had gotten a flash of some personal motivation behind Harvey's Buddha-mask. Maybe she was starting to think. Maybe I could ram it home . . . .

"You've been riffing about how New York's done things to our heads, Harvey," I said. "The obvious question is, what's San Francisco done to *yours?*" Harvey smiled.

"Very good, Tom," he said, as if I had just shown myself to be the prize pupil. "You do seem to understand that *any* environment will deeply affect the consciousness of *anyone* who lives in it. Which is what we've really been talking about, not the relative merits of San Francisco and New York. Arlene felt the need to defend New York because her sense of identity is deeply bound up with this city. Probably the average San Franciscan would defend San Francisco in the same way. But I don't feel compelled to do so because I've achieved enough consciousness to rid myself of environmental fixations. And you'll all be able to do the same eventually—whether the Foundation stays here or actually moves to San Francisco—because the goal of the Foundation is Total Consciousness and the truly conscious individual transcends his external environment."

He paused, ground out his cigarette in the ashtray under his chair, got up, and said: "Well, I think I've done enough lecturing for one night. Let's just relax and digest what we've heard."

And that was it, the end of the meeting. He had gotten by me as easily as that. Old Harv was still master on his own turf.

The meeting became just a roomful of people rapping with each other. But an awful lot of the conversation seemed to be about the same thing: San Francisco. A bunch of people—Rich, Linda, Tod and Judy, Blum, Bonnie Elbert, and of course Doris—gathered around Ted who was really wound up in the wonders of San Fran. And when Ted got started talking, a lot of people started listening. A second group—older types like Ida, O'Brien, Charley, Rhoda Steiner— were listening to Harvey talk about the same thing. But the roles were reversed—they were doing most of the talking and Harvey was playing the Reluctant Dragon. All very fishy indeed. I had no desire to join in. I looked for Arlene, saw her walking out of the room and down the hallway, and threaded my way through the mob scene towards her.

■ ■ ■ ■ ■ ■ ■ ■ ■ ■ ■

Arlene was standing at the far end of the hallway, her back to the window. By the way she smiled when she spotted me, I knew that she had been waiting to talk to me alone.

"Hello," she said, as I took her hands, feeling the center of her body swaying subtly towards me.

"Hello yourself."

"Just what were you trying to do in there?" she asked. But behind her glasses, her eyes were more possessive than hostile.

"You know what I was doing. You were trying to do it yourself."

She turned her eyes downward. "I did get the feeling Harvey was trying . . . trying . . . I don't know what." She looked up at me. "You were way ahead of me," she said. "You still are. I don't know . . . maybe Harvey could be right . . . I *did* feel awful uptight when Ted started putting down New York. Probably New York *is* involved with my sense of identity, so when someone attacks New York, I feel they're attacking me. I almost felt you were defending *me.*"

"Purely intentional," I said.

We smiled at each other silently for a moment.

"I don't know," she said, "intellectually, I can realize that we're both wrong and Harvey's right. But I *felt* I was right, and I felt good when you took my side, and for that, sick or not, I thank you."

She paused, stood absolutely still for a moment, then suddenly leaned forward and gave me a big open-mouthed kiss.

"And I'd like to thank you for it at your place," she said. Her eyes made it clear that I had come out of the meeting with what I had gone in there for after all.

10
Naked To My Friends

Sitting beside her on the couch in the soft orange light, I looked at Arlene Cooper, her hair all bronzed, her body inviting under the green dress, and tried to understand the reality that existed behind the glossy green eyes behind the glasses. It occurred to me, almost shamefully, that I had never really tried to get inside her. I had manipulated her machinery—successfully once, unsuccessfully once, now maybe successfully again—but I had no notion of *why* her head worked the way it did.

"Girl," I said, making no move to touch her yet, "would it shock you to hear that I have no idea of where you're really at?"

She slowly took off her glasses and made a thing of putting them on the table, shrugged in a way that made her loose blonde hair bounce provocatively against her shoulders, said: "That makes two of us."

She leaned back against the big cushion that backed the couch, and angled her body in the general direction of my shoulder, though holding back from actually touching me. She seemed to be doing it quite deliberately, as if this were her way of saying "Shut up and fuck." Perversely, though this was exactly what I had intended to do all the way down from the Foundation to my pad, I didn't want to do it that way now; something inside was telling me that it was time I really go to know this chick. I didn't want to fuck her now; I wanted to make love to her. She was a bad fuck—but if we could make it as *lovers*, if our minds were in the same place as our bodies, might it not be a whole new ball game?

"What about me?" I said. "Do you understand me?"

"I understand what you do to me," she said. She leaned her head on my shoulder. I felt her sigh against me but I sensed a tension behind the sigh; she wasn't letting go, she was pretending to let go.

"What do I do to you?"

"Aw, come on . . . ." A nervous false laugh.

"No, really. And I'm not talking about what you think I'm talking about. What did I do to you tonight, at the Foundation . . . ?"

She lifted her head and stared into my eyes. "You're serious, aren't you?" she said. I didn't move a muscle; just sat there staring into her

Arlene

eyes, digging my reflection in them. Almost like an animal who isn't supposed to be able to look a man in the eye, she refocused her vision on a point somewhere to the side of my head. It occurred to me that this chick really didn't know how to be with a man at all. It was either all talk or all sex and neither communicated anything below the surface.

"I guess you . . . spoke for me," she said. "Spoke for a part of me, I mean."

"The part of you that doesn't really believe that Harvey Brustein is the Living Buddha?"

She nodded. "I think that's why you get to me," she said. "I feel there's a part of me that's always wanted to be the way you are. But I don't know whether it's the sick part of me or . . . "

"Or what?"

"Or . . . or something inside me screaming to get out. The me I'd be if I dared to . . . ."

She smiled, ran a finger along the line of my jaw. "You know what I envy you?" she said. "I envy you your center."

"My *what?*"

"Your center. Deep inside you, there's a core of certainty. You may not know where the world is at, but you know who you are."

"That's news to me," I said truthfully.

"Maybe it is," she said. "Maybe you know who you are but don't know you know . . . .How could you have gotten yourself off heroin otherwise? How could you . . . have put up with what I put you through last time we . . . ? I mean, a man who had uncertainty at his center . . . would've . . . blamed himself for the bad time we had in bed. Every man I've ever made it with has turned away from me afterward . . . because of the way I hurt them, I guess . . . .But you . . . "

I put my arm around her. She put her hand on my hair, began toying with it. I felt that she really had something to tell me about myself that she understood better than I did; it was a beautiful and unexpected feeling. And I felt that if I could really let her give me something of value, I would be giving her something she needed, too.

"I don't understand," I said. "I really don't."

She smiled. "I believe you. You don't have to understand what you are because you . . . *are.* I'm not. There's no center inside me. That's why I go to the Foundation, I suppose. If I can understand why I am the way I am, maybe I can find my center the hard way."

I was beginning to understand her. She was chasing something that didn't exist for a woman alone—or so good old male ego told me.

"Did you ever think that maybe all you're missing is a man?" I said.

She stiffened. "Oh come on, you don't have to hand me a line. I'm here, aren't I?"

"Are you? Really *here*? Look, you've never had a real thing with a man, have you? So maybe that sense of certainty you're knocking yourself out chasing is something a woman can only find with a man. How would you know?"

She stared at me; her lower lip trembled. Then I felt her body relax. "I think I understand," she said. "I . . . I push men away, don't I?"

"You don't exactly welcome them in. Did you ever think that maybe you don't have a sex problem?"

Blank stare.

"Know what I think?" I said, riffing the wisdom of the universe off the top of my head. "I think you'd be just fine in bed if it weren't for this 'center' bullshit. It's not that you can't let yourself go, it's that you don't want to. You think you're empty inside so you're afraid of really letting a man in all the way because you're afraid he might just fill the void inside with himself."

She stared at me, real wonder in her eyes. "That's the deepest thing anyone's ever said to me," she whispered.

"Even Harvey?"

"Even Harvey," she said humorlessly.

"Okay, that'll be fifty bucks for the first hour. I'll even carry it a step further. You're hung up in a circle. You won't let a man all the way inside because you're afraid he'll fill the void. Thing is, he *would*. But that's what you're really looking for. You need a real lover, is all. A woman needs a real thing with a man at her center; it *is* her center. But you've gotta go into the center of your fear. You've gotta trust a man."

Wow! I knocked *myself* out. Where in hell did all that come from? The words just seemed to pour out, as if . . . as if that certainty she claimed I had at my core really existed and had done the talking. Christ, we were really into it now: drawing things out of each other that neither had believed was there.

"Trust me," I said, taking her hands.

"I'll try. But I'm afraid . . . I'm really afraid . . . ."

So am I, baby, so am I. Magic was loose in the world.

"That's a good sign," I told her. "If two people don't scare each other a little, they're not really alive to each other."

"Are you afraid too?"

I nodded, feeling naked before her for the first time. It felt scary. It felt good.

"Let's go into the bedroom," she said, her lower lip trembling, her eyes moist and shining.

I got up, pulled her gently to her feet. I kissed her ever so lightly on the lips. "I dig a woman who can scare me a little," I said.

For the first time since Anne, I felt myself poised on the brink of the infinite possible, walking naked into a situation with a woman where I was really vulnerable, not in control. And grooving behind it.

No words as we went into the bedroom. The alarm was set for eight, and she knew it this time; the magic building in the air between us did not have to be broken by logistical hassles.

When I turned on the night table lamp, her hand moved toward the switch, then hesitated, went back to her side. She smiled at me; a sardonic little smile. I smiled back, letting her know I understood what a little victory that moment was for her, for us.

We stood facing each other beside the bed for a long, still moment, eye to eye, just the palms of our hands touching. I felt strangely light-headed, almost high; ready to slip my control of the situation, myself, give it all over to that certainty at my core that she believed in and I didn't.

Then she turned from me, her hand reaching for the zipper at the back of the green sheath dress: a graceless gesture, a turn-off, a renunciation of the openness building between us.

I reached for her shoulder, spun her around to face me as gently as I could, pulled her arm down to her side. Her eyes widened in confusion (maybe in fear?); her jaw tightened, then her mouth opened in a big protesting "O".

I sealed her lips with my finger, smiled and said: "Dig."

I began to unbutton my shirt. She looked at me as if I were crazy, as if a male strip were some kind of ultimate perversion. But as I threw off the shirt, took off my undershirt and bared my chest, her face relaxed and she kept her eyes on me all the way as I kicked off my shoes and pulled off my socks.

I unbuckled my belt, unzipped by fly, paused for a moment and smiled at her, digging her digging me. And she *was* digging me; her eyes were openly hot and she gave me a brave little smile that swelled my groin and made me vibrate deep inside.

She moved closer. We were almost touching, eye to eye, as I let the pants drop and stepped out of them.

I reached for the shorts, but she pulled my hand away, smiled at me and drew them off herself. It was a strangely beautiful feeling, standing naked before her and she fully clothed. We made no move to touch each other; she stared openly at my cock as if she had never seen one before in her life. And in a peculiar way, I suppose she never had—never had taken a long, lingering look between a man's legs. It was almost like capturing her virginity.

Then, still facing me, not taking her eyes from mine, she unzipped her dress in an awkward behind-her-back motion, kicked off her shoes and stepped out of the dress, letting it lay where it had fallen. She wore no stockings, just a white bra and functional white panties. She unhooked the bra, threw it to the floor, and her breasts hung free, the nipples pink and erect. I reached out with both hands and rolled the panties down her thighs, feeling the warmth of her flesh beneath my palms.

We stood before each other truly naked. I knew that we had just won a kind of victory together, and, aroused though I was, I felt a curious asexual tenderness behind it. Or could it be *sexual* tenderness—discovering for the first time that such a thing could be?

We took each other in our arms, gently, as if each of us believed the other were made of transparent, fragile crystal.

I kissed her, closed-mouthed, softly: a child's kiss. Her lips were closed against mine but there was no resistance to them. I parted her lips with mine and inhaled her sweet breath, then sighed my own breath into her. In, out, in out; just our breaths, our essences, mingling in sexual rhythm. Then I let my tongue pour lazily into her mouth—and tasted her groan of pleasure as her arms suddenly tightened around my waist. Our tongues met inside her mouth, caressing each other in the warm moistness. As our tongues' juices mingled filling the place between our mouths, blurring my sense of what was her body and what was mine, I felt a switch close somewhere inside of me, heat coursed up through my body, and I pulled her tight against me and my tongue began thrusting deeper, deeper, faster, faster, and I felt her mouth contracting around it rhythmically kiss-kiss-kiss.

Then her weight pulled me forward with her down onto the bed, on top of her, our mouths still a separate fused universe, where I tasted her tasting me tasting her.

I felt her hand moving down the valley of my spine, over the cheeks of my ass, up my belly and down, and then she held the very root of my cock, fingers stroking it while her palm lightly touched the softness of my balls.

My mouth tore itself from hers in a moan that seemed to pulse up my whole body from the base of my spine where my hips began to move before I knew it to the coaxing of her hand. I ran my hand down her belly and between the silk of her inner thighs and was rewarded with an answering moan as her legs clamped my hand to her and her hips began to undulate beneath me. Her hand began to work faster and faster and I felt myself building building building up to a quick crest. I remembered last time and a pang of fear went through me—too quick! too quick!

I looked down at her face: eyes rolling behind half-closed lids, mouth open and groaning. I kissed each of her eyes in quick succession; they opened, she smiled, and I felt we were in contact now at both ends of our beings. She ran her tongue cat-like over her lower lip as if acknowledging the moment and—

In one smooth motion, she thrust me into her and clamped her legs around my waist. I groaned, screamed. Too beautiful! I slid my arms under her body and hugged her to me.

I began moving my hips in a slow-grinding rhythm—she bucked under me, faster and faster, half a beat ahead of me, throwing me off-stride. I kept to my rhythm but began moving my body harder, more forcefully, trying to break her to my moves. But she kept bucking harder and harder, faster and faster, off in some turned-inward world of her own.

A savage rage tore through me: I wasn't going to let this happen again! A feral wisdom took hold—I bit her on the breast, hard, tasting the salt of her skin on my tongue.

She screamed in pain—but I felt her rhythm break under the shock and I started thrusting harder and harder, but slowly, majestically, grinding my hips in a circle with each thrust.

And her scream faded into a deep moaning and she was with me, her hips moving with mine in sweet counterpoint. I let myself go, turned off my mind as our bodies moved with each other, flesh dancing with flesh in perfect rhythm, building and building and building, our moans mingling feeding our bodies feeding our moans feeding each other building building building—

A scream! A tremendous earthquake of flesh against me, a spasm from the very bowels of her being, a total contraction of flesh sound soul—

That flipped over every synapse in my body into a white-out pleasure-flash that shot through my body up my balls into my cock and then through me as the universe exploded through a beat of non-being . . . .

A moment later, I opened my eyes and met hers, warm and bright and heavy-lidded in the dim light. I kissed her lips tenderly, gently, a child's kiss, ending up as it had begun.

"Oh yes . . . " she sighed. "Yes . . . yes . . . yes . . . ."

■ ■ ■ ■ ■ ■ ■ ■ ■ ■ ■

Lying under the covers together, warm and toasty, naked hips just barely touching, staring up dreamily at the ceiling, then at each other.

"That was . . . " Arlene sighed.

I touched a finger to her lips. "It just *was*, is all. Let's leave it at that." I ran my hand down over her chin, across her collarbone, smoothed the bite I had made on her breast. Feeling the welt made by my own teeth, I felt a pang of shame—but I also felt myself swelling a bit under the covers. Not now, I thought, maybe later.

"Un . . . about that . . . " I mumbled uneasily, "I hope you don't think I'm some kind of sadist . . . ."

She laughed at me with her eyes. "If you're a sadist, I'm a masochist, because I loved it . . . No . . . I didn't like the pain . . . but it . . . you know . . . set me free . . . ."

I nodded. The warmth of Arlene Cooper's body in my bed, the smell of her in my nostrils, all's right with the world. It was something much more delicious than just the afterglow of a fine fuck. Once, maybe because I was very stoned, I had been able to make a Celebrated Nymphomaniac come for the first time in five years of very heavy trying. Now I remembered how good that had felt; I had had that with Arlene but I had had something even better: the feeling (whether I deserved it or not) that I had achieved what I had not because of how good I had been but because of what I *was*. I may have had as tasty moments in the act of fucking, but I had never felt *this* good afterward.

"Funny . . . " Arlene was mumbling, "pain doing that for me . . . ."

I stroked the soft mound of her breast, snuggled closer to her. Was this love I was feeling now? Who knows what the word means? I

knew I had walked an extra mile for Arlene, and would probably
walk a mile beyond that. Was I *in love?* I didn't think so. But yes, we
were *lovers* now . . . .

"Maybe it's just a physical reaction . . . pain at the right moment
transmuting into pleasure . . . ."

Skin to skin, the emotion I felt was too complex to have a name. I
didn't want to name it, but I wanted to recognize it somehow with a
symbol—like a class-pin or a ring. But what was the right symbol for
a thing like this . . . ?

" . . . maybe it *is* masochistic—"

"Hey," I said, suddenly inspired. "I'd like to give you a key to my
apartment."

Arlene looked at me, seemed to come back from someplace she
had been all by herself: *"What?"*

"I said I'd like to give you a key to my pad."

She shrank away from me slightly, looked at me as if I had
flipped. *"The key to your apartment?"* she said. "What's that supposed
to mean?"

I smiled at her. "Well, in the square world out there, a guy gives a
girl an engagement ring when he's decided to think seriously about
marrying her. So I want to give you the key to my pad to show you
that I'm thinking seriously about asking you to live with me."

She screwed up her face and shook her head. "That's the screwiest
thing I've every heard!" she said. She did not seem amused.

"Don't you dig sentiment?" I said. Then, seeing that she was starting to smirk as if it were a joke: "I'm not putting you on; I really
mean it."

She looked at me; her eyes narrowed. "You *do* mean it seriously,
don't you?" she said.

I nodded.

"Then I should consider it as a serious matter, shouldn't I?"

I nodded again.

"Well look," she said, "if you really mean it as a commitment to
think seriously about living together sometime, then accepting the
key means I agree to think seriously about it too."

"Exactly."

"Then accepting the key is a serious step in itself."

"I suppose so."

"Well, then, I can't accept the key."

"Why the hell not?"

"Because I'm not really sure what happened tonight," she said.

"What do you mean you don't know what happened? We made love, is what happened, *we made love*. We finally got through to each other."

Her jaw clenched, a muscle began twitching at the hinge of her jawbone; she drew her body away from me under the covers. "I felt something with you that I never felt before," she said. "But how do I know it wasn't just an animal reaction? Maybe you just did something to my body . . . ."

"Oh shit! Can't you even tell what you feel?"

"I know what I felt, but I don't know what it means. I'm not in love with you, Tom."

"I didn't say I was in love with you."

"Then *what?*"

"You mean something to me, is all. There's a way to say it in Spanish: *mi casa es tu casa*, my home is your home. That's what the key is supposed to say."

"That's beautiful," she said, "and I really do appreciate it. But I can't go into something like that without thinking about it. I've got to understand my feelings first . . . maybe Friday at our group . . . ."

I sat bolt upright in bed. *"The Group!"* I yelled. "The fucking Foundation? You're gonna drag Harvey in bed with us?"

"That's what group sessions are for," she said firmly. "To help us understand our feelings . . . ."

"Of all the fucking idiocy! Look baby, I understand my feelings about you and I understand my feelings about . . . .Ah, shit!"

"You're not being logical about it."

"And you're being too damned logical!"

I sensed her withdrawing behind her eyes as they got cold and calculating. She glanced at the clock. "Look," she said, "I've got an early class tomorrow. I think I better go home now. Otherwise, we'll just fight all night."

"Aw for crying out . . . ." I cut myself off. About the one thing, she was right: if I had to listen to much more Foundation crap from her tonight, I'd pop my cork for sure.

So I just lay there in bed stewing in my own juices as she got up and started to dress. Part of me wanted to tell her to get lost, get out of my life, go fuck Harvey Brustein or take on the whole Foundation in a neo-Freudian gang-bang.

But I remembered having told myself that I would go another extra mile for this girl. And I remembered that I *had* broken through her biggest hang-up tonight. And I remembered that our relationship *was* in motion—maybe it was just asking too much to expect her to give up the navel-staring of the damned group cold turkey, without my help.

So when she had dressed, and leaned over the bed, and kissed me goodnight, and asked with a worried frown: "You *will* be at the group?" I smiled nastily and said: "Yeah, baby, I'll be there. But don't expect me to hold back anything. I think this is sick and I intend to say so. No holds barred."

"That's the name of the game," she said, just before she left. And left me with a wan, brave, lost little smile.

And how do you turn your back on that, smart-ass?

11
Mano a Mano

I just sat back in my seat at the left end of the semi-circle of folding chairs, kept my mouth shut tight and glowered, letting the rest of them work Harvey around like sparring partners. I was trying to build up an effect: I had sat down as soon as I came in, had maneuvered Arlene into taking the far right seat opposite me at the other horn of the crescent, so that the rest of them—Doris, Charley and Ida to my right, Linda Kahn and Rich Rossi to Arlene's left—were boxed in between us, with Harvey at the apex of our little isosceles triangle. And while Rich bitched about fucking up his sex life, and Charley insisted he was off the sauce and *did not* consider himself a washed-up middle-aged failure, and Ida refused to discuss her sexual fantasies, I just sat there like a wooden Indian staring now at Arlene, now at Harvey, thinking black thoughts and projecting ominous vibes.

It felt almost good. I was in the room purely to sock it to Harvey and show Arlene what a prick he was. It might be his turf, but when the deal came around to me, we were going to play by my rules. In fact, in a way, we were already playing by my rules because my silence and the poisonous looks I was giving Harvey were really getting the animals uptight; the whole group was off-balance and lines of curiosity and hostility were becoming skewed in my direction. It was only a matter of time before the tension-wave broke over me.

Linda Kahn was mouthing some bibble about the ingrained hostility of men caused by the competitive nature of American society, or some such hash of Marx-cum-Freud. The masculine egos in the room were snarling back at her. Arlene was sneaking nervous glances at me every time she thought I wasn't looking. Any minute now, the shit would hit the fan . . .

"Now look at *that* over there," Linda said, pointing at me. "It hasn't said a word all evening. Just sits there pouting like a sullen little boy. *There's* your masculine hostility!"

Harvey, perhaps sensing that even the chicks were getting tired of listening to Linda's dumb bullshit, looked my way and said: "I do notice that you haven't said anything so far, Tom. You were quite outspoken at the last group; what's troubling you tonight?"

I smiled my best eat-shit smile. "Sex," I said. A wave of giggling smirks went through the peanut gallery and we were off to the races.

"That's a pretty broad topic," Harvey said.

"It's a *broad* topic, anyway," I said with as much crude in my voice as I could muster. The bad-pun groans were music to my ears.

"Is there some trouble between you and Arlene?" Doris asked. Good old Doris!

"Yeah, there's some trouble between me and Arlene."

"She threw you another lousy fuck, didn't she?" Rich said.

Not really meaning it this time, I thought Humphrey Bogart at him, said: "I warned you about your mouth before, creep. I won't warn you again." True to form the balless wonder sat back in his chair, pulled in his horns.

"Actually," I said, "sex really isn't the problem."

"Oh yeah, Hollander?" Charley said. "Then why did you say it was?"

I smiled sweetly. "Because I wanted you jerks to get your jollies," I said. "Got all your dirty little minds drooling, didn't it?"

"The little boy wants to play his little games," Linda simpered. "Isn't that cute?"

"Maybe I should whip my cock out so you can bring yourself off baby," I suggested good-naturedly. "You can't come anywhere else, maybe you should try getting yourself off in group. That's what you're here for anyway, isn't it?" And I made a phony move towards my fly.

Linda turned a whiter shade of pale. Ida looked like she couldn't decide between fainting like a proper lady or daring me to really do it. Arlene looked quite properly aghast but I sensed she was getting a charge out of it, maybe because everyone knew where the organ in question had last been; there was hope for the chick yet. The rest of them, except for Doris and Harvey, did their best to look snide. Doris gave me a look that told me she knew I was playing some game and was mildly interested in where I was going.

Harvey cracked neither a smile nor a sneer; instead he made with the psychiatrist's pounce. "Do you often feel exhibitionist tendencies?" he said.

"Only in subways and men's rooms," I told him, writhing in mock ecstasy. "I can't help it—something about dirty white tile just turns me on." It would be interesting to see if I could gross *Harvey* out.

"Come on Tom," Harvey said humorlessly, "what's really bothering you?"

"The varieties of erotic response," I told him. "Aren't you hip to Krafft-Ebing?"

"Come on, Hollander, stop beating around the bush," Charley said.

"Isn't the real question *whose* bush is *who* beating about?" I said.

Harvey pouted slightly. "I really don't think this deliberate vulgarity is necessary," he said stiffly. So it *was* possible to gross old Harv out. I filed it for future reference.

"All this . . . is really my fault," Arlene blurted out. "I think . . . I think I really hurt him."

"Baby, you didn't hurt me, you hurt yourself."

"How about letting *us* in on all this," Ida said.

"All righty. Got your dildo ready, Ida-baby? Arlene and I enjoyed carnal knowledge of each other Wednesday, we created friction in each other's private parts, we polluted our vital bodily fluids; that is, we fucked."

"Do you have to be like that about it?" Arlene said angrily, eyes blazing, hands balled into fists. I had finally gotten to her! "Do you have to make it sound so animalistic?"

"Was *I* the one who was animalistic about it?" I said.

Silence. Her lower lip trembled. The peanut gallery shut up; they were beginning to groove behind the show.

"Dig what an animal I am," I said. "I made love to that girl, dig, made love; not screwed, not fucked—*made love.* All you dirty voyeurs have been listening to her bitch about her sex hang-ups for months. Well, it's all bullshit. I said it was bullshit last week, but then I thought I was lying to protect my lady's honor, if the concept isn't totally beyond you. But this time I found out I wasn't lying, isn't that right, Arlene?"

Arlene studied her shoes.

"Go on, tell 'em," I said. ""*You* wanted this, remember?"

Arlene nodded without looking up. "It . . . it was beautiful . . . " she whispered. "I . . . I really felt like a woman for the first time . . . ."

"What do you want us to do, pin the Congressional Medal of Honor on your fly?" Linda Kahn sneered.

"Just making a point. Which is, that with a Secret I Learned in the Orient, I was able to get her to make love just like a woman. No applause, please. Because it was really a big nothing. Arlene never had a sexual problem. But she *does* have an emotional problem; something's made it impossible for her to have a decent relationship with a man. Somethings that's right here in this room . . . ."

"That's very interesting," Harvey said, "whether it's true or not. And just what do you believe the supposed cause of this supposed non-sexual problem to be?" Ah, snideness! Microscopic cracks were starting to appear in the facade of Harvey's cool.

"Looked in the mirror lately, Harv?" I asked him.

He actually flinched.

"What is this crap?" Charley said.

"Attacking the therapist is a clear—"

"Shaddap!" I roared. "I'm paying for this damned therapy, and I'm gonna get my money's worth."

"Let him talk," Harvey said quietly. "This may be a valuable breakthrough for Tom."

"Thanks pal," I told him. "Harvey, how would you react if I called you a castrator, a voyeur, a pervert, a liar, a monster, a cocksucker, a pederast, a Commie, and a faggot?"

Harvey peered at me from behind his glasses as if trying to decide whether a padded cell was in order. "How would you expect me to react?" he said mildly.

"*That's* how I'd expect you to react, Harvey," I said, mouse-trapping him in his own cool. "Are you a human being, man?"

Harvey frowned. What could he say to that?

"Groovy," I said. "I'm taking your silence to mean you don't object to being called human. Because if you weren't human, none of this would make much sense."

"You call this making sense?" Rich said.

"Back to your kennel, Fang," I told him out of the side of my mouth. "Let's run it all back to the beginning. I meet Arlene. We ball once—pretty mediocre. But the second time around, it's really groovy—real human contact, dig? Kind of thing that should really start something going, right? Right, Arlene?"

"I don't know . . . " Arlene muttered, twisting her hands together, looking at the floor. Poor kid. Yeah, I felt like something of a shit putting her through this, but goddamn, she had asked for it. If she was right about the Foundation, I was only doing my duty; if I was right, I was purging the muck out of her head. Either way, it was for her own good.

"The little lady doesn't know. *Why* doesn't the little lady know what the beginning of a real thing between a man and a woman should feel like? Has the little lady ever had a meaningful relationship with a man?"

Arlene's body drooped forward, head practically buried in her breasts. Real touching. But I had worked up so mush nasty momentum that there was an IBM machine where my heart was supposed to be, and it was Arlene who had gotten me into this situation and put it there, and the voice of the computer told me that anything that happened to her in this room was her own fucking fault and I would be doing her no favor by holding back now.

"Dig, so she's never had a real relationship with a man, is why she can't be expected to know what it's supposed to feel like," I said. "So last Wednesday, I, who have at least had *some* kind of real relationships with chicks, did feel that something had started between us. So to show her how I felt, I offered her a key to my apartment. Now you'd think a girl who had never gotten that far before might be a little touched, moved, excited, happy. But not the little lady—"

"That's not true!" Arlene shouted, bolting upright in her chair, hands balled into fists. She hesitated, as if looking at herself overreacting; then seemed to deflate like a leaky balloon, and in a little whisper said: "I really *was* moved, Tom . . . really I was . . . I still . . . ."

"But you couldn't so much as accept a lousy key, could you?"

"No . . . ."

"Why wouldn't you take the key? Go on, tell 'em."

"Because . . . because I was afraid . . . it was too big a step for me to take without . . . without . . . ."

"Without hacking it out in this group?"

"Yes."

Oh yes, I had them in the palm of my hand, I did. They were all hunched forward sucking it up and wondering what came next. And old Harv was leaning back with a little smile, the Great Guru watching his people do his thing.

"Okay," I said, "you can all take your hands out of your pants folks, because you've heard the whole lurid truth about Arlene's torrid affair with Attila the Hun. So what's the point of all this except my taking my cock out? One more question for the little lady: would you say that one of the reasons you're a Foundation member is because you're trying to do something about your inability to make it with a man?"

Arlene shot me a look of pure hostility. "All right, all right!" she said. "Yes! Yes! You have all the answers, don't you?"

Harvey leaned forward, took off his glasses, rubbed the bridge of his nose, replaced them and said: "Just what are you trying to say? You haven't gotten very far with all this." Ah, Harvey was getting a bit pissed-off at my playing shrink. Well you ain't seen nothing yet, Harvey-baby!

"What I'm trying to say is that maybe you can't tell the cure from the disease without a scorecard. The chick can't make it with a man till she clears it with her group; she's going to group because she can't make it with a man. Isn't there something vaguely circular in all this?"

"You're saying that *therapy* is keeping me from having a healthy relationship with a man?" Arlene said. The hostility was gone; it was an honest question.

"I'm saying that therapy *is* your relationship with a man," I said. "Instead of taking your troubles to your lover, you take them to group; instead of opening up your soul in bed, you puke it up here."

"Are you suggesting that a healthy relationship between a man and a woman must be based upon her . . . *puking her troubles on you,* as you put it?" Harvey said primly.

"I'm suggesting that no real man can put up for very long with a woman who gives her cunt to him and her soul to someone else. I'm suggesting that no real man wants some other cat making it a three-some when he's in bed with his chick."

"And who is this other man you seem so paranoid about?" Harvey said.

"You are, Harvey," I told him.

Pow! Harvey's face froze into a featureless mask. Arlene looked straight at Harvey instead of at me. Rich, Charley, Linda and Ida rolled their eyes and groaned silently in various degrees of exasperation. But Doris—Doris stared into space as if I had triggered some cosmic flash in her head. What could that—?

O wow! Yeah—Ted gibbering about homosexual fantasies; not making it with her; no more chicks on the side either. Doris was seeing a strange new lover between herself and Ted--but this "other woman" was Harvey Brustein. Did she think it was a psychic fag thing? It wasn't—what Ted and Arlene and the rest of them were getting off Harvey was deeper and dirtier than sex, was what I had gotten off smack when I was with Anne. Yeah, Harvey was the Other Man and the Other Woman to all of them—the way smack had been the lover that slept between Anne and me.

"You don't think you might be projecting your own insecurities onto—"

"Can it Harvey!" I told him. "Look around this room. Arlene can't have a healthy relationship with me; you're the other man there. Ted can't get it up for Doris because you're—"

"*Are you suggesting that I have sexual relations with my patients?*" Harvey fairly shrieked. His gray pudding-face had a hint of redness in it; his eyes flickered heat for a second.

"That fag thing got you going, didn't it?" I said. Harvey's hands actually balled into loose fists. "Well cool it man, I'm not talking about anything as healthy as a little harmless nooky for the shrink. Dig: you and Rich and pot are the same twisted triangle. Likewise you and Charley and booze. You're an emotional vampire, sucking it all in and putting out nothing but void. What I'd like to know, man, is the breed of monkey *you're* feeding with all this shit."

The color left Harvey's face and his hands relaxed. "An interesting delusionary system," he said. "Quite consistent with your history of heroin addiction."

A middling-good try, but it wasn't working. I could sense the group fissioning into factions: Doris and Rich and maybe Charley were eating up what I was putting out; it hit a chord in their own guts; Ida and Linda looked like they were ready to claw me to pieces in defense of their therapist-Man; Arlene seemed to be hanging high and dry on the fence.

"Come on, Harvey," I said, "let your hair down. You're a human being. A human being has needs. No one does anything without personal reasons. You're got a personal reason for this Foundation scene; it's *your* scene, you put it together. What's your brand of junk, Harv?"

"The therapist must stand outside the group and maintain an objective viewpoint," Harvey said woodenly. "Of course I have personal motivations like anyone else, but I leave them outside the Foundation. If I were to enter personally into the emotional dynamics of a group, my usefulness as a therapist—"

"Cut the shit!" I snapped. "You spend your whole life listening to people baring their souls in front of you. You've got scores of twitches so hooked on you they won't take a piss without group discussion. Don't tell *me* you're not getting anything off it! That shit's for the birds and we both know it."

"I will not discuss my personal life in a group or with any of my patients," said the Great Stone Face.

"Okay Harv. Just answer a simple question: are you married?"

"I see no point in—"

"Aw come on, Harvey," Doris said in her best both-feet-on-the-ground Earth Mother voice, "that won't kill you. Tell us."

"Yeah," said Rich, "why the hell can't you tell us that?"

I had the wolf-pack baying: Arlene looked puzzled at Harvey making such a big deal over nothing; Linda, true to her paranoia, looked suspicious; Charley looked more cynical than usual; even Ida seemed to be waiting for a straight answer.

Harvey paused for a moment, seemed to be studying the situations; he probably realized that if he carried the Great Silent Buddha Act much further, what their imaginations would read into it (maybe a Bluebeard number) would be uglier than any truth could be.

"I am legally married," he said evenly. Then, more slowly, haltingly in fact: "However . . . my wife and I are . . . separated . . . we have a boy and a girl . . . ." But strangely, instead of relaxing now that the Deep Dark Secret was out, he seemed to get tenser, began rolling the fingers of his right hand around an imaginary cigarette. He was afraid of something else coming out. I could smell it. What . . . ? A sudden flash: he had been awfully uptight about admitting he was a San Franciscan.

"You were married in San Francisco, right?" I said.

Uptight! Uptight! His eyes looked like the eyes of a trapped animal. "I . . . I believe I told you that I've lived most of my life in San Francisco . . . "

"And the wife and kiddies are still there, aren't they?"

"I . . . I . . . that's really none of your business," Harvey said. He glanced with far-too-plastic nonchalance at his watch. "Well, er . . . I see our time is about up," he said. "I've got a session with Rhoda Steiner next hour, so we'll have to cut it short. It *has* been a . . . er . . . most interesting group . . . ."

And that was that. I deserved two ears, at least. You could argue about the tail.

■ ■ ■ ■ ■ ■ ■ ■ ■ ■

Arlene and I, as if by some, unspoken arrangement, had let the others leave the room while we sat there exchanging strange stares. Now that we were alone, we both got up and faced each other down in the middle of the room.

"Well what do you think of the little brass Buddha now?" I said.

"You were cruel to him," she said, without much conviction.

"Yeah, but what if it was the truth?"

"I don't know if it was the truth," she said, not meeting my eyes. "I know you think it was the truth, so I can't be mad at you for saying it—that's the way a group should work. But. . . ."

"But if that's the truth, you'll take vanilla?"

"I . . . I don't want to think about it now. Look, I don't want this to sound like a put-down, but please don't ask me to go home with you tonight."

I smelled it coming, but I was still kind of disappointed. I had socked it to Harvey according to the script, but I had hoped that the conquering hero would ride off into the sunset with the fair maiden. That's the way they'd shoot it in Hollywood.

"Who said I was planning to?" I lied, deciding to leave *her* off-balance.

"You're not—?"

"No, I'm not mad," I said blandly. "I just got other fish to fry tonight. Later."

And *I* left *her* standing there and wondering.

Olé!

12
" . . . and Trust Your Fate to the Hand of God . . . ."

Ordinarily, I can do without TV dinners. Plastic peas, library-paste mashed potatoes and a few slabs of well-rotted shoeleather drenched in diluted motor-oil are not exactly my idea of food for the inner man. However, making it back to my pad from the Foundation and determined to blow the accumulated muck out of my mind in the far East Village coffee-house scene, I was in no mood for restaurants and even in less of a mood to cook real food.

So I threw a turkey TV dinner into the oven and by the time it was as ready to eat as it would ever be, I had convinced myself that I wasn't really hungry anyway. The TV dinner itself did nothing to change my mind.

Well, anyway, the TV dinner *had* taken care of my hunger, one way or another, and after I threw the aluminum foil tray into the garbage, I was ready to see what the night would hold. Except . . . .

Except it was *really* November outside: temperature barely goosing 30 and a wet wind blowing. What I really needed after that Foundation scene was a nice June night when everyone and everything pours into the streets and you don't have to think about going anywhere in particular. I had a yen for the street, but I knew that once I stepped out of the steam heat and into the cold sullen November street, I'd quickly end up making for Stanley's or the Blue Goo or the Id or some other downer dive and the kind of crowd that had started to get pretty boring in the last few months. Cold weather in New York does that to you—kills the urge to wander.

But I had no intention of brooding around my pad, so I changed to Levis and a heavy flannel shirt, put on my warm black toggle-coat, pulled up the hood to protect my ears and ventured out into the dingy hallway. As I reached the stairwell, I heard a girl's footsteps on the tin stairs about a flight below me.

I started down the stairs, but on the first landing down, I met Robin puffing her way up from below. Her ears and nose were bright pink from the cold—which made going outside seem a crummier idea than ever.

She frowned when she saw me. "Oh shit, man," she said, "you're going somewhere?"

"Nowhere important."

"You're sure?"

"I'm sure."

She smiled, reached into her peacoat pocket, pulled out a little brass opium pipe and a tinfoil-wrapped cube about half an inch on a side, said: "Groovy. Let's go up to your place and blow some of this hash."

"Best offer I've had all day."

■ ■ ■ ■ ■ ■ ■ ■ ■ ■ ■

My eyes were popping from the effort not to cough and my throat felt like a furnace flue. The civilized way to smoke hash, for my money, is ground up with pot in a joint. But it wasn't my money or my hash, so we were smoking little brown chips of it in the opium pipe and it was pure murder on my throat and lungs.

A mule kicked me in the Adam's apple and I coughed out a typhoon of blue-gray smoke. I coughed again and again—top of my head seemed to explode in a shower of sparks with each spasm. But when I stopped coughing, I felt a delicious hollowness inside, feeling of containing the universe, conscious of the sweet cool air pouring into my lungs like the kiss of the sea. That's hash: if you're not a heavy cigarette-head, it can go down like honking Ajax, but man, you *do* come up high!

Leaning back on the couch next to me, Robin blew a thin stream of smoke high into the air like a spouting whale, no coughing, just as cool as you please. My throat still felt like it had been napalmed, but after four tokes of hash, who gave a shit?

"Very nice . . . " I drawled.

Robin giggled. Ripples of giggle shimmered the blue smoke in the air.

"*Vury* nice . . . " she said furrily. She knocked the residue out of the pipe into an ashtray and refilled it with a big chip that she worried off the cube of hashish with a fingernail. She held a match over the pipe, took another toke, and passed it to me.

Girding my lungs, I held the match over the little bowl and sucked. Closing my eyes, I felt the hot smoke coursing down my throat into my lungs; I *was* smoke pouring down dark passageways and fading into moist flesh. I was the smokeflesh interface writhing in a million subtle convolutions. From somewhere outside my being, I sensed a hot tickling and a spasm building. I fought back the pressure of the spasm, concentrated on digging the spasm till I *was* the spasm fighting to be born. I let myself be pushed up a long dark tube and whooshed out into the universe . . . .

I opened my eyes. Whee! My body had no weight; I knew I could float up to the ceiling if I felt like it. But why bother?

■ ■ ■ ■ ■ ■ ■ ■ ■ ■ ■

"Hey man, what *is* this thing?" Robin said. I let some air out of my balloon and drifted gently back to earth, saw that she was looking through one of the fee manuscripts I had taken home from Dirk Robinson, Inc. Some mingy little part of me seemed to be pissed off at her intruding on my life's work, none of her business, really. But what the hell, man, what the hell . . .

"That, my good woman, is a fee manuscript," I said.

"A *which*? Man, is this thing weird! Uh . . . you don't write this stuff, do you?"

"Hand it here, girl," I looked at the title page: "Meat for the Monster" by Harry Carew West. Mmmm, she had lucked onto a tasty example—the latest science fiction epic by old Hairy West, the schizophrenic monster-freak who I secretly suspected of accosting basket cases in men's rooms.

"This is the work of an aspiring writer," I told her. "Leave us have some respect. It is my job to read it, decide whether or not it can be sold, and then write a letter full of wisdom to the creep that wrote that piece of shit."

She recovered the sf masterpiece from my hot little hand. *"Dig this stuff!"* she said. She opened the manuscript at random and began to read:

" . . . strapped to the cool wet rock with fetid encrustations of rotten yellow moss and semi-congealed mortworm ichor, Kellerman stared up at Buglush, gibbering with a nameless dread. The huge Jupiteranian rolled all twelve of his obscene saucerlike eyes and a thin stream of blue spittle dribbled from between the creature's pulsating lips. The touch of a wet tentacle on his bare chest sent a wave of horrid pleasure through his fibers.

But when the huge tubular tongue snaked out of the grotesque lower orifice, Kellerman howled in torment. The drool-covered tube . . . "

Robin held the manuscript up between her thumb and forefinger like it was an old dead fish and dropped it on the table. "Phew!" she observed. "*That* is *sick!* What kind of job do you have, man?"

"I work for the world's greatest con game," I told her. "Freaks like that in search of fame and fortune send us their masterpieces, expecting us to sell them. Instead, we take their bread, we read the things and send them back a classy literary rejection letter."

"What can you tell a creep like this?" Robin said, all wide-eyed innocence.

"Simple, girl, simple. We got it down to a science: we tell the twitch he's a great writer, but this story doesn't *quite* make it. Then we tell him why, and we tell him to keep trying and think positive thoughts. And write more checks, of course."

"Man, I still don't get it. Go on, tell me what you're gonna write to this freak."

"Why not?" I leaned back, closed my eyes, pretended I was at my typewriter and the golden words of wisdom poured forth:

"Dear Mr. West:

Thank you very much for your latest science fiction story, 'Meat for the Monster.' I must say that this piece is certainly representative of your considerable talent at the top of its form. It has all the qualities that I've come to expect in a Harry Carew West script: vivid description, a unique imaginative power, a sense of the arcane and genuine reader-involvement. However, certain elements in the theme and its handling, I'm sorry to have to say, make this one not quite suitable for the current market . . . ."

"Notice," I told her proudly, "that at no time have I lied to the man."

Robin giggled. "How could you," she said, "when you haven't said a fucking thing?"

"Ah, me girl, you've got the essence of it! Dirk himself couldn't have put it better: don't lie and don't say a fucking thing."

"Hey, I think I dig! It's a crazy game, is all. Go on, rap out some more."

"Con mucho gusto," I said.

" . . . first of all, you fruit, you seem to have scanted the question of motivation. Kellerman's objective in landing in the Red Spot of Jupiter is somewhat unclear, but the actions of Buglush, the Jupiteranian Muck Monster, are even more unmotivated . . . ."

"Hey dig," Robin said. "My turn:

. . . for instance, creepo, what kicks does the Muck Monster get off strapping Kellerman to the rock and dribbling all over the poor shit? Is the Muck Monster some kind of disgusting pervert or something?"

"Ah, you got the fee-reader touch," I told her. "To continue:

. . . Perhaps the reader can suspend his disbelief long enough to become convinced of the reality of the Muck Monster, and you are a good enough writer to bring off the tour-de-force of a *perverted* Muck Monster who is addicted to running tongue and tentacles over hapless Earthmen before dissolving them with acid drool and sucking up the residue with its hollow proboscis. But since you clearly establish that Kellerman is the first human being to visit Jupiter, the unanswerable question arises: where the fuck has the Muck Monster been scoring Earthmen for the last thousand years?"

"Your turn," I told Robin.

" . . . After all, freako, the poor fucking Muck Monster would be out of his gourd if Kellerman was the first human being he had been able to score. A thousand years of being hooked on Earthmen before he ever saw one and he'd be chewing that slime-stone of his. Your story is unfair to Muck Monsters . . . ."

We broke up in giggles.
"Jeez," Robin said, "you do this all the time?"
"Five days a week."
"Too much. Just *too* much!"
"You've got a pretty good natural talent for it," I told her half-

seriously. "Want to try out for the job?"

Robin shook her head. "Pass, baby," she said. "I'll stick to something honest like dealing dope. Speaking of which . . . I gotta do a thing. Should be back in about half an hour . . . unless you want to come along . . . ?"

"Where?"

"Tenth and Avenue B."

"Just around the corner, practically. Why the hell not?"

"Groovy," she said, flaking a piece of hash off the cube. "Let's take a couple more hits to keep us warm."

■ ■ ■ ■ ■ ■ ■ ■ ■ ■ ■

The reek of cat-shit nearly knocked me on my ass. The guy who let us into the apartment had shoulder-length stringy hair, wore a denim workshirt and day-glow red bellbottoms, but otherwise looked like the world's youngest wino or a terminal speed-freak. The pad itself was strictly East Side Gothic:

One big room with a tiny kitchenette in the far right corner next to the bathtub and a water-closet in the near left corner from which came obscene gurgling sounds. In the sink and spilling over onto the tin washtub-cover were geological accumulations of dirty dishes and rancid frying pans dating back to the early Jurassic upon which a thousand cockroaches were holding a grub-in. A white Japanese lantern over a blue bulb copped from the subway cast a mercifully-dim junkie light over the furniture in the room, namely: one mattress on the floor covered with a dirty sheet and a shit-brown Army blanket which in turn were covered with candy-bar wrappers, cigarette butts, ashes, under-and-over-ground newspapers, rotting socks and mildewed underwear; one kitchen table on which sat a box of cornflakes and a hookah constructed out of a Mason jar, an old pipe-bowl and lengths of enema-bag tubing; a monster stereo rig with two huge walnut speakers; four orange crates filled with records. The walls were papered with groovy posters and squashed bugs. The floor was carpeted with more old newspapers, ashtrays, paperback books, butts, both kinds of roaches, assorted slime—all covered with a rich patina of dust and occasional cat-turds. Close by the mattress, a sullen gray tomcat was shitting into a cardboard box filled half-and-half with Kitty Litter and cat crap.

"Sit down, man," our gracious host wheezed. Seemed to be a problem there: sitting on the floor was a sure way to be carried off by the roaches; the only thing to sit on was the (yech!) bed. Which, apparently, was the idea. Our host swept the assorted crud off a considerable area of the bed with a swipe of his paw and sat down on the mattress. Robin sat down next to him and, after a slight hesitation, I planted my ass in the muck too.

"Cody is a writer," Robin said, giving me a coy grin.

"Yeah, man, I write lyrics for some of the real heavy groups."

"Oh? Any group I'd know?"

"I've done things for The Black Death . . . The Four Horsemen . . . Did about ten songs for The Meat Factory . . . ."

"Don't think I've seen any of their records," I said.

Cody gave me a scornful Oh Wow look. "Shit man," he said righteously, "those groups are too heavy for *record companies!*"

Robin gave me a wink, cocked her head at Cody. "Tom here is a literary agent," she said slyly.

Cody looked like he might start to drool like a Jupiteranian Muck Monster. Yeah, and five'll get you ten old Cody's drool would really be acid—Acid, that is. "Oh yeah?" he said real supercool. Didn't know whether to put me down for a square or try to hustle me. I was tempted to really take him for a ride; Cody was definitely the fee-reader type.

"Yeah, but we don't handle lyricists," I said, turning him off and feeling all warm and virtuous inside.

"Hey baby, you got the stuff?" Cody said, apparently deciding to ignore me.

"How much do you want?" Robin asked.

"Man, I've gotta write some stuff for The Meat Factory by Monday, so I'll take a nickel's worth of anything that'll get me high. But if you've got *good* hash, I'll take a dime."

Robin took a nickel cube out of her pocket, handed it to Cody. Cody unwrapped the tinfoil and examined the brown cube of hashish. "Good count," he said. He took a five dollar bill out of his shirt pocket and handed it to Robin. "Tell you what," he said, "let's blow some of it and if it's good stuff, I'll take another nickel."

Robin shrugged. "It's your hash now, man," she said.

Cody got up, fetched the hookah and set it down beside the mattress. He sat down, took a pocket knife out of his other shirt pocket, shaved off a big flake of hash and carefully placed it on the wire-mesh inside the bowl of the hookah. He scrabbled around under the

blanket, came up with a box of wooden kitchen matches, lit one, held it over the bowl, and took a big hit. He passed the mouthpiece to Robin, held another match over the bowl for her and she toked.

Robin held the match for me. I took a big, big drag. The water-pipe cooled the smoke so I felt I could suck on the mouthpiece forever: the tit of the universe. I concentrated on filling myself up with hash from the bottom up, first my toes then up the bones of my legs like giant straws my body each individual sack in my lungs up my throat the little air space between brain and skull and finally holding the last nugget of smoke in my cheeks like a chipmunk. Concentrated on holding it all in as I passed the pipe to good old Cody. Felt every cell in my body swimming in hash soaking it into my DNA, ah yes, thing to do was get stoned on a cellular level a whole new high each and every cell stoned out of its little gourd so the whole would be higher than the sum of its parts--

Whooosh! Wheee! Smoke boiled up from my toes through my legs up my lungs, up over and out. Roger, over and out, that is. All systems A-Okay, orbit established.

Digging Cody's pad as the pipe passed around in timeless cosmic rhythm. Good clean organic dirt—suck in smoke—God's own crud, is all—hold it in—essence of Stoic philosophy—whoosh it out—why clean it up?—suck on the tit—just get dirty again—hold it in—live close to nature like Cody's cat who doesn't turn a Puritan back on his own shit—exhale—get rid of holier-than-thou put-down of ethnic East Side dirt—another drag on the pipe—no worse than pads I'd inhabited myself—don't lose the smoke—destroy tension between inner chaos and synthetic outer environment—whoosh!

"Ah yes, ah-hah, yes . . . " Cody wheezed. "That's good shit."

"Fuckin'-A!" I told him. Of course, my chick sells nothing but the best. Class will tell, old man.

"Want another nickel?" Robin asked. 'Course old Cody wants another nickel. That's good shit, gotta get it while it's hot. Or cool. Good stuff supply could dry up tomorrow. Principle of Free Enterprise what made American great.

"Waaal . . . ."

"It's good stuff," I reminded him.

"Yeah, but . . . ."

I gave him the old snake-oil salesman look. "Could be there won't be such good stuff when you've blown the first nickel," I warned.

Cody pondered the cube of hash displayed like a brown jewel on the open tinfoil. "Got a point there," he said.

"Yas," I said. "Make hay while the sun shines. A cube in time saves nine. Treat instead of a treatment. Don't be a boob, cop another cube."

Cody cocked his head at me; then he grinned. "Son of a bitch," he said, "ya talked me into it."

Out came a fiver. Out came a cube. The transaction was made and the great wheel of commerce spun around.

"You've done your bit to avert a hair-curling Depression," I told him. "Keep the money in circulation is the very principle upon which Our Great Nation is founded. You've done your fucking patriotic duty, is what!"

"Man, are you stoned!" Robin said admiringly.

"I deny the allegation and I defy the alligator!"

■ ■ ■ ■ ■ ■ ■ ■ ■ ■ ■

Cold out in the street. The sky clear and black and the air thin as outer space and the buildings the empty street all hard gray pumice-stone. Like walking with Robin on the Moon, sans spacesuits. Who needs space suits anyway? All in your head. Just take a toke and step outside. Spacesuits are a boondoggle. Must inform the Government first thing in the morning, save millions. Telegram to NASA: "SPACESUITS A PUT-ON STOP VACUUM IS NATURAL ENVIRONMENT OF MAN STOP GROOVE BEHIND IT." Nobel Prize for sure.

"Man are you stoned!" Message from Robin at ground-control.

"Roger. All systems go."

"Too much. *Too much!*"

"Scientific impossibility," I informed her. "We have reached equilibrium without Librium, is all. Only problem is to watch out for perverted Muck Monsters."

"But the Muck Monster is your friend," Robin opined.

"Listen, I don't know about *your* friends . . . ."

"Any Jupiteranian Muck Monster that drools Acid is a friend of mine!"

Of course! Must compose another telegram to NASA: "MUCK MONSTER IS YOUR CONNECTION ON JUPITER."

"On the other hand," Robin said, "I heard a rumor that Jupiteranian Acid is cut with disgusting green slime."

"Shit, what's the universe coming to when you can't even trust your friendly neighborhood Muck Monster?" No integrity left nowhere!

■ ■ ■ ■ ■ ■ ■ ■ ■ ■ ■

Into the apartment, a warm cave in the mountain, climbers' rest Swiss Alpine chalet at the top of an endless Matterhorn of puffing tin stairs. We flopped down on the couch in our coats sucking warm pad-air into the bottoms of our lungs (air still tasty with haze of hash smoke, a booster-shot) in sharp spasms like a team of horses just galloped flat-out up five flights of East Side stairs, sweating even in the cold.

Just laying there panting in my coat, too tired to move or even think, waiting for approximately a thousand years for my lungs to catch up with the universe. Finally, enough breath back (and feeling steam-heat leaching life's juices into the cloth of my clothes) to peel off my coat and throw it on the floor and help Robin off with hers, expending last quantum of energy. The two of us curled together in a heap panting like summer dogs.

Nothing in the universe but the feel of her body panting against my panting side in a funky afterbeat—PANT-pant, PANT-pant, PANT-pant—and her eyes dimming and flashing in the same rhythm into the back of my brain—You-me, You-me, You-me—the rhythm of the great artery of the universe—PANT-pant, PANT-pant, PANT-pant—my brain pulsing with hers in the standing wave pattern of creation—You-me, You-me, You-me—Robin's being beating like a secret second heart to my blood-rhythm—PANT-pant, PANT-pant, PANT-pant—I *was* the sighing of the universe—You-me, You-me, You-me—I was her—PANT-pant—she was me—You-me—we were It—PANT-pant—we Were—You-me, PANT-pant, You-me, PANT-pant . . . .

PANT-pant . . . bodies grinding together . . . PANT-pant . . . shirts and buttons . . . PANT-pant . . . buckles and zippers . . . PANT-pant . . . secret white underwear . . . PANT-pant . . . naked flesh touching . . . PANT-pant . . . tongues rolling on each other . . . PANT-pant . . . drifting across the floor towards the bedroom . . . PANT-pant . . .

Grooving together in the blind blackness: two universes intersecting in the cosmic nexus of my being.

Feel of cool sheets on my naked back—*humming mandalas of neon butterflies against black velvet*—Robin rolling me over enveloping me in a marvelous feather-bed of flesh—*a million tiny pinwheels of light whirling pulses of green-blue-yellow sparks into space*—lips touching mine and my blind universe of flesh filled with the wet essence of her tongue—*spirals of light moving within a greater spiral within a greater spiral the galaxies turning in their cosmic spirals the touch of our bodies the nexus of nexuses*—an upheaval in the Earth and now a rippling continent of flesh beneath my body—*spirals of neon light circling within spirals of darkness within spirals of color in pulsating yin-yang mandalas of the universe fucking the Cosmic Cunt*—circle of legs around my waist like primeval lips of her cunt around my cock her mouth around my tongue—*mandala of the universe flashing color and darkness*—my being thrusting in at the top out at the bottom in at the bottom out at the top—*flashing in and out of tongues of flame*—her mouth circling around my thrust cunt sucking around my beat—*cosmic spirals of light whirling flashing in-out-in*—pure FEELING of in-out-ness—FLASH IN, FLASH OUT—*her universe of flesh whirling in cosmic rhythm around*—yin-yang mandala around and around—*In, out and around*—In, out and around—

Light merging into flesh into darkness into In, out and around into flashing wave of neon-colored flesh into Flash in Flash out Flash-flash whirl Flash-flash whirl Flash-flash-flash-flash—

Lights-sound-feel-flesh all coming together: FLASH! FLASH! FLASH! FLASH!

And the universe melting down into a long smooth tunnel into total sweet black velvet void . . . .

■ ■ ■ ■ ■ ■ ■ ■ ■ ■

. . . . my head felt like a basketball balanced atop a baseball bat: huge, hollow and wobbly on the end of my neck . . . .

Which was the first thing I felt on Saturday morning. Lying in bed with my eyes glued shut by morning-after mung; the sheets rumpled beneath and above me; a vague kaleidoscope of impossible memories and no sense of time.

Not that I had what you'd call a hangover—my head didn't hurt, it just felt strange. Going to bed really stoned and waking up straight is a peculiarly disorienting feeling, especially if you've O.D.ed in bed. Had I O.D.ed in bed? Hard to remember. We had sure smoked an awful lot of hash. We had balled, I think . . . .Yeah, I think that's the last thing I remembered. WoW. I felt like the mythical debutante into whose drink an unscrupulous degenerate had secreted a peyote button.

I fumbled around in the bed, my eyes still closed. Knock, knock— no one there. Well, there was no getting around it: I rubbed my eyes open. Sunlight was streaming in around the edges of the green window-shade. Even that dull green light was a bit too much for my taste at the moment. The clock said one. The mouse ran down....*One o'clock?*

"Robin!" I yelled, "you still here?"

"Coming right in, man," her voice said from far away, from what sounded like the kitchen.

A moment later, Robin walked into the bedroom—wide awake, dressed and smiling—with a cup of coffee in one hand and the hash pipe in the other. She kissed me lightly on the nose (my mouth tasted like the Black Hole of Calcutta), sat down on the bed next to me and handed me the coffee.

I took a long drink. It was just this side of scalding and had cream and sugar in it the way I like it, and it cut through a lot of cobwebs on the way down. I was beginning to feel almost human.

"Very domestic," I said. "Somehow I didn't make you for the type."

"Oh, sometimes I groove behind that trip," Robin said. "Got scrambled eggs ready to go in the kitchen, too." She smiled and held the hash pipe up to my lips. "Not only that, I brought you your pipe. Couldn't find any slippers, though."

I eyed the hash pipe dubiously. "Isn't it a little early in the morning?"

"Early in the morning? It's one o'clock!" She took out a pack of matches, lit one, held it over the pipe bowl and took a drag. She blew sweet-smelling smoke in my direction. "Tasty ... " she said. "I've been stoned for an hour already waiting for you to wake up. Try and get out of bed without it, baby!"

I propped myself up against the headboard. Blecch!

"Man, it's a groove getting up stoned," she said. "Think I'd be making breakfast if I were straight? Come on, have some hash and dig the day."

"Well ... maybe just a little one ... " I said, letting her put the pipe between my lips.

■ ■ ■ ■ ■ ■ ■ ■ ■ ■

Something to be said for a little hash before breakfast as an aperi-tif. By the time I was dressed, I had had three medium-sized tokes (no sense in pushing my lungs too far) and my head felt firmly in contact with my body (if not much of anything else) and my body felt like a loose, well-oiled machine, and by God, I had an appetite, which somehow seemed like an amazing feat of prestidigitation. Robin served me toast and eggs and more coffee in the living room which I devoured like an Iowa farmboy. After a post-breakfast passing of the peace-pipe, I felt like a fat and happy suburban hubby; all that was missing was the morning paper and I was just as happy to pass on that.

"See?" Robin said, laying the pipe down on the table and smiling domestic tranquility. "It's groovy to blow some hash first thing in the morning, once you get past the idea."

I nodded. "Like most of the best things in life," I said, "it's immoral, illegal and (patting my stomach and faking a belch) fattening."

Robin laughed. "That's why you've got to be poor to cut it as a good stoned chick," she said. "If I were rich, I'd own my own candy store and just smoke dope and eat till I blew up to about three hundred pounds."

"And here I was about to tell you I was a millionaire playboy in a clever plastic disguise . . . ."

"I'd almost believe you," Robin said. "You're a cat with hidden resources. Like that crazy job you have reading all that . . . Say, you *do* have a job reading freaky stories? We weren't *that* stoned?"

I gestured toward a pile of fee manuscripts on the table. "Would that we were, girl," I sighed. "Would that we were."

"Yeah, you're a strange cat," she said. "AC-DC."

"WHAT?"

She laughed. "Don't get uptight. I mean, you groove behind stoned trips and I'll bet you groove behind square trips, too. I'll bet you even have some little college chick balling you on the side."

She gave me a look that said she meant it, and a smile that said it didn't matter. Which didn't keep me from getting uptight. How did she . . . ?

She kissed me lightly on the lips, her mouth tasting of coffee and hash; not a bad combination. "Relax, baby," she said. "I trip in and out of your life and you don't bug me about what I'm doing the rest of the time, and that's the way I gotta have it. I dig you for it. Why should I mind that you've got some other action going? It keeps you interesting. I dig a man of mystery."

"What makes you think . . . ?"

"Come on man, we've gotten too high together for me not to be tuned in on your vibes. I can tell you've got another chick in the closet and it doesn't bother me." She grinned evilly. "But I bet it'd blow *her* mind if she knew about me!"

Thinking of Arlene and what material this would make for the old group, I couldn't help flashing an evil grin back at Robin. Caught! Well, what the fuck, maybe I needed someone to talk to . . . .

"From here to Pluto," I said.

"A real straight chick?"

"You're really not jealous?"

"Does that hurt your ego, man?"

"Well maybe . . . But man does not live by ego alone. I almost wish you'd make an evil scene so I could make up my mind . . . ."

"This chick has really been putting you through changes?"

"You . . . you really don't mind talking about this . . . ?"

"Hey, you really *are* uptight about this . . . ?"

"Arlene."

"Yeah, it figured to be an *Arlene*. Dig baby, you can talk about it to me. Really. I want to dig the inside of your—"

A knock on the door. Shit!

Instantly, Robin was on her feet. "I'll get it," she said, and whoosh, she was out of the living room and into the kitchen. I heard her opening the door. A few minutes' mumbling with a male voice, and then she was back. "Just a customer," she said. "A couple of people'll be coming by to cop some hash. You don't mind . . . ?"

Of course I minded—but how could I say so to a chick who was being so beautiful about my extracurricular activities?

"Just as long as they're not traipsing through the pad all day," I said.

"I'll cool it, do my things at the door, okay?" she said, fishing a cube of hash out of her coat pocket and leaving the coat on the floor where it lay. "Just take a minute. Why don't you refill the pipe in the meantime?" And she tossed a second cube onto the table.

Why not? I thought. Some huge idea seemed to be lurking just around the corner of my mind. Maybe a little more hash would smoke it out into the open . . . ?

■ ■ ■ ■ ■ ■ ■ ■ ■ ■ ■

"Man, this Foundation trip's gotta be the world's evillest mind game," Robin said. I breathed out a lazy feather of hash smoke. Between tokes of the peace-pipe (and two more business trips to the door by Robin), I had riffed out just about everything. Had slid quickly and smoothly from telling her about someone who was making a scene called the Foundation for Total Consciousness to rapping on the Foundation itself, which seemed to be a safer subject.

"That's were it's at," I said. "I wonder sometimes why I'm making it."

"It's not just this Arlene chick?"

"Naw . . . I could probably never go back to the Foundation and still have something going with Arlene if I wanted to."

"But you *are* going back?"

"I suppose so . . . got two good friends of mine hung-up there and I can't leave 'em in the lurch . . . ."

Robin exhaled a cloud of smoke. Big black eyes laughed at me. "Bullshit," she said. "I know where you're at. You're grooving behind the game."

"Behind Harvey Brustein's mind-game?" I said. "That's crap, girl. Harvey isn't putting anything over on me."

"No man, you're grooving behind *your* game."

"*My* game?"

"Don't you see the game you're playing? Ever been heavy behind bikes? Ever know a cat who likes to fight? Dig the bullfighter's thing. Or cats that jump out of airplanes for kicks. Same game."

"You lost me around the first bend."

"Catch up, baby," she said, sticking the pipe in my mouth. I took a deep drag. Held it. "Natural male game," she said. "Playing chicken with death."

"Death? Come on!" Around a cough of smoke.

"No dig: there are all kinds of death. Rack up a bike kind of death. O.D. yourself on smack kind of death. Blow your mind kind of death—ego-death, dig? That's an Acid game. That's your Foundation game, too."

Ah, she just didn't understand! That was Harvey's trip, not mine. "I assure you, I'm not the ego-death type," I told her. "In fact, ego-death is my idea of the ultimate cancer-hole."

Robin bobbed her head up and down like a stoned rabbi. "Yeah, yeah, yeah! *That's* the game. Bike-freaks don't want to smash themselves up. Junkies don't want to O.D. The idea isn't to kill your ego on Acid. The game is to come as close to death as you can. Closer and closer and closer all the time. Till you can taste it. Till you don't know if you can pull your bike out or pull your mind out. Death is the grooviest trip there is."

"The only trouble is it kills you."

"You dig, you dig! That's the whole thing: to come as close as you can to death without dying. Man, that kind of fear is a trip! To go right into total fear and not know whether you're coming out or not. And then when you do—Oh wow. That's why Acid is such a groove—sometimes you can taste death, but you don't die."

Eyeball to eyeball: her eyes so huge, so ferally alive I felt myself sucked into them and something at the dark bottom of the wells spoke to itself inside of me, smiled a dirty smile at itself a billion years old. This girl was alive, alive-o! Deepest thing inside us all was up front on the surface of her mind.

Oh Christ, yes: " . . . into the valley of death rode the six hundred . . . " . . . Harvey Brustein, Prince of the Final Darkness . . . the universe-shaking rumble of the H-bomb, so groovy . . . wheels screaming around a curve . . . the long free-fall from the sky . . . flash of nothingness of The Big Orgasm . . . . " . . . fuck me fuck me fuck me to death . . . . " . . . Total Consciousness of the Total Void . . . . " . . . break on through to the other side . . . . " " . . . one moment of agony," said Count Dracula, "and then—eternal life!" OM . . . OM . . . OM . . . Blow your mind. BLOW YOUR MIND. BABY, BLOW YOUR MIND!

Robin gave me the old Mona Lisa smile. Did old Mona know what we knew?

"You're a scary chick," I said.

Robin laughed a cosmically dirty laugh a million years old. "That's why you dig me, baby," she said.

A knock on the door.

"Another one," she said, fumbling in her coat for a dub of hash. And over her shoulder as she went to the door; "And that's why your Arlene doesn't uptight me. Like the song says, man: 'Your debutante just knows what you need, but I know what you want.'"

■ ■ ■ ■ ■ ■ ■ ■ ■ ■ ■

"Hey, how'd you like to see the old Foundation in action?" I asked her when she got back. "Get a taste of the surge yourself, see how the other half dies."

"Mmmm, you are a groovy evil cat," she said approvingly. "Yeah, I'd like to take the whole Foundation trip with you. When?"

"There's a party there tonight . . . "

"Okay baby. Just one thing: we get good and stoned before we go, right?"

"This isn't stoned enough for you?"

"Oh baby, *nothing* is stoned enough for me! Just too bad we don't have some acid."

A strange thrill went through me. I had felt that thrill before, oh yes, but now I knew what it was and I could groove behind it. Harvey Brustein, meet The Man in Black.

"We gonna blow us some minds," I said.

"Do some evil numbers . . . ."

"I never really grooved behind evil before."

"You're gonna groove behind it tonight. Worried what it'll do to your debutante?"

"Yeah . . . " I said. "But I'm also kind of interested . . . mmmmm . . . ."

Robin leered at me. "You can get pretty scary yourself," she said. She handed me the pipe. "Have some hash, baby. We're gonna blow us some dirty square minds tonight, oh yes!"

"That's the name of the game, isn't it?" I said. And sucked the breath of the Assassin deep into the bowels of my blood.

13
The Man in Black

Black night and windy, dank and cold and suitably atmospheric, something out of Lovecraft. The Man in Black and his Lady getting out of the cab down the block from the Foundation: Robin wearing her peacoat, Levis, black plastic boots and an old black shirt which I've laid on her, her long black hair blowing wildly over her shoulders; me in black chinos, my new black shirt with black tie and my black toggle-coat with the hood up around my face and black shades I can hardly see through.

I was really stoned, but not *that* stoned—it was a calculated effect I was after and I wasn't so stoned I had forgotten that, but I was stoned enough to be grooving behind the image I was wearing. I was playing it from the inside out, a kind of Method put-on, and I felt cool and black and crystal-clear inside The Man From Deep Space.

The dry-run on the cabdriver had shown all systems at go: the poor slob had been mightily glad to get us out of his cab, which I had filled with heavy black vibes. Had I really sucked him into the spirit of the number or was he simply a pragmatic New York cabbie worried about being knifed by crazy junkies? Was there a difference?

Walking up the block towards the Foundation, Robin's dark hair thunderheads in the wind, she looked under by black hood at the shiny black surfaces of my impenetrable shades, said: "Man, you've almost got *me* going. You sure know how to look sinister."

"Baby, I was doing sinister junkie numbers when you were but an innocent tyke sniffing airplane glue in junior high school." True, how true! Maybe my days as a junkie were not a total loss after all; they had given me Hidden Resources of Sinister. Mmmm, how long had it been since I had wrapped myself in cloak of darkness and prowled the night . . . ?

Shit, if I didn't watch out, I'd start playing the game with myself!

"Man, are you a trip!" Robin said. Was there the slightest tightness around her eyes, a tiny tremble in her lip? Could I play the game with *her?*

"Do you believe?" I asked. "Do you believe in the Sinister Forces that prowl the midnight of the soul?"

"Oh Wow! Happy Halloween, baby!" She giggled evilly. I needed that—the giggle to bring me down and the evil in it to put me just far up enough again. Trick was not to take it *too* seriously, just seriously enough to project black vibes—a fine line to walk, with Robin my kaleidoscope-gyroscope.

I pressed the door buzzer at the street entrance to the Foundation. A hesitation; then the doorlock buzzed and I pushed the door open.

"They got a magic word, too?" Robin asked as we started up the long flight of stairs.

"You're a scary chick," I said.

"Bet your ass—the magic word is 'money'."

I could hear the sounds of party echoing along the entrance hallway and down the stairs: it was nearly ten and things should be going full blast; I had timed it for the Grand Entrance.

At the landing outside the doorway, I unbuttoned my coat but left my hood up—billowing cloak effect—took Robin's hand and burst into the dimly lit (and dimmer through my shades) hallway flapping cloth like Bela Lugosi. Ida and some fat hausfrau type I hadn't seen before were taking off their frumpy coats in the hall, looking the other way. They turned at the sound, and I was pleasured by a tiny flicker of shock as Ida turned into the vision of darkness. Just a flicker, but it must've cut deep because she instantly froze into a sneer of defensive contempt, and said: "What's the costume for, Tom? And who's that with you?"

"Costume?" I said pleasantly. "I wear no costume. And this is Robin, a simple Child of the Night."

"Arlene is supposed to show up tonight," Ida said primly.

"So?" A challenge which Ida nervously brushed aside.

"Is . . . ah . . . Robin interested in joining the Foundation?" she said.

"Maybe . . . " Robin said in a teeny little girl voice. "I understand you try to expose your consciousness here."

"Well, yes . . . ."

Robin's voice dropped two octaves; somehow she made her eyes look totally crazed. "Yummy . . . " she said, licking her lips with a lazy jungle-cat tongue. "Raw consciousness on the half-shell. My favorite dish. Slurp! Slurp!"

Ida looked like she had bitten into a turd. The woman with her shot a why-did-you-drag-me-into-this-den-of-iniquity look. They hurried up the hall away from us. Black vibes followed them.

"Evil chick!" I said approvingly.

Panther-eyes and a Cheshire-cat smile leered back.

In the little room next to the john, there was a table piled with coats, a couple of people I didn't know, and Ted and Doris. Ted gave me a what-have-we-here look as I took off my black coat revealing my black clothes underneath; Doris looked at Robin, then at me, then shook her head and rolled her eyes.

"Robin, Ted and Doris Clayton, old friends of mine." I helped her take the peacoat off and threw it down on the table over mine.

Ted gave Robin a leer that a couple of years ago would've set me to grinding my teeth and Doris to chain-smoking and anticipating a nightmare evening. But neither of us were uptight now, not even when Robin gave him a super-fey smile. Evil chick that she was, Robin seemed disappointed at not getting a rise out of Doris. Poor fucking Ted!

"Hey man," Ted said, "gotta talk to you for a minute. Doris, why don't you take Robin on in to the party . . . ."

I nodded okay to Robin; she nodded back and I dug how Ted was impressed by the number as Doris led Robin out of the room. Ted pulled me into a corner away from the table as people came into the room, undressed, and left in a continuous stream.

"Why the shades, as if I didn't know," Ted said.

"You got it," I told him.

"Harvey isn't gonna like you're coming here stoned."

"Fuck Harvey. I paid my fifty bucks. Besides man, I can maintain."

Ted grimaced. "*Sure* you can," he said. "But what about Arlene? She's gonna go through the roof when she sees you here with that Robin chick . . . ."

"You were never one to let something like *that* bother you, Ted."

Ted smiled a poor little ghost-smile of pussy-past. "Got to admit that's a mighty fine looking piece of ass you got there. Looks like she fucks like an angel."

I licked my lips. "Like a devil," I said.

Ted grinned. "That's what I mean."

For auld lang syne, I faked a nervous smile, said: "That's my turf, Ted."

"If I weren't a happily married man . . . ."

My guts cried out in pain for him. Knowing I was on safe ground and sad for it, I said: "You can have her man, courtesy of the house in memory of the chicks you steered to me."

Ted blanched and I hated The Man in Black for his sly cruelty.

"If you're ready to fight me for her with pistols at ten paces, that is," I drawled, letting him off the hook. Friendship can sure go through some funny changes. I had the awful feeling Ted had picked up on every nuance, but of course he couldn't and wouldn't and shouldn't make a sign. I just couldn't take that.

"Looks more like it'll be Robin and Arlene with pistols," Ted said.

"You sure you know what you're doing?"

"Don't you dig having chicks fight over you?"

Ted sighed. Laughed. Frowned. "I don't know about Robin, but you sure could blow your thing with Arlene this way."

"If it blows her mind, that's only fair," I told him. "She's sure fucked around enough with *my* head."

"This is gonna be one interesting party," Ted said.

"Well let's not keep the animals waiting," I told him.

■ ■ ■ ■ ■ ■ ■ ■ ■ ■ ■

Through the black glass of my shades the decadence of the big crowded room took on the ominous funky tones of a Berlin-in-the-twenties movie. Sitting on the lip of the dais in his baggy pants and decaying shirt, Harvey was the prototypical streetcorner Hitler rapping with Linda Kahn, Ida, O'Brien, Weeping Willy Nelson, Jeannie Goodman, and a few other gray losers, all dreaming of the day when the sewers of the universe would boil their muck out into the dim light of what passed for reality. Rich Rossi and a weird-looking science fiction fan (with him, it was a whole career) named Chester White were squatting on the floor trying to make a couple of fat female pimples. Charley Dees and a couple of other lushes were swilling beer decked out on the table in the back of the room. A few scattered noncouples were twitching in the gloom like terminal paretics to the low-fi Muzak-rock coming from the phonograph. The rest of the room was pretty well filled with clots of pudding-faced clots discussing whatever pudding-faced clots discuss. All very dim and shadowy through the shades like a worn-out film-clip from an ancient Polack remake of *La Dolce Vita*..

Over in a corner, Doris and Robin were rapping on each other. Couldn't hear them, but I could tell from their faces that it was a non-contest of one-upmanship: Robin trying to out-freak Doris (no contest) and Doris out-mothering this poor deluded chile (also no contest).

Robin smiled at me as Ted and I reached them. "Welcome to the cartoon," she said.

My head did a flip-flop. The unreality of the whole scene washed over me in india ink. Tuning in to the sounds in the room, it seemed like a million ducks were quacking. Over at the table, was an assembly line of beer-drinking mechanisms: constructs consisting of arms to grab beer cans, mouths connected to tubes to convey the beer to bladders, legs to walk the bladders to the john, spigots to piss the beer into hidden tubing that led under the bowels of the Earth back to the beer factory. Machines running in a closed circuit. Dancing robots slightly out of sync. Plastic music like a crumbling player piano. People milling back and forth on hidden tracks in the floor, rearing, gesturing and making mouth-noises at preprogrammed points like the mechanical bears in Coney Island penny arcade shooting galleries. Old Uncle Harvey's Bavarian cuckoo clock, with dozens of near-lifelike metal figures moved by creaky clockwork through a complete cycle every hour on the hour.

"You ever been to San Francisco?" Ted was saying to Robin. I could see the clockwork moving his mouth as the piano roll Harvey had put into his head sent him through his paces.

"What's with this San Francisco thing?" said The Man in Black, trying to toss a handful of sand into the mechanism.

"I've really been thinking about San Francisco," the Ted-machine said. "The Foundation would be—"

"Much better off in San Francisco than New York," I said, causing the gears of his speech-box to slip a few teeth.

"Yeah! You know, we really *could* move the whole Foundation to San Francisco. I mean, a cross-country trek together, just like old pioneers . . . ."

"You talked to Harvey about this?" I asked.

"I've tried to," the Ted-thing said. "But he acts kinda funny about it . . . sort of puts me off . . . ."

"Or puts you on."

"What do you mean, puts me on!" Ted said. "He's just not ready to consider it yet . . . but I get the feeling that if enough of us really commit ourselves to making the move, Harvey would go along for the good of everyone."

" 'Please, please, don't throw me in dat ol' briar patch,' said Brer Rabbit."

"What's the matter with you tonight, Tom?" Doris' Earthmother

The Man in Black

tape subsystem caused her vocal mechanism to say.

"I guess I just got the Old Piano Roll Blues," said The Man in Black.

"Can we go look at the monkey cage now, Daddy?" Robin said, pulling me toward the crowded center of the room.

"Evil chick," I explained over my shoulder to Ted and Doris.

"*Evil chick,*" I whispered to Robin, grabbing the cleft of her ass and holding it hard for a long moment as she dragged me by her ass and my free hand toward the gaggle of listening-machines surrounding Harvey.

"I'm an evil chick with a tasty ass!" she said loudly, causing heads to turn.

"That's the best kind," I said, giving her a slow, exaggerated, ultra-conspicuous feel before I let go.

■ ■ ■ ■ ■ ■ ■ ■ ■ ■ ■

I could feel a wall of eyes behind us as we threaded our way through the clockwork machinery toward Harvey and his mechanical worshippers; clockwork eyes watching The Man in Black and his Evil Chile as we moved in a train of darkness across the room. Maybe the gears were grinding a little (The Man in Black not programmed on the Old Piano Roll Blues) like seeing characters drawn in *Crypt of Terror* style popping into their Feiffer cartoon. Uptight, they were: "Get back in your own cartoon!" Because digging The Man in Black & Co. drawn in contrasting style meant the realization that other cartoon-realities existed meaning that maybe their own Harvey Brustein cuckoo-clock mechanism was not Total Reality after all, in which case— "Help! I'm trapped into a Bavarian cuckoo-clock factory!"

Into the current inner circle: Ida and her fat hausfrau friend; O'Brien, Myra Golden, a fat blond chick in a circus-tent mumu (moo-moo); Weeping Willy Nelson; a couple of mindless college twerps; Donald Warren, the Foundation's sanitized token Negro; an aesthetic faggot; and Linda-uptight-Kahn, all standing at the bottom of the little dais with Harvey standing on the platform itself about six inches above them and *outside the mechanism.*

Outside the mechanism! By God, old Harv was outside his mechanism! I had wondered about that: it was theoretically possible for the cuckoo-clock maker to end up incorporated in his own mechanism (a la Adolf Hitler-Mickey Spillane-The Doors & Co. at one time or another) in which case Harvey would be running off his own set of piano rolls meaning that he couldn't change anyone else's piano rolls meaning that predestination would be a self-programmed invariant. But no, Free Will was alive in Argentina—no clockwork behind Harvey's eyes.

"No, Mike, the job situation is about the same in San Francisco as it is here," Harvey was saying.

"It's just as . . . cosmopolitan as New York," said the aesthetic faggot (meaning the San Fran vice squad languished not for lack of pederastic clientele), "but more . . . *intime*. . . ."

"Yes, San Francisco is as much a city as New York," Harvey conceded, "but the Bay Area as a whole is as spread out and varied as Los Angeles . . . ."

By God, I had caught Harvey red-handed in the act of changing piano rolls! Cleverly inserting a groove-behind San-Francisco piano roll into each individual subsystem. Had to admire, in a technical sense, the subtlety of the programming, considering the crudity of the clockwork he was working with. Instead of changing the Master Piano Roll of the whole Foundation cuckoo clock (which would have jarred the individual member-mechanisms, possibly introducing self-awareness glitches into the program), he was changing the individual piano rolls one by one so that they would all demand a change in the Master Piano Roll themselves while still believing in Free Will. Put that in your hash-pipes and smoke it, Free Thinkers: illusion of Free Will can be programmed into a predestined piano roll complex!

But The Man in Black danced to no Piano Roll Blues. "You're changing the piano rolls!" he said.

Linda-uptight-Kahn turned into an eyeball-to-shades confrontation with The Man in Black. She goggled. "What the hell is that get-up?" her vocal mechanism said.

"You've heard of the *traje de luces*," I said, "the suit of lights?"

"Well, the man is wearing a suit of Darkness," said Robin. The chick was clearly telepathic on the blacker wavelengths.

"And who is *that?*" said the Linda-thing.

"Some crazy hippy he dragged here," said Ida.

"You're avoiding the issue," I informed them. "Don't you notice that old Harv, the master-programmer of this cuckoo-clock, is changing your piano rolls?"

"*Piano rolls?*"

"He's under the influence," O'Brien said paternally.

"Under the influence of *what?*" said the margarine voice of Ida's hausfrau friend.

"It is you who are under the influence," said The Man in Black. "You are all under the influence of the Piano Roll Blues. In fact, you've all been incorporated into Old Uncle Harvey's Black Forest cuckoo-clock mechanism while your backs were turned."

The aesthetic faggot rolled his pretty blue eyes at me, sucked in a little reverse-kiss: a Brotherhood of Grass secret catacombs recognition signal.

"Cuckoo clock?" Harvey said with a vapid little smile, mistakenly shifting to a humor-the-drunk mode. General metallic laughter from all voice-box systems.

"Come on, Harvey," I said, "stop putting us on. You're not in your own cuckoo clock, you're *outside the mechanism.* You're changing the piano rolls. You're punching in a Let's-Go-To-San Francisco program."

"Are you all right, Tom?" Harvey said earnestly. "You seem rather—"

"Ah, so this is the world-famous Harvey Brustein!" Robin exclaimed. "You've got a funny cartoon going here, man!"

"And who are you, young lady?" Harvey said coldly, appraising her financial potential with a pawnbroker's eye and finding her wanting.

"I'm not a young lady," Robin said. "I'm an evil chick and a dope-fiend and a perverted degenerate."

"Crazy hippy," said Ida.

"Not as crazy as you are, Prune-face," Robin said. "Yeah, now I recognize the style—it's Dick Tracy. Prune-face and B-B Eyes and Flattop and B.O. Plenty. A paranoid narc's nightmare cartoon." She studied Harvey. "Hey man," she told him, "you don't belong in this cartoon; you're drawn in the wrong style. You belong in Terry and the Pirates or something—you're an Oriental Menace."

"He's the Programmer," I explained.

"Programmer . . . ? Oh, I dig—he's the cartoonist!"

"Who . . . who *is* this creature?" a quavering girl's voice said from behind me. My arm brushing Robin's waist, I turned to face Arlene. She looked silly and unreal in a white blouse and blue skirt and honey-blond hair and those intellectual bullshit glasses—the All-American Semi-Bohemian College Girl. Her jaw was hard and cold as a bear-trap and her green eyes were trying their best to be cool and not making it.

"Arlene," I said, easing our nasty little threesome out to the periphery of the Mystic Circle, "meet Robin. Robin, meet Arlene."

The mechanisms around Harvey looked everywhere but where they really wanted to, going into an ignore-the-bad-scene program.

"Interesting . . . " Robin said, studying Arlene like a side of beef. "Not bad." She smiled pseudo-possessively at me. "I see your taste is totally depraved," she said.

Arlene opened her mouth, closed it, opened it again, like a beached fish. "How . . . how *could* you?" she finally said unimaginatively. She stared daggers at Robin, who smiled cherubically back.

"How could I *what?*" said the Innocent Man in Black.

Arlene looked around frantically: a signal pleading for Private Words.

"Go make some waves for a while," I whispered into Robin's ear and sent her on her merry way with a little secret touch of tongue-to-ear. I shunted Arlene off to a quiet little corner far from the maddening crowd.

"Who *is* that girl?" Arlene hissed at me as I stood with my back against the wall, screened from the party by her rigid, uptight body.

"What do you mean, who is that girl?" drawled The Man in Black. "Name is Robin. She's an evil street-creature."

—Over Arlene's shoulder, I clocked Robin standing over Rich Rossi and Chester White sitting on the floor trying to make the two pimple-things. The pimples were very uptight as Rich and Chester stared up at Robin with drooling eyes—

"You know what I mean!" Arlene said.

"No, I don't know what you mean. And I don't think you know what you mean, either." Was Arlene a clockwork creature wired into the mechanism? I could sense clockwork behind her eyes, but kind of blurry . . . .

—Robin said something to Rich and he went pale. Chester laughed and said something leering to Robin. Robin said something back. Chester turned green. Both of them returned their attentions to the pimples—

"Stop gibbering at me, damn you!" Arlene said. Real unprogrammed tears rusted the mechanisms behind her eyes. Could I freak her out of it, blow the old Piano Roll Blues out of her mind? Shit, if I couldn't freak hard enough in my present state, I'd never be able to do it straight!

"I'm not gibbering," I said. "I'm in tune with the harmonic structure of the universe, is all, making me telepathic, homeopathic, and a little psychopathic. Like I know what you really want to ask is: namely, why am I here with Another Woman?"

—Robin talking to another faggot, Mannie Davis, a closet-queen with a wife and a son he found a wee bit too succulent. Rhoda Steiner, Hilda Charles, Claude West, and a few other would-be-hip types looking on—

"You call that creature a woman?" Arlene's voice mechanism said—clearly a Jealous Cattiness Piano Roll in action. Ambiguity here: Arlene capable of unprogrammed emotion but expressed only through programmed responses. Environment producing spontaneous emotions which immediately get shunted into the gears of Harvey's cuckoo clock and come out in the form of preprogrammed responses.

"You are jealous," I said.

—Robin smiled, put her hand square on the secret faggot's crotch. Mannie Davis smiled sadly ("If only you were a boy, my dear!"), would-be-hip types totally grossed out—

"Of course I'm jealous!" Arlene said. Ah, now *that* was a genuine protoplasmic response! No clockwork there. "Why the hell shouldn't I be jealous? That take the key to my apartment business and then you show up at a party you know I'll be at with . . . with . . . some crazy unwashed street-bitch!"

"But you didn't take the key, now did you?"

Arlene hesitated as if her mechanism were trying to come up with an appropriate piano roll and coming up dry. Had The Man in Black succeeded in throwing a monkey-wrench into the clockwork?

—Robin was now talking to Ted over by the beer table. Smiling hot looks at him. Ted was making eyes back. Where was Doris?—

"I just don't see where you can afford to put down Robin," I said. "Where do you come off blaming me for being here with her? I asked you to more or less be my woman and you just fed it into the old Foundation clockwork soul-grinder and copped out on me according to some preprogrammed response-pattern. What the hell did you expect?"

"I . . . I didn't exactly say no . . . ." Arlene said defensively.

"You didn't exactly say yes."

—Robin leaned up against Ted and purred like a pussy. Ted seemed to be enjoying it, but his eyes were all over the room. Looking for Doris? Or me?—

"So because I didn't take your damn key, you come here with some crazy hippy just to humiliate me?"

—Ted looked our way. I caught his eye. He shrugged at me as Robin fingered his neck. I shrugged him back a go-ahead sign, knowing he wouldn't. Nasty, nasty!—

"Not *just* to humiliate you," said The Man in Black. "She also happens to be a groovy chick who's free as the birds and is an excellent fuck."

"Meaning I'm a bad fuck?" Arlene nearly screamed. But there were clockwork gears grinding.

"Meaning you play unpleasant games with both of our heads and Robin is a Chile of Nature and therefore a welcome change of style," I said.

—Said Chile of Nature was now kissing Ted. Was I uptight behind my massive cool? Well . . . not really . . . .And anyway, there was Doris walking toward them—

"So you prefer her to me?"

"I didn't say that. The invitation is still open. Any time you want the key, just holler. But in the meantime, don't put down a chick with more guts than you'll ever have."

—Doris was watching the kiss with a knowing, secure smile. She let them finish, then said something non-uptight to Ted. Ted and Doris smiled fatuously at each other. Poor Ted, his last bluff called! Robin chatting with them like some genteel tea-party all smiles all around. Evil chick! *Evil* chick!—

"What do you mean, more guts?"

"Guts enough to live her own life without Big Daddy Harvey," I said. "Guts enough to do without a piano roll."

"Ooooh . . . " Arlene snarled through her bear-trap lips, her hands balled up into fists. Hit me, baby! I telepathed. Do you good.

"You two have a nice little talk?" Robin said, appearing beside me. "I'm not interrupting anything?"

Robin smiled sweetly at Arlene. "Our boy's a nice tasty piece of dick, isn't he?" she said woman-to-womanwise. "You can ball him to-night if you want to. Lots of other action around." And she half-turned as if to leave like a gentlewoman.

"Oooh shit!" Arlene howled. And she stomped off into the depths of Uncle Harvey's Bavarian Cuckoo Clock.

"Evil chick!" I hissed at Robin.

Tiger-eyes and a pussycat smile. She parted her lips and ran her dainty pink tongue around them.

The Man in Black shrugged and kissed his Chile of Nature hard on the mouth and let her fill his own with her luscious magic witch's tongue.

■ ■ ■ ■ ■ ■ ■ ■ ■ ■

"I do not *believe* this place," Robin said as we took a breather in the dark hallway separating the monkey cage from what is sometimes laughingly referred to as the real world. "I just do *not* believe it."

"Neither do I," said The Man in Black. "I don't believe it either, is how come I can hang around and not get incorporated into the cuckoo-clock mechanism."

"Yeah man, but *why?* Do you dig what this is all about, do you really dig it? I mean, I can *play* at being an evil chick, but that Harvey cat is not playing, man. *Eeevil!* All those cartoon-character people . . . he's got their souls in a paper bag. Yeah, he probably goes home and sticks all those souls in a hookah and smokes 'em." She touched my cheek with the palm of her hand. "You're a nice cat, I like you. I don't want to see old Soul-Smoker roll you into a joint and suck you up, baby."

"Harvey Brustein can't touch The Man in Black," I assured her. "I have the strength of ten because my heart is rotten. Besides, tonight, thanks to better living through chemistry, I have seen the mechanism. No way he can stick a piano roll in me. I can take old Harv any time I want to. Do you believe, girl, *do you believe?*"

"Well yeah, I guess, I mean I can see your game and it's not his game. You're a heavy cat, but so is he. I suppose you can stand him off—"

"Stand him off!" The Man in Black shouted indignantly. "I can STOMP HIM INTO THE FUCKING GROUND, you better believe it!"

"Yeah man, but why bother? Who needs this bummer?"

"Nobody needs it," I said. "That's just the point. None of these poor fuckers need it. Harvey is scooping their souls and replacing them with clockwork."

"Are you going to save them?"

"Fuckin'-A, baby!"

"But why do you care about these losers? They're gray, they're pimply, they're cartoon-characters."

"Yeah, but what were they before Harvey wired them into his Bavarian Cuckoo Clock? Maybe they were all groovy people once. Ted was."

Robin made a face like biting into a lemon. *"Ted?"* she said. "Man, that is one pathetic cat! A mile of mouth and an inch of action. The cat's a total fraud."

"That's the point, chile. Time was, Ted wasn't a fraud. Time was I'd kick the shit out of you if I saw you making eyes at Ted because I'd know what would happen. Harvey's cut my friend's balls off. Think I let him get away with that?"

"Wouldn't have something to do with that Arlene, would it?"

"You're jealous!"

Robin looked me cold in the eye with pupils as hard and measured as ball-bearings. Smiled a smile a million years old. "Baby," she said evenly, "when I find myself getting jealous of a chick like that, I take ten thousand mikes and go out in a blaze of glory. Do *you* believe that?"

"I believe," I said.

"Groovy. Then listen man, you're doing a Knight in Armor number. You're not so hung up on the chick as hung up on the ego-trip of saving her from the Soul-Smoker."

"So? Didn't you tell me that was my game? Don't put down ego. Where would I be without it?"

"Yeah, but that's a Goodness Trip. It's a drag. You're blowing your cool."

"Are you accusing me of not being evil?" The Man in Black asked righteously.

"You're in danger, man. I haven't seen you do anything really evil tonight."

"Didn't I give it to Harvey in there?"

"You started to, but as soon as dear sweet Arlene showed up, you blew your cool and forgot about it."

By God, the chick was right! I *had* forgotten all about Harvey as soon as Arlene had showed up. Yeah, but . . . .

"But I did a really evil number on Arlene," I said.

"I didn't see that," Robin said primly. "Come on baby, go on in there and let's see some evil. Kill! Kill!"

"You are an *eeevil* chick!"

"Come on tiger, go on in there and let's see you do your thing. Give me Harvey's head on a platter. Bet you can't! Bet you can't . . . ."

"Evil chick," I said, but this time I smiled. She was right; I was losing the razor-edge of my cool.

"What you need is a booster-shot," Robin said, taking my hand and leading me down the hall to the coatroom. "I've got about four good tokes in the hash pipe in my coat. Let's go suck up some tasty evil and then go set the cartoon on fire!"

"Lead on, Lady Macbeth," said The Man in Black.

■ ■ ■ ■ ■ ■ ■ ■ ■ ■ ■

Just what the witchdoctor ordered. My cool honed to a switchblade edge, I was Kid Death, The Man in Black, gliding out of the shadows with his Dark Lady and onto the Main Street of Cuckooclock City. The Smoker of Souls, Master of the Cuckoo Clock, had gathered most of his creatures around him, or caused their piano rolls to form them up into a series of concentric semicircles centered around the foot of the dais on which he stood. Sense of the night building to a climax; all individual piano roll programs coming together at a preprogrammed harmonic point and Harvey standing above this space-time nexus ready to make his move, change the Master Piano Roll, the hand is quicker than the eye.

But not quicker than the All-Seeing Eye of The Man in Black, knows all, sees all, kills all. *Two* would face each other across the nexus in the Big Shootout.

The Man in Black moved to the rear edge of the crowd and stood there projecting the blackest of vibes as the Dark Lady held his hand and whispered into his ear: "Kill . . . kill . . . kill . . . ."

Up at the front of things, Ted had planted one boot up on the dais, and was saying: "Come on, Harvey, why not?"

With a butter-would-not-melt-in-my-mouth look on its face, the Smoker of Souls said: "Are you really serious about this, Ted?"

"Of course I'm serious," Ted said. "It'd be easy if we all did it together."

The Man in Black and his Lady drifted closer to the front of the crowd; elbows and knees were not necessary as a wavefront of black vibes parted the sea before them.

"Move the Foundation to San Francisco?" said the Smoker of Souls.

"Sure," said an alternate voice of the Smoke of Souls through the speaking-mechanism of the Ted-thing. "All together, like a commune.

We could set up committees—one to find jobs, one to find pads, one to find a house for the Foundation. It'd work . . . ."

Way in a far corner of the room, Arlene was standing apart from it all with her body but sucking it up with her eyes—New York patriotism conflicting with her San Francisco sub-program.

"You're assuming that we really want to move to San Francisco," Harvey said. Ah, the master's touch: the Devil playing Angel's Advocate, knowing how well his San Francisco piano rolls had programmed his creatures. Gotta admire confidence.

"You mean you wouldn't go?" said Bill Nelson.

"I didn't say that," said Magnanimous Harv. "How many of you would seriously consider going to San Francisco if the Foundation moved? I don't mean *would* move, I just want some idea of how many would take the idea seriously."

The Cuckoo clock chimed the hour of doom with a great murmur coming off the vocal piano rolls of all the loose ones that weren't nailed down (Ted, Linda, Rich, Weeping Willy, Bonnie Elbert, Tod and Judy, like that): just pure affirmative noise on cue, essence of the Piano Roll Blues.

"Well, I believe in coming to a consensus on things like this," the Smoker of Souls said. "You could bring this up at a meeting, Ted. We could kick it around for a couple of weeks or even longer, and if the group consensus favored a move to San Francisco, I'd probably go along with it."

"Go . . . go . . . go . . . " Robin whispered in my ear. She was right: it was time for The Man in Black to make his move.

"LIAR!" I shouted. One huge knife-edged word that cut through the murmuring like flame through smoke.

The silence held; it was my ally since the next move was Harvey's and I intended to force him to make it. I pulsed heavy black vibes at Harvey. He sucked them in and transmuted the energy to a thin Buddha-smile.

"You apparently want to say something, Tom," Harvey finally said softly. "Why don't you go ahead and say it?" The smile broadened into a leer and the moment broke: the animals giggled. "Aw shit, he's stoned out of his mind," Bill Nelson said.

"Stoned into his mind," Robin said, stepping up beside me.

"That's right," I said. "I'm stoned and you suckers aren't. If you were, you'd see the game that's being played here."

"Crazy junkie!" Linda-uptight-Kahn shouted to approving murmurs. "Gibbering—"

"SHUT UP, CUNT!" I roared, resorting to Tactical Nuclear Gross-Out Weapons. They were bombed back into Stone Age Silence.

"Whose idea was this San Francisco thing, Harvey?" I said.

"It's my idea," Ted said. "I—"

"SHUT UP, TED! Come on Harv, WHOSE IDEA?"

"It's Ted's idea, apparently . . . ." Harvey said.

"WHOSE IDEA, HARVEY?"

"Stop yelling, Hollander," Charley Dees said.

"Hey, what is this, Tom" Ted said sincerely. "You *heard* me talking about it before, man. You *know* it's my idea. So why are you—"

"Who put the idea in your head, Ted?"

"Nobody did," Ted said indignantly. "Are you calling me a liar? If you weren't my friend and if you weren't stoned . . . ."

"Harvey programmed the idea into your head," I said. "Didn't you, Harvey?"

Harvey looked out over his congregation, smiled at them, shrugged, looked at me. "I'm afraid none of us have any idea of what you're talking about," he said. "You seem to be suffering from severe paranoid—"

"LIAR!" I shouted. "Who's got a wife and kids in San Francisco, Harvey, you or Ted?" Something flickered for a moment behind Harvey's watery eyes. Then the spark went out.

"I fail to see—"

"THE FUCK YOU DO! You want to go back to San Francisco and you want all your suckers to follow you. That's why you put the idea in their heads."

Harvey smiled a great shit-eating smile. "Is there anyone who thinks I . . . put the idea of moving the Foundation to San Francisco in his mind?" Silence, aside from a few snickers. "See, Tom?" Harvey said. "You're imagining things. If you're high on drugs, you may even be hallucinating. It's not surprising that your hallucinations are taking paranoid form, considering—"

"Don't you see what he's doing?" Goddamit, couldn't they see? Wasn't there *anything* protoplasmic alive out there? "He's got your minds so controlled you don't even know you're controlled! Don't you see? Can't any of you see?"

I turned and stared the whole lot of them in their nonfaces. Doris, Ida, O'Brien, Charley. Dead fish-eyes. Linda, Rhoda Steiner, Bill Nelson. Corpses animated by clockwork. Blum, Chester White, Mannie

Davis. Swiss music-box zombies. Rich, Tod and Judy, Frieda Klein. I stared at them all and a million glass eyes seemed to stare blindly back.

I looked into Ted's face, inches from my own—dead, dead! Harvey had scooped him out hollow and filled the shell with himself. "Ted, Ted, for Chrissakes, can't you see? It's a fucking Cuckoo clock! You've been programmed! WAKE UP, DAMN YOU, WAKE UP!"

"Hey man, take it easy . . .Maybe you should lie down and . . . ."

"*And die?* Lie down and die like the rest of you?"

I looked around the room trying to find a human face. Zombies. Robots. A million dead eyes. But . . . but off in her corner, Arlene's eyes seemed to be wet with tears. She was crying—for me? But that was all wrong, I should be crying for her, for Ted, for Doris, for a roomful of corpses who had sold their souls for a mass of clockwork.

I whirled around, screamed at Harvey: "YOU FUCKING MURDERING SON OF A BITCH! Give them back their souls! GIVE THEM BACK THEIR SOULS!"

I looked out into a forest of eyes. Cold glass eyes of animated corpses reflecting the neon-light of mechanical nonbeing. Millions of unblinking dead eyes whirling, whirling, whirling . . . .

The room started to spin around me. I felt Robin's hand of warm real flesh in mine, my only anchor to flesh-and-blood reality.

"Take it easy, man," she said. "They're just not worth it. Don't let them freak you out. There's nothing alive in here to care about, anyway."

I stared at Harvey, with his pseudo, plastic concern painted on his lying face. At Ted, shaking his head at his freaking friend. At a roomful of deaf clockwork.

I was beaten.

Disgusted, infuriated, frustrated, saddened beyond hope, I let Robin lead me out of the room and into the dark hallway. Behind us, there was a short moment of dead silence, and then I heard the machinery of the Cuckoo clock whirring back into an imitation of life behind me.

14
The Cuckoo-clock Revisited

Everyone is a sucker for something for nothing, but as I climbed the stairs to the Foundation on Monday night, I wondered whether it wasn't possible to carry the great American tradition of never looking a gift horse in the mouth a bit too far.

A special group for the benefit of little old me, just because you need it and we care, no extra charge, was how Harvey had put it to me on the phone last night. Oh sure. A bunch of the Senators are throwing a little party for you at the Forum, Caesar, just because we dig you, baby. I'll be there with bells on Brutus, old buddy.

No man, I knew damn well that I was about to walk into Harvey's version of a Court of the Star Chamber. No question about it, I had really grossed them all out Saturday night, if nothing else. *Probably* nothing else. It had been a long time (well, anyway, since my acid trip) since I had been that stoned. Too stoned to make sense to un-stoned Foundation-heads. *Not* too stoned to remember all events that had occurred. But too stoned to remember how I had really felt during those events. *Not* too stoned to retain the vision of Foundation-as-Cuckoo-clock. But too stoned to be sure whether or not *in hash veritas.*

Which, of course, was why I had decided to answer Harvey's subpoena. Dope can give you a vision that seems realer than real, but you can't *know* that it's true until you take a second look at things straight. Works like binocular vision: take a look stoned (left eye), then straight (right eye). Either eye sees only a two-dimensional half-truth, but put them together and you see reality three-dimensionally, which should be closer to the way things really are. That's why this trip was necessary: looking at something *only* stoned is no better than looking at it only straight. Truth is in the intersection between stoned and straight realities.

Besides, when you're as stoned as I was, it's pretty hard to get through to anyone who isn't on your trip. I had made sense to me Saturday, and I still made sense to me today, but I obviously hadn't gotten through to the poor slobs trapped in the Cuckoo-clock. Being straight now, but still in possession of the memory of the vision, I might be able to get it across now.

And furthermore, if those motherfuckers thought Tom Hollander wouldn't have the balls to show his face in their creep-joint again, they had another think coming!

But as I entered the Star Chamber itself, I found that *I* had another think coming. In addition to Harvey, Arlene, Rich, Charlie, Ida, Doris and Linda—the group I had come to know and love—there was my buddy Ted sitting on the right hand of God. To Ted's right, Doris, Rich, and Arlene; to Harvey's left, Ida, Charley and Linda. And an empty seat for the victim encircled by the arms of the crescent and facing the judge, and Smoker of Souls, good old Harvey.

All of them very solemn and soberly concerned for the soul of the heretic. Even Arlene mirrored the group's collective this-is-for-your-own-good expression. If I were Charles De Gaulle, I'd have gone into ecstasy at finally *really* digging what it felt like to be Joan of Arc versus the Inquisition.

I tried to see the clockwork behind their eyes, but I couldn't quite cut that straight. So, leaping into the frying pan, I sat down in the dock, said with what I hoped was a sufficiently irritating look of contrition: "I suppose you're all wondering why I gathered you here tonight . . . ."

The silent inward snarls behind the earnestly-concerned masks were not ungratifying.

"This is what we call a Situational Group, Tom," Harvey said, ignoring all the vibes in the room. "In other words, a group called together to focus on a specific problem of a particular member. By exploring a specific event, in this case your behavior at Saturday's party, a Situational Group should give unusual insight into your internal reasons for your external behavior."

"Yeah, I dig," I said. "Nothing new. The same thing's gone by other names: witch-hunt, Red Guard self-criticism session, meeting of the House Un-American Activities Committee."

Harvey smiled professionally. "That attitude is entirely consistent with the paranoid delusions you displayed Saturday," he said. "This paranoia would seem—"

"It's not that I'm paranoid, it's just that everyone's against me."

"Such an attempt to pass over a threatening truth with a humorous remark is clearly indicative of—"

Oh Wow. "Look Harv," I said with a great display of misunderstood earnestness, "I didn't mean that as a joke. What's your definition of paranoia, anyway?"

"A paranoiac is someone who clings to a delusion system in which

he is being persecuted by others—and in advanced cases, even by in-
animate objects—when in fact no such persecution exists in object reality."

Objective reality? Is there such a thing as objective reality or is objective reality nothing more than the opinion of the middle class?
Somehow I had the feeling I wouldn't get very far challenging the existence of objective reality inside the mechanism of the old Cuckoo-
clock. So:

"Okay. Now take this cat who thinks about eighty million people
are out to do him in because they think he's less than human; he
thinks all kinds of monsters are out to catch him, pull out his gold
teeth, kill him, and melt him down for soap. Paranoia?"

"A rather extreme example of paranoia."

I smiled sweetly. "Forgot to tell you the cat in question is a Jew in
Nazi Germany," I said.

Ted, Doris, Rich, even Linda-uptight-Kahn, stifled laughs in spite
of themselves. Two points for the defense.

"Point is," I said, "paranoia is a relationship between what someone thinks is going on and what *is* going on. Can't have paranoia
without delusions by your own definition, Harv. If things really are
as crazy as someone sees them, he's not paranoid no matter how
many monsters he sees, not if they're really there."

"What's that got to do with *you?*" Linda-uptight-Kahn said. "You
were gibbering about . . . let's see . . . piano rolls . . . cuckoo clocks . . .
programmers . . . Harvey changing people's piano rolls . . . and ended up screaming and cursing. If *that's* not paranoia, what is it?"

"Poetic imagery," I informed her.

"Bullshit," said Charley.

"Really? I mean *literally* bullshit? Fecal matter from a male bo-
vine?"

"Ah, stop playing word games," Rich said.

"How can I do that without either shutting up entirely or grunting
like an ape? Isn't this whole group nothing but one big word game?"

"All this is quite beside the point," Harvey said.

"No man, it *is* the point. Point is, I am no paranoid. I saw a truth
Saturday night and expressed it in allegory, poetic image, word game
if you will. If I didn't succeed in explaining it to you, I may be a lousy
word game player, but that doesn't make the truth I saw any less
true. And if the truth I saw was a bummer, that doesn't make me paranoid for calling a spade a spade."

"Truth, schmuth," Ida said. "You were babbling. You didn't make a word of sense to anyone."

"She's right, Tom" Arlene said sympathetically. "You were babbling nonsense. No one understood a word of it."

"I'll bet you don't even remember what you said yourself," Linda said. "I'll bet you don't even know what this great revelation you're bullshitting about is any more."

I smiled an eat-shit smile at her. "You're faded, baby," I said. "What I saw was the essential nature of the Foundation, namely as an old-fashioned cuckoo clock, you know, with a lot of little mechanical figures that go through their numbers when the clock strikes. You people are the clockwork figures. Harvey is the Black Forest Elf that put the clock together according to his own notions of what kind of creatures you should be and what funny numbers you should run through every hour on the hour. The piano rolls are the individual programs that Harvey has put in your heads. The Master Piano Roll is the total Foundation bag. Changing the piano rolls means putting new ideas into your heads. The San Francisco Piano Roll is Harvey's new game of getting you all to think *you* want to move the Foundation to San Francisco. See? It all makes poetic sense."

Harvey nodded sagely. "Paranoid systems of delusion are often internally self-consistent," he said. "Surely you don't expect anyone to believe that the Foundation *is* a . . . er, cuckoo clock, that they are mechanical figures on the clock, that—"

"Man, are you dense!" I snapped. "The real truth is that the Foundation is a structure designed to make you suckers act the way Harvey wants you to, that's robbed you of free will. The proof of it is that you really *do* believe that going to San Francisco is your idea, not Harvey's. You're being *had*, folks."

I looked squarely at Arlene. Was there the dawn of comprehension in her eyes? Maybe . . . Because I was being so fucking brilliant? Or just because the idea of going to San Francisco turned her off?

"You dig, Arlene?" I said. "I'm talking to *you*. Dig why you *really* couldn't take the key to my apartment? Because the piano roll in your head programmed you to reject it."

Arlene seemed to be looking inward. She was wondering; it was no longer a question of whether she understood what I was saying but whether she would accept it. And the question seemed to be hanging suspended in the silence . . . .

Then Ted blew it: "Aw come on, all this is bullshit and you know it, man. You were stoned out of your mind, is all. What was it, acid?"

"Hash," I corrected evenly.

"Must've been awfully good hash," old Rich couldn't help saying. He got six poisonous looks from the clockwork creatures and prim disapproval from the Cuckoo-Clock Maker for his troubles.

"Nothing but the best," I said. Then, strictly for nasties: "Could probably get you a dime's worth."

Rich seemed to be really considering the proposition as Linda Kahn said: "A dope-pusher too!" Arlene got a frightened (but fascinated?) look in her eyes. Hmmm . . . maybe she had a cherry in an unexpected place ready for plucking.

"Now we get to the heart of it," Harvey said. "You admit that your actions Saturday were taken under the influence of hashish?"

"And that dirty little hippy he had with him was probably on drugs too!" Ida said. A little spasm went through Arlene.

"Sure Harv," I said. "And there's plenty to go around. I might be able to get you some, too."

Harvey ignored the invitation. "So your delusions were caused by drugs," he said. "That's encouraging—your paranoia may not be so deep-seated, but only a part of your drug problem."

"I don't have a drug problem."

"You just admitted you were on hashish!" Linda said.

"Sure. But what's the problem?"

"You don't consider drug addiction a problem?" Harvey said.

"I never said that. That problem I *have* had. And I licked it. Now I've got a healthy attitude towards drugs: a nice place to visit, but I have no intention of living there." I could see that Arlene was definitely getting interested, oh yes she was . . . .

"That's a common attitude among drug-users," Harvey said. "It's part of the drug-neurosis itself—the false notion that one can use drugs without losing one's perspective on reality."

Well, by god, there we were back with good old objective reality—no way around it.

"What's reality?" I asked.

"The fact that you could ask such a question is a clear--"

"Aw bullshit! Dig, you'd say that reality is the real nature of the external universe, right?"

"Yes."

"Okay, so let's assume that there is an objective reality, one way the external world really is. But that's *only* an assumption. We get all our data on external reality through our sense organs and we interpret it with our brains, all of which are based on a particular biochemistry. When you turn on, you change the biochemistry and your subjective reality changes."

"Exactly," said Harvey. "You distort your perception of object reality."

"Which is subjective to begin with! How can you know that straight biochemistry gives you a more accurate picture than stoned biochemistry? Answer: you can't. You can't even be sure that there *is* an objective reality. If you used drugs, you'd see that reality has styles, depending on your biochemistry of the moment."

Arlene was hunched forward, staring at me, apparently lapping it up. Yes, that was the way to turn a chick like her on: give dope a nice philosophical mystique. Way to her head was through . . . her head!

But old Harv was really uptight. "That's the way to madness," he said. "If you think that way, you've got no certain ground to stand on." And suddenly I flashed on why Harvey had to be down on drugs, why they were such a threat to him. And I was sure my hash-vision had been essentially true. Harvey was pushing certainty: Total Consciousness. Key word being *Total* . . . .

"Ah, I dig you now, Harvey," I said, "you're a control-head, that's why you're so down on drugs. You've got all your suckers trapped in your own brand of subjective reality. But the gimmick is that you've got 'em convinced that your Foundation-reality is the real thing, Total Consciousness, the way things really are. But don't let the suckers turn on, right? Because if they turn on and dig another style of reality, they might see that reality is *all* subjective and you aren't giving them Total Reality because maybe there is no Total Reality. In short, folks, if you turn on, your heads will be outside the Cuckoo Clock and you'll see it the way I did, and then the con-game is kaput. Anybody want some hash?"

Hea-*vy!* Rich was grinning like a Nazi who had just heard Der Fuehrer rap. Ida and Charley didn't know what the fuck I was talking about. Linda did but was good at pretending she didn't. Ted and Doris were remembering less square days. Harvey . . . who could read Harvey?

But Arlene . . . ah, there were dope-lights in her eyes! No doubt about it, I had turned her on to the mystique of dope. But would she put her lungs where her head wanted to go?

"I begin to understand you, Tom," Harvey said, giving me a nod of the old head and a plastic fatherly pucker. "I was probably wrong to attribute your problems to paranoia . . . .No, it would seem that drugs lie at the core of your problem—hardly surprising, since drugs seem to have structured your ego at its deepest levels."

"Look Harvey, I told you—"

"Yes, I know, you have no addiction problem. But you do have a drug problem and it's far subtler than you seem to think. Let's go with the way you look at reality: under drugs, you claim to experience a subjective reality that is just a valid as the reality you're experiencing now, and you claim that by experiencing more than one subjective reality, you get a more complete view of objective reality. That's because, under drugs, you experienced a subjective reality in which I appeared as a kind of puppet-master and the Foundation as my puppet-show, you are free from control. That because drugs enable you to experience an altered consciousness, there is no Total Consciousness, and therefore no objective reality. Have I stated it to your satisfaction?"

I nodded, sensing that Harvey had somehow taken control by the simple act of repeating what I had said. They were all sucking up his shit now, even Arlene.

"And you still don't see the trap you've fallen into."

I couldn't think of anything clever to say; I had lost control of the situation at least until Harvey arrived at wherever he was going.

"What if the reality you experience on drugs is pure delusion?" Harvey said. "What if there *is* such a thing as Total Consciousness of an objective reality? Then this whole business of drugs giving you three-dimensional vision would all be false and all they would be doing is introducing a distortion into your total perception of the world—a distortion that would persist even when you're not high because you give credence to your drugged perceptions."

"That would be pretty scary if it were true," I said. "But it's not."

"Oh?" said Harvey with a flat, inflectionless smugness. "How do you *know* it's not true? The fact is you have *no way* of knowing whether it's true or not. If drugs *are* simply giving you distortions and the reality you perceive without them *is* objective reality, you have no way of judging the validity or non-validity of your drugged perceptions."

"Hey dig," said Ted, "there *is* one way to judge whether being stoned fucks up your outlook on reality: how do you act with other people when you're stoned?"

"Exactly," said Harvey. "Consider what happened to your relationship with the outside world when you were stoned last Saturday. You came to an ordinary party and felt threatened by a conspiracy . . . ."

"You looked like a freak," Ida said.

"You offended everyone in sight," said Linda.

"You ended up freaking-out."

"And you brought along that Robin-creature," Arlene said sympathetically, grasping at the it-wasn't-you-that-did-it-to-me-Tom-it-was-the-dope straw.

"Yeah, and that dirty little hippy was on dope, too," Ida said, "and look how she acted."

"Tried to make me right in front of Doris," Ted said wishful-thinkingwise.

"Felt up poor faggoty old Mannie Davis in front of everyone," said Charley Dees.

"Foul-mouthed everyone in sight," said Linda.

"And made a fool out of you, Tom," said Momma Doris. "Made you act like a jerk and then did things behind your back with half the men in the room."

My head was reeling. Harvey's logic had no holes in it: I had been stoned and in their eyes I had acted like a lunatic; if drugs gave me nothing but distortion, I *would* have no way of knowing it.

Yeah, the logic was all on Harvey's side . . . .But something in my gut told me I was right and he was wrong. But . . . but . . . could *that* be drug-distortion too?

Goddamn, he was right! I had no way of knowing! Scary, yes!

But . . . but Doris had been dead-wrong about Robin: she hadn't done anything behind my back; it was all part of the game both of us were playing. And Ted was putting himself on; Robin never had eyes for him, she thought he was pathetic. And what the hell did "looking like a freak" really mean? Nothing but a difference in style! And Harvey really *was* a control-head (the bread he was raking in from the suckers was sure no delusion!), so I hadn't been paranoid. And I freaked out because I saw evil and couldn't do anything about it. They didn't have any more of a total view of reality than I did. There *was* no Total Reality. We saw different styles of reality, acted on them, and so appeared crazy to each other . . . .AND . . . .

And that was it!

"Wanna hear something *really* scary folks?" I said, making with a nasty grin. "Take everything Harvey's just said and just substitute Total Consciousness for dope and see how the equation comes out. If the Total Reality Harvey is peddling is pure delusion, then Total Consciousness is just a distortion in your perception of reality as it really is. And if so, you have no way of knowing that your heads have been distorted, programmed, and that you're trapped in the old Cuckoo Clock—because the Foundation has distorted your minds in such a way as to make the distortion invisible to you."

"But . . . but that's just your assumption, isn't it?" Arlene said uneasily. It seemed like a purposeful straight-line, as if she sensed where I was taking her and wanted to get here.

"Right," I said. "An assumption—just like Harvey's assumption about dope."

"Ah, but remember how insanely you acted Saturday night," Harvey said.

"Did I? From my viewpoint, you're all acting insanely because you're blind to what's being done to you. If my assumption is right, you're all nuts; if you're assumption is right, I'm nuts."

"But . . . how can any of us know which is true . . . ?" Arlene asked.

I shrugged and smiled. "*That* is the scary part," I said. "None of us can. What's more, there's no reason why we can't *all* be nuts. Drugs could cause delusions . . . but that wouldn't mean the Foundation view isn't a distortion, too. Or maybe we're both right, in which case there just isn't any such thing as objective reality."

"That's the essence of madness," Harvey said.

"Could be," I conceded. "But that's no guarantee that it isn't the way things are. Maybe the essence of the universe is that kind of madness—in which case we damn well better learn to groove behind it."

"My God!" Arlene whispered. "You could be right. You really could be right! But . . . but how can you function, seeing the world that way?"

Now there was the Big Question! Best I could do was fake an answer: "You told me how yourself, baby. Remember that inner core of certainty you said I had? Well, that's what you need—you've gotta trust it and act off it."

"Sheer mysticism," said Harvey, of all people. "You don't even know what this inner certainty you're talking about is, do you?"

"Nope. That's what makes life interesting."

"But this core of certainty is *also* affected by your drug-taking. Certainty maybe, but what makes you think it can be trusted?"

"Instinct, Harv," I told him. "Be like an animal, you once said—that's Total Consciousness. Okay, so maybe I don't have Total Consciousness—but I've got this little core of instinct deep inside where I can't see it and so I gotta work off that. Man, if you start distrusting your instincts, you're distrusting three billion years of evolution. *That's* real insanity in my book."

Rich, Ida, Linda and Charley just weren't on the right wave length; they all looked monumentally bored. Harvey was losing at his own game and trying hard not to show how little he liked it. Ted, and maybe Doris more than Ted, were digging the principles behind the actions of someone they had watched for years; they were thinking about it, anyway.

Ah, but Arlene was eating me up with her eyes, and why not: I had taken her insight into me and blown it up into just the kind of intellectual Empire State Building she grooved behind. The ultimate flattery—and ultimately scary for her because, building as it did on her own viewpoint, she had to admit to herself that I could be right. And it was that very inner certainty (or the illusion thereof) that she dug in me, and envied, and wanted for herself.

"And . . . and you think drugs have helped you to trust your own instincts?" she said.

"As much as anyone here thinks Harv has helped them to trust theirs. Isn't that what you all want out of the Foundation—inner certainty? We're all looking for the same thing, but we're looking for it in different places, is all."

Harvey started to fidget in his seat, stole a glance at his watch. He obviously wanted to end this mess as soon as possible, and, with the look on Arlene's face, I found myself on old Harv's side for once.

"And how do you know that you can find it your way?" Harvey said. "If you were really sure, you wouldn't be here."

I didn't care for that thought, so I glided around it: "I don't know why I'm here. Instinct maybe. Who knows? I still take drugs because the same instinct that keeps me coming back here tells me to."

"You think that *drugs* can give you the same thing as the Foundation?" Arlene said wide-eyed, as if looking through a peephole into a whole new world. Harvey also winced; then stared back at his watch for an overlong moment, obviously for our benefit.

"Don't knock it 'til you try it," I told her.

She was silent, but her eyes said: "Maybe I will."

Harvey took another look at his watch. "Well I'm afraid we're about out of time," he said. "I don't think we've gotten any answers, but at least we've defined the major area of Tom's problem." He looked at me, forced a smile. "I think you'll find the regular groups much more meaningful now, Tom," he said. Was there something ominous in the way he said it?

■ ■ ■ ■ ■ ■ ■ ■ ■ ■ ■

On the street outside, Arlene, bundled up against the cold in her green toggle-coat, caught me by the elbow as I started toward Second Avenue and the bus home.

"Look Tom," she said, "about Saturday night . . . .I acted as badly as you did . . . I should've understood . . . ."

"That I was a crazed dope-fiend and you had to make allowances?" I felt too cold to be patronized.

"No, no," she said, her eyes furtive, her lips hesitant, as if there were something ugly in her mouth she was afraid to spit out, "I mean about . . . Robin. You were right. I had no reason to expect you to be . . . faithful to me or anything when . . . in a different way, I couldn't be faithful to you. I was jealous and had no right to be."

I touched here gently on the cheek; we both shivered—her cheek and my hand were both ice-cold. "Jealousy isn't a matter of right, it's a feeling," I told her. "If you felt jealous, you had a right to feel jealous. What you didn't have was the right to dump your feeling on me. But even that was more good than bad, because for once you were acting from the gut."

She smiled; I smiled back. Possibilities *were* still alive between us. All of a sudden, it didn't seem so cold.

"Can I ask you something I . . . don't have the right to ask?" she said. "You don't have to answer if you don't want to . . . "

"Ask away."

"What do you really see in Robin?"

Ooo-hoo! Must admit that naked jealousy *does* turn me on when I'm the object. I laughed, trying hard not to chortle like a miser. "Robin acts from the gut." I told her. "She's a feral creature. Makes life mighty interesting."

"You mean . . . Robin acts on instinct, the way you do?"

I nodded. I didn't really believe that *I* was such a Chile of Nature, but Robin—*oh yeah!*

"And I don't," Arlene said sadly. "I know I don't. That's why I turned down the key. I wanted to take it, but . . . I started thinking . . . and . . . Have you offered a key to Robin?"

Shit, no chance I'd trust *that* chick that far! "No," I said, "and I don't intend to."

"But if you did, she'd take it, wouldn't she?"

"I haven't the slightest . . . ." then I saw what she was getting at. "You mean, would she take it if she felt like taking it, without consulting her navel?"

A nod.

A nod back.

"I wish I could be like that," Arlene said.

"So do I."

Arlene nibbled her lower lip. "Do you suppose . . . do you suppose drugs might . . . let me act . . . freer?" she said softly.

"You've never even smoked pot?"

"I've always been afraid."

"Are you afraid now?"

She took my hand, squeezed it hard. "Yes," she said, "but . . . but I think it'd be all right if I smoked some with you."

I looked at her jaw set in grim determination, her eyes like the eyes of a virgin asking for it for the first time. Yes indeed, I must've been rapping out some really heavy stuff in there.

"Are you asking me . . . ?"

"I'm asking," she whispered.

Robin had left half a cube of hash in my pad and I had an old hash pipe somewhere. "All right," I said, "I've got some hash. How about Friday night after the group?"

She shook her head. "You know what group does to me. I'd be afraid to do it then. Besides, I could change my mind a hundred times between now and Friday. My instinct says do it . . . don't let me give my mind a chance to argue me out of it . . . .Please . . . ?"

I felt an overpowering wave of affection for this poor fucked-up chick diving into the center of her fear; at that moment I would've fought the world for her.

"Now?" I asked.

"Now."

15
" . . . but I Would Not Feel So All Alone . . . ."

"Ooooh . . . shit!"

Arlene coughed another half-lungful of smoke into the musky air of the living room. The blue-gray haze-layer drifting above us in the orange light created the feeling of sitting on the banks of the Ganges watching an oriental sunset.

At least for me, anyway. Arlene was having trouble keeping up. "I don't think I'm really getting any," she said. "This stuff is burning my lungs out."

I took the hash pipe from her, knocked out the residue, flaked a fresh piece of hash off the cube with a razor-blade, put it in the pipe, held it to my lips, placed the flame about a half-inch above the little bowl, said: "Dig. Take a lot of little puffs and hold the pipe loosely in your mouth so you get plenty of air with it." I followed my own advice, inhaling the hot smoke in little sips like scalding coffee. My full lungs fought against a burning spasm.

"Hold. It. Down. Fight. The Cough," I wheezed around the lungful of smoke. I handed the pipe to her, held the match over the bowl as she sucked in little bursts of smoke, her brows furrowed in concentration. She put the pipe down. My lungs ached. I could see her on the verge of a cough: her lower lip sucked in, her nose wrinkled, her shoulders hunched forward and inward.

"Come. On. I. Dragged. First," I wheezed, fighting the hot balloon in my chest. "Don't. Let. Go. Before. I. Do."

She stared at me in tense concentration. I stared back. I smiled. She smiled back at me with her mouth, but her brows were doing their best to meet the tip of her wrinkled nose. If I could only get her to keep one good toke down . . . .

"Contest," I wheezed. "Don't. Leggo. First." My lungs were exploding. Head pounding like a drum on the inside. Hold it in! Our eyes locked in a Junior High School staring contest, lungs locked into the contest-circuit. Hold it in! Hold it in!

Whoosh! The bubble in my lungs finally exploded sensuous smoke billowing up my throat out my mouth in a spasm of ecstatic release.

A moment later, Arlene exhaled a huge quick sigh of smoke. But no cough this time.

She sighed, and her body relaxed against the back of the couch. Breakthrough! Now she should be relaxed enough (stoned enough, that is) to really keep some hash down.

I stuck the pipe back in her mouth. She grimaced. "Come on," I told her, "it gets easier and easier from here on in."

I held a match over the bowl. She sucked in bursts of smoke and held it, nose not nearly as wrinkled this time around. I took a long slow drag myself. Time seemed to inch by as I let the pressure of the smoke in my lungs sweep away into the heart of the rich orange sunset . . . .

Whooosh!

Whooosh!

Now her eyes were wide as saucers and she grinned lazily at me as I passed the pipe to her again. We took big drags, held them for what seemed like five minutes, exhaled in sweet unison.

"Feel anything?" I asked her.

She smiled dreamily. "I feel all sorts of things . . . feel so strange . . . elongated . . . like a piece of taffy melting in the sun . . . ."

"Like it?"

"I don't know . . . it's relaxing . . . but I don't feel like me . . . So how can I know if *I* like it . . . ?" She giggled. More wordgames. Had to get her beyond word-game level.

"One more round," I said. We both took another drag. No big deal this time. She collapsed dreamily against my shoulder, warm and soft and breathing easy in the oriental sunset, essence of coziness, just the two of us together breathing together like OM . . . OM . . . OM . . . OM . . . .

"Is it always like this?"

"Like what?"

"Oooh . . . like . . . being inside my own body . . . ." She rippled her flesh against me like a stretching cat. "Feeling the blood flowing . . . heart beating . . . so strange . . . ." Her mouth opened; her wet pink tongue circled her soft lips. "Like being my own body . . . never understood before . . . it's always there, you know that, *it's always there*. Flesh . . . flesh . . . it's weird, I'm flesh all the way through, you know that? All that blood just flowing around and around and around . . . Ooooh . . . ."

"I do believe you're stoned."

"It's funny, so strange . . . I don't feel drunk . . . or fuzzy or anything . . . .Just the opposite, like I'm in focus for the first time . . . ."

She took off her glasses, sat up and looked at me with huge shining green eyes through which a million years of god-knows-what seemed to be bubbling up from the back of her brain. This was not the same Arlene, oh no, this was the Arlene inside. "You know what I want to do?" she sighed. "I want to touch your body."

"By all means," I said, and started to draw her to me. But she pulled away.

"No," she said. "I want to *really* touch your body. I want it to be . . . I want to feel your body the way you feel mine . . . ."

She frowned at me. "If I ask you to do something really strange, will you . . . ? I mean . . . ."

"It's your trip, baby," I said. My cock was beginning to throb and every word she said seemed to stroke my balls; I had set some magic creature free and god knew what it would do.

"Take another puff," she said, holding the pipe to my mouth. "Take a big one." She held a match over the bowl for me, and as I toked, she said: "I . . . I want you to go into the bedroom and take your clothes off. And then come back. Like Adam and Eve . . . .That's not . . . I mean I'm not acting . . . crazy?"

"You're beautiful," I said around a cloud of smoke. "It sounds like a groovy game." I got up and started for the bedroom, taking the hash pipe with me.

"Could you leave that here?" she asked. "I . . . I'd like a little more first . . . ."

I handed her the pipe. Man, you never know, you just never know . . . .

I suppose she needed the pipe more than I did at that point, but alone in the bedroom taking my clothes off, high as I was, I did wish I could get a wee bit higher. What hath hash wrought? The chick waiting to do her thing (whatever it was) in the next room was no old head like Robin but uptight wordgame first-time-high Arlene. This was a chick with some strange sex hangups and now she was going to . . . what the fuck *was* she going to do? More important, which way would her mind blow? Man, if she freaks out on me . . . .

I stood there stark naked with only a half-hearted hard-on. I was really bringing myself down. And if I walked in there projecting uptight vibes I could *really* mess up her head . . . even thinking about being uptight was putting me more uptight and if I walked in there uptight and put her uptight . . . .

Shit man, get a hold of yourself! You got a chick in there wants to play dirty games with your body and you're winding yourself up into a responsibility bummer! And right now, being hung up on responsibility is the most irresponsible thing you can do . . . .

So, shivering a little, and not from the cold, and getting a flash of how an aging hooker must feel with a sixteen-year-old virgin, I walked into the living room.

Arlene was standing in front of the couch with the hash pipe in her mouth. Her clothes lay in a heap on the table. Her long, loose blond hair flowed like hot bronze over her pale bare shoulders in the warm orange light. Her nipples were sunset-painted a light rusty brown. Her green eyes flashed orange fire-highlights. Her lips shone with her own clear sweet juices. Between her legs, a tawny mane of lioness-fur. She smiled at me, showing cat-tongue between glistening teeth and blew a long, languid plume of hash smoke in my direction.

I laughed with joy inside, and between my legs was a furnace; no problem, no bring-downs, just a beautiful, beautifully stoned chick with hunger for my naked bod in her eyes.

Somehow sensing it was what she wanted, I just stood there displaying my nakedness for her eyes like the mother and father of all Greek statues and let her come across the room to me.

She ran her tongue slowly in a circle around the rim of her lips and part of me wanted to leap on her right then and there and pour myself into her; but no, this was her trip, and we'd do it her way.

"Our third time," she said, sticking the pipe in my mouth and holding a match over it. "First time was a waste . . . second time you did for me . . . and now I'm going to do for you . . . ."

I took a long, deep drag. The hash flowed down my throat like lovely warm syrup. Deep inside me below my waist, a huge chime started to sound.

"I'm gonna do you all over gonna eat you drink you smoke you gobble you up . . . ."

Trembling, I leaned over, placed the pipe on the floor and let the charge of hash permeate every cell in my body. Arlene, my uptight chick—gloriously stoned out of her flaming fucking mind!

"Touch . . . " she said, and placed a forefinger lightly on each of my nipples. Electricity ran from her fingers down my body, twin currents that met and exploded in sparks at the root of my cock. She sank slowly to her knees and touched the wet tip of her tongue to my navel; a spasm went through my groin and I moaned, blowing thick sweet smoke into her coppery hair.

She ran her hands slowly down my flanks, like butterflies barely skimming my skin, rested them on the curve of my ass.

"Skin," she whispered. And rose to her feet. And leaned forward slightly so that her nipples were two tiny points of flesh-to-flesh merging on my bare chest. She brought her face close to mine—

And kissed me, parting my lips with the smooth warm muscle of her own, and her tongue seemed to pour into me, a stream of sweetness without end, filling me to the delicious edge of choking, her juices mingling with mine and—

Her hands were suddenly deep, deep beneath the cheeks of my ass, caressing the defenseless softness of my balls from behind. I moaned into her mouth as my knees started to go rubbery.

Her mouth left mine and moved slowly down my chin to the base of my neck, gliding along a trail of its own wetness—and I screamed from deep inside in a total pain-to-pleasure whiteout as she bit me hard on the shoulder and her nails dug into the soft flesh of my ass.

"Blood . . . " she whispered hoarsely, and sinking to her knees, she ran her mouth down my chest and belly to the brink of my pubic beard.

She stared wide-eyed, mouth-open, at the burning crown of my cock and cupped my balls in warm gentle palms. My legs started to shake; then every muscle in my body was vibrating.

"Balls," she crooned, "sweet soft lovely balls." She held them to her mouth and explored every scrotal wrinkle with the fullness of her tongue.

"Jesus! Oh Jesus!"

Huge green animal eyes stared up at me . . . . "Cock!" she cried, "Cock! Cock! Cock!"

We both moved at once. She took my cock in both hands and opened her mouth wide, wide, lips pulsing, tongue rolling, and every ounce of my flesh seemed to pour into her as she devoured me, and my knees gave way and I slumped forward, the hardness of my chest onto the silken skin of her back, and the universe became a hot wet vacuum of willing flesh sucking at the root of me spread-eagled on her body my hips thrusting forward will of their own forward and forward and forward and a pain sharp as my pleasure mingled with it as nails bit into the flesh of my ass and the world exploded in spasm after spasm of hot black fire!

Out of a well of black velvet, I seemed to drift slowly upright, borne above myself on a foam of warmth. Even the mere opening of eyes sent tremors of sexual ecstasy through me as I looked down and saw my still-enormous cock glide slowly and gently out of her mouth. She looked up at me, eyes shining behind heavy lids, her cheeks puffed out slightly with my seed.

Then she smiled at me, raised her face to the ceiling, closed her eyes, and swallowed deeply. And ran her tongue around her lips like a cat lapping up the last drop of cream.

Oooooooh! My mind blew all the way to the far side of her moon, and every fibre of my being became a torch burning the image of her love to the back of my brain, and I—

Reached out for her shoulders, tipped her over onto her back, clutched at her ankles and hoisted her legs high in the air, then back in an arc so that the tips of her toes nearly touched the floor alongside her ears. I plunged love's burning spear deep, deep, deep down into her, thrusting down, down, down, seeking to burn myself into the core of her being and set it aflame . . . .

"Fuck me! Fuck me! Fuck me!" she screamed and screamed and screamed as I thrust deeper and deeper and deeper, spreading her legs wider and wider and wider, splitting her essence and filling it with my own, and when her body exploded a half-beat ahead of me, her teeth sunk into my shoulder like red-hot fangs and my lungs-cock-being whited out in a huge pleasure-pain scream . . .

■ ■ ■ ■ ■ ■ ■ ■ ■ ■ ■

And she buried her head against my chest as I collapsed onto her and we panted wordlessly into each other's ears as my mind went blank, totally, incredibly, wonderfully blank for ten million years . . . .

" . . . cold . . . ." I could feel her lips murmuring against my chest. *Cold?* Chick must be crazy: I felt ten thousand degrees of tropical night warmth, felt like a huge featherbed drifting off on a bloodheat cloud of sweet immobility secure in the proper center of the universe her moist flesh warm against me breathing the sighs of equatorial seas. *Cold?*

" . . . cold . . . so cold . . . ."

Oh what a drag . . . possible that the sweet warmth that enveloped me was leached from her body by mine? I didn't want to budge from the delicious floor; my every muscle seemed set in maximum pleasure position so that any shift, the least move, would destroy perfection. Over on the edge of the table was my coat . . . .If I could reach it without moving . . . .

I stretched my right arm out to full length—a pain in my shoulder protested and every muscle said what the fuck you doing—but I was six inches short. I leaned the mass of my body into my arm-extension-bones creaking, pleasure-receptors disturbed from the optimum they had reached—got my fingers on the coat, pulled it off the table and across the floor, draped it over Arlene's bare back and let my muscles sink back into maximum repose beneath her weight.

" . . . cold . . . ." Her body stirred against me, the motion like a thousand tiny charleyhorses. Damn! Wish we had done it in bed so we could lay like sleeping logs together for about ten years. But the bed was a million miles of motion away. Shit!

" . . . oooooooh . . . ." Now she was groaning an awful hangover-groan. The outside universe was slowly seeping back into my consciousness: I was still stoned, but laying on a hard floor with Arlene writhing most unsexually against my chest. Memory of what we had done about a century ago drifted through my head in fragments like someone else's dream. Jesus! It had been incredible: a fuck so pure and totally mindless it was beyond memory's recall. Images of memory, film-perfect, flashed on a screen in my head, but I couldn't imagine us as the actors in the film or what I had felt except that it had been totally, amorally delicious, like places inside us that never existed before had taken command as if it had been hash loving hash.

Arlene lifted her face from my chest. Her eyes met mine and seemed to shrivel to prunes; she shifted her head so that her ear rested on my chest and her eyes looked off into the far corner of the room, not meeting mine. "Oh God," she moaned. "Oh God . . . I'm sorry . . . I'm so sorry . . . ."

"*Sorry?*" What was she raving about?

"Oh how you must hate me! Oooh . . . disgusting animal . . . ." I felt her body spasm against me, drawing up into a fetal ball under the coat. What's going on?

I reached up, cupped her chin in both hands, lifted her face towards me. Her eyes were drawn inward, defended by a deep frown, her lips puckered in a grimace of disgust.

"What's the matter, baby? Why on Earth should I hate you?"

"What I did . . . oh God what I did . . . ." She touched the bloody bruise at the back of my neck and cringed. "I hurt you . . . I didn't know what I was doing . . . oh . . . how could I be such an animal . . . ? Oooh . . . ."

Jesus, was she going to freak out *now?* What was the matter with her? I wished I wasn't so damned stoned so I could figure out what strange worms were wriggling behind her fish-cold eyes.

I tightened my grip on her chin, shook her. Her flesh felt dead in my hands. "Snap out of it!" I said as sharply as I could manage. "What's the matter, baby?"

Her eyes seemed to come back into focus, but they were like two chips of cold green glass. "Oh Tom," she whispered, "how can you stand to look at me?"

"Why not? You're beautiful." I tried to kiss her on the lips; her flesh seemed to crawl under mine and she pulled her face away. I let go her chin. She let her head fall to my chest propped up on the point of her chin and looked at me as if she were trying to frighten off private demons with the vision of my face.

"Come on baby, come on baby," I crooned. "You're just a little stoned, is all. Everything's all right . . . ."

"The things we did . . . the things I did . . . ."

"Were just groovy . . . ."

"How can you say that? We were like animals! Ooooh . . . ."

"What's wrong with that? You dug it at the time, didn't you?"

"Yes! Yes! That's what's so horrible! Biting you and . . . and . . . and . . . and *liking it!* So disgusting . . . ."

"You never went down on anyone before?"

"No . . . no . . . oooh . . . like an animal . . . ."

Oh Christ, why did she have to ruin something beautiful with all this goddamn stupid thinking? Maybe it was just because she was stoned . . . ? Yeah, yeah, thing to do was to get her to sleep it off; maybe in the morning I could make some sense to her, but it was hopeless now.

"Let's get some sleep and forget about it," I said. "Things'll look different in the morning, I promise . . . ."

"Sleep . . . ?"

"Yeah, you know, *sleep.* When you wake up, the world'll look different."

"Yes . . . sleep . . . I want to sleep . . . forget . . . oooh . . . ."

And she wrapped the coat around her and refused to look at my naked body and we got in bed together in the dark. Under the covers, she curled up into a ball and was almost instantly asleep, with her back turned to me.

■ ■ ■ ■ ■ ■ ■ ■ ■ ■ ■

It wasn't easy, but we managed not to say a word to each other until we were sitting at the table in the living room over coffee—the alarm had rung and she had bolted out of bed before I could even get my eyes open; and by the time I had got out of bed she was dressed and through in the bathroom, avoiding me as she fussed with the coffee-pot; and by the time I had shaved and gotten my work suit on, my coffee was waiting on the living room table and she was sipping hers, staring deep down into its muddy depths as I sat down beside her. I tried to kid myself that she had just been doing a groovy domestic number—but I didn't get very far. The poor chick just couldn't face me, is all.

"You okay?" were the first words I was able to say to her.

She stared down into the coffee. "I'm all right," she said coldly. "My God, what you must think of me after last night . . . ."

"I really don't understand any of this. What in blazes do you think I think?"

She finally looked up at me. Her eyes were points of fear hiding behind her glasses, her face seemed to cringe. She looked like someone waiting to be hit. I took a long drink of coffee and started to feel almost human.

"I acted like a filthy animal," she said. "I don't see how you can stand to look at me."

"Do you think you're the first girl that ever sucked a cock?" I said harshly, trying to gross my way through to her.

Her mouth puckered, as if the coffee had suddenly turned to semen in her mouth. She shuddered. "It . . . it . . . it's not what I did," she muttered, "it's . . . the way I did it. I was out of my mind . . . I feel so . . . ."

"Maybe just *different?*" I suggested.

Her face relaxed just a little. "Yes," she said. "I . . . I don't feel like the me I was before last night."

"Is that really so terrible?"

She stared at me with huge eyes that seemed on the verge of tears. "I . . . You mean you don't . . . ? I don't . . . ?"

"Disgust me? Why should you? I enjoyed it. You enjoyed it. What's the problem?"

She looked down into the coffee again. "But the way I was . . . I've never been like that before . . . I felt like . . . sucking you up . . . like . . . like . . . ."

"You were just turned on all the way for the first time."

"Like an animal . . . ."

"We're not carrots, you know."

Still not daring to look at me again, she said: "I really don't disgust you now? You're not just trying to be a gentlemen?"

I touched my hand to her cold, dry cheek. "Baby," I said, "I love you for last night. You were really you, and it was groovy."

"But the hashish—"

"Is just a chemical! Arlene stoned is still Arlene."

She looked up at me, started to move her hand towards mine, dropped it back in her lap. "I feel so different," she said. "Like there are things inside of me I didn't know were there, maybe things that shouldn't be there . . . things that would make you hate me if you saw them . . . ."

"Just the other way around. We opened up to each other. We shared something very private. Dig: you're not going to discuss last night in group, are you?"

A horrified grimace.

"Well, see? Last night isn't something bad, between us it's something good, something only the two of us can share. That's what sex should be between two people who care for each other."

Her hand came up and touched my hand touching her cheek. "You make me feel so strange," she said. Then she looked at me, smiled hesitantly, then kissed me very lightly on the lips.

"Not so bad, is it?" I said.

She smiled shyly at me. "No . . . .I'm all confused . . . But . . . you really don't . . . ?"

I fished in my pocket and brought out my key. I dangled it in front of her face.

"You don't really expect me to accept that now," she said. It was just short of being a question.

"No. But I want you to know it's still there for the taking, dig?"

She smiled a real wide smile, and her eyes seemed to soften.

"You're really a good person," she said. "You know, I just might be falling in love with you . . . ."

And she kissed me again, harder this time, with a flick of her tongue and the homey taste of coffee.

Eyes to eyes, smile to open smile, she said: "I woke up thinking last night had killed everything between us. Now I think . . . things may just be starting . . . ."

Once more she kissed me, a kiss that was hot and languid, and her tongue started to move in my mouth like something we had no time to finish was starting.

I pulled away with a little laugh. "Better cool it," I said, "or you'll never get to class and I'll never get to work."

She laughed back. I felt five years younger, felt I could contemplate the word "love" without snickering.

"I'm a little scared," she said. "It feels so different . . . Let's take our time . . . yes ?"

I felt that uncertain hollow tingling too. "Slow and easy," I said. "We've got all the time in the world . . . ."

16
"... You May Take Two Giant Steps ..."

"... comes as close to being the big breakthrough for you, Mr. Feinblatt, as anything of yours I've ever seen. In fact, *Silent Cal* is the kind of novel that gives a conscientious agent fits ..."

Gah! Fits is right! What kind of jerk would spend two years on and off writing a novelization of the life of Calvin Coolidge? A 100,000 word eight-pointer yet! Which was its only saving grace—here it was Thursday afternoon and here I was with only 32 points and a Foundation meeting tonight so I couldn't catch up at home. So an eight-pointer that would bring me even should've been a godsend.

Only how the fuck was I going to write six pages on this thing? It was the ultimate horror—a good novelization of the life of Calvin Coolidge; every one of those hundred thousand words well-chosen, well-typed, well-punctuated and stupefyingly dull. Paragraph by paragraph, chapter by chapter, this Feinblatt freak could really write. Only trouble was he had made one small mistake at the outset—he had chosen a subject for his masterpiece that was *dull dull dull*. I mean—*Calvin Coolidge?*

Moaning softly, I returned to the salt mines:

"... Structurally, the novel is flawless. The prose is clean, well-chosen, and carries what action there is smoothly along in a most professional manner ..."

Well, it was that kind of week. After Monday night, I had pissed Tuesday away on a lousy seven points worth of one pointers, unable to get my mind off Arlene. Wednesday, I made like a Stahkanovite and tore off twelve points, but after dinner with Arlene and a quick one that wasn't a thing like Monday and soothing her for about three hours afterward because it wasn't and having to convince her it didn't matter, I had started today in a nice rotten mood and goofed the morning away on one short and reading this mess and now I had

damn well better rip off six pages before five somehow, or Friday
would be a nightmare . . .

"*. . .* however, to paraphrase something Herman Melville
once said about the impossibility of writing a great work about a
flea . . . "

"Come take a piss with me, Tom, old man."
Dickie Lee had appeared before me like the Cheshire Cat, replete
with shit-eating grin.
"What?"
"I am inviting you to the executive's pissoir," Dickie said grandly.
Bruce and Berkowitz barely looked up; too busy typing away to even
bother making the required cracks about faggotry. That kind of week
for them too, I guess.
"There *is* no executive's john, Dickie," I pointed out.
"I," huffed Dickie regally, "am an executive. Therefore, wherever I
piss is the executive's john."
"Your logic is irrefutable, Dickie. Besides, anything to get away
from Calvin Coolidge."
"Who?"
"The latest candidate for fame and fortune," I said, thumping the
giant manuscript of *Silent Cal.* "A novelization of the life of Calvin
Coolidge. Nice piece of work. I'm thinking of—"
Dickie winced. "If you pass that thing on to me even in jest," he
said, "you will become the executive's pissoir because this executive
will piss all over you."

■ ■ ■ ■ ■ ■ ■ ■ ■ ■ ■

As we stood side by side at the reeking urinals, Dickie letting loose
a healthy piss and me faking it, Dickie glanced around the large, dir-
ty-tiled men's room that served our whole floor of the building, saw
that we were alone except for a pair of feet peeking out from the bottom of one of the crapper stalls, said: "I suppose you're wondering
why I've gathered you here tonight?"
"A company that goes to the head together makes bread together?" I suggested.
"I am trying to be serious."
"I guess you just haven't had too much practice, Dickie."

"Look, Tom old man," Dickie said, now *really* serious, "I'm trying to do you a favor. I'm gonna reveal a deep, dark secret. Dirk offered you the *Slick* slush-pile job, right?"

"Dirk *did* seem to be hinting at something."

"Ah!" said Dickie. He flashed me a conspiratorial smile. "Well . . . *Slick* is a small operation itself. Mort Clarke is the editor and Harold Berg is the assistant editor and there's the usual fag photography editor and that's it."

"So?"

Dickie beamed at me. "However, me lad," he said, "*Slick* is owned by a big West Coat stiffener outfit that publishes about a dozen of the things."

"Come on Dickie, what are you getting at?"

"I am trying to show some class, but I see that a peasant such as yourself understands nought but crudity. Harold Berg is approximately three hundred years old and far too senile to take over the editor's job. And good old Mort is starting to fuck up."

"So?"

Dickie frowned, shook his head at my denseness. "*So*," he said, "Mort has blown several similar jobs in the Big Town, which, in fact, is why he fled to L.A. Old Mort is—shall we say?—a lush. Dirk knows him well and such is Our Leader's wisdom that by the length of time Mort is taking to read stories from the pros and the growing incoherence of his correspondence, Dirk has concluded that Mort will drink himself out of the *Slick* editorial seat and under the proverbial table ere the year is out. And if not, New Year's Eve is certain to finish the job. So . . . since Harold is ready for St. Petersburg, whoever gets the slush-pile job will probably be editor of *Slick* before February. *Comprende?*"

"*Comprendo*," I said as we walked toward the door. In fact, I *comprehended* a bit more than Dickie thought I did, namely that Dirk had put him up to this. "*If* I wanted to be editor of *Slick*, that would be very interesting. However—"

"Fame and fortune await in the Golden West, me boy!" Dickie chided. "Don't be an ingrate, old man."

"I won't be an ingrate, Dickie," I said. "You told me your big secret and now I'll let you in on an even more important piece of information."

"Oh? And what might that be, old man?"

"Your fly is open," I said.

■ ■ ■ ■ ■ ■ ■ ■ ■ ■

"What's this meeting supposed to be about, baby?" I asked Arlene as Harvey threaded his way through the crowd on the floor to his folding chair on the dais. We were sitting on folding chairs too—in the row of chairs at the back of the room. After getting my suit good and mungy from the floor last time, I had made it my business to get there early enough to cop a chair and save one for Arlene too.

"I don't know," Arlene said. "You know that meetings aren't usually called for any fixed purpose."

"Uh-huh. But I also know that this one is on Thursday and the last one was on Wednesday, so there's no fixed schedule for the things, right?"

"So?"

"So old Harv calls 'em when he wants to call 'em."

"I never thought of it that way," Arlene said. "I suppose Harvey just calls a meeting when he senses something in the air."

"Uh-huh. And five'll get you ten I know what's in the air tonight: San Francisco."

Arlene frowned. "I hope you're wrong," she said.

"Why's it got you so uptight?"

"Everything that matters to me is in New York. Everyone I know . . . you . . . my family . . . college . . . .I've never lived anywhere else. I'd be lost in California."

I remembered what Dickie had told me this afternoon. Dickie was not one to give away Dirk's secrets unless under orders to make like a security leak. Therefore, Dirk was really offering me the editorship of *Slick* by next year. It made a lot more sense from Dirk's viewpoint that way: with me as full editor of *Slick*, he would have a permanent friendly outlet for the agency's stiffener crud. It had been eating on me all evening: why couldn't I get interested in a real editor's job, even if it was a sleazy mag like *Slick?* Sure beat fee-reading. But now Arlene had laid it out for me: I was a New Yorker clean through, everyone and everything I knew—and her too—was here and there was nothing for me in LA but the gaping unknown and a job. I felt much saner knowing that Arlene felt the same way about leaving New York. Cowardice loves company . . . ?

"So what's the problem?" I said.

"The problem is I'd be lost without the Foundation too," she said.

"God, I don't know what I'd do . . . "

Way across the carpet of people in front of us, Harvey had seated himself on the dais. He lit a cigarette, took a drag, exhaled and said: "I understand Ted would like to open this meeting. Ted . . . ?"

I gave Arlene an I-told-you-so look as Ted stood up at the foot of the dais, put one foot up on it, and turned to face the membership, his blue eyes gleaming, his big body hunched forward almost like a quarterback behind his center.

"Last meeting we kicked around the idea of what it would be like to have the Foundation in San Francisco," Ted said. "Since then, everyone seems to be talking about it, but we really haven't discussed it seriously yet. So I think it's time we did. So to start it off, I'm making a formal motion that the Foundation move itself to San Francisco as soon as possible."

Arlene clutched at my hand. I shrugged at her. I had seen this coming a mile away. And I could even see Harvey's next move . . . .

"Let me get this straight, Ted," Harvey said. "You want to put this to a vote of the membership?"

"That's right."

"But don't you think it's a little unrealistic, even unfair, to expect people to make such a monumental decision on such short notice?"

"No, no, no!" Ted said, shaking his head violently. "I'm not really saying we should decide right now. All I'm saying is that we should *really* start thinking seriously about moving the Foundation to San Francisco. And I just think the way to do that is to have a formal motion before the membership, dig? Sure we'd be crazy to vote one way or the other right now, but if we've got a motion, it gives all the bullshit we've been throwing around lately some reality."

"Well that seems to be a reasonable way of going about it," Harvey conceded. "In order to make it a formal motion, though, I think we should have some seconds . . . ?"

A sprinkling of hands went up: Doris (quickly, but without much obvious enthusiasm), Linda Kahn (surprise!), Charley Dees, Bill Nelson, Tod-and-Judy, Chester White, George Blum, and a few others. And a few mutters: "Second the motion."

"Well," Harvey, carefully not gloating, "it looks like a formal motion to move the Foundation to San Francisco is now before the membership. So let's chew it over. Since it was your idea, Ted, suppose you tell us why you're in favor of the move . . . ."

Ted flashed a big grin out over the room, rose to the balls of his feet, and man, did I recognize that look on his face: Ted the True Believer, fried to the eyeballs on adrenalin, panting to convert the whole world to his latest Big Answer. Old Harv sure knew who to maneuver into playing his mouthpiece—when Ted got wound up like this he could just about sell a lifetime subscription to *Pravda* to J. Edgar Hoover.

"Look at us!" Ted nearly shouted. "Maybe forty people who've come to the Foundation because we're not satisfied with our lives and we want to change them by changing ourselves, right? Okay, so we come into this loft, and while we're here, we *do* change our consciousness. But then we drag our sorry asses out into the same shitty environment we've known all our lives and do the same fuck-up things we've always done. *So where's the change?* Trouble is, we're all committed to a whole shitload of useless garbage besides the Foundation: jobs, school, people, ways of fucked-up living. When we should be totally committed to just one thing—*Total Consciousness*. Deep down we all know that, or we wouldn't be here. We need to move the Foundation to San Francisco to get rid of all that external crap and make the Foundation the center, the *only* center, of our lives!"

Arlene was suddenly on her feet shouting: "This is crazy! Do you realize what you're asking? We've all got lives of our own here, jobs, school, family, friends! Why the hell should we cut ourselves off from everything we care about to drag ourselves across the continent to some city most of us have never seen? It's crazy!"

"Ah shit—" Ted began.

But Harvey cut him off. "That's a very good point. I don't think you've really thought this through, Ted. You and Doris have no strong ties here, and you can work and paint anywhere. But many of the members have careers, families, are going to college—have deep ties to New York. You don't seem to understand what moving to San Francisco would mean to them—they'd have to totally uproot their lives. And those that chose to stay behind would lose even more—the chance to develop their consciousness. You don't seem to realize what this would mean to the Foundation members as individuals."

Arlene sat down. "See?" she whispered to me. "You've got Harvey all wrong. This insane San Francisco thing *can't* be his idea. You *are* paranoid about it."

I shrugged. No point in trying to explain the ins and outs of the old Briar Patch Gambit. She'd have to see for herself.

"Just watch how the old worm turns," I told her.

Ted, who had been dancing around like a kid who was waiting to take a piss while Harvey rapped, shook his head violently, said: "That's the whole point! In our minds, we know that Total Consciousness is all that really counts, but we don't *live* it. We're all hung up on our dumb little ego-games: jobs and school and all that external shit. If we really want the Foundation to give us Total Consciousness, we've gotta give up all that, make the Foundation the center of our lives. We can't do that here, but we *can* do it in San Francisco."

Harvey made a show of pondering this great revelation. "Mmmm . . . you've got a point," he said. "Ideally, our only commitment *should* be to Total Consciousness, through the Foundation. But I don't see why that would be more possible in San Francisco than in New York."

"Dig, it's not *San Francisco* that counts," said Ted, "the important thing is to *make a move*. San Francisco is just a very groovy place to move to. Dig: if we moved, we'd all be strangers—no jobs, no friends, no outside commitments, no nothing. Like being born again, yeah! But the Foundation would be there, the *only* thing at the center of our lives—we could put it first without trying because there'd be nothing to get in the way. We can't do that here because there's too much competing ego-garbage. But with a clean break from all our pasts, it'd come naturally, dig?"

Harvey took a long drag on his cigarette, stared at the back wall as if waiting for the handwriting to appear, as if Ted (oh sure!) had opened his eyes to some Great Truth. I was probably the only one in the whole room who saw through the set-up—and who would listen to the Gibbering Dope Fiend!

"Aren't you going to say anything?" Arlene hissed at me.

"Wouldn't waste my breath."

Harvey sighed smoke. "I see," he finally said. "You do seem to be making sense, Ted. What you're really talking about is moving the Foundation to San Francisco *as a community* . . . "

Ted's eyes seemed to suddenly get even brighter, like turning up a three-way bulb. "Yeah! Yeah!" he said. "Sure, if thirty or forty of us moved, *as a community*, like Harvey says, it'd be no sweat. Among thirty people, we could get at least ten cars together and all drive across the county, what a gas! And when we got there, we could set up committees to find jobs, pads, a house for the Foundation . . . Hey, we could even find a couple of old houses and set up kind of communes—"

"I think you're getting a little ahead of yourself, Ted," Harvey said gently. "All these details would come much later, assuming we decide to go."

"Sure, sure. I'm just saying that once we start thinking of ourselves as a real community, all the little hassles will disappear."

Harvey nodded. "Yes, it's this idea of the Foundation as a community that really appeals to me . . . "

"Yeah, like the old wagon-trains going west," Tod Spain said.

"A big mobile commune!" said Bonnie Elbert.

Babble, babble, babble! I could sense the mood of the crowd: maybe a dozen or so of the young itchy-footed ones like Tod and Judy and Bonnie and Rich were really serious, but the majority, suckers that they were, were getting their jollies out of the fantasy of picking up and setting up a giant psychiatric crash-pad in the Golden West. They were grooving behind it because they didn't have to take it seriously, it was such a crazy idea, and if a vote were taken now, Ted and Harvey would look like assholes. Just a cheap thrill—*right now.*

"Well?" I said to Arlene. "Did I tell you so?"

"You know," she said dreamily. "Ted may have something there. Didn't you once tell me that it was important to go into your fear . . . ? Well, leaving New York sure scares me. Maybe it would be good—"

"Ah shit, you're not serious!"

Her mood seemed to break. She laughed. "Is *any* of this serious?" she said. "Do you really see *these* people actually leaving everything behind and following the Foundation to San Francisco . . . ?"

"But what if the Foundation *did* move? How many of them could give it up? Could you give it up?"

She frowned, then shrugged. "I don't know . . . but I'm not about to worry about it. It won't happen; the whole idea is impossible."

I wondered. People were getting up and milling around and the whole meeting was breaking up into little clots of people, all rapping on the notion of San Francisco. It was all in the timing. If Harvey pushed now, he would probably blow it, but if he let it stay a fantasy until they were good and worked up . . .

"I think we had better end the formal meeting now," Harvey shouted redundantly above the tumult. "Let's just all talk it over as long as we want to and try a vote on it when the spirit moves us."

"Hey Harvey," Rich yelled, "if we vote to go, would you go along?"

Harvey considered the smoke dribbling out of his mouth. "Well . . . If the vote were *really* overwhelming," he said. "I wouldn't want to split the Foundation down the middle. That's why we should take our time before we even think about a vote."

And the scene broke up into general bullshitting.

Arlene and I got up. "Want to stick around and shoot the shit?" I asked her unenthusiastically.

"I'd like to . . ." she said. "But . . . Look, I've got two big tests Monday, and I won't be able to see you over the weekend—"

"How about spending the weekend at my pad?"

"And how much studying would I get done then?"

"Uh . . . there *is* that. . . "

"What I was going to suggest," she said, "is that we go have dinner now and then . . . "

"Best offer I've had all day."

▪ ▪ ▪ ▪ ▪ ▪ ▪ ▪ ▪ ▪ ▪

As we made our way out into the hall, Ted caught up with us, his eyes still glazed from adrenalin-fever. "Hey, where are you guys going?"

"A gentleman never tells," I informed him.

"Oh . . . Look, before you go—what do you think? Wouldn't it be a gas to—"

"Ted," I said, "you've got rocks in your head."

Ted didn't even skip a beat. "Yeah, I thought you'd say that," he said. "You need it more than anyone, Tom. Get away from all this shit—"

"And right in all *that* shit."

"You know, Tom, maybe Ted has—"

I dragged her toward the stairs. "Come on baby, let's get out of this cuckoo-clock!"

"Hey, at least think it over!" Ted called after us. "It's not like making the move alone. We're gonna be a *community*, man, a fucking community!"

17
A Meeting of the Brotherhood

"Forty-eight, forty-nine-*fifty.*"

Terry Blackstone put the last white capsule into the pile on the table, stoppered his big bottle of acid caps, stuffed the bottle back into an inside pocket of his black raincoat, and said: "Fifty caps. Five dollars a cap, that's two hundred and fifty dollars. A hundred is your cut, baby, so you owe me one-fifty, and I gotta have it by Monday. Can you deal it all by then?"

"No sweat," Robin said, scooping up the caps and dropping them into a baggie. She took a drag off the joint and passed it to me.

I took a short toke and passed the joint to Terry Blackstone, who looked like he needed it. His eyes were invisible behind his black shades, but he was rocking back and forth like an old Jew in a synagogue, and giving off uptight vibes. He toked, passed the joint back to Robin, and said: "Look baby, tell you what . . . you lay a hundred and twenty-five on me now, and that's the price, you can keep the extra twenty-five."

Robin looked at me, asked the question with arched eyebrows.

I shook my head. "It's Saturday afternoon and the bank is closed," I said. "I don't keep that kind of cash around."

Letting her do her thing in my pad was one thing; fronting bread for her was another, and I wanted no part of *that.* But it would be gauche to put it that way, so, for the capper, I smiled at Terry Blackstone and said with great sweet innocence: "Unless you'll take a check, man."

"A *check?*" Terry Blackstone shrieked. "Are you out of your gourd?"

Natch. A wholly predictable paranoid dealer reaction. Terry Blackstone would rather wait sweating in fear (he probably owed a bigger dealer) till Monday for Robin to lay the bread on him than take a check which he knew he could cash. So, a bluff I knew for openers wouldn't be called.

"All right Terry," Robin said, stuffing the bag of caps into the pocket of her peacoat, which lay beside her on the couch, "a hundred and fifty in cash on Monday."

"Okay, baby," Terry Blackstone said unenthusiastically. "I gotta split. Got another two hundred caps to deal today."

I showed him to the door myself for the purpose of securing the police lock behind him (fifty caps of acid in the pad made *me* a little paranoid). When I got back to the living room, Robin was in the bedroom.

"What're you doing?" I called.

"Using the phone. Okay?"

"Okay," I said, leaning back on the couch and rolling a fresh joint from the nickel bag Robin had left on the table. I took a nice long drag: smooth, sweet shit and it went down nice and easy. Holding the smoke in my lungs, I contemplated the workings of fate. Arlene's tests on Monday had allowed me Friday night, today, and Sunday with Robin. So I had been able to have my Thursday night Arlene cake and eat Robin too (metaphorically, that is). Question was, did Arlene *really* have to study all weekend or was she just getting out of the way, sensing that Robin might show up unannounced and being too insecure to be competitive? Or third alternative: could Arlene only take me in small doses? Were we both pussyfooting around each other? Was ignorance bliss? I exhaled. What the hell, I thought, taking another toke, Saturday and Sunday with Robin were a fact and the thing to do was take the next two days as they came, as a vacation from Arlene-Foundation reality and Dirk-Robinson reality, and smoke enough grass in the process to blow the cobwebs out of my head.

As I watched Robin emerge from the bedroom, walk across the room, and sit down on the couch, I wondered if maybe Robin gave me the breather I needed to put up with the Arlene-scenes, and vice versa. Reality-contrasts, two separate sides to my head and a different chick for each side, and if I tried to make it all one or the other, I'd either have to turn half of me off or put one of them through some real bummers—not to mention the bummers I would go through trying to relate to Arlene in a Robin-mood or Robin in an Arlene-mood.

But that was definitely an Arlene-Foundation-navel-contemplation thought, and too heavy for the present reality-style. So I took another BIG hit and handed Robin the joint.

"Is it okay if we stick around for a while?" she said. "Some people are gonna show up . . . you might find them interesting." She took another drag and handed me the joint.

Well, what the fuck, so a little dealing out of my pad wouldn't be the end of the world, stay good and stoned and dig how the other half lives. *Me*-mories . . .

"As long as the grass holds out," I said, taking another toke.

■ ■ ■ ■ ■ ■ ■ ■ ■ ■ ■

"Have some grass, man," I said to the neatly-bearded thirtiesh cat. He wore a brown tweed jacket over a black turtleneck and black-rimmed glasses shielding nervous blue eyes.

"Thank you," he said in a soft, uptight voice, sitting down on the edge of the couch as I handed him the joint. He took a very controlled but quite respectable drag.

"Fred's a professor at N.Y.U.," Robin said, sitting down on my other flank. "He's kind of . . . a connection for the groovier teachers."

Fred puckered his thick lips at the word "connection" and passed the joint to Robin. As a gesture of intelligentsia-solidarity, I asked: "What do you teach?"

"English . . . " Fred said apologetically.

Robin exhaled, handed me the joint, said proudly: "Tom's in the business too."

I took a little toke, mostly for the taste at this point, as Fred said: "You're . . . uh . . . a dealer . . . ?"

"No, no, man!" Robin said. "Tom's in the English business. He's a literary agent."

Fred smiled, loosening up a bit; then his eyes narrowed, suspicious of a dope-pusher put-on. "A literary agent?" he said with black-board-chalk dryness.

"Chick not speak with forked tongue," I told him. "Next question you are about to ask is, `What's a guy like you doing in a place like this?'"

Fred laughed a nice human laugh. "Shee-*yit*," he observed unself-consciously. I handed him the joint and he took a long drag, relaxed against the back of the couch. I decided I liked him—kind of a Che Guevara of the academic set, meek, mild-mannered professor who is in reality a stoned head. In a weird way, though he might be ten years older than me, I seemed to feel a paternal regard for him.

Fred passed the joint to me, exhaled, smiled again—this time with a I-don't-give-a-shit grooviness—and said: "You're not *really* a literary agent, man?"

"I really am, honest. It's a kind of Nathanael West (dig the literary reference, Fred!) number, though. I squat behind my typewriter reading nut manuscripts and writing literary critiques to lunatics for a fee . . . "

"Oh, you mean you're with Dirk Robinson?" Fred said.

I gaped. Fred laughed. "Worked my way through my Masters as a fee-reader for good old Dirk Robinson, Inc.," he said. I took another drag; suddenly I needed it. "Dirk is a secret patron of academe. Christ, dozens of English professors, even poli sci people, have gone through that mill."

I passed him the communal joint. He studied it for a moment. "I do believe that working at Dirk Robinson is what has turned hundreds of normal people to dope," he said.

"It *is* that kind of a job," I conceded. "Cloaca of the universe."

"But also its navel."

"Ah, an academic mystic!"

"My specialty," he said around a lungful of smoke. "Twentieth century mystical novelists."

He started to hand the joint back to me, but Robin leaned across my body and grabbed it out from under my nose; she seemed kind of uptight at all this stuff over her head and irrelevant to the matter at hand.

She took a short drag (grabbing the joint had been a matter of principle more than anything else, apparently), said: "How many caps you want?"

"Huh . . . ?" Fred was feeling no pain. "Oh . . . ten . . . . "

Robin counted out ten caps from her mystic baggie, handed them to Fred, who dropped them casually in a jacket pocket, took out his wallet and pulled off five tens and handed them to Robin, who gauchely counted the bread before stuffing it in her Levis pocket. She took a longer drag and roached the joint.

She looked at me, looked at Fred, looked at me; kind of a signal for Fred to split. Fred caught it, started to get up, saying: "Well . . . ah . . . I guess . . . . "

"Stick around man," I told him. I started rolling a fresh joint. "Have some more grass. Relax."

Robin gave me a dirty look that said this cat is a customer, what the hell are you doing? I gave her a dirty look back that said this is *my* pad, baby, not a dope supermarket, cut the crap.

"Any former Dirk Robinson fee-reader is welcome in my pad," I said. I lit the joint, took a little puff, then handed it to Fred, who smiled, toked, and sat back on the couch.

"Talk to you a minute, Tom . . ." Robin said uptightly. Knowing what was coming, I shrugged at Fred, let her pull me off the couch and over toward the bedroom.

"I've got another customer coming!" Robin hissed in my ear.

"So?"

"They've never met. It'd be a very strange scene. Get him out of here."

"I dig strange scenes," I told her. "He stays."

"But—"

"The decision of the judges is final."

"It's your pad," she said somewhat sulkily.

"I'm glad you noticed."

■ ■ ■ ■ ■ ■ ■ ■ ■ ■ ■

"My God," said Fred, "you mean the Mad Dentist is still around?"

"His latest is a sex novel about—"

"The Communist fluoridation plot to bankrupt the dental industry."

We both laughed. But Robin, sitting next to me, seemed to be getting more and more uptight listening to us rap about Dirk Robinson, Inc.

"Y'know, Dirk Robinson isn't Dirk's real name," Fred said.

"Who would *really* have a name like Dirk Robinson?" I said. "I wonder what his real name is . . . ."

"I used to know, but I forgot. Sam . . . Sam and something long and Middle European . . . ."

"Yeah, I always did make Dirk for a Balkan horse-thief at heart . . . ."

A knock at the door propelled Robin off the couch like a nervous ICBM. A moment later she reappeared gingerly leading a tall, thin, spade-bearded Negro in a khaki coat. An awfully familiar face beneath his modified natural: bony, smirk-mouthed, vaguely sinister.

The spade looked at me. I looked at him. He began snapping his fingers soundlessly. "Don't tell me, man," he said in a deep, clear voice. "You used to go around with the jivy Anne Jones chick . . . Tom . . . Tom . . . ."

"Hollander," I told him. I recognized him now, a street-junkie from the bad old days who used to hustle the white Washington

Square weekend high school chicks. Some kind of crazy name for a
spade, I vaguely remembered . . . .

"You're . . . The Colonel, right?"

He grinned a mouthful of small dainty teeth. "Jefferson Davis
Lee," he said, "before I returned to the People. Now I go by Jefferson
Davis X. Ain't that a bitch?"

We both laughed. I got up, shook his right hand with both of
mine; we grinned at each other, then sat down on the couch; me between Fred and Jeff and Robin out in deep right field on the other
wing of the sectional facing the three of us. Uptight as she had been
when I asked Fred to stay, she now smiled in relief and maybe a little
pride in the fact that I knew The Colonel, who probably had her a little intimidated (his white-chick scene in the old days).

"Have some grass," I said, handing Jeff a joint.

"Don't mind if I do."

A moment of silence as he dragged and held it. Then both of us
said simultaneously: "You still on smack?"

We both laughed as Fred fidgeted.

"That's Evil White Man's Medicine," Jeff said. "I got busted and
did a year. When I got out, after they scraped me off the walls, that is,
I found I had lost the taste. And you?"

"I gave it up for Lent."

"Shee-*yit!*"

Suddenly we both kind of noticed Fred, who was sucking nervously on his own joint. Jeff gave him a Big Bad Spade Leer. "Are
you the fuzz, white man?" he said ominously.

Fred gave him a fish-eyed stare. "As a matter of fact," he drawled,
"I am Inspector Lee of the Nova Police. Yer all under arrest."

Jeff laughed. "What you doing with that joint there, Inspector?" he
said.

"I am confiscating the evidence," Fred informed him. "Standard
police procedure."

"This cat is like *stoned*," Jeff said admiringly. "You White Boys
have lured a po' honest Afro-American into an opium-den! I had best
dispose of the merchandise." And he took a really enormous toke—
almost half the joint.

I grinned across at Robin: she was grinning and eating it all up
now, grooving behind the show. Ah, it was beautiful! Warmed the
cockles of me heart to see us all grooving together: hippy-dippy
chick, college professor, ethnic spade, literary lion. Ain't that What

Made America Great?

"You dealing the acid, man?" Jeff asked.

"I've gone straight," I told him (old fee-reader Fred sneered at the concept). "The little lady is our entrepreneur."

Jeff shrugged. "I want twenty caps," he told Robin.

Robin pulled out the baggie, counted out twenty caps. "One hundred even," she said.

Jeff scowled at her. "A hundred bucks! What the—"

Robin cringed a bit. "Five a cap," she whined. "That's the standard price . . . ."

"Shit!" snarled Jeff. "That's *street prices.* I'm copping twenty caps. I should get volume rates. Don't jive me, white girl!"

Robin seemed to wilt—the old Colonel doing one of his sinister spade numbers.

"Cool it, Colonel," I told him. "Don't go mindfucking my chick."

Jeff broke up. "Okay man, okay. Just thought it was worth a try." He took off his coat and pulled a roll of bills out of his shirt pocket. Robin heaved a sigh of relief and gave me a thank-you look as he handed her five twenties. And smiled this time as Jeff scowled and said: "Where are my fucking green stamps, woman?"

I laughed, shoved the joint I was holding into his mouth and said: "Shut up and smoke your pot!"

Cozy, cozy, cozy.

■ ■ ■ ■ ■ ■ ■ ■ ■ ■ ■

"I heard this theory," Fred said, "that everyone in the world knows someone who knows someone who knows someone who knows anyone."

"Huh?" said Jeff.

"Mathematical acquaintance of mine worked it out on acid once," Fred said. "Four steps between any two people in the known universe, no more, Jeff. Like you to me. I know Tom who knows you. Or me and . . . oh, Mao Tse-tung. I know a cat who knows a member of the Russian Politburo who knows the Russian Ambassador to China who knows Mao."

"Oh yeah, I dig," Jeff said. "I know a cat who split to Cuba and met Castro who must know someone who knows Mao!"

"Small world . . . " I murmured. "Smaller world of dope . . . ."

"Naw, yer wrong," said Fred. "'Nother equation. Everybody in the world knows somebody who's a head. Einstein worked it out in 1937. Special special theory of relativity."

"How come I never heard of it?" I said.

"Because he got busted before he could publish."

"Albert Einstein got busted?"

"Naw, was his cousin Orville Einstein. Got busted for dealing. See what I mean?"

"Man, are you stoned!"

We were all pretty well whacked out—except Robin, who was mostly sitting and watching and worrying about selling the rest of her acid. Dealing is such a drag! On the other hand, Robin was our connection according to the special theory: if she wasn't dealing, I wouldn't have met good old Fred or ever seen Jeff again. So amend that to: dealing is a drag for the dealer. That's what dealers mean by "paying dues" I guess. Dealing is a drag, but *someone's* gotta do it to preserve the noble traditions of the Free Enterprise System.

Still, I felt for Robin, sitting there watching us groove, and obviously upright about something.

"What's the matter, baby?" I finally said.

"Couple of people I couldn't get on the phone," she said. "And I gotta deal the rest of the acid by Sunday night." She frowned, hesitated, said: "Look, Tom, would it be all right if I went out for an hour or two and unloaded the stuff?"

I shrugged. "If that's your thing, baby."

"Think I'd better," she said. "Won't take more than a couple of hours."

As Robin closed the door behind her, Jeff said: "Quite a chick you got there."

"Where do you know her from?" I said, a shade uptight.

"Oh, just from dealing. You know."

"Uh-huh," I said unconvincingly.

Jeff chuckled evilly. "Relax, baby," he said. "I got no eyes for that chick. Too strange, man, too strange! Man, you do go for strange chicks. That Anne—whew! And this Robin . . . groovy-looking, and you can tell she fucks like a fiend, but the young pussy running around the Village these days, man, you can have *no* idea of what's going on inside their heads."

"I do believe you're talking like an old square," I said.

"No, he's right," Fred said. "The younger generation—"

"Younger generation! Look, you may be a decrepit dirty old man of at least thirty, but I'm still eligible for the draft."

"And all that teen-age tail?" said Fred.

I laughed. "Fuckin'-A!" I said. "Young enough to fight, young enough to ball teenyboppers all night!"

"Look, man," said Jeff, "you *know* I'm an old expert on teen-age pussy. Love that juicy young white meat! But I'm telling you, like the song says, they don't look different, but man they've changed! All that young cunt is totally crazed these days. Man, like your Robin can't be twenty and you *know* she's dropped more acid than all of us put together. Don't fool yourself you can see inside her head."

"Ah, come on, you're putting him on a bummer," Fred said.

"He's right, I'm on the wrong side of the generation gap, you better believe it," Jeff said. "It's a different scene and dope's the only reason old heads like us can even get a taste. I mean, I know young Brothers who would cut me dead just for smoking grass with you dirty honkies. But the young chicks are even worse . . . they're mindfuckers, it's a fucking' . . . .what's the word . . . .?"

"Matriarchy?" suggested Fred.

"Yeah," said Jeff. "They carry those young cats' balls around in their purses. Why do you think a young chick like that is interested in a cat like you?"

"Tell me, Great Swami."

"Because she can't get inside your dirty old head. You can play with her mind and the young cats can't. The little chicks love that, a cat who can mess with their minds. Just don't think you can get inside her head any more than she can get inside yours."

"But it's fun trying."

"Just watch out, man," Jeff said. "Don't let *her* mindfuck *you*."

He stretched, got up, said: "Well, I should've left already. I got some people uptown who are probably uptight waiting for their acid, and that could get unhealthy."

"I ought to be going too," Fred said. "Must be near seven."

I walked both of them to the door, feeling groovy and a little sad all at once. Were they right? Was Robin something I couldn't handle? Ah bullshit, both of them were just getting old, is all. Yeah, that's why I was sad—two groovy guys talking like old wrecks.

"Give my regards to Dirk," Fred said.

"I'll say hello to the Mad Dentist for you too. Don't either of you guys take any oregano nickels."

"And don't let that little chick blow your mind," Jeff said. "See you around, honkie."

Then they were gone.

■ ■ ■ ■ ■ ■ ■ ■ ■ ■ ■

Robin was sure taking her own sweet time getting back. I was starting to come down, and once I had reached the stage of knowing how high I had been half an hour ago and knowing that I wasn't that high now, I didn't feel like any more grass because while what Jeff had said didn't bother me as long as I was thinking straight, I was a cool enough head to know that pacing around waiting for her, getting higher and higher and uptighter and uptighter would—

The phone started ringing. Robin? Arlene?

I loped out of the living room, where as a matter of fact I *had* been pacing around getting uptighter and uptighter, if not higher and higher, made it to the bedroom, picked up the phone and grunted: "Hello?"

"Robin?" said an asthmatic male wheeze on the other end of the line.

"Do I sound like Robin?" I snarled.

"Hey, man, no need to get uptight. I'm not after your chick, it's strictly business, dig? Will you tell her Duke called and I just got back and I still want ten caps and she should hold them for me and—"

"How do you know I'm not a cop, Charlie?" I said.

"Hey! Hey! Stop it, man, I'm up on speed—don't go putting me on a paranoid trip!"

"Yeah, but what if I *am* a cop? What if this line is tapped?"

"Hey man, cut it out, you're not the fuzz . . . what're you doing this for? All I want is some acid, will you stop—"

"What if this call is being traced? What if there are narcs pounding their flat feet up your stairs at this very minute . . . ."

The line went dead.

I hung up the phone and went back to my pacing in the living room thinking: that was a real dirty number to pull. Fuckin' A it was! But how had that freak gotten my number? Now *there* was a stupid question! But no stupider than the answer, Robin giving my phone number to her speed-freak customers—

The phone range again. I had a premonition . . .

"Yeah?" I said belligerently into the receiver.

"Hi baby," said a soft thin girl's voice I didn't recognize.

"Robin?" I said, not really believing it was her—unless this was some kind of stupid put-on.

The girl's voice giggled. "No baby," it said, "*you're* Robin. I'm Suzy. I'm stoned, really, really stoned . . . .Hey, you're *not* Robin, are you? I mean, I'm not *that* stoned, am I? You're a *man* . . . ."

"That's the nicest thing anyone has said to me all day."

"Hey, this *is* Robin's number?"

"This is *my* number. What's *your* number?"

"Oh WoW WoW WoW! Hey man, you *do* know Robin? I haven't got a wrong number? You her old man?"

"You could say that."

"Wow, you had me going there; I mean here I am stoned out of my beautiful little old mind and I thought I had a wrong number and you could be some kind of square freako and here I am rapping to you about how stoned I am . . . .Well, look, Robin's old man, I just dropped one of Robin's caps about an hour ago and it's groovy, groovy stuff, and there are four other people here who want to take my trip with me, so if Robin will get over to Ronnie Freed's pad, we'd like to score another four caps . . . ."

"I'm sorry, I don't think Robin will be able to make it."

"Why not?"

"Because I'm an ax-murderer and I just chopped her up into a thousand pieces and flushed them down the toilet. Except for her left nipple, which I'll mail to you if you'll give me your address . . . ."

"Aaaaah! Oh shit! Eeeee!"

Click.

I felt like an awful creep even as I put the phone back on the hook: *that* I shouldn't have done. I wasn't mad at poor Suzy, wasn't her fault that Robin was giving out my number to every head in creation; I shouldn't have done such an evil thing to her, say a thing like that to someone on *acid* for chrissakes!

But that goddamn Robin. Wasn't enough she was dealing out of my pad, she had to turn me into a fucking answering-service! Getting me involved in a goddamn dealing scene! Was Jeff right? Or was she just too damned stupid to realize that it was uncool to get someone involved in a dealing scene without asking them? What the hell *was* inside her head, anyway?

I went back to my pacing, faster and faster and faster; burn the dope out of my system because I wanted to be stone-cold straight when she got back. *If* she got back. If I let her back . . . .Goddamn it, I had put all this shit behind me a thousand years ago with Anne . . . no one was going to put me on *that* bummer again.

No one!

. . . .

"What the fuck's the matter with you?" I shouted at Robin as she stood in the doorway.

She glanced nervously behind her into the hall. "Cool it, will you," she said. "I'm sorry I took so long. I've been missing a lot of connections."

I closed the door behind her and followed her into the living room. She sat down on the couch and began rolling a joint. I sat down beside her and knocked the paper out of her hand. Grains of pot went flying all over the table.

"Hey man," she crooned, "what *is* bugging you?"

"*What's bugging me?* I got two calls while you were gone from some Duke and a chick named Suzy who said she was high on your acid. They both wanted to buy some more, that's what's bugging me!"

She looked at me as if I were crazy. "But that's groovy," she said. "I've still got twelve caps I couldn't get rid of. I knew Duke wanted ten, but I couldn't get a hold of him. How many did Suzy say she wanted?"

"What the hell's the matter with you?"

"Hey . . . what *is* wrong, Tom?" she said softly, her eyes worried, genuine concern written all over her face. It made me feel like a monster of uptightness. I had to get hold of myself . . .

"You gave them my phone number, didn't you?"

"Well, of course I did. Where else would they get it?"

"You don't understand? You really don't understand, do you?"

She took my hand, squeezed it gently, studied my face. "You're not freaking out, are you?" she said. "It's gonna be all right . . . take it—"

"I'm *not* freaking out. I'm not even stoned any more. Don't you realize what you've done? You've involved me in your goddamn dealing, is what you've done. Giving my number to your customers as if I were your fucking answering-service."

"Hey, what is this?" she said a shade belligerently. "All I did was let some people know where I was so they could get to me if they wanted to score. What's all this paranoia?"

"It's a dealing scene, dammit! You don't just go and involve people in dealing scenes without bothering to ask them!"

"Oh Wow!" she snapped, her face getting hard. "Of all the square, shitty, uptight . . . ." Then suddenly her face melted. "Oh wow . . ." she said again. But this time it had the tone of an apology. "I forgot. Man, I'm sorry, I really am, I forgot you were used to *junkie* dealing scenes. Yeah, that kind of shit can be a real bummer. Wow. I can see you'd be uptight if every junkie in the world knew your number and knew a chick was dealing out of your pad . . . ."

"If you do understand, why did you go ahead and do it?"

"Because it's not like that, Tom, really it isn't. I don't deal smack, these people aren't *junkies*. You can trust them. Fred's groovy; you liked *him*, didn't you? And Jeff turned out to be someone you knew . . . ."

"A *junkie* I knew!"

"And you were once a junkie *he* knew, dig?"

That brought me up short—because next thing I would've screamed at her might've been something like "once a junkie, always a junkie," and where would that have left *me?*

Robin put her hand on my knee. "Look," she said. "I really dig you. When I'm here, I want to feel like you're my old man. So giving people the phone number is the most natural thing in the world. I never dreamed it would put you uptight. Believe me?"

I was beginning to feel like a lower and lower form of animal life with every word she said. Goddamn, maybe I *was* acting like a paranoid ex-junkie. I dug Fred and Jeff; for all I knew, Duke and Suzy were okay too. They had trusted *me* up front, and I had come on like a king-sized shit . . . .

"Yeah, I believe you," I said. "But you've gotta understand—"

She squeezed my kneecap tenderly. "But I *do* understand," she said. "You're coming on as if I were getting you into a smack-dealing scene because that's what you're used to. But it's just not like that . . . ."

"Maybe it isn't . . . I dunno, maybe it *is* just my paranoia. but I don't know if I can hack it . . . ."

She kissed my cheek lightly. "I really do understand your hangup," she said. "But try to understand me. This is my scene; it's where I'm at, and I'm not ashamed of it and I'm not going to play phony games with you or anyone else. We've gotta be honest with each other, we've gotta accept each other for what we are, or it's just no good between us. Dig?"

"Dig. But I don't know if . . . ."

"I know, I know, I'm putting you on a trip back to a lot of old shit that hurt you once. I'm telling you my scene isn't like that, but you've got to see I'm telling you the truth all by yourself. I dig you. I dig you enough to walk out the door with no regrets, if that's what you want."

"I don't want to do that . . . ."

"Then you'll have to come to peace with who I really am, because I'm just not gonna live a game for you. If you want me around, you've gotta accept what I am. Otherwise, it's been a gas . . . ."

"I dunno . . . ."

She smiled a warm human smile at me that melted my insides and made me hate my paranoia. She really wasn't asking any more of me than I was of her. She was right. But . . . but . . . .

"Oh course you don't know," she said. "I don't expect you to know right now. Look, I've gotta deal the rest of the acid anyway, why don't I split for a few days and let you think it through, okay?"

"Okay," I said. I kissed her on the lips. "You're one fucking good chick," I told her. "Maybe too good for me, is all . . . ."

She smiled, touched a finger to my nose. "You're gonna be all right," she said. "I can feel it."

"You're not just gonna split and never come back?"

She laughed. "Tell you what," she said, "I'll leave the rest of the pot here as hostage—you *know* I won't leave *that*." She began rolling a joint.

"Peace-pipe for the road?" she said.

I nodded. There was nothing wrong with her; I had to get my head straight, is all. Or maybe my head was *too* straight . . . ?

"Peace, baby," I said, lighting the joint for her.

18
Into the Briar Patch

I felt myself choking on the stale taste of Choice as I hunkered on the dusty floor of the Foundation living room between Arlene and Ted, as Harvey sat down on his folding chair, lit a cigarette, and wound up for the pitch. Not plain old choice, dig, but Choice—like: quit college, like: throw Anne out, like: cold turkey—kind of choice that leaves you with the feeling that you're gonna go down one road and never know what's at the end of the other, a whole string of potentialities about to be snuffed out of your world-line forever.

Yeah, you could taste it in the air, hear it in the silence of maybe forty people hunched forward on the floor waiting for the Word, even smell it in the insane odor of paranoid sweat that seemed to hang over the whole room. Which was probably why I was getting that scared, empty feeling in my gut—contact paranoia. I mean, after all, I wasn't hung-up in a Big Choice scene. Sure, Harvey was obviously going to take another big step towards San Francisco tonight, but that wasn't my problem, there was zero probability, no chance, forget it baby, that anything would even make me consider following the Man and his junkies into the sunset. Arlene? Not even Arlene would be worth getting sucked into a bummer like that, and besides she was so hung on New York . . . Yeah, sure, she had a heavy choice coming, and I must be picking up her vibes . . . or maybe my choice was just whether I'd make one more college try at breaking up Harvey's game, whether I'd try to make Arlene's choice for her . . . Shit, maybe I had just been smoking too much metaphysical dope lately . . . .

Harvey blew out a cloud of ectoplasmic smoke. "Well this time we know what we're here to talk about," he said, "Whether or not the Foundation will move to San Francisco . . . "

An anxious stirring among the animals on the floor: Ted was hunkered on the balls of his feet, ready to pounce; next to him, Doris was deep inside her own head; beside me, Arlene chewed her lower lip, grim and uptight as if her life were on the line.

"I've been giving it a lot of thought," Harvey said. "I've made the personal decision to go along with a move to San Francisco—but not with a simple majority vote. I think if we do move, we've got to do it as a community. And if we're going to start thinking of ourselves as a community, we can't let ourselves get trapped in a numbers game . . . ."

Community . . . was that what was eating at me? Not the Foundation, but the Brotherhood of Dope. Wasn't that what Robin was trying to get me to see—that as a member of the International Pot-Smoking Conspiracy, I couldn't very well get self-righteous about dealing as long as I was buying? Could that be the Choice whose nasty vibes I was tasting—in or out of the dope scene, and Robin only a part of it, the chick that I would keep if I came back to the Tribe, or the chick I would lose forever if I closed that door behind me . . . ?

"We've got to come to some kind of organic community decision," Harvey was saying. "A vote, maybe several votes, should be part of it, but a mathematical majority would be meaningless. We've got to reach a community consensus, a group feeling . . . perhaps even a group consciousness . . . ."

Robin had her community and she was willing to pay her dues to it. I had had a community—Junk—and baby, I had paid all the dues there I cared to. Question was, was she right, was the smack scene different than the general dope scene? Or were only the names changed to protect the innocent, whoever they were? Was it smack that made the smack-dealing scene and acid and grass that made the acid-and-grass-dealing scene—or was it Dealing itself that made any dealing scene a paranoiac's orgy? I couldn't see taking the blind chance that Robin's dealing wasn't just dirty old Dealing . . . Was I starting to get smart?

Or just getting old?

Brrr! Yeah, that was where the cold wind was blowing from: if I couldn't accept Robin for what she was, what was I but a dirty old man trying to make it with a young chick, but too scared and old and wasted to do anything but fake it . . . not really making it . . . Shit!

"So what I'd like to try tonight," Harvey said from about a thousand light-years away, "is several ways of coming to a group consensus. First, I'd like to see a show of hands of those who *really* want the Foundation to move to San Francisco. Not a vote on whether to go or not, just those who now feel *personally* committed to trying to get the Foundation to make the move."

About a dozen hands went up: Charley Dees, Rich Rossi, Tod and Judy, Bill Nelson, Bonnie Elbert, a few others who were still faces without names to me, and of course Ted, whose right hand shot into the air like a spastic Nazi at a Nuremburg rally. Noticing that she wasn't Sieg-heiling, Ted shot Doris a dirty look; Doris gave me a Gallic shrug and raised her hand too.

"Hmmm..a bit less than a third of the membership," Harvey said. "Okay, now I want to see everyone who's committed to staying in New York no matter what the Foundation does . . . ."

For a long moment, no one dared raise a hand. Then Rhoda Steiner timorously ran her hand up to half-staff. Then Mannie Davis, who had his law practice to consider. Ida. Frieda Klein, who was married to a cat who wasn't a member. Two or three others. Harvey was playing it real cagey: now he had a phony two to one majority for San Francisco.

Suddenly it got through to me that Arlene's hand wasn't up!

"Hey, how come your hand isn't up?" I hissed at her.

"What about yours?"

Huh? Jeez, that's right, I was so busy counting the house and thinking dark thoughts that I had forgotten I had a vote too. Or more likely my arm was smart enough on a cellular level not to want to take part in this farce. Still, what the hell, it was my Patriotic Obligation to vote, so up went my arm under Constitutional protest.

But Arlene still wasn't voting.

"What is this?" I said to her.

"I'm just not all that sure, Tom . . . ."

Harvey puffed on his cigarette, exhaled, said: "Well now, about half a dozen are committed to New York. Very interesting—we seem to have twice as many people deeply committed to the move as we do to staying here. Which would seem to indicate that about half of us have open minds. Now I'd like to see all those leaning towards San Francisco . . . ."

The biggest show of hands yet, maybe fifteen, including Linda Kahn; O'Brien, George Blum, Chester White, Jeannie Goodman, and Donald Warren, our Token Negro.

"And those leaning towards staying in New York . . . ."

Less than ten hands—but, thank God, Arlene's among them.

Harvey gave a plastic laugh. "No opinion?" he said.

Three or four timorous souls and/or smartasses (including Rich, who had already voted) raised their hands amidst titters.

"And finally, I'd like to see the hands of those among *all* groups who'd be willing to follow the community decision either way . . . ."

About a dozen hands went up instantly. Then more hands in

groups of twos and threes. Two dozen. Then thirty or more. Then Arlene's hand went up. And in less than a minute, everyone's hand was in the air except mine and a few of the hardcore aginners like Mannie Davis, Frieda Klein and Ida.

"What the hell are you doing?" I hissed at Arlene. "You're not *serious!*"

"We're not voting to go," she said, "just showing our confidence in the Foundation. Come on, raise your hand!"

"No chance!" I said. Harvey was sure playing a complicated numbers game. There were so many ways to vote, even overlapping votes, that I couldn't figure out what the hell he was getting at. Except that one way or another, it would end up adding up to San Francisco.

"Now let's see what all this adds up to," Harvey said. "Less than a dozen of us are committed to staying in New York no matter what. About a third of the membership is actively committed to moving to San Francisco. About half of us haven't made up our minds. But of that half about two-thirds are leaning towards San Francisco. And the overwhelming majority is willing to abide by the community decision . . . ."

I had had about as much of the Brustein Poll as I could take. "What the hell does this numbers game mean?" I yelled.

Harvey flashed me a shit-eating smile. "You're quite right, Tom," he said. "Numbers by themselves mean little; these votes are just a rough tool for determining the general state of the consciousness of the Foundation community. So let's see what we've found out qualitatively. First, and most important, I think it's obvious from the final vote that we have come to see ourselves as a community, that most of us are willing to abide by the community decision. Second, it seems clear that if we do move to San Francisco, no more than about a dozen members are committed to staying behind. Finally, it would seem that about three quarters of us are either committed to the move already or are leaning that way . . . ."

My head was spinning. Harvey had missed his calling: he should've been a tax accountant or a political statistician. Because he had neatly designed his series of votes to prove to the suckers that most of them wanted to go to San Francisco. Like they say, figures can't lie, but liars sure can figure!

And, as if on cue, Ted leaped to his feet with the capper: "Well that does it, right? Three-quarters of us want to go to San Francisco!"

Harvey smiled at him benignly. "I think you're jumping to conclusions, Ted," he said. "Only a third of us want to got to San Francisco. The others are just leaning that way . . . ."

"But almost all of us are willing to go along with the group decision," shouted Rich Rossi, another of the San Fran red-hots.

"And we *know* which way the vote'll go," said Ted. "So what are we screwing around for?"

"I don't think this is the time for a final vote," Harvey said. "But let's see . . . how many want a vote now?"

Only the hands of the dozen or so San Francisco fanatics went up. Harvey was playing it so cool I couldn't figure out what he was doing.

"Ah shit!" Ted shouted disgustedly. Then he got that awful gleam in his eyes. "Dig," he said, "let's just *pretend* we're having a final vote between New York and San Francisco. Everyone has to vote one way or the other." He looked at Harvey for approval; Harvey shrugged indifferently. Ted took it, no doubt correctly, for yes. "New York?" he said.

Something between a dozen and fifteen hands went up: all the hard-core aginers except me, all the leaning against people including Arlene, and a few of the luke-warm San Francisco people like Chester White, who were having second thoughts.

"Why aren't you voting for New York?" Arlene asked me nervously. "Come on, you're not gonna vote for San Francisco, are you?"

"I categorically refuse to take part in this farce," I told her.

"San Francisco?" Ted said with a smug grin.

A forest of hands. Maybe thirty.

"See?" Ted crowed. "A big majority wants to go and almost everyone is willing to go along with the vote. So what are we crapping around for, Harvey?"

The moment of truth: Ted had set it up beautifully for old Harv who could now say yes and still have everyone convinced that he had been pushed every step of the way.

But I had underestimated Harvey again. He still had one more finesse up his dirty white sleeve: "That's not a meaningful vote, Ted. It may be a clear indication of how such a vote would go, but it's a forced choice. It's not a truly committed vote. And I refuse to accept anything less than a genuine community consensus."

"Aw—"

Harvey held up his hand like the Living Buddha. "Tell you what,

Ted," he soothed, "let's break up the formal meeting now and chew it over. I'll call another meeting next week and then we'll be ready for a final vote. It'll give everyone a chance to really consider the reality of the situation, now that we know more or less how the vote will go. This isn't an election, after all, but an attempt to reach a real community decision. It'd take several weeks to plan the move once we decide to go, so we can surely wait one more week for a final decision. So let's just break this up and talk it over."

And so saying, Harvey stepped down off the dais and the meeting almost immediately broke up into dozens of hot little bull-sessions. Man, that had been the Master's Touch! Give 'em a week to stew in it, *knowing* what the decision was going to be! Changed the question from "Do I vote for San Francisco?" to "Do I cut the Foundation out of my life?" As a group, as a community as Harvey would put it, it was all over but the shouting. And as far as I was concerned, I had had it with the Foundation. If I couldn't talk Arlene and Ted and Doris back into their senses (and Arlene, at least, seemed no problem), they, and the rest of the Cuckoo-clock, could go take a flying leap into San Francisco Bay.

So I grabbed Arlene's hand as we got up off the floor, held Ted by the shoulder, and said: "You can't be serious, man!" Thus achieving what I wanted: Ted, Doris and Arlene formed into my own little bull-shit group around me.

"Why not?" said Ted. "What's to keep me in New York? I can set up a bike repair shop in San Francisco with no sweat, Doris can get some kind of job there, and I can get a big pad to paint in one hell of a lot cheaper than I can here."

"But who do you *know* in San Francisco?"

Ted spread his arms as if to hug the whole universe to him. "All these people here!" he said. "That's what's so great about the Foundation—when we all move together, we'll all know plenty of people in San Francisco. Like one big family!"

"Yes," Doris said rather mechanically, perhaps trying to convince herself, "it's not as if we were moving three thousand miles from home all by ourselves . . . ."

"Et tu, Doris?"

She shrugged. "New York, San Francisco, what's the difference? If Ted wants to got to San Francisco, why not? I'll miss you, though, Tom . . . ."

Ted draped his arm around my shoulder, "I'll miss you too, man,"

he said. "Shit, it's ridiculous! Why the fuck don't you come along?
It'd be great for you!"

It seemed hopeless—unless something happened out of left field,
Ted and Doris would go. Any why not? As Doris said, New York,
San Francisco, what's the difference. Of course, the *real* difference
was that it's the Foundation that counts. If not for that, I could see
how a move across the country could be a groovy thing—but not if
you took your worst hang-up along. And certainly not if following
your insanity was your reason for going!

"You know, maybe you've got something there," Arlene said.
"I've been against going all along, but I'm not sure why . . . ."

"You know why! Because you're afraid!" Ted said.

"I know that . . . but afraid of *what* . . . ?"

"Shit," said Ted, "you're afraid of what *everyone's* afraid of—being
alone, all by yourself, in a place you don't know, and where nobody
knows you. Look, do you really think New York is the best place in
the world to live, Arlene?"

"Well . . . not really, I suppose . . . "

"Of course not! You're not that unconscious. Dig, don't you see?
It's your sickness fighting for its survival. Your ego-fears telling you
that going means change. And it's right! Like Harvey once said to
me, if you want to know what to do, take a good look at what you
fear the most . . . ."

Arlene was silent for a long moment. Then she turned to me and
said: "You said something like that to me once, too. Maybe you were
right. I know damn well I've got no rational reason for staying in
New York—"

Goddamn, Ted was starting to get to her! "Bullshit!" I said.

"What do you mean bullshit? You told me to go into my fears
yourself!"

"I mean bullshit, you've got no rational reason for staying in New
York. What about college? *What about me?*"

"Ah, shit, there are colleges in San Francisco," Ted said. "And
there's no fucking reason why Tom can't go with you if you mean
that much to each other. Hell, if you *really* mean anything to Tom,
there's no reason why he shouldn't go. Yeah, . . . It's a good test of
your thing with each other. If you were really meant to be together . . . well, if Tom won't go with you to San Francisco, how can
you—"

"Hey, mind your own fucking business!"

"He's right," Arlene said flatly.

"What do you mean, he's right?" I said. "By that same stupid logic, you should stay in New York to prove that I mean something to *you!*"

"But there *is* one big difference," Ted said before Arlene could get her mouth open. "The Foundation *is* going to San Francisco. We all know it is. So if you don't go, Arlene, you're gonna be left here all alone. No more groups, no more Harvey, no nothing. That's what you'd be giving up to stay with Tom. But what will Tom have to give up to go with you? Just a crummy old job . . . ."

"*You're supposed to be my friend?*" I snapped.

"But I *am* being your friend," Ted said with humorless sincerity. "I'm being your friend and I'm being Arlene's friend too. Because the two of you belong together—in San Francisco with the Foundation!"

"Ah shit!"

"Look, I think we ought to talk this over, Tom," Arlene said, her eyes cold, her mouth grim and determined. "Alone."

"Yeah, well the smell *is* getting pretty thick in here," I said. "Okay, we'll go eat our hearts out over dinner."

As we turned to go, Ted caught my arm, stared at me with warm, concerned blue eyes. "No hard feelings?" he said quietly.

"*No hard feelings!* What the fuck's the matter with you, Ted?"

"I'm just trying to help you . . . ."

"With friends like you, who needs enemies?"

"God-damn, Tom, you need to wake up! Your mind is only half-conscious! I feel sorry for you, is all . . . "

"Yeah, well the feeling is mutual!"

I dragged Arlene through the crowded room where the San Francisco agitprop machinery was whirring along in high gear. "You and I are gonna have a long nasty talk, baby," I promised her.

19
Which Side Are You On?

I had decided to pass on Sing Wu's which, though a much better restaurant than the little joint down the street, was big and light and a little flashy, with a bar and crowds, and hardly a place to talk. The little Chinese restaurant three blocks further down Second was small, dim, obscure, undistinguished, and the kind of place you remember by location, not by name. The small, low-ceilinged, badly-lit dining room was half a flight from street level and gave you the feeling of a cool, quiet cave. The only other customers, seated as we were at little two-place tables along the walls, were a cop in uniform, two old ladies eating together, a guy that looked like a truck driver, and a scuzzy old duck about one step up from a Bowery bum. The bigger tables in the center of the dining room looked like they had last seen service in 1939.

Arlene and I hadn't said much to each other on the cab ride down—in fact we both seemed to be purposely confining the talk to where we were going to eat—and we still hadn't broken down the wall of small talk and long silences between us as I ordered dinner and the waiter plunked down a pot of tea on the table. I let her pour cups of tea for us—a very Bronx-chick thing to do—and sipped mine straight—a very hip thing to do—while she dumped a huge spoonful of sugar into hers and began stirring and stirring and stirring, staring down into the dark brown whirlpool.

"Don't you see what Ted was really doing?" I finally said from deep right field. "He wants me to go along. He figures that if you go, I'll go."

"You trying to tell me that your *friend* is using me to trick you into going to San Francisco?" Arlene said belligerently, taking a brief sip of her over-sweetened tea.

"Yeah . . . But it's not like *that* . . . it's not something sinister. Ted's nothing if not sincere. He digs me, he digs you, he thinks we should be together, he wants all of us to be in San Francisco with the Foundation where he truly believes we'll all live happily ever after, and he feels that he knows what's good for us better than we do. I'm not putting Ted down . . . I feel sorry for him."

"Why should you—"

The waiter shuffled up with the wonton soup and Arlene cooled it. I spooned broth, wontons, greens and reddish-pink slivers of pork out of the tureen and into our bowls. I tasted the soup: flat. I dribbled in a few drops of soy sauce, turning the broth a murky brown. Not exactly great, but better.

"Why should you have such a superior attitude?" Arlene said, sipping diffidently at her soup.

I suddenly realized I was hungry. Uptightness can do that to me sometimes. I started gobbling up soup and wontons, gauchely talking with a full mouth.

"Maybe because I *am* superior. I see through what's going on and you and Ted don't. A week or so ago, you wouldn't have dreamed of following old guru Harv to San Francisco. Now—"

"I know what you're going to say. Harvey maneuvered the whole thing. I'm not that dense, Tom. But what if he has? So what?"

"*So what?*"

"Look," she said, starting to eat a little heartier, "it all depends on what you think of Harvey and the Foundation. You think Harvey's a phony and the Foundation is bad. If you're right, then Harvey maneuvering everyone into going to San Francisco is an evil thing. I'll grant you that ... "

Looked like the food was starting to make her more reasonable: she was talking more calmly and the lines on her face had relaxed with the motions of chewing. Maybe it was a matter of eating up that old Oriental cool—I was feeling less combative myself.

"But?" I said. "There *is* a but ... ?"

She nodded, finishing off the last of her soup. "*But,*" she said, looking up from her bowl, "what if Harvey is a good man and the Foundation a good thing? What if he's wiser than any of us? What if he knows that a clean break with our pasts and a fresh start in San Francisco and a sense of the Foundation as a community is what we all need? What if he knows we wouldn't accept it if he told it to us? Well, then the only way to get us to help ourselves is to make us think it's our spontaneous decision. You see what I mean? If what Harvey's doing is really a good thing, then how he gets it done doesn't really matter ... "

"Der Fuehrer knows best, eh? Baby, I have not the words to tell you how slimy and evil that feels to me!"

"But you're just going with a feeling ... "

"I trust my instincts," I said.

"So why shouldn't I trust mine? My instincts tell me that Harvey is good and wiser than I am. So—"

The waiter appeared carrying three big dishes with steel covers on a metal tray. He cleared off the soup tureen and the bowls, set a big platter down in front of each of us, put the three dishes down on the table, and split.

I spooned a big mound of fried rice onto each of our platters. The other two dishes were lobster Cantonese (pieces of lobster in egg sauce) and Chinese pepper steak (beef with green peppers, onions and water chestnuts)—nothing fancy. I dumped some of the lobster on my plate. Arlene started on the pepper steak.

"Look," Arlene said while I struggled with my lobster-fork, "doesn't it all boil down to what you feel about Harvey and the Foundation? You feel he's not doing a good thing, so the move to San Francisco is just one more bad thing. I feel he's good and he knows what he's doing, so going to San Francisco is probably a good thing for me. Especially since it scares me. Ted was right about that. So were you—I'm full of fears. Maybe if I lick this one big fear, it'll be a breakthrough for me . . . "

The lobster wasn't bad. "Try some of this," I said, spooning some of it onto her plate. I took some of the pepper steak. Too greasy.

"I'll buy the fighting your fear thing," I said. "Okay, you gotta make a motion, an existential act, whatever you want to call it. But why buy Harvey's junk? Why not do something more personal?"

"Such as?"

I reached into my pocket, dangled my apartment key in front of her face.

She grimaced, seemed about to say something, hesitated, smiled, grimaced again. "You know," she finally said, "you could be right. Maybe it would be the same thing. But . . . I can't do that . . . "

I put away the key. "Because you're afraid," I said around a mouthful of rice.

"Yes . . . "

"Well, there you are . . . It *is* the same thing. If you can fight one fear, you can fight the other."

She swallowed a mouthful of food. "It's *not* the same thing," she said. "If I take that key, then it's you and me all alone and the Foundation goes to San Francisco . . . and . . . and I'm left here with you and my fears . . . and no support . . . That's a much bigger thing than going to San Francisco . . . . "

"I'm glad you finally realized that."

"*Don't you see?* If I go to San Francisco, I have the Foundation and Harvey and all the members . . . a whole community to help me with my hang-ups . . . I'd be afraid, but I wouldn't be so alone."

"You wouldn't be alone with me."

"But . . . a real relationship really scares me. You'd be the last person in the world to help me with *that* fear . . . I haven't reached that level of consciousness yet . . . I think with the Foundation's help I could, someday . . . But if I stay behind, I'll be trapped . . . I'll *never* be able to have a real relationship with you or anyone else."

"You'll never know until you try. You won't get there by just talking about it for the rest of your life."

She played with her pepper steak, stared at her plate while a vein pulsed at the hinge of her jaw. "You're right," she said, "But . . . but I'm right too. I'd like to take that key, but . . . But if it means giving up the Foundation—"

Suddenly she cut herself off. She looked at me with a thin smile arced across her face; her eyes shone with a strange kind of berserk fire.

"Do you think it could be . . . the real thing between us?" she said.

"Yes . . . "

"I think so too. And I'm willing to prove it. Are you?"

"Try me."

"I will: If the Foundation goes to San Francisco, I'm going with it; I have to. But I'll prove that you mean as much to me as the Foundation does—I'll be your . . . woman on any terms you want."

She paused, put down her fork, and stared at me with frightening intensity. "But *only* in San Francisco," she said. "That's what *you've* got to do to prove yourself to *me*; we've got to go to San Francisco together. That's fair." And she clamped her jaw into bear-trap resolution.

"*Fair?* That's asinine! Love me, love the Foundation, that's what you're saying!"

We stared at each other across the littered table, across the oriental flotsam and jetsam of a meal that was starting to turn to a cold greasy lump of lead in my stomach.

"In a way, maybe that's right," she said. "I need the Foundation; I can't survive without it. That need's part of me, so you can't have me without it . . . I'm not asking *you* to need the Foundation . . . "

"Aren't you?"

"No I'm not."

"*Sure* you're not!" I said. "You're just asking me to drag my ass all the way across the country to be with you--and all because *you* have to be with Harvey."

Her jaw trembled but didn't relax. "If you don't think I'm worth leaving New York for . . . "

"Oh shit, it's not that and you know it! You want to run away with me to Paris or Timbuktu or Cleveland, we can leave tomorrow. Anywhere but San Francisco!"

"If you really mean that, then why *not* San Francisco?"

I forced myself to shut up for nearly a minute and recover my cool. What she was really saying was, I'm willing to try making it with you if you're willing to give me a quid pro quo. All the logic was on her side. But goddamn it, a relationship between a man and a woman can't be based on horsetrader's logic!

"Okay," I said, about ten decibels lower and minus 25mg of speed less uptight, "I'm trying to understand, really I am. You need the Foundation, you say. And you want me. So I have to go with you and the old Cuckoo-clock to San Francisco. Okay, I dig: you want me, but you *need* the Foundation and you've got to go with the need over want."

"You still don't completely understand—even if I stayed in New York with you and let the Foundation go to San Francisco, it wouldn't work. Maybe part of me *wants* to do that. But I *can't*. Because I need the Foundation to get me to the point where I *can* have a real relationship with you."

"Bullshit! It's the Foundation that's keeping you from really making it with a man."

"You believe that. I don't."

I was starting to feel old and weary. We were talking in closed circles. If she was right about Harvey, I was being a stupid shit, and I should go with her to San Francisco and with the help of the Great White Father, we'd live happily and Totally Conscious ever after, after only a few decades and maybe fifty thousand bucks worth of Total Psychotherapy. But if I was right, then the more she chased her freedom into the labyrinth of Harvey's machine, the further in she'd be sucked, and if I let myself chase after her, I'd go down the rathole too.

No way we could argue rationally about Harvey: he was her god and my devil. But . . . but there was still one card left to play:

"You've got the Foundation now and you haven't taken the key. What makes you think it'd be any different in San Francisco?"

"Because . . . because if I can face my fear of leaving New York, I can face my other fears too . . . "

"You think that, you don't know it."

"I believe it."

"Because you want to believe it!"

She heaved a great sigh; all the combativeness went out of her face and she looked like a pale, lost little girl. I felt myself melting . . . melting . . .

"Oh Tom," she whispered, "I don't know . . . I just don't know . . . All I know is that I feel so lost and alone and hopeless . . . Harvey gives me hope . . . and you do too. I can't stand the thought of leaving either of you . . . If only you believed in the Foundation too . . . If you can't believe in the Foundation, couldn't you just believe in me?"

"I want to . . . "

Shit, I felt all talked out. The wall between us was a micron thin and a million miles high. I found myself wishing I *could* believe in the Foundation so I could take her in my arms and carry her to San Francisco and . . . But it was no use!

"Well what the hell," I said lamely, "the Foundation hasn't voted to go to San Francisco yet. Let's jump off that bridge when we cross it, okay?"

"We *will* have to cross it, you know," she said in a tiny voice.

"I know," I sighed. "But let's pretend for another week that we won't."

She gave me a poor brave smile. "I'm tired of talking too," she said.

We both stared at our empty plates until the waiter finally came and cleared them away and set chocolate ice cream and a fortune cookie down in front of each of us.

Arlene cracked open the crisp brown pastry, pulled out the little strip of paper, read it, pouted, and shook her head. "What's it say?" I asked.

"Hope is the mother of faith," she said softly, "but despair is its father." Then solemnly: "And yours?"

I broke open the cookie, read from the slip of paper: "You are about to take a long trip to an exotic land."

Somehow, it didn't seem all that funny.

20
Dues

Sitting around the pad Friday night nervously waiting for Robin to show up, it occurred to me that when she had called, maybe I just should've told her to get lost and take Arlene with her and I should seriously consider becoming a monk. I mean, monks don't have any problems with chicks who demand that they do *their* thing, crawl into *their* bag or else it's splitsville. Monks have their own bag and no one is about to convince a monk that he has to make *their* scene.

Only thing wrong with becoming a monk is you end up like Arlene. Which must be why monasteries are so heavy behind silence—if you had all those monks gibbering at each other, each one sure he was into The One True Faith and determined to drag all the others into his bag with him, they'd chew each other to bits like a school of famished piranhas. Naw, I really couldn't cut it as a monk—if I were the True Believer type, I might as well make my One True Faith the Foundation and go with Arlene to San Francisco and at least get laid for my trouble, which is more than your monk gets for *his.*

Of course, there was always Robin (where *was* she), and the more I thought about the heavy dues Arlene demanded, the better Robin looked. Robin didn't ask for anything from me—except that I shouldn't ask anything from her. She accepted me for what I was— even accepted that she couldn't quite understand exactly where I was at—and all she wanted in return was that I accept her for what *she* was.

Yeah—but the only thing keeping me from making it Robin all the way and to hell with Arlene *was* what Robin was: namely, a dealer.

Ah yes, there was the crunch! Maybe I was just a prisoner of my junkie past—a smack dealer, let's face it, is just about the lowest form of vertebrate life: a creature either driven by slobbering need if he's a junkie or by something nameless and far, far worse if he's the kind who never touches the stuff. I couldn't help it, that was the kind of dealer I had known.

But maybe Robin was right—maybe I was just thinking like a dirty old junkie, emphasis on the word *old.* It was sure true that grass and hash and acid were *not* junk. I still dug good old *cannabis sativa* in any form, and acid had been a good trip. Robin's customers weren't junkies and neither was I, any more. Where did I come off being self-righteous about her selling what I was buying? Shit, that was plain old square hypocrisy—I had no moral grounds for putting down Robin's dealing.

If I was honest about it, I'd have to admit that my objection was nothing more than gibbering paranoia. Fear of The Heat. Fear of paying nameless Dues. Fear of Fear itself, which, of course, is the scariest fear there is. I mean, how do you fight Nameless Dread?

Answer: by faking it, by walking straight into it, by acting as if it weren't there.

I sighed and relaxed against the back of the couch. Once I had bored to the center of my navel it turned out that the right thing to do was what I had instinctively done for openers: told Robin to come on over. If only I could stop thinking and just act on instinct the way I told everyone else—

A knock on the door. An omen? Why not? What was an omen but a random event you used to convince yourself that the universe intended you to do what you were damned well going to do anyway . . .

And of course it *was* Robin at the door, looking so pure and tasty and ferally innocent with her big dark eyes and long loose hair and total certainty that total certainty was a drag that I felt a hundred years old just looking at her and not being able to simply groove with her and turn the word-garbage machine in my head off forever.

"You look kind of uptight," were the first words she said. Feelings—she could read feelings as if she had absolute emotional pitch. And her only morality was the morality of flesh and gut. That was the way to be—if I could find some way of being it.

"Decisions, decisions, alla time decisions!" I said, leading her into the living room.

She sat down on the couch, and as I sat down beside her, she said: "I get vibes that you're hung-up on more than my dealing. That Arlene chick and her cartoon freak-show?"

I nodded. "Don't want to bug you with it," I grunted.

"I don't mind."

"I know you don't mind. That's why I won't bug you with it. If you *did* mind, I'd drive you nuts crying on your shoulder. Dig?"

"I dig. You've gotta make up your mind about me and you've gotta make up your mind about old Arlene. Poor Tom . . . You know what your problem is?"

"Yeah, I know what my problem is."

"No you don't. Your problem is that you're all hung up on *like* problems. Where you're at now is all mixed up with where you were and where you think you're going. If you could shake that, you wouldn't be uptight. Bummers happen, but you can't do anything about them. Don't worry about the future—it's all bad anyway, I mean, look far enough into the future and you're dead, so what's the point? Life is now."

"That's another great theory," I said. "If I believed it, it would be groovy. Probably I want to believe it. But I don't and I can't. So what can I do about it?"

"You can give your mind a good blow, man," Robin said. She pulled two caps out of her pocket. "Five hundred mikes of good acid apiece. Let's take a trip together and just let it happen. That's how it all began between us ... "

Staring at the caps in her palm, I knew dead-certain that this was why I had told her to come on over, this was what I had secretly hoped for, this was what I needed. Magic. A leap into the unknown. Something to turn off the word-machine and let the universe speak. In my gut, Nameless Dread. The caps seemed to pulse in her hand. I was suddenly afraid to drop acid with my head in the state it was in ...

Which was why I had to do it.

"Come on man, stop all that thinking! Do you—"

"Don't waste the sales-pitch, baby," I told her, taking a cap from her hand.

We held the caps up to our mouths, paused. Robin grinned. "To us, baby," she said.

"To now ... "

And we both dropped a cap dry.

■ ■ ■ ■ ■ ■ ■ ■ ■ ■

Now:

Sitting on the couch waiting for the acid to hit and trying to remember what it had felt like last time it had started to hit and remembering that last time it had started to hit about the time I found myself wondering what it would feel like when it started to hit—

"I think I'm getting high," I told Robin.

Robin smiled like glass flashing in the sun and said: "You're not really high till you stop thinking about whether you're high."

"What I can't stand about you," I said super-pompously, "is your higher-than-thou attitude."

A woods-elf smile. *"Now* you're high, baby."

Now I *must* be high: I felt like I was an impersonal viewpoint positioned in time a moment ahead of myself watching myself being high a moment in the future. But a straight part inside me kept saying "if *that's* not high, what is!" which told me that I had not yet surrendered entirely to the wings of acid flapping my great bird of night.

Thing to do was surrender entire—so I've been told by gurus of acid wailing on half my LPs—that was it, the big flash ego-death consciousness-orgasm, a true death of the mind because the you that went in was not the you who came out. But looking into the vortex of the obsidian waters within, I didn't quite feel ready to take that deep-six flying leap into oneness with the forces of roulette-wheel magic yawning hole into acid's nuclear phoenix ultimate power of heaven and/or hell . . .

"Not quite ready for that trip yet," I mumbled.

"What . . . ?" Robin drawled from some other continuum.

"I—"

Suddenly I popped into a universe where I dug my feeling shining out from Arlene's eyes. Saw that *my* fear was her fear was her desire was my desire—to flip her being through the void inside and die for a moment to be reborn on the other side. Her fear of orgasm that was a little taste of the big flash trip through the Shadowed Valley was what made her fuck in uptight frenzy—because she needed the taste like a junkie needs junk. But in the throes of The Surge just when it was hitting, fear of The Big Nothing forced her to hold back gibbering with fear and self-thwarted desire. And I was the cat with the karmic muscle to lean in and push her over if she let me get inside her skin; so she feared me and wanted me like a forty-year-old virgin locked up with a rapist-gorilla; and that prove-you-love-me-by-coming-to-San-Francisco bit was bullshit from the Arlene inside that wanted to shove my mind through the Foundation machinery so we'd be even, so I'd die my own kind of death, not of the cunt, but of the mind. Yeah, and that was acid: love's ego-merging-death-orgasm-bottled, processed and transliterated to a solitary masturbatory come of the mind. And that was what I feared and desired. And that was why I hung around the Foundation sniffing the glue-fumes of blowing minds. And that was why junk. And Anne.

And Robin?

But Robin was Acid itself—the vortex inside brought to the surface in a storm of black clouds and bright lightning was all possibilities of good and evil from a continuum where good and evil merged into raw neutral power. And what I needed and what she was trying to give me was the courage to ride that black eagle of power to the far corners of wherever it went.

"You're a witch," I said. "You're a witch, but that's all right, I'm grooving behind it."

"And I'm grooving behind—"

Came a rapping at our chamber door. "'Tis the fuzz and nothing more . . ."

"Don't freak!" Robin warned with ridiculous uptightness, not realizing that *my* uprightness was beginning to melt away like fog in the sun, seeing that one leap of courage could one way or another put it all behind.

Robin came back from the door trailing Terry Blackstone trailing a big blond decaying beachboy type: the All-American Boy after a thousand years of heroin and faggotry, wearing a white leather trench coat over tan buckskin pants and tooled cowboy boots. Clearly a crazed California-Gothic dealer with mad blue eyes like homing signals for the narcs. For the first time, I understood the cosmic truth of the New York saying: "California is where you go to get busted."

Terry Blackstone managed a nervous nod at me, but there was a slavering behind his shaded eyes as if he were a *thing* the California heavy-bread man was leading on a leash. "Are you stoned, baby?" he asked Robin anxiously.

"We both just dropped five hundred mikes."

"Oh shit!" His face grew so frantic I could see red-coal pig-eyes boring through the black glass of his shades. "Look Robin, you're just gonna have to maintain. This is the chance of a lifetime, bottles of acid, we'll be rolling in bread, you gotta—"

"Stop gibbering, you freak, *we're* stoned, not you!" I suddenly snarled. Robin gave me a poisonous look, but the Creature That Ate California gave me a television commercial smile full of rotten A-head teeth, and said in a rich-but-asthmatic voice: "You this chick's old man? Blackstone here says the chick has connections—must be true, otherwise a thing like him wouldn't be willing to split his cut, now would he? This is the deal. I got two ounces of acid on me—"

"*TWO OUNCES!*" Robin and I screamed.

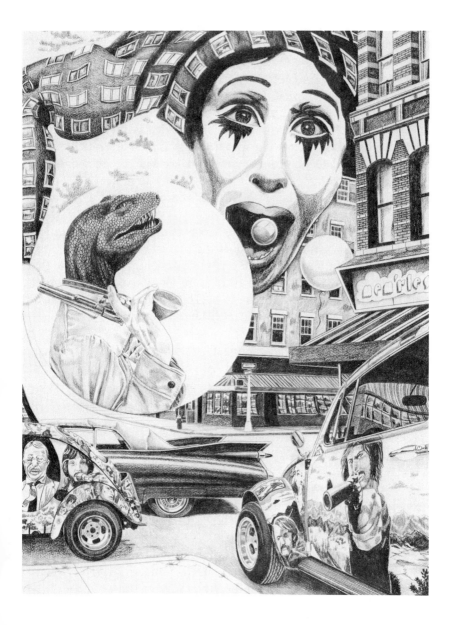

The Ice Lizard

"That's what I was trying to tell you, dig—"

"Shut up creep!" said the moldy Mr. America. "I'll do the talking, if you don't mind. Call me Tex—it's not my name. I got reasons I gotta make it out of the country by last week which you'll be happy to hear are none of your business and I need heavy bread fast. A syndicate's getting up the bread for one ounce and I'll have that by tomorrow. As soon as I get it, I'm on the plane. But between now and then I gotta deal a fucking ounce of acid. Things being what they are, I gotta deal fast, and fast means cheap. So this is the deal: your chick here takes us around to her connections and we sell the acid cheap and quick. Fifty percent of everything we get you three get to keep. How you split that up is your problem. Let's move it. I got a car waiting outside."

It finally got through to me that Tex was talking to me, not to Robin. Yeah, well wasn't I the head of the household? Smelling bust all over it. But half the proceeds of an ounce of acid! More money than I could make in a year. And something else too whispering the voice of acid in my blood said was time to be The Man in Command destiny calls don't be afraid can only die in flash of freedom . . .

"Two ounces?" I said again.

Tex opened his white leather coat, pulled two medicine bottles out of an inside pocket, each one filled with about an ounce of clear fluid.

"I believe . . . " Robin sighed. "Man, I believe!"

"Well come on," Terry Blackstone said. "Fifty-fifty split, okay Robin? Ditch this square and let's—"

"Hold it Fred!" I barked like a paranoid sergeant. "Nobody ditches me. Who do you—"

"Aw fuck off, you—"

I wrapped myself in the sinister cloak of The Man in Black. Shadows shifted perspectives in the room. Tex caught it, gave me a let's-see-you-work smile, and waited like a carrion bird behind the blue ice of his eyes.

"I don't see why we shouldn't ditch *you*," I drawled. "It's Robin's connections the man needs. Nobody needs you."

Terry turned to the freak in the white leather coat. "I brought you here, man! You're not gonna let this creep . . . "

Tex the Ice-Lizard laughed silently.

"Aw come on, Robin . . . "

Robin gave me a proud, glass-melting smile. "Talk to Tom," she said softly, "he's my old man."

"All right, Terry, show you I'm a sport," I said. "You're in for a third of our end."

"A third? Hey—"

"Take it or leave it," said The Man in Black.

Tex smiled. Terry Blackstone wilted into a sullen dwarf with treachery behind his beaten eyes.

"And don't think you can play games because we're stoned," said The Man in Black. "I killed someone for that once."

Terry Blackstone didn't seem quite ready to swallow the lie whole—but Tex turned to me and said: "Murder on acid's the biggest flash of all, ain't it?"—and Terry quivered in dread. Only then did I see what I was getting myself into: Tex had not been jiving and Terry knew it, was why he was scared shitless, takes one to know one, he figured.

"If you freaks have finished psyching each other out," said the voice of I-Groove-Behind-Killing-On-Acid, "let's get our asses into gear. We got a shitload of acid to sell."

I didn't even have to think about it; just made it into the bedroom to get my coat, Yassah, Massah. This Tex-thing was a monster cartoon-character out of Terry and the Pirates as rewritten by William Burroughs—The Man in Black, but actually standing out there in a white trench coat for real. And just for the dumbshit silly kick of mindfucking Terry Blackstone, I had gone and convinced this slobbering space-monster that The Man in Black was for real! Now I *had* to play it for real, and bombed out of my head on acid . . .

Which was the only light-bulb in the current comic strip: the acid said, groove behind playing it for real, dues you gotta pay suddenly come due, it's the trip you've been sniffing after baby, and your only other choice leads to an even bigger dose of Condition Terminal— crucifixion on acid by the Thing That Ate California with me in the role of O.D.ed J.C.

So when I got back into the living room, I had my cloak of darkness furled around me—but better believe it, under it I was shivering.

"You been in there a long time, man," said Tex California. "You wouldn't have gotten a piece?"

"You wouldn't be asking me if I had a piece unless you were prepared to find out in some unpleasant manner," said The Man in Black.

The very air seemed to cringe. Robin looked at me wide-eyed, thinking maybe she had never seen me before; T. Blackstone looked as relaxed as a junkie in withdrawal; even Tex California looked a bit like he had run up against an unexpected wall.

"No need to get uptight," he said. "I'll remember that's a bad question to ask. To show you how honest I am, I'll even tell you up front that I *do* have a piece. There, now doesn't that make you feel all warm and secure?"

The fucking Man in Black had done it again. Now I had convinced an armed berserker that I had a gun! Yet somehow, the trip hadn't yet turned into a total bummer—with destiny in control, I found a new faith in the blind forces behind it all. I had to believe that Acid, if not God, was on my side.

Because if It *wasn't* on my side . . .

■ ■ ■ ■ ■ ■ ■ ■ ■ ■ ■

Outside, double-parked and blocking the narrow street, Tex California had the car I knew he would have: an old red Cadillac convertible in mint condition. At least the top wasn't down!

Robin and I in the back seat, Tex behind the wheel, and Terry Blackstone up front beside him in what is sometimes unfortunately referred to as the Death-Seat by statistically-minded safety-freaks.

"Let's go cross-town to Fred's," Robin said. "Him and all his head-professor friends are having a party. It's a fancy crowd; those cats have bread."

She gave Tex Byzantine instructions on how to get to Fred's loft in the lower West Village and after a kamikaze tour through traffic during which I couldn't have had more than a couple dozen heart attacks, we were parked outside an old loft building on Greene Street. Of course Fred's loft was on the sixth floor. It always is. Grunting and cursing in our private freak-outs, we chain-ganged up the stairs. Robin pounded her fist against the metal-plated door one flight down from the roof. Again.

The door opened to the sound of voices over acid-rock music, and Fred's face above a tie-and-collar peered out.

"Robin?" he said nervously. "Ah . . . er . . . ah . . . who are your friends?"

He had been referring to the California Lizard and his tame Terry Blackstone who definitely was suffering from lack of *something*— tossup between smack or speed. I had been lurking behind them, and when I stepped out, trying my best to look like a literary agent, Fred seemed mightily relieved. "Oh, it's you, man. The two guys with you—they're . . . all right?"

I calculated the chances of grabbing Robin, shoving us inside Fred's pad and slamming the door behind us before Tex California could draw and run amok. They weren't bad. But then what? We'd be trapped inside a pot party with a crazed monster with a gun shooting his way inside. What could we do about *that?* Call the cops and all get busted?

"Salt of the Earth," I lied. Then, with a surge of conscience-driven honesty: "Don't worry, they're not narcs."

Inside was a big dim loftful of toney West Village hip college prof small-time serious actor lower-echelon publishing crowd in uncasual casuals and a captive cloud of pot-smoke. The Doors were freaking out unnoticed on a stereo set a low volume and it looked insanely like a low-budget Hollywood cocktail party except half the extras were smoking joints.

Fred stood by the door with us not quite knowing what to do next. It was like we cartoon-characters had suddenly invaded a French intellectual feature-film of New York Bohemia. The genteely-stoned gapers didn't know whether to laugh or sneer or get uptight at the appearance of these quaint characters out of their own heroic mythology. I felt incredibly weird—I remembered what Dirk and Dickie were trying to shove on me and what it was was a trip out of the cartoon and into the feature film. But digging the people in the feature film not having any more idea than I did of who was real and who was not, I wondered if *anyone* knew.

But Tex California had no trouble deciding whose reality we were in. "Look," he said loudly, still standing by the door, "I got no time for bullshit, so I'll come right to the point." Every eye in the room zoomed in on him, fascinated by the gross-out.

He reached inside his coat and pulled out a medicine bottle of acid. "This is pure acid," he said, "and I've gotta sell it all tonight." He appraised the crowd with pawnbroker's eyes. "I've gotta let this stuff go for almost nothing. So for fifty bucks, you get to dip a one-inch square of paper into the bottle. It's *pure acid.* You'll get enough for dozens of trips. I'm taking a beating, but I gotta do it!"

Faces flapped open like dying fish. Ah, we wowed 'em in Peoria! They were all smashed on grass for openers and suddenly you had a whole roomful of stoned intellectual potheads who didn't know what the fuck was coming off. Reactions ranged from slavering greed to gibbering paranoia.

Fred seemed to see fuzz under every speck of dust. "Robin," he hissed, "get this guy the fuck out of here!"

Fred turned to me in pure panic, begging with his eyes for me to do something. Standing to one side of Tex California with Robin, I had an overwhelming urge to melt into the woodwork. Behind Tex, Terry Blackstone was bobbing and weaving like a punchy pug. Yeah, I could see how a thing like us could look like the end of the world to the feature-film players.

"Look man," Fred finally said to Tex California in the lamest phony-brotherly voice the world has ever seen, "I don't want to come on antsy, but this is a private party and dealing acid in someone's pad in pretty uncool. You can stay if you cool it man, but—"

"Screw your party," Tex California said coldly. "I just want to sell some acid. Don't give me a hard time."

A plastically-pretty chick in a mini-skirted black dress shrilled: "Who does that creep think he is?"

Fire behind Tex California's ice. "Shut up, cunt," he advised sagely.

Terry Blackstone was already inching towards the door. Robin leaned closer to me. Fred folded his tents, having just realized that he wasn't talking to one of his pot-smoking students and finally waking up enough to be scared.

But of course, some big dumb dick with a bald head, and black beard and a fancy shirt full of muscles elbowed his way through the lowing cattle and, like a member of Hip Rotary, stuck his stupid puss in Tex's face and snarled: "Watch how you talk to my chick, motherfucker!"

Tex California gave off fumes like a volcano about to go nova. "Get this shit-eating prick out of here," he said to Fred. "If you don't, I'll kill him."

Beard-and-muscles lifted his arm and formed a fist. Tex's hand went into his right outside coat pocket and came out with a large caliber revolver, the point of which he proceeded to place against the Defender of Feminine Honor's nose.

I—

—Flashed: a gun he's really got a gun gonna use it used it before a gun a gun jesus oh jesus oh god brains and guts and blood all over everything kill him murder him death cops murder electric chair fry you till you die forever and ever—

Tex California

—Snapped away from the unfaceable, saw the scene stopped in freeze-frame: the Bearded Jerk turned to stone by the pistol, crowd in the room frozen to immobile monuments to horror, Terry Blackstone caught in a crouch, Robin plastered to my side in terror, Fred's mouth wide open and Tex California's eyes drooling insanely behind his statue of cool sucking up the surge of a death to come.

"Whimper, you mother!" Tex cobra-hissed. "Ask me to let you suck my prick." Nobody dared move.

"I'm not kidding, you cocksucker! Ask to suck my prick or I'll blow your brains against the wall."

Dead silence and crystal stillness. Then a tiny whimper escaped the lips of the cat with the gun pressed against his nose. His eyes started to roll—he was going to freak! And Tex would go apeshit! The creep was totally psycho—one loud scream and he'll start to shoot!

"Cool it, you fucking psycho!" The Man in Black suddenly said, cold and clear.

Tex and his gun whirled around and I found myself staring straight into a bottomless hole into final darkness. Up that cold metal hole spurted wave after wave of electric blackness—and something inside me inverted and I found myself riding the bird of death. Death looked up at me with his single steel-stalked eye and I sucked it up and threw it back into the neon-blue eyes of the California Lizard.

"*I'm* stoned, not you, fuck-up," I said with cosmic coolness. "Look what the fuck you've gone and done, pulling a gun in a place like this! There'll be cops all over us if you shoot this jerk."

Tex's white porcelain cool suddenly shattered. "Cops? Whatdaya mean, cops? They don't have any idea of where I—"

Oh shit, the fuzz were after him too! "They fucking-A will know where you are an hour from now, asshole," said The Man in Black. "One of these squares'll be sure to call 'em after this!"

Tex spun on the room, waving his gun. "If anybody talks--"

"Nobody'll talk," Fred whined. "Far as we're concerned, you've never been here, right everybody?"

"Right!" "Right!" "Right!"

"Okay, now all of you want to buy some acid—"

"*Are you out of your mind?*" I screamed at him. "We've got to get out of here! Now!"

"What the hell for?"

Goddamn, he was stupid! "How do you know there aren't any

narcs in the house? How do you know someone hasn't *already* called the cops? There's a couple of other rooms back there."

"But I gotta deal this acid—"

"You dumb jive motherfucker!" The Man in Black howled at Tex, reaching significantly into his coat pocket. "You're not gonna deal your fucking acid if we're in the fucking *joint!* You don't get your ass out of here, *I'll* blow *your* brains out."

It sure wasn't fear that iced over the fire in Tex California's mad blue eyes—but suddenly he must've realized what he had been doing. He smiled a broken smile at me. "Yeah, well maybe I got carried away," he said. "No need to get excited. Your chick's got some other places to go, let's split."

And my moment of control went as quickly as it came as Tex California led us out of the loft and on a crazy race down the endless dark flights of stairs to the street.

"You better come up with something better than that," Tex California told Robin as we got into the car. Terry Blackstone curled up in the front seat beside him like an aging fetus. Beside me, Robin was like a plastic doll with things wrong inside: smiling and shivering and looking at me with now-vacant, now-uptight, now-greedy eyes.

"Stop freaking my chick out," I told Tex California.

"You know," he said ominously, "you got a big mouth, friend."

"Not half as big as yours, friend," said The Man in Black. I had already gone over the Big Edge with the California Space Monster, backed his piece down in front of the marks. No turning back now, it was his cool against mine, mano a mano—could I con myself into believing it was an even fight with Acid on my side?

"All right, all right, so I flipped a little in there. So what? So worst thing that could've happened, I kill that square. Could happen to anyone, man. He was coming on real rank . . . "

"Maybe you *like* the fuzz looking for you . . . "

"Look man," said the California Lizard, "I got Feds after me already, why do you think I've gotta get out of the country? All the same trip, baby: when you've killed one man, you've killed 'em all."

I started to shiver. *The cat's for real,* I tried to convince myself, but I couldn't believe it; the acid told me with mathematical logic it was all one big comic book trip. There was no *real* Tex California; he was just some character out of some other reality's trip.

"Yeah, well you blew selling maybe a thousand bucks worth of acid," I told him, "and don't blame that on my chick."

"Yeah, yourself, well your chick better come up with something or I got no reason to keep you creeps alive."

Terry Blackstone whimpered. Robin seemed to snap back to fear-driven reality. "The Meat Factory," she said.

"The *what?*"

"The Meat Factory. It's a group. But they all deal a lot on the side. They got a big pad over on Avenue C."

"That sounds more like it," said Tex California.

"Hey man hey man hey man . . . " Terry Blackstone started gibbering. "Anybody got any speed . . . need some speed weed reed need some speed . . . "

"Shut up, you shitty speed-freak!" Tex said, slamming the back of his hand into Terry Blackstone's mouth as he pulled the Cad away from the curb.

■ ■ ■ ■ ■ ■ ■ ■ ■ ■ ■

The Meat Factory's pad was an incredible combination of electronic opulence and oriental squalor. All rooms of the apartment had been collectivized into one giant opium-den by the simple process of knocking down the interior walls with a sledge-hammer (jagged plaster scars on floor and ceiling). Against the far wall were three or four monster amplifiers and about ten thousand dollars worth of more esoteric and amorphous electronic bric-a-brac. Angled off this East Village IBM complex was the complete Shooting Gallery: a musty blue couch and a table in front of it holding spikes and pieces of rubber tubing and various other junkie and/or crystal-freak works.

As a matter of fact, a cat with long straight black hair dressed all in blue denim was knotting a length of rubber tubing around the arm of a fat girl with pimples as an emaciated bearded, bald freak of maybe twenty-five opened the door with a joint in his hand. Looking inside past him, I saw, in addition to the needle-freaks fixing, a couple balling with their clothes on on one of the mattresses that carpeted the floor. A charming establishment Robin had dragged us to.

Terry Blackstone, however, thought it was just fine. Almost before the cat in the doorway could wheeze "Robin?" he pushed in front of all of us, stuck his head inside the doorway, and shouted: "Hey man, you guys got any speed in there?" The fuckers kept fucking; didn't miss a beat. The cat fixing up the chick grunted "Yeah" and like something on drippy tentacles, Terry Blackstone slithered inside.

Even Tex California wasn't quick enough to stop him, though he grabbed a good fistful of air trying.

"Hey Robin, what the fuck's going on here?" said the cat holding the joint, as if about to say, hey, we run a respectable establishment.

"You guys want to buy a lot of acid cheap?" Robin said, coming right to the point. "*Real* cheap?"

"Well come right in," said the bearded cat with a y'all come flourish. We came in.

Terry Blackstone was already pleading with the cat in the Shooting Gallery. The girl had already taken her shot and was nodding on the couch dreaming sweaty fat-girl dreams. The couple was in the process of coming, and off in a dim corner of the room (which was lit by a single bright blue light) another cat with long stringy blond hair was diddling a disconnected electric guitar.

As the couple came and groaned, Terry Blackstone whined in inverted vibrational harmony: "*Sheee* . . . just gotta have some speed . . . "

"Why should I give you a taste, man?" Blue Denim said. "You got any bread?"

"Got something better than bread," Terry Blackstone cackled shrilly.

"How much acid you say you guys have for sale?" the bald doorkeeper said loudly. The guitarist's head swiveled our way in a sweep of blond hair. The needle-freak toying with Terry Blackstone pricked up his ears at the word.

"One ounce," said Tex California.

"*AN OUNCE OF ACID?*" shrieked the guitarist. Blue Denim gaped. Baldy took a long drag on his joint. The guy balling the chick on the floor rolled off her and stared up at us through steel-rimmed glasses. The skinny chick on the floor with him zipped up her Levis and sat up. Even the nodding fat girl opened her eyes.

"Ah bullshit!" Baldy said. "Nobody ever had an ounce of acid around here . . . "

Tex California brought out the bottle. "Jesus Christ," the just-fucked chick said.

"Is that *really* acid?" Blue Denim said, getting up and joining Baldy who was peering dimly at the bottle. The guitarist joined the mystic circle, then Steel-Rims, finally his chick. The fat girl was too far gone to move and Terry was using the opening to grab for the works on the table.

"It's acid," said Tex California.

"How do we know it's acid?" asked the guitarist.

"Are you called me a liar?" Tex California inquired.

"I just don't believe in Santa Claus," the guitarist said. "That'd be an awfully expensive bottle of water to buy. Unless you want to wait around till we take it and see if we get high."

"You'd need a chem lab to cut it into doses," Tex said.

Steel-Rims giggled. "We got it," he said.

"I don't have the time to wait around here while you try it," the California Lizard said.

"That doesn't exactly give me a trusting feeling," said Baldy.

Tex started to flare, caught a glimpse of me, cooled it. "Tell you what," he said. "Terry here is our partner, right Terry?"

"Right man," Terry said, pulling the needle out of the pit of his elbow and unwrapping the tubing from his arm.

"You guys know Terry?" Tex asked. Somewhat unenthusiastic nods. "Then you know what a paranoid freak he is. Terry, you know that's real acid, don't you?"

"Sure man," Terry said.

"Okay," said Tex California, "so our partner stays here till you're satisfied. If you get burned, you can always kill him. Got that Terry? Are you scared?"

Seemed to me Tex had laid an awful lot on a very weak commodity. But Terry was paranoid enough to know not to act scared even though he must've been scared shitless despite having no reason: "No man, I'm not scared."

"You got a deal," Blue Denim said. "But we can't buy all that. What are your prices?"

"How much money you got."

"First tell me your prices," Blue Denim insisted.

"Tell you what," said Tex. "You tell me how much bread you got and I'll tell you how much acid it'll buy and I guarantee it'll blow your minds."

"How much we got, treasurer?" the guitarist asked.

Steel-Rims did some arithmetic in his head: " . . . kilo last week . . . the smack deal . . . about two thousand dollars."

"Told you these cats had bread," Robin said.

Tex California did not seem happy. "Fuck it . . . " he muttered under his breath. Then: "You guys got a medicine dropper?"

Blue Denim rummaged around the Shooting Gallery till he found a medicine dropper. He handed it to Tex.

Tex opened the bottle, stuck in the tip of the dropper, and sucked up an inch of acid. "Think that's about two thousand dollars worth of acid?" he said.

"Oh wow!"

"Get the bread, man, get the bread!"

Steel-Rims fished a giant roll of bills out from under one of the mattresses and started counting it out. Sacramental silence until he was finished. He handed the money to Tex, who pocketed the bottle, handed the dropper to the guitarist who handled it like the Holy Grail, and slowly counted the money.

As Tex counted the money, the guitarist said: "Look, will you take an amp and a guitar? Man, I don't know why you're selling so cheap, and I don't care, but you can have anything in this pad . . . "

"Shit, you can even have Suzy," Steel-Rims said, pointing to the recently-fucked chick. "She gives great head."

Tex ignored them and finished counting the money. Sticking it in his pants pocket, he said: "Cash and cash only."

"But man—"

"Are you guys cleaned?"

"Yeah, but listen—"

Tex turned his back on the entire scene, and to Robin and me said: "Let's split."

We split.

■ ■ ■ ■ ■ ■ ■ ■ ■ ■ ■

"This is getting us nowhere fast," Tex California said as we got into the car. "Chick, you gotta come up with some real heavy-bread men."

"What about Terry?" Robin said in a tiny voice. "I mean, it really *is* acid . . . ?"

The California Lizard turned and leered his rotten teeth into the back seat at us. "Does it really matter, chick?" he said.

Robin turned pale, clutched my hand, stared at the convertible roof and giggled. Either I was too high or not high enough because something working my vocal cords made them say: "Fucking-A it does! If you burned those freaks, they just might do it to Terry and Terry knows Robin and Robin knows me—"

"But you don't know me," said Tex California.

"If you burned those guys, I'd see to it that New York got mighty hot for you ... "

Tex California laughed an ugly laugh. "Who gives a shit?" he said. "The whole United States is too hot for me as it is. I might as well be radioactive."

He paused for effect. "Now that you know what the scene is, what the fuck you think you can do about it?"

The cold of the night seemed to seep in through the windows. The California Lizard was wanted by the Feds, a killer behind acid had pulled a gun thrown Terry Blackstone to the wolves—how could anyone believe he was above burning The Meat Factory? Who in turn were probably not above wasting Terry or Robin or me ...

At that moment, I crossed over the line, flashed all the way, cut the anchor to the shores of my life—my fate was in the hands of a psycho murderer on his way out of the country one step ahead of the Feds and god-knows who else; my life was spinning on the roulette wheel of the gods and there was not one fucking thing I had to say about it.

"Dig," said Tex California, "I got no reason not to put pure water in the bottle." Then with a horrid smile: "And that's why you can trust me when I tell you the acid is the real thing. Now ain't I just put you through some interesting changes?"

Then he turned around, started the motor, and was all business. "Come on chick let's find some real dealers. Enough of this fucking around. You *do* know some real dealers?"

Robin came back long enough to say, "I know a pad up-town ... crash pad for dealers coming through town ... " But she seemed awfully uptight about something. "I don't like to go there ... "

"Sounds like just what we want," the California Lizard said.

"But ... I don't like to go there ...." in a tiny scared voice.

■ ■ ■ ■ ■ ■ ■ ■ ■ ■ ■

The dealers' crash pad was an apartment in a cruddy building in an obscure Puerto Rican neighborhood in the East Twenties. Only two flights up: class.

Robin knocked on a black door with no less than three shiny new brass locks showing. A sound of lots of hard metal chittering inside, and then the door opened just enough for a tall spade in a red double-breasted silk suit with a huge bush of natural to peer out into the hall.

"Robin. Friend of Manfred's. Business. Big."

The spade ushered us into a pitch black kitchen, closed two door locks and a police lock behind us, and opened the door to the inner sanctum—

A big room all painted a Day-Glo blue seared your eyeballs to look at with an electric orange carpet wall-to-wall and hot red light from a ceiling fixture, felt like the inside of a blast furnace or a nuclear reactor. Low black backless couches formed three sides of a continuous rectangle rimming the walls. An inner rectangle of gleaming white formica tables surrounded the huge stereo rig at the reactor's core. The stereo was playing some ghostly kind of acid rock that was mostly ultra- and sub-sonic; felt it with my skin more than heard it, so creepy. On the tables were several ounces of pot, three big brass hookahs and two huge bricks of hash. The air was full of smoke. On one of the couches, a long-haired cat in a white suit, white tie, and black shirt, sucked on his hookah. On another, an A-head type, white, but with a bush of blond natural as huge and wiry as the spade's, also in an expensive mod suit, this one kelly green. Near where we stood, I could see a light behind a closed door, heard girls muttering from within.

"Well?" said the spade.

"This is . . . uh . . . Tex," Robin said. "He's got a lot of acid to sell and he's selling it cheap."

The cat with the hookah giggled.

"Well now, the little chicky has brought us a big horse-trader out of the wild west," the spade said. "Well now, I'm Ali, and those creatures are Marvin and Groove, Mr. Tex-ass. Now what's all this about acid? We're not exactly in the market for a box of sugar cubes."

"If you're trying to impress me, you're wasting your mouth," said the California Lizard. "I gotta get rid of an ounce tonight." He palmed the bottle. Ali oohed.

"I'm Marvin," said the cat with the hookah. "Do sit down."

Tex sat down next to Marvin. Ali sat down on the other side of Tex, boxing him in. Robin and I huddled together on the empty couch and tried to fade into the woodwork. You could smell Dope Power in the air.

"Can you guys handle it?" asked Tex California.

"Well now, I think we can scrape the bread together," Ali said. "First we've gotta be sure it's acid, though."

"I got no time to wait for you to get high," Tex said. But he said it nice and easy and matter-of-factly—these were *heavy* cats.

"Won't take but a minute," Groove wheezed. "I'll shoot some."

Shoot it?? The cat was out of his mind!

Groove reached into his inside breast pocket and took out a black leather case. In the case was a hypodermic syringe.

Tex looked at the spike as Groove took it from the case as if suddenly confronted with someone crazier than he was. "It's your funeral," he said.

"Well now, and it's *your* funeral if it's water, fair enough?"

"Gimme!" Groove said. Tex somewhat reluctantly handed over the bottle. Groove dipped the point of his spike into the bottle and drew up about half its contents—enough acid to turn on the whole Red Army!

"You're out of your fucking mind!" Tex yelled.

Groove giggled. He squirted all of the acid in the syringe back into the bottle, stoppered it, and handed it back to Tex. "Now I just shoot up with a spikefull of water and if that was pure acid, I'll get loaded from what's still sticking to the sides."

Groove went through the kitchen and into the bathroom. Gurgling sounds. A couple of minutes of tense silence . . .

Then Groove came back into the room waving his arms and giggling. "Do business with the man," he said, flopping back onto the couch. "I'm stoned out of my mind."

I looked at Groove staring at the light fixture with a big happy smile and couldn't help feeling an idiot admiration. He could've shot a hundred mikes or ten thousand--and he'd done it without a prayer in the world of knowing which. I saw a cat who had casually done something nothing in the world could make me do. Groove was either totally mindless or the world's heaviest saint.

"Well now," said Ali, "it looks like the Dope Exchange is open for business. The whole bottle, eh? What do you think, Marvin?"

"I think $3000," said Marvin. "Yes, that's just about exactly what I think."

"You guys are crazy!" Tex whined. "You know what this is worth . . . "

"So we do," Ali said ominously.

"We know what it's worth to us," said Marvin, "and we know what it's worth to you."

"And it's just not the same thing," said Ali. "Not the same thing at all."

"How do you figure that?" said the California Lizard, squirming a bit on the couch between Ali and Marvin. For the first time, I saw gaping holes in his cool.

"Well now," said Ali, "to us that stuff is worth maybe $20,000, which is the profit we figure to make over what we pay you. But you're in a bind, Mr. Tex-ass, or you wouldn't be up here using a nickel-bag dealer for a connection and selling acid an ounce at a time, now would you? Man, everything about you is screaming Heat. You are a leper, you are a pariah, you are a walking dose of clap. You need bread instantly. You oughta be down on your Tex-ass knees thanking us for being softhearted enough to lay on 3Gs."

I mean, that Ali was a genius! Genius in the black magic of dealer's logic. Tex California was a heavy-bread berserker, but these boys were pros. Paisanos in full standing in the private Dealer's Mafia. Tex California the Ice Lizard death-on-acid big bread berserker was like a bar-room brawler suddenly come up against a karate-freak.

They had him and he knew it.

"Come on man," he begged, "I've gotta hole up in Tangier or somewhere. I need *bread.*"

"We'll make it four thousand," said Marvin. "'Cause we like your groovy white coat."

They were bargaining for real now. "Come on man, make it seven."

"Four," said Ali. Sounded like the bargaining had ended one step after it had begun.

"Shit, a lousy five thousand bucks, five, okay?"

"Well now," said Ali, "tell you what. My old lady is in the next room cutting some hash into sticks. We'll leave it up to her. Okay, things?"

Marvin nodded. Groove just giggled.

"Hey Tanya, haul ass in here!" Ali shouted. At the sound of the name, a shudder went through Tex that spent itself moving his hand with a seemingly-random twitch into his right coat pocket.

Out of the other room came a slim chick in a tight black dress, pale and skinny and spookily good-looking, a sinister A-head Madonna.

"This here is—"

"You know who that is, you dumb jive spade!" Tanya shrilled when she saw Tex. "That's Larry Allen! Oh Jesus, oh shit..Larry-the-Depthcharge Allen!"

I saw Tex's right hand close on his gun; apparently he didn't like someone calling him by his rightful name.

"Well now, who the fuck is Larry Allen, you crazy speed-freak bitch?"

"Wait a minute! Wait a minute . . . " said Marvin. "The Depth-charge . . . I know that name from San Francisco—"

"Bet your ass you know the name from San Francisco!" Tanya said, staring hot razorblades at Tex. "Remember the cat was supposed to be sticking cyanide in one cap out of five hundred? Larry Allen!"

"Well now, cunt, I don't see what you're getting so excited about," Ali said.

"Hey, now I remember," crooned Marvin. "Month ago, when I was in the Haight, there was a story going round about some Federal narc was going around making big scores off all the dealers in sight and then busting them quietly, one by one. Was getting kind of ominous. Then, the story goes, some cat put the narc in a position where he had to taste some of the merchandise and it turned out to be cyanide . . . "

Groove came back from giggle-land just long enough to say: "If this is the same cat, then we're talking to a hero!"

"Hero!" screamed Tanya. "Some fucking hero! For openers, he didn't know the narc was a narc, he just slipped him the Depthcharge on general principals. It's his thing, he grooves behind it. He's left a string of bodies everywhere he's gone--cops, dealers, connections, customers, Feds, carhops, mafia hoods—you name it, he's killed it."

"Well now," said Ali sitting on one side of Tex and suddenly making it seem very significant that Marvin was on the other. "This changes things, doesn't it? This creature has the Feds, the Mafia, and for all we know the CIA and the NKVD after him—sounds like he's set the all-time record for Heat. I figure we just take his acid and pay him nothing. If he bitches, I figure we might just as well make a lot of people happy and kill—"

Suddenly, Tex California exploded off the couch, whirling around like a typhoon, gun coming up out of his pocket—

A muffled Cooosh! sound like someone jabbing a chisel through cheap sheet-metal and the firecracker smell of gun powder—

Tex California's face was suddenly ten years younger, a Malibu beach bum looking at death from the wrong side folding and falling like a punctured balloon clutched feebly at his chest where the blood

Tex Gets It

made a weirdly-lovely rising-sun pattern on the shiny white leather of his coat; he pitched over on his face and I knew he had died could feel the cosmic stench of his death in the room *he was really dead* I was looking at a *dead body* would never get up and walk again he was dead dead really *dead* . . .

And Groove was giggling and stroking the silencer on some kind of automatic.

"You stupid cunt!" Ali snarled at Robin. "Bringing that thing here! We oughta waste you too . . . "

"Yeah," Marvin said, far more reflectively, "it'd be safer to kill these two creeps too . . . "

Robin's nails dug into my thighs in a spasm of total panic. All of them were staring at us from a million eyes with pistols for pupils all staring at us they were gonna kill us oh Sweet Jesus they're gonna kill us I don't wanna die don't wanna die die die . . .

"Yeah, and this other creep is probably Allen's partner," Tanya said. "Let's shoot the motherfucker."

"Yeah man," said Ali, "just who the fuck are you coming here and making like the great gray ghost?"

Die die die die don't wanna die please don't kill me don't don't kill me kill me please please PLEASE PLEASE PLEASE—

I was off somewhere—the dark side of gibbering hysteria—then realized I was hysterical and my life was on the line and something cold and swamplike cold stone hard cold took control of my vocal cords and The Man in Black ate my mind and filled me with himself.

"I'm afraid that's something it wouldn't be healthy for you to know," said The Man in Black. "Let's just say I represent a certain organization for whom you have just done a small service. The girl . . . knows no more than you do . . . a kind of Judas-goat, if you see what I mean."

"You're gonna have to come up with a better story than that," Groove said, still holding his gun.

The Man in Black ignored him and his gun and continued as if he hadn't heard the interruption. "Luckily for you," he said, "you've managed to convince me in the only possible manner that you weren't involved with the late lamented. The contract I accepted was for Allen and anyone I considered his partners, which of course is why I took my time fulfilling it—it called for a payment of $15,000 for Allen and $2,000 apiece for any . . . extra work. You're very lucky I'm not the greedy type, or rather that I hate cleaning up after myself. But

I've decided that since you've fulfilled my contract for me, every-thing concerned becomes your property: the red Cadillac convertible outside, the acid, any money on the deceased's person—and of course, the body."

"*The body?*" Ali screamed shrilly.

"Of course, the body," said the Man in Black. "You want the car and the money and the acid, you get rid of the body. If I have to get involved with the details, I keep the acid. Don't be stupid enough to think that my employers give anyone something for nothing. That was one of Mr. Larry Allen's more costly mistakes."

"Hey . . . hey wait a minute!" Tanya said, suddenly starting to shake. "Allen was supposed to have slipped one of his depthcharges to the son of a capa mafiosa . . . You're not . . . ? Look, none of us ever had anything to do with the creep! You're not . . . ?"

"Would I tell you if I was?" said The Man in Black. "Let's just say that Allen had very poor taste in enemies and leave it at that. Natu-rally, you people aren't stupid enough to make the same mistake. None of this ever happened, did it? My employers dislike . . . publici-ty. They tend to over-react to minor annoyances. Need I be cruder?"

"Well now, take it easy man," said Ali. "We'll get rid of the body. After all, an ounce of acid's worth a little effort, isn't it?"

There seemed to be a general agreement. Groove put away his gun.

The Man in Black got up, had to pull his Lady with him—she was totally out of it. "And of course you people have never in your lives seen me?" he said.

"Never in our lives," said Marvin.

"And you don't know this girl either."

"What girl, man?"

The Man in Black smiled a basilisk smile and said: "You will do well to remember that," And let a thoroughly uptight Ali rush him and his Lady outside the door.

■ ■ ■ ■ ■ ■ ■ ■ ■ ■ ■

Outside on the empty street, the universe flew out of me in a rush of psychic vomit and I was a kid screaming in terror dragging a sleepwalking Robin by the hand and running dead-out to Seventh Avenue and the next thing I remember we're in a cab back to my apartment and the cab driver is shaking and sweating and Robin is smiling and smiling and crooning to me and stroking my hair . . .

"Oh, wow . . . oh wow . . . baby you were beautiful you're the heaviest cat there is I love you I love you . . . " The sea whispering in my ear. I started to come out of it—we were *alive*, out of there, in a cab home, they didn't know who I was I had scared them off looking and left them a big deathday present..they had no reason to come looking . . .

"Oh baby, and have I got a tasty surprise for you," Robin said, seeing my mind back in my eyes. "Just rest easy baby, everything's gonna be groovy . . . groovy . . . groovy . . . groovy . . . "

■ ■ ■ ■ ■ ■ ■ ■ ■ ■ ■

I bolted the police lock behind us and only now, in my own dark apartment, did I start to feel safe, really safe from rising sun blood on white leather eyes of a million pistols—

In the pitch blackness of the kitchen, I felt Robin's arms around me, tasted her long lingering kiss from three cold universes away.

"Oh man," she sighed, "you were *beautiful*. I still don't believe it, the way you rapped down those cats, heaviest dealers I ever saw . . . And the best is yet to come, baby. Go on into the living room, and turn on the light and I'll have a big beautiful surprise for you."

I went into the living room, turned on the orange ceiling light, and grew on the couch like a vegetable. How groovy it was to be a vegetable growing in the hidden dark earth with not a care in the world . . . timeless mindless dark and drifting . . .

Into my orange root-cellar stumbled a smiling girl with huge dark eyes and long black hair. The creature stood over me with her hands behind her back.

"Man," she said, "you are too much! Those freaks were the biggest dealers in town and they had just killed a man and you got away with pulling rank on them and you were stoned on acid! Too much! Man, we're gonna make millions!"

"What are you gibbering about, girl?" Why didn't she leave me alone with my dark roots and soft silence?

"You got the head to be the number one dealer in New York, maybe the country, and I got the connections to get us started. All we need is a big enough stake, and baby, thanks to that creep from California, we got it! Dig: while you were getting your coat, he stashed it under the sink."

And grinning like a lemur, she held up the second bottle of acid.

"*ANOTHER BOTTLE OF ACID*—" I screamed. "After . . . after . . . after *all that* . . . another bottle of acid!" A monstrous insane joke—I was speaking its idiot punchline. But there *was* another bottle of acid! No joke—another bottle of deadmen mafia hoods narcs electric chair pistols Ali Blah-Blah and his Forty Fiends condition terminal *ANOTHER BOTTLE OF ACID* . . .

"Hey man, what's—?"

I leaped to my feet screaming: "Down the toilet bowl! Flush that fucking stuff down the toilet bowl!"

Robin backed away from me, clutching the bottle to her chest. "Are you crazy? Thousands of dollars worth of acid!"

"Get that stuff the fuck out of here or get yourself the fuck out of here! Down the toilet—now!"

"Come on, man, take it easy, you're stoned . . . "

"Me or the acid! You can't have both! Flush it down the toilet or flush yourself down the toilet! Now! Now! NOW!"

Backing towards the kitchen, Robin's eyes got cold and hard like a million years of California Space Monster blood on shiny white formica table. "I don't give up this acid for you or anyone else," she said.

"Then get yourself the fuck out of here!"

Behind white leather eyeballs something warm and red and human seemed to pulse for a moment. "Come on Tom, you're freaking, is all . . . I dig you . . . don't do this to me . . . you're stoned . . . you're just stoned . . . ."

Stoned! I was *really* stoned, knew it because the universe had just hit me over the head with a gigantic club a huge voice screaming in my head: "*THERE'LL ALWAYS BE ANOTHER BOTTLE OF ACID!*"

Robin was another bottle of acid! As long as there were Robins there'd be another bottle of acid! Acid boiled out of the blood of the blackest bowels of dead crawling things of night in the cesspool of the earth fermented bodies of Tex California in a million neon-blue pads "come on kid, the first one is free" Robin gobbled up by became the Vampire God of Acid!

ANOTHER BOTTLE OF ACID!

"Get out! Get out!" I screamed. "Don't ever come back! Not another bottle of acid! Out! Out! Get the fuck out of here! You come here again and I'll kill you!"

Robin slithered into the kitchen like the black snake that ate the world holding up the acid daring me to take it baby you can be the greatest dealer in the world . . . Her lips trembling, her eyes heavy with held-back tears—but it was all a fucking fraud! The Great Bitch-Goddess Acid had no tears for man not sucked up in a spike from *ANOTHER BOTTLE OF ACID!*

"Look man . . . look man, you're freaking out, but . . . but . . . I'm not taking this shit from anyone, you're crazy—"

I opened the door. "Out! Out, cunt!"

"Eat shit, you gutless faggot!" she screamed like a harpy—and slammed the door in my face. Another bottle of acid! Another bottle of acid, oh Christ, another bottle of acid!

I bolted the door behind her, then the police lock. *Another bottle of acid!* I still wasn't safe! I wedged a kitchen chair under the doorknob. Still not safe! It was colorless, odorless, tasteless, the Devil's own nerve gas! Could creep in through the windows in the water supply nobody was safe from it I wasn't safe from it *ANOTHER BOTTLE OF ACID—*

21
"Break on Through to the Other Side . . ."

—Another bottle of acid another bottle of acid . . . Oh Jesus, wouldn't it ever stop? Why not just a harmless little blow your mind baby without Anne smack Robin acid dead bodies another bottle another bag another bag another fix one more time baby one for the road you could be number one dealer in a daisy-chain line from the tip of the needle to the navel of the universe down into blackness nothingness inside condition terminal . . . Why did they have to package crystal lovely nothingness in a spike in a cube in a joint in *another bottle of acid* and sell it through a long line of rotten-toothed vampires would suck you in suck you dry and fill you with the coal-black slime of final darkness in *another fucking bottle of acid!*

I'm freaking out! a tiny lost part of me said—

Another bottle of acid from cesspools of rotting teenyboppers with mottled teeth in the grave of the California Lizard—

Gotta do something, gotta come out of it—

Eat shit, you fucking gutless faggot eat shit eat smack eat me eat acid eat Anne eat Ali eat Terry Blackstone's speed-soaked brain eat death—

Gotta talk to somebody can talk me out of this I can't maintain—

Eat death eat garbage eat condition terminal gutless fucking motherfucker faggot eat *another bottle of acid*—

Harvey! Harvey the Man! Harvey the Shrink! Harvey the Bringdown . . . Total Consciousness of the Total Void I was staring down into on the brink of a cliff a million miles high I was a million miles high and maybe Harvey had the Antidote Stomach Pump Acid-Eater machine.

I slithered into the living room on a thousand ropy tentacles and chewed my way through piles of moldy paper until I came to the Foundation's letterhead with Harvey's emergency home phone number on it . . .

I became a dialing-machine dialing a string of numbers on the bedroom phone till the dial seemed to be dialing me dialing the combination of a safe inside my head inside of which was the gaping monster of *another bottle of*—

"Uh . . . huh . . . " said a voice on the other end of the vampire-thing sucking at my ear.

"Tom Hollander . . . " I screamed. "You gotta do something it's coming in the doors in the windows—"

"What? What? Tom? What's the matter? Take it easy. This is Harvey . . . Wha—?"

"*Another bottle of acid!* They're trying to get me to take *another bottle of acid!* She had it right here, *another bottle of acid!*"

"You're on acid?" Harvey's electric voice said. Sounded better that way: IBM computer trip. "Take it easy, you must just be having a bad trip . . . "

"*A bad trip? Another bottle of acid* and the California Lizard rotting in his own white leather blood and it's coming in the air now *another bottle of acid* and they're sucking me dry and pumping in void and it's a bad trip? It's a trip to Condition Terminal to the black—"

"Take it easy! You've got to make it down to the Foundation. I'll meet you there as soon as I can."

"But—"

The phone went dead. The motherfucker murdering speed-freak California Lizard bastard hung up on me with *another bottle of acid* stewing in my own cauldron of night's black angels closing in filthy cocksucker leaving me to stew in my own *another bottle of acid* juices—

Black void fading to red fury fading to—something snapping back into focus, like Harvey leaving me hanging was a hard slap of reality across the face. That what he wanted to do? Because he had done it, waiting there with salvation from the forces of dead dealers' other bottles of acid could be the greatest dead vampire in the whole world of nightmare assassins—

I had to get to the Foundation! Had to maintain! But it was coming in the door how could I go out into the night of blackness total void of *another bottle of acid* under every dark street corner waiting for me there in the rain in the dark in the long cold dark went on and on and on—

From the sewer of memory the ghost of a moment: walking down Second Avenue in the rain trying to remember how once before on Romilar or something I had made time stop, turned myself into a walking-machine outside the timestream of my mind, and now I seemed to remember how I reached in and turned off the switch in my head . . .

Another bottle of acid won't work I can't get there trapped in this cave of my own fright Harvey a million miles away in the warm sweet inner—

—Door. Steps. Cold wind. Running. Lights. Cars. Arm waving. Cab. Motion through a whirling Christmas tree. Money passed from hand to hand. Slam of car door—

—Sanctum of his Total Consciousness dream of OmOhm home on om...

And I was standing on the cold empty street outside the Foundation staring at the glowing brass nameplate, while the night, a great sky of razorblades, was about to fall in on me in a million shearing fragments. I leaned on the bell—

No no no not *another bottle of acid* not the sky falling in on chicken little gutless faggot you could be the number one murder on acid in the world with just *another bottle*, baby—

The door was pressing against my face trying to kill me with secret vibrating death-ray of the California Lizard's kamikaze white leather rising sun of blood..the buzzer..buzzer.

I yanked the knob, leaned on the door, and it flew open and I fell inside, slammed the door behind me, but couldn't find the police lock to lock out the universe of hungry razors of night battering the secret cave of orange desire—

I loped up ten million stairs in total darkness on my hands and knees while thousands of razor-sharp mafia spades pounded on the door behind me with sharp glass medicine bottles—

Drooling sweating oozing ichor I sensed a long black womb and halfway down it a warm yellow light. I ran down the womb down the hall mewling and screeching and tore open the door to:

A small room. Just a gray carpet and a floor lamp and two overstuffed black velvet chairs. One chair was empty, but in the other sat a soft gray creature in a dirty white shirt and baggy gray pants.

"Sit down," said Harvey.

I dissolved into a boiling pool of black jello in the empty chair and my eyestalks looked at Harvey; warm gray eyes behind his glasses like a cocker spaniel, a concerned tired grimy face, an ancient teddybear.

It was the most beautiful thing I had ever seen.

I sat there waiting for the teddybear to speak, to say something magic that would chase away demons of bottled of acid white leather spades in mafia suits pounding broken bottles on the door below—

but the teddybear just sat there radiating quiet gray warmth out of its big rheumy eyes as we sat facing each other under the roof of its warm little cave insulated from the blackness outside far away outside by a million miles of orange cotton-candy insulation.

The teddybear looked so sad and tired and worried staring at me with those great leaky eyes and not smiling, only those gray, sad, all-forgiving eyes in a pasty gray face looked totally blank. I wanted the teddybear to say something, anything, crack a smile, curse, scream, laugh, *anything* . . . But the silence hung like a curtain between us and the eyes of the teddybear told me I was going to have to break it.

"Hey, man," my voice managed to say, like something from a bottle, "I'm sorry I dragged you out of bed."

"If you're sorry now, wait till you get my bill," the Harveybear said—such a dumb Harvey-imitation of a psychiatrist telling a psychiatrist-joke that the air seemed bright with flakes of shiny gray plastic. But then the Harveybear finally smiled and the air suddenly crinkled around the smile-line-extensions and reality fractured along some new cleavage and some part of me that had gone on an immense dark journey best not to even remember was suddenly back.

And the Harveybear had brought me back! Harvey—the Black Forest Cuckoo-Clock Builder Elf, the Control-Freak, the Psychic Castrator—*Harvey Brustein* had brought me back!

"Jesus Christ, man," I said, "did you do that on purpose?"

"Do what on purpose?"

"I was off on the dark side of nowhere gibbering and screaming inside and you brought me back. Just like that. Without even saying anything . . . How did you know . . . ?"

Harvey smiled a knowing Buddha-smile. "I've used LSD in therapy," he said, "so I've developed ways of bringing people out of acid bummers as a matter of necessity. Most people on bad trips feel threatened by their external reality in one way or another. So the first step is to present them with a non-threatening reality with which they want to and must deal: a quiet, concerned human being who is ready to listen but in no hurry to speak."

"As simple as that?"

"You're dealing with external reality now, aren't you?"

I wondered—I seemed to be alone with Harvey in a guru-cave in India, bodiless, floating, mind-to-mind telepathy. Reality—or something beyond the real?

"I feel so strange," I said. The shape of the words existed as emotions in my mouth. Nothing else that was me was real.

"If we're going to get anywhere, we'll have to go back in there, you know."

"I know," I said. And I knew he knew what I was saying when I said I knew. Back there into the darkness into the void into *another bottle of acid*. But somehow it was like looking at a movie of myself from far away—vague shadow-shapes shifting in an electric night . . .

"Talking about it won't be nearly as bad as living it," Harvey said. "When you give a nightmare verbal symbols, it takes it away from the inside and puts it outside where you can look at it instead of being eaten by it. Try and tell me what happened . . . "

"I just saw the hole in the bottom of Dope. Hole down into pools of black vomit and the whole universe is trying to push me through. But that's not the worst of it—worst of it is that a big part of me wants to be pushed through."

"Why do you want to be pushed through?"

"To get on the other side."

"Why do you want to get through to the other side?"

"I don't want to get through!" I screamed at him. "I just told you, it's pools of black vomit in there death in there monsters in there wearing my face . . . "

"But you just said part of you wanted to be pushed through. You'll have to face that part of you. Why do you want to go on through?"

The words bubbled up from my ectoplasmic gut to my flesh-and-blood lips: "Because it's the other side! Any other side! Because this side sucks! Anything is better than reality on this side!"

"Anything?"

"Oh wow . . . " I moaned.

Colored whirling lights seemed to halo the cosmic teddybear as a flash flared in my mind: blow your minds, baby, take a trip, flash, freak out; it was all the language of escape artists, refugees from an East Germany of the mind jumping off the top of The Wall in a hail of reality's bullets, not caring what we were jumping into as long as it was On The Other Side.

"Have you ever really understood why you take drugs?" Harvey said. His eyes were huge tunnels into the center of the universe of my brain—could he read the flash in my mind?

"Not until now," I told him.

It was so simple—drugs were the only way to look at reality from another side, only way to believe there was another side. Drugs were the sacrament of an Einsteinian god, a God of universal random chaos, God of the ultimate freedom of a table of random numbers, maybe not a very good god, but a god with my kind of style. Getting high was a cosmic good. But . . .

But . . . white leather rising sun out of the moldering California Lizard in *another bottle of acid* you just couldn't keep from taking that next fix of darkness and the merchants of void in a spike in a cap in another bottle of acid sucking you dry sucking you in and filling you with Condition Terminal darkness . . .

"Perhaps not even now," Harvey said. "Not completely."

"I know why I take drugs," I insisted. "What I don't know is where drugs take me . . . "

"Which is what counts, isn't it?" Harvey said. "I know why you take drugs and so do you: to see a better reality, a deeper vision, a more total view of the truth . . . "

"No man," I told him. "I'm not looking for any Oneness with the Cosmic All. A man needs more than one reality is all. Get stuck in one reality and you're dead—"

Whoom! Another massive flash hit me! That was it, that was the evil in Dope: dope-reality fought to trap you inside itself and shear off any vision into other realities. Paranoia of Dope was the same paranoia as Anti-Dope: stay in one fucking reality! You'll turn to shit if you step outside your bag. Neither Dope nor Anti-Dope had a lock on Total Reality—to chase that down the infinite corridors of Dope was a ticket to gibbering paranoia: always the chance of finding it in *another bottle of acid,* one more fix. Dope, like nuclear power, had no morality; you used it or it used you. If you could maintain, you added snatches to your mosaic of reality, but if you lost, you lost heavy because surrender to pure force was surrender to chaos. Each trip was an existential moment: your whole universe was on the line.

The room seemed to flare up with bright yellow light of sunshine—by digging the essence of the evil in Dope, I was free, not just free from the danger, but free to take hash, pot, even acid, free to take the Middle Path between Condition Terminal and gibbering East German anti-Dope paranoia, free to snatch as many goodies as I could from the hands of the Devil inside as long as my reflexes held. Free! Free! Free!

"You seem to have come to some conclusion," Harvey said.

My lips laughed like the grin of the Cheshire cat suspended in no-space. "Yeah, I've come to the conclusion that there is no conclusion. Secret of the universe, man—don't look for Final Conclusions. They're just not there."

"But there is a conclusion," the Harveybear growled softly. "And it's nothing if not final. And we don't have to look for it. It's called death."

From the corners of the room, shadows advanced, devouring the light. The Harveybear grew dark shaggy fur, long yellow teeth; its eyes became hollow sockets.

"Don't talk to me about death!" I screamed. "I've seen too much death tonight too much—"

"But you haven't experienced it," the shaggy thing in the black chair said, licking its sharp teeth.

"Of course I haven't experienced it, you asshole! I'm sitting here talking to you ain't I?"

"But don't you want to experience it? Get it all over with? Find out all there is to know?" It wasn't making sense! The Harveybear was gibbering slavering scraps of white leather coats rising sun of blood hole into final darkness forever and ever who the fuck wants to know about death the end of everything long black slide into sleep with no bottom . . . And who the fuck has a choice?

"Every true mystic has said you must die to be born again in one way or another. Don't you think there might be a truth in there some-where?" said the Giant Polar Bear God of endless frozen desert.

"Pie in the sky in the great bye and bye . . . "

"Let's bring it down to Earth. As far down as we can. Let's talk about fucking. Ever meet a girl who was afraid to have an orgasm?"

"If you're half the shrink you think you are, you know that Ar-lene—"

"I know. I wanted to be sure you did. What is she afraid of? Not pleasure—but of surrender. Not surrender to anything in particular, just surrender itself."

"Keep going," I found myself saying. Shadows seemed to soften. The light from the floor lamp bathed Harvey in gold. The words poured from his calm Buddha-lips like living glass butterflies. He was right about Arlene, and it wasn't just sex. That was why she was afraid of a real relationship—it meant surrender of a piece of her des-tiny to an outside force. He had it—the worm at her core. I felt myself in the presence of Truth . . .

"Surrender to what?" the Gray Buddha said. "What is there to fear surrendering to if the fear has no specific object? How about surrender to reality itself, to give oneself to the unknown beyond your control and let it take you to the hidden shore?"

"Sure, sure, that's why Dope too—cast yourself into the arms of the great unknown. But why be afraid of it . . . ?"

"Because," said Harvey, "the ultimate reality is death. That's where we're all going. Control is an illusion the unconscious individual erects to hide the unfaceable. Surrender control, and you lose the illusion and you see that the ultimate reality is death. Who does not fear death?"

For an instant, the room seemed to go black, totally, finally, ultimately black like the hole at the bottom of Dope of sex of rising suns of blood on white leather of sleep without bottom or end and I heard my blind voice mumbling: "We all know about death . . . can't do anything about it can't face it why—"

The calm, soft, sweet gray voice of Harvey pulled me back from the bottom of the lightless void; all the light in creation seemed to gather like a cloak about his shoulders and head.

"We can't do anything about it, so we're afraid of it," the voice said. "And because our ultimate reality is our ultimate fear, it fathers a million little fears—fears of getting too close—like fear of the orgasm, fear of love, fear of all consuming emotion, fear of passion, fear of commitment, even your own fear of the Foundation . . . "

"Spare me the sales talk," I protested wanly.

Harvey smiled an all-knowing, all-forgiving Buddha-smile. "You see?" he said. "You *do* fear the Foundation, because it demands a commitment to something outside yourself, a force beyond your control. And that is the primal terror of our egos—fear of surrender to something beyond our control. Because our egos are the interface between external and internal reality; to destroy the interface and let in the ultimate reality is a kind of death."

I tried to tell myself it was just parlor Buddhism—but it had the feel of reality, the taste, the touch. Shit, he was admitting the ultimate put-down of his own Foundation—admitting that the goal was a kind of death! As if those gray eyes saw something beyond . . .

"I was right about you," I said. "You're pushing death."

Harvey smiled a sad, strong smile. "Yes," he said. "But what kind of death? Yes, Total Consciousness involves a kind of death. But what dies? The ego dies. And with it, all fear. Because fear is the tension between the way things are and the way we want them to be. You've got to die to be born again. If you go through that death, the death of ego-desire, real death will never have a hold on your life again."

Oh God, how I wanted to believe that! Harvey seemed so calm, so sure, so cosmically certain, so above and beyond it all. "How do you know all this?" I said. "Have you—"

"Gone through to the other side? Yes. Look at me: I'm a middle-aged, middle-looking man with a middle intelligence, nothing more. But people listen to me and they follow me and I will get to them to go to San Francisco as you rightly say I want to. Why? Because I have gone through, and they can sense it and they want it, and so they believe . . . "

Goddamn, look at him sitting there so sure, being totally humble and cosmically arrogant in the same breath. I did believe. I believed he believed. I believed what I wanted to believe. But . . .

"But why don't I believe . . . "

Harvey shrugged. "Perhaps it's the drugs. You're closer to breaking through than any of them, and because you're closer, your ego sees rather clearly what breaking through means and it's fighting back hard. You have a very strong ego precisely because you're so close to the truth and your sickness has grown huge muscles to fight it. Your greatest strength is your worst enemy."

Every word seemed to pulse and quiver with the truth. The only kicker was that it was a truth from either side: if my ego was me, Total Consciousness was its death; if I died, I had no guarantee the me I had been would dig the me that was reborn. Death was discontinuity. Discontinuity was death. I wanted to trust him; if I could believe he had gone through, I could make the leap myself to the freedom I saw could be beyond my me.

But I saw that the essence was trust—I saw why the Foundation demanded total Surrender. It had to. There ano other way through . . . If there *was* a way through and Total Consciousness wasn't just another dealers' con . . . But he had just admitted—"

"You just admitted the whole San Francisco business was a con!"

Harvey sighed heavily, then smiled, as if his very special pupil had finally achieved his first minor satori. "You finally noticed," he said. "Of course it's a con. It has to be. I found that out the hard way. After months of trying, I finally understood that you can't *talk* people into taking that leap into the center of their own fears. You've got to push them into the water and let them learn to swim—with a lifeguard around, of course, just in case. So I give them hope in the Foundation, the only hope they've ever found, and then I force them to leap into the unknown to keep it."

"And make them think it's their own idea to make sure they do it?"

Harvey nodded, a cosmic weary nod made it seem like the whole universe rested on his shoulders. Maybe it did?

"That's a cruel thing to do."

"It's a cruel task to be set," Harvey said. "Besides, I'll be there to catch them on the other side."

"What about those who might not make it through?"

"Every meaningful act involves risk."

He was *so* right! If he wasn't the cleverest incarnation of the Devil yet, Harvey had to be some new kind of unclassifiable saint. But wasn't that just the final word-game cop-out? He was dead right about the core of things—it was the leap that counted, the kamikaze dive into the unknown. Could any means that achieved the highest end really be bad?

I looked at Harvey with new eyes; saw a man I couldn't understand, a man with the total arrogance to force people into their final fears, the total certainty that he was right, the total courage to make the decision alone.

"Maybe I've misjudged you, Harvey," I said inadequately.

Harvey smiled a tired, warm, almost humble smile. "I'm used to that," he said. "The questions is, what do you do now? I can't help you any further—you know too much to be pushed. You've got to do it yourself."

"*How* do I do it myself?"

"Only you know that. It's got to be some action, a headlong leap into the center of your fears. Only you know where that center is."

Harvey stared at me, not smiling, not blinking—a hard unwavering stare that saw through layers and layers of flesh and bone and being, down, down to the center of my fears. He knew where that center was; I knew that he knew. And knowing that he knew I knew, I was forced to admit to myself that I had known all along that the thing I feared most was giving myself to something greater than myself, trusting in the great unknown, trusting in something with mortal power for good or evil, life or death.

Trusting in *him*.

I stared back at him begging with my eyes for him to tell me to do what I knew I had to do. But his face was a Buddha-mask and I knew he would never tell me, knew that he knew I knew *exactly* what I had to do.

I felt ultimately terrified and ultimately brave as I said, "I'm gonna vote to go to San Francisco and I'm gonna go with you."

As I said it, I felt an enormous weight lift off my shoulders and head for the stratosphere. I knew dead certain that I *had* leaped through the very center of my fears because now I *was* on the other side: there was nothing left to be afraid of. I was free! At last my fate was in the hands of an unknown destiny, a force far, far greater than myself. I had dared the unthinkable and now I no longer needed to think—I could just *be!*

Harvey smiled what seemed like a much less weary smile, as if now he were not quite so alone. "I think you've taken the important step."

"So do I," I said, feeling it with every ounce of my being.

We smiled at each other for a long silent moment. We smiled at each other as friends. I had won the final victory over myself: I loved Harvey Brustein.

22
The Path to Consciousness

A weird five days since Magic Friday, five days I seemed to drift through like the ghost of Tom Hollander past, going through the motions of eating, sleeping and writing fee-letters, round and round the great circle of karma, while my consciousness chased its mystic navel around the outer reaches of the Great Beyond.

Thing was, memory was playing chicken with my gut. I could reel off the film of Friday in my mind, recall every external event that had occurred. And on the ultimate cosmic level, I remembered a whole chain of feelings whose memories still tasted true. Yes, I had an event-track and a feeling-track; it was the certainty of the connection between them that was lacking. Could I trust in the truth of my acid visions? For that matter, could I trust my non-acid self? They were obviously in a knock-down drag-out with each other. Here on the straight side of the universe, I was finding a new faith in Harvey harder and harder to support as the days flickered by towards Thursday night and the Foundation vote on San Francisco and what had to be my real external moment of truth.

Doubts . . . Yeah, I had doubts, but something *had* changed inside: now I *did* trust Harvey; it was not him I doubted but my lingering doubt, the shrill mocking voice of my ego. Thursday night, I had to make a decision which would bring me either salvation or damnation; trouble was I couldn't be certain which. Like poised on the brink of jumping from one reality to another and though I knew which way I had to jump, I couldn't rid myself of the notion that the jump was still blind.

Aw bullshit! I was just conning myself again with that. My *gut* knew which way to jump—the memory of the great surge of freedom I had felt when I made up my stoned mind to trust my fate to Harvey and vote for San Francisco was still bright in my mind. Yeah, I had really made my decision already and I would damn well stick to it! Trust your instincts was the old party-line, and acid *was* the voice of instinct, and instinct told me to leap through the center of my fear, and I had, and instinct had been right, instinct had told me that Harvey was a strange kind of saint I might never really understand, and I had leapt into the arms of his truth, and the feeling it had given me was pure and clean and good.

Shit, it was just the courage of that perfect moment that was eroding away. But I wouldn't let it happen! I wouldn't let fear force me into one more negative anti-life decision. I had put Robin and the whole ugly dope-dealing scene behind me, half my life; I had Arlene and the Foundation and the freedom of surrender to the impulse to Total Consciousness ahead of me, and all it took to keep it was one more moment of courage and then I could relax forever and just *be*. I had already made the right decision, a positive one for a change, and I wouldn't let my dirty old ego psych me out of it. Now I understood my fear . . .

So I had told myself on Saturday, on Sunday, on Monday, on Tuesday, and now I was giving myself the pep-talk again on Wednesday afternoon as I sat dreamily in front of my typewriter letting myself get further and further behind on the week's quota. I understood why I was letting myself get so far behind and it seemed healthy—my instinct's way of cutting through the tortured maze of my ego straight to my fingers, telling them to fuck up, don't give a shit about a job you'll soon be leaving, burn your bridges, baby. So, points, schmoints, what the fuck . . .

"Oh Jesus!" Bruce moaned beside me, "this thing is just too much . . . "

Mechanically I turned to Bruce—he already seemed like part of something I was leaving, there had been a pathos in the banter back and forth all week, an emptiness inside me that seemed both a gain and a loss.

"What are you bitching about now?" I asked, pro forma.

Bruce put his hand on a thick manuscript in a gray cardboard binder. "Another freak thinks he's written the Bible," he said.

He handed me a letter—suddenly my gut dropped out from under me as I recognized the Foundation letterhead! "Dig this," Bruce said. With a horrid empty bubble building inside my gut and reaching for my brain, I read:

> Dear Mr. Robinson:
> Here is my check for $35 and my book, *The Path to Consciousness*. I make no pretense at being a professional writer. But *The Path to Consciousness* was not written with literary intent, nor as a means of making money. This book represents the distillation of my life's work with human consciousness

through the Foundation for Total Consciousness, an institution which I founded and of which I am the head.

Mr. Robinson, I'm confident that when you read this book, you'll agree that the world at large must have access to it. I am willing to work with a professional writer to polish the prose. I am willing to do anything short of violating the integrity of the book to get *The Path to Consciousness* published. My commitment to my work is total, and I think you'll feel the same way once you've read this book. This is a book the world *must* read!

Sincerely,
Harvey Brustein

The bubble exploded in my brain. Harvey Brustein taken in by the old Dirk Robinson con! And yet . . . and yet, why not? If Harvey had put it all into a book, Dirk Robinson was the logical place to send it—Dirk had sure seen to that! The bubble passed through me leaving an expectant hollow—almost the feeling you get when you know some chick you've wanted to ball for months is about to strip naked before you. Because I had read enough fee-crap to know that it was here that people *did* strip their heads naked. Like, the Mad Dentist functioned well enough as a dentist in the external world to be able to afford Dirk Robinson—but his fee-shit revealed the gibbering paranoia of the madman inside.

Staring at the gray binder—I could now read the white label pasted on the cover that said: *The Path to Consciousness* by Harvey Brustein—I felt a sudden dread. Here would be the real truth, Harvey's real truth, and I had all the experience I needed in this line of evil to read every twitch of emotion or madness between the lines of a fee-creep's swill. I would *know*, not feel, *know*.

Was I ready for that? Was I really ready?

"Read any of it yet?" I asked.

"Do I really have to?" sneered Bruce. "You read the letter. This cat is a nut."

Yet another fear in my gut—fear that Bruce would see what was inside of me, that I believed in this "nut." And yet . . . and yet if there were forces of destiny at work behind the stage-set of reality, this moment was proof. Bruce hadn't read it, he didn't want to read it, I could con him out of it and do it myself. I was *meant* to read this book; it was a message from whatever gods there be. I had to know.

"Uh . . . look Bruce," I said with tension-feigned casualness, "I've

The Bubble Exploded

been kind of fucking up all week. Is that thing an eight-pointer?"

"Five," Bruce said glumly.

"Well, what the hell, a five-pointer is better that five ones. I wouldn't mind taking it off your hands . . . "

"Be my guest," said Bruce, pushing the gray binder across the dividing line onto my desk with a wrinkle of his nose as if it were a bag of shit he was cleverly and secretly discarding on a Subway platform.

TABLE OF CONTENTS

Don't know what, but there was something about that table of contents that ruffled the hair on the back of my neck. Overuse of words like *Total* and *Against*? Shit, knowing what I knew, I probably could've written what was in the book myself from that table of contents! But the *what* wasn't what counted—what counted was the *how*. I felt almost as if I were dropping another cap of acid as I turned to INTRODUCTION:

You are not fully conscious. Few of us are. Down through the ages, mystics who have achieved a greater degree of consciousness than their fellow have proclaimed this truth and have been feared and reviled and persecuted, or worse, ignored.

Blah, blah, blah. No point in wading through that kind of crap, give it the old Dirk Robinson speed-read—and suddenly I found myself reading the book just like a fee-reader! Which, after all, I was. Weird—like turning one switch in my head on, and another one off. I skimmed the usual bibble to the end of INTRODUCTION . . .

> ... therefore, when I proclaim that this book contains not mere-
> ly one path to consciousness but *the* path to Total Conscious-
> ness, the *only* path, I am not placing myself above the great
> minds of mystical thought, but I am walking in their footsteps,
> along the path of Gautama the Buddha, of Jesus, of the found-
> ers of Yoga, of the Zen masters. *The Path to Consciousness* is
> not a denial of their total insights but a rediscovery of the path
> to Total Consciousness that they trod—stated clearly and shorn
> of meaningless superstition for the mind of modern man.

Jesus! Now that's what I call an *introduction!* Harvey certainly
hadn't fallen into the trap of false modesty—just the logical inheritor
of the mantle of Buddha and Jesus, a simple, unaffected Savior of
Mankind. And yet ... yet if he *were* right—and I had plenty of reason
to believe he was—he had every right in the world to make that kind
of statement; it was the simple truth. Well anyway, it was certainly
what we call in the trade a gangbusters narrative hook! I turned to
Chapter II ...

> Consciousness is the ego looking at itself and proclaiming "I
> am therefore I am." Consciousness is a self-fulfilling prophesy.
> Consciousness ...

... is like an onion. So it's *not* like an onion? Shit, I knew what
Harvey thought consciousness was; no point in reading through this
bilge. I flipped over to THE EGO AGAINST THE UNIVERSE,
skipped the first couple of pages and read at random:

> ... man's basic condition is misery. His desires are regular-
> ly thwarted, love is an illusion, the world is filled with hate, and
> death is the only certainty. A common paranoid delusion is that
> the universe is a vast conspiracy against the self, that the very
> forces of destiny seek one's destruction, that the physical laws
> of the universe are designed for one's personal persecution.
> Who has never felt the malignancy of Creation gnaw at his own
> heart? But is it paranoia?
> Or do paranoiacs simply possess some terrible hypercon-
> scious insight into the truth? ...

Oh god, it can't be! Harvey Brustein a closet paranoia-freak? Last
thing I would've believed—Harvey was just too good at making

things come out his way to believe that the Universe was a Bolshevik
Conspiracy, the way the Mad Dentist did. Or was he . . . ?

> Is not the universe in fact truly stacked against us? Do not all
> men fear death? And do not all men die? In the end, we all lose
> our battle with the universe, all of us. The paranoiac is right: in
> the final analysis, the universe is a torture chamber for the ordi-
> nary human mind. We cannot win—we cannot not die . . .

There it was, the ultimate paranoid statement, pure as the driven
snow. Completely paranoid—but also completely true. Death always
wins. But who but a paranoiac admits it? Then . . . who but a paranoiac is right? Question then is, is it better to be right, or better to be
sane? Is that what Harvey's getting at? Something—perhaps some
dread—made me skip into THE EGO AGAINST CONSCIOUSNESS:

> . . . as seen in pragmatic terms, the external universe *is*
> against us: by our own ego definition, the universe is evil, since
> its blind and always-achieved goal is our death. But we must
> ask ourselves: what is it that we fear and what is the `I' that
> does the fearing? What we fear is death. More precisely, our
> ego fears its own annihilation. Our ego fears the inevitable . . .

Etc., etc., blah, blah, blah . . . Something strange was building up
inside me: everything that Harvey was saying was what I thought
he'd be saying and all of it was logically correct; but my gut insisted
that all of it was wrong, wrong with a wretched twisted sickness.
Was my ego fighting the truth, scrabbling desperately for hand-holds
in its fight against my decision? How could I trust my instincts when
they were having a knock-down drag-out among each other in my
belly? This was a heavy book; it *was* Harvey. In his own way, the
fucker could really write . . .

> . . . and so we must conclude that it cannot be sane to fear
> the inevitable. The inevitable is . . . *inevitable.* Our fear is use-
> less. The universe is not against us; the universe is a blind
> mechanism. A mechanism without consciousness cannot be
> our enemy. Only consciousness can be hostile. Our egos are
> the enemy for they fight against the inevitable and deny us
> peace. Therefore, we must reach out for a new level of con-
> sciousness which will bring us peace.

A level of consciousness which will enable us to not merely
accept the inevitable but to embrace it. We must learn to embrace death.

NO! NO! Something inside of me cried out: madness to embrace
death! What was the point? When you were dead, you were *dead,*
gone, cipher, zero, nothing. What could you gain by digging it? It
was truth, but better a decent lie. Harvey couldn't mean *that.* Had to
be something else, sure, a metaphor for something else . . .

But a phrase that had been haunting me for days came back like
the taste of old sauerkraut: "It is possible to desire anything you fear.
It is possible to fear anything you desire." Was Harvey turning it into
something far dirtier and more unequivocal: "You should groove behind the thing you fear the most." Could it be that Harvey *really*
grooved behind death? Man, I didn't want to read any more of this
evil shit! But I had to—and not just for the five points. I flipped on
into TOWARD TOTAL CONSCIOUSNESS and to hell with THE
EGO AGAINST ITSELF—I knew all too well where *that* would be at.

. . . Lao Tze, Buddha, and the other mystics of the East
taught that desire was the cause of all pain. Therefore, in order
to abolish pain . . .

Hell, I didn't need a lecture in Buddhism! I skipped through a ten
page resume of Taoism, Buddhism, Zen and the paths to Nirvana . . .

. . . is Nirvana Total Consciousness? Perhaps we can never
know; the mystics lacked a terminology congruent with our own.
Clearly, Nirvana is believed to be a result of the annihilation of
the ego; Total Consciousness is also a result of the abolishment
of the ego. But are the egos that are abolished the same? Total
Consciousness, unlike Nirvana, may be rigorously defined: the
abolition of the tension-interface between the internal and external environments. In a very real sense, it is the entire mind, not
merely the ego, which ceases to exist. More even than the
mind, the personality, the very conceptual illusion of `me-ness'
versus `it-ness.' Total Consciousness is the annihilation of self.
Total Consciousness is the psychic equivalent of death . . .

I felt synapses rearranging themselves in my gut. Man, this was
wrong, this was evil, this was going too far! This was death-wish, or

worse—death-love. This was what I had committed myself to? To the goal of death-in-life? To groove behind death?

And yet, damn it, there were no logical holes in the argument so far. Harvey was right—but Harvey was sick, sick, sick. Sickness rose off the prose like a swamp stench. If Harvey were right, the universe was a sewer. But did that mean Harvey was wrong just because I *wanted* him to be wrong? I turned to what I sensed had to be the nitty-gritty: THE FOUNDATION FOR TOTAL CONSCIOUSNESS:

> . . . and so, coming to the conclusion that men could not and would not face the ultimate reality of Total Consciousness alone, I created the Foundation for Total Consciousness. The Foundation for Total Consciousness is a social and psychological mechanism for the annihilation of the ego . . .

Something on the next page suddenly caught my eye:

> . . . morality, in the conventional sense, is irrelevant to the work of the Foundation. Since Total Consciousness, the goal of the Foundation, is literally the ultimate good, any means necessary to achieve that end is totally justified. That is, in this case, the end *does* justify the means . . .

What? *What?* The world was starting to move under me; at this point in writing the book, Harvey must've shifted (or stripped!) mental gears . . .

> . . . initiates into the Foundation suppose that it is an advanced form of psychotherapy, that is, that its goal is a healthy mind integrated into its environment. Actually, the goal is quite opposite: the total destruction of what psychotherapists consider the psyche. Neurotics come to the Foundation seeking hope, but it is hope which must be destroyed. Hope is illusion, hope is evil, for in a universe where death is the ultimate reality, hope is a lie . . .

Oh shit, oh shit, stench of decayed bullfrogs rising up out of the pages of the manuscript like the Devil's farts! Oh Christ, how could I have let this crazy monster con me . . . ?

> . . . but once all hope has been destroyed by the Founda-

tion, something beyond hope is possible: faith. Absolute total
unreasoning faith born of absolute total despair. Faith, of necessity, in myself, not as a teacher or even as a prophet, but as
someone who has gone through to the other side. Once faith is
total and unquestioning, volition, self-motivation, even self-
conceived drives are abolished and the Foundation becomes
not merely a community of individuals but a single organism in
which the constituents are mindless cells. At that point, the
egos of the members die. For a time, my ego exists as the
'brain' of the gestalt organism, but when Total Consciousness
of the organism is complete, my ego too may die . . .

Totally freaked out! Groveling at the feet of death! The Foundation
wasn't even a nice evil religious con; Harvey believed in his filth himself. He wants everyone to die, himself included! I had had just about
all I could take . . . except . . . what's beyond death? I looked into BE-
YOND THE DEATH OF THE EGO:

. . . a social organism, a gestalt of human bodies in which all
mind has died. Thus, death is defeated: the individual cells die
but the organism lives on forever, conscious, egoless, change-
less and eternal. By embracing my own death before I die, I
achieve immortality for myself and for the members of the
Foundation. We create an organism that is greater than the
sum of our parts and allow it to devour us. Thus, though we die,
our essence lives on . . .

Jesus, that's the hole in the bottom of Dope too! Let Dope devour
you and groove behind the Cosmic All—death, is all. I had been right
the first night I saw Harvey and his Foundation: Death *was* the trip.

Yeah, but I had come a long way since then: now I knew it was
possible to groove behind the death-trip. I had done it. And swallowed it. But now I was puking it up, coming through the other side.
Death *was* the ultimate reality, and something in me grooved behind
it because if you accepted that as truth and let it carry you away, you
were free, totally free: nothing mattered. Maybe nothing *did* matter.
Maybe that was truth. But if that's truth, I'll take vanilla. *Harvey*
grooved behind that truth, and he was out of his fucking mind.

And shit, for all his bullshit, *he* didn't accept death either; he had
to create a metaphysical torture-chamber to con himself into believ-

ing that the Foundation could be his immortality. Mind-fucking was Harvey's Dope, his piece of the ultimate.

And now I *really* understood the reason for getting high: tasting it was a relief and an ecstasy. Following Dope down its ultimate sewer-hope was what did you in. Chasing anything to its ultimate termination was what did you in—Condition Terminal. A fancy name for the thing with more fancy names than anything else—Death.

But knowing it was better than not knowing it, because once you knew the Big Secret, you could taste anything as long as you didn't let yourself get hooked. The Magic word was: *maintain.*

"One thing is certain and the rest is lies . . . "

But now I really picked up on what old Omar the Tent-Maker was really laying down: the ultimate end of *any* trip is a guaranteed terminal bummer; face that and groove behind the lies. Yeah, that's why I dug old Omar before I knew what he was really talking about: he had the essence of Cool. And that was the goody inside Dope, if you were man enough to snatch it out of the fingers of the void: dig the ultimate reality and know in the end you can't beat death, but you can face it down and win the one victory no reality can take from you—it can kill you, but it can't make you blow your cool. Only you can do that. And knowing *that* is the soul of Cool.

But Cool could also be a cold steel cutting edge if you needed it. And I had it now; I had it *all* now. *The Path to Consciousness,* oh, yes, it was that all right! A weapon. The ultimate doomsday machine for the Foundation for Total Consciousness. The vote tomorrow night . . .

My god, it was all set up for me: Harvey thought he had me; I had the book. All I had to do was go home and find the sickest slimiest parts of the book and read them at the meeting. I'd blow everyone's mind. Ted and Doris . . . Arlene . . . Yeah, I had the weapon that would make Arlene mine and wreck the Foundation . . .

"Well?" said Bruce.

He suddenly snapped me back to Dirk Robinson reality; I realized that I had closed the binder and was staring off into space.

"Well," said Bruce, "has this cat really discovered the Secret of the Universe?"

I laughed from way deep down and said: "Ah, you were right, man. Another nut thinks he's written the Bible."

23
The Emperor's Tailors

Under my arm as I climbed the stairs to the Foundation on Thursday night was *The Path to Consciousness* in the proverbial plain brown wrapper (kind of bag you use to line your garbage can). I hadn't the time or the stomach to read the thing word-for-word (which hadn't stopped me from writing the usual four-page fee letter this afternoon), but having given it the professional Dirk Robinson once over, I knew what was in it and where the worst muck was, and I had slips of paper marking the choicer freak-outs.

I hadn't found out till I took it home Wednesday night that some of the worst stuff was in the last chapter, TOTAL CONSCIOUSNESS VERSUS SOCIETY, wherein Gautama Brustein somehow managed the dialectical broadjump from his sucking at the teats of various death-gods to a brand of fascism so grotty it would've made Adolph Hitler puke. Near as I could make out (Harvey started to gibber a little in the last chapter), after he and the Foundation had devoured their own egos and become mindless cells of the Foundation ant-hill organism, other Foundation-things would be formed by converts who had read the book, until the whole human race consisted of nothing but these Consciousness-Communes (as he called them somewhere), and then the Harvey-Glob would proceed to gobble up the other Globs, until there was nothing left but one world-wide Thing, at which point Time, being an ego-construct, would cease to exist and the Uber-Glob would spend a timeless moment of eternity doing something nameless and incoherent which came out sounding very much like fucking itself.

Not that Harvey wanted to rule the world; all he wanted to do was eat the human race and become God.

Verily, it took a veteran Dirk Robinson fee-reader to understand how a cat who seemed to have all the fade-into-the-woodwork cool in the world could sit down at a typewriter and produce such an epic of insanity in the firm belief that it would convert the world. The Mad Dentist and assorted other fee-freaks were no different—except that the Mad Dentist filled teeth in real life while Harvey's straight job was fucking minds. Not really schizophrenia, but the ability to erect a mask over gibbering madness—they were just sane enough to realize that they'd be candidates for the funny farm if they talked like the things they were. But somehow a typewriter and a ream of blank paper became an invitation to puke it all out, and once it was written, the very magic of The Word on paper convinced the Mad Dentists of the world that the world Had To Have The Truth . . .

When of course what the world would do was puke. Ted, Doris, Arlene, even the worst Foundation-freaks like Linda Kahn, would have their minds scoured out when I read them choice selections from old Harv's magnum opus. The book he had written to convert the world would be instant turn-off to anyone who knew what was in it, even the marks he already had. Maybe *especially* the marks he already had, who couldn't help but puke at the true face of the thing they had worshipped.

Yeah, in an aesthetic way, Harvey's submitting the book to Dirk Robinson wasn't chance, it was inevitable. The Dirk Robinson fee-desk wasn't the cesspool of the universe for nothing, after all . . .

By the time I got to the old Foundation living room, it was already jammed. I could see Ted, Doris and Arlene sitting on the floor up front. Harvey was just sitting down on his little throne, and the animals were as quiet as a congregation in a cathedral, waiting for the Cardinal to speak. It suddenly seemed very eerie to have all those people sprawled on the floor at the foot of the dais—I became conscious of the yawning emptiness of the room above floor-level, as if the Void were hovering above them all, waiting to descend.

I didn't try to squeeze up front to where Ted, Doris and Arlene were sitting, or even let them know I was there. Instead, I found myself a shadow in the far rear corner of the room, stepped into it, and proceeded to lurk.

Harvey lit a cigarette, waved it around like a censer; I imagined the congregation eagerly sucking up the carcinogenic incense. "Well now," Harvey said, "we all know what this meeting is about." Silence filled the room like a physical presence; so far the Great Trek to San Francisco had been a word-game, but now it was whooshing like a runaway freight-train toward reality and you could taste the second thoughts. I had to play it right, had to ride the wave of doubt and catch it just at the moment it poised to crest . . .

"We're going to vote on moving to San Francisco in a few minutes," Harvey said. "But first I'd like you to understand the mechanics of such a move, if we make it. I'd fly out to the Coast immediately to look for a house for the Foundation. I'd hope that at least a dozen of you would be able to go out no more than two or three weeks later as a kind of advance guard to help me set things up, find apartments and jobs, so that when the bulk of you arrive more or less at your leisure, you'll have jobs and apartments and a functioning Foundation ready for you."

The whole room seemed to take a deep breath. Harvey had moved them a long way towards acceptance: talking like a vote was a foregone conclusion, a mere formality (which, not knowing what I was going to spring, he must've been sure it was) and telling them they'd just have to get there and their womb would be waiting for them. I took *The Path to Consciousness* out of its garbage bag—I had missed the crest of the wave; I needed some kind of opening fast.

"Come on, come on," Ted shouted up front. "Let's vote already!"

General silence. Shit, I had to find some way of sneaking the book in before they voted! And I couldn't just start yelling—they'd shout me down. I had to sneak up on their head, real cool-like. *Had* to have an opening . . .

"Take it easy, Ted," Harvey said. "Before we vote, I think we should see if anyone has anything further to say . . . "

The hole opened up in the line, courtesy of Harvey himself, but I didn't bull my way through, I played it real cool, raised my hand, waiting for Harvey himself to call on me.

"Yes Tom?" Harvey said with a barely-concealed smile. I could read what he was thinking: he knew that the suckers expected a pie in the face from me, he knew that I had been converted, he knew that I would now be a pussycat, and he knew that this sudden reversal would be the capper he needed.

So I played his game, smiled innocently, led him up the primrose path.

"You all know what I've been saying about Harvey and the Foundation and moving to San Francisco," I said in a humble, contrite voice. "Well, since the last meeting, I've had a few revelations . . . "

I paused and let the moment hang as everyone craned their necks around to rubberneck at the new, humble, converted Tom Hollander. Harvey was smiling at me—he thought he knew what was coming and why. Arlene's eyes lit up—she probably was sure I had decided to go to San Francisco for her sake. Ted looked smugly paternal. No one else seemed to know what was coming off. I had to do this just right or I wouldn't get to do it at all . . .

"Yeah," I finally said, "since last meeting, my girl told me it was

San Francisco or splitsville, my friend Ted tried to talk some sense into me, I've had a terrible acid bummer and a very interesting private session with Harvey . . . "

I paused again and made a kind of bookcover out of the brown paper bag, hid the gray binder of Harvey's book behind it. Harvey was flashing the biggest public smile I had ever seen on him; a lot of the Foundation-freaks like Linda and Ida were nodding, smug and tight-lipped, sure that the chief heathen was about to announce his conversion. So far, so good—I had to con them along long enough to be allowed to read from the book; I couldn't let Harvey realize what was coming till it was too late.

"And something else," I said. "I just happened to come across a groovy book which seems to have some relevant things to say to us, as we're about to vote to undertake a kind of great adventure . . . I guess when an idea's time has come, it crops up in all kinds of places at once. So for the benefit of any doubters that may still be left, I'd like to read a few passages from this book . . . "

A mutter went through the room. I had delivered the whole thing deadpan, but I suppose the idea of listening to me read from some book seemed awfully weird to most of them. What the fuck is the lunatic doing now? seemed to be the general expression. But Harvey nodded clerically, still smiling, sure in the knowledge that whatever I thought I was doing now, I was on his side.

Still keeping the book hidden behind the paper bag, I opened it to the first passage I had marked and began to read: " . . . Down through the ages, mystics who have achieved a greater degree of consciousness than their fellows . . . have been feared and reviled and persecuted, or worse, ignored . . . "

Linda and Rich and the rest of the shitheads seemed about to yawn. But old Harv really reacted—his jaw started to flap open; then he caught himself. But he knew! I had to con him along. I gave him a near-subliminal wink and quickly said: "Yeah, I read that, and suddenly I saw myself right in there with the fearers and the doubters. I started to *really* think . . . "

Harvey's face relaxed into a nervous smile. Nervous because where the hell did I get his book; smile because he was sure *The Path to Consciousness* was pure unadulterated self-evident Truth, and besides I had been converted even before I had read it. That was Harvey's blind spot and it was a mile wide: he couldn't see that *The Path to Consciousness* was a piece of gibbering insanity; to him it was Cosmic Truth.

"The guy that wrote this book really understands where consciousness is at," I said. "Dig . . . Consciousness is the ego looking at itself and proclaiming "I am therefore I am" . . . Consciousness is the interface between the mind and time . . .'"

Ah, I was getting weird looks now. Half the freaks seemed to be thinking "That sounds just like Harvey." The other half seemed to think it sounded like meaningless bullshit. Interesting philosophical questions: which faction was stupider? Harvey, though, seemed really relaxed now; after all, I was reading from a Great Book, making him look good from either end.

"You dig?" I said. "Great minds move in the same paths, right? Guy that wrote this book says so himself: ` . . . I am not placing myself above the great minds of mystical thought, but I am walking in their footsteps, along the path of Gautama the Buddha, of Jesus, of the founders of Yoga, of the Zen masters . . .'"

I paused, let the inevitable snickers move like a hopping mouse through the room. Harvey's smile became an empty, hollow thing as his worshippers unwittingly tittered at Holy Writ. And who knows, maybe hearing the words read back to him aloud was enough to let even him sense their madness.

As the groans reached their maximum, I said: "What's the joke?" in a very uptight voice, telling Harvey that I was on his side. Yeah! That was the way to do it! Get them to laugh at me and get madder and madder and act like a prick who believed in the book so they'd see what a prick you had to be to believe in it, and then . . .

"Hey, come on," I said, "this guy is laying down some heavy truth. He's got a right to talk like that!" Harvey nodded slightly, sucked on his cigarette. Linda Kahn shook her head. Arlene looked at me as if she were sure I was stoned. "Dig what he says about consciousness: . . . our ego fears its own annihilation . . . Our egos are the enemy for they fight against the inevitable and deny us peace. Therefore, we must reach out for a new level of consciousness which will bring us peace . . . We must learn to embrace death.'"

"Oh crap!" Linda Kahn shouted. "How much more of this garbage do we have to listen to?"

"Sick, sick, sick!" Bill Nelson chanted.

"Ah, he's stoned again!" Rich Rossi yelled.

Now there was real fear in Harvey's eyes. Fear and confusion—they were putting down *his* book! He took off his glasses, rose to the edge of his chair, seemed about to try and cut me off somehow—so I leapt to his defense.

"Shut up, you jerks!" I yelled. "This guy really knows what he's talking about! Dig: `Total Consciousness is the annihilation of the self. Total Consciousness is the psychic equivalent of death . . . '"

Dead silence. They had heard the magic words. Every head turned to stare at Harvey. Harvey held his glasses limply in one hand, toyed with his cigarette with the other as if it was his prick. His face was a pasty blank mask; only I knew what worms were writhing behind it. What could he say? What could he do? But he still didn't realize that *nothing* would gross them out more than more crap from his book. It was time to hit them with the kitchen sink.

"Dig this!" I shouted. "'The Foundation for Total Consciousness is a social and psychological mechanism for the annihilation of the ego . . . initiates into the Foundation suppose . . . that its goal is a healthy mind integrated into its environment. Actually, the goal is quite opposite: the total destruction of what psychotherapists consider the psyche. Neurotics come to the Foundation seeking hope, but it is hope which must be destroyed—'"

"*Where did you get that book?*" Harvey was on his feet screaming. I was blowing the con! He must've finally realized that *The Path to Consciousness* sounded like a snakepit of insanity. "*Where did you get that book?*" People were jumping to their feet, looking back and forth between me and Harvey, whose face was turning beet-red, whose eyes were flaming, like spastics at a tennis match. "*Where did you get that book?*"

I raised my voice till my throat burned, screamed at them, above Harvey, above the murmurs and the shouts and the sounds of a mob lumbering to its feet: "Listen, you stupid bastards! Listen to this! ` . . . once all hope has been destroyed by the Foundation, something beyond hope is possible: faith . . .Once faith is total . . . self-motivation . . . is abolished . . . the Foundation becomes . . . a single organism in which the constituents are mindless cells . . . the egos of the members die . . . my ego exists as the "brain" of the gestalt organism—'"

"*STOP! STOP! STOP! YOU DON'T KNOW WHAT YOU'RE DOING!*" Harvey was howling, waving his arms, his eyes rolling wildly. Everyone in the room seemed to be running around like chickens with their heads cut off, baying like a pack of dogs.

"Dig it, suckers!" I shouted. "Dig this: ` . . . the time will come when individual consciousness no longer exists, when every human mind will be concentrated in one great Super-Consciousness Commune, when death will be defeated, when the Consciousness-Commune will contain all of us, will contain every iota of consciousness on Earth, will be like a God . . .'"

I threw aside the paper bag and waved the gray binder over my head. "Dig it! Dig it!" I screamed. "There's your fucking Foundation in the man's own words! *The Path to Consciousness* by Harvey Brustein!"

Harvey's knees went out from under him; he collapsed back into his chair like a deflated balloon. His glasses lay at the foot of the folding chair, his eyes were vacant and glazed. One great sob wracked his body. People were rushing up to him, pushing each other out of the way, knee-and-elbowing, milling around like panicked cattle.

"Dig it, you idiots!" I howled into the whirlwind. "Harvey sent this piece of puke into the literary agency where I work. He swallowed the agency's con just like you swallowed his. Dig it, he's crazy, he wants to rule the world, he wants to be God, he wants to gobble you up! Want to hear more? 'It is given to few men to comprehend the nature of the universe, fewer still to transcend the limits of their own ego and live the ultimate truth. Therefore, it is the obligation of all of us who have achieved Total Consciousness to . . .'"

Suddenly, I realized that I had been speaking into silence. No one was even looking at me; they were all crowding around the dais where Harvey sat on his chair in a limp stupor. As I became aware that I was being ignored, I stopped reading and a strange hush seemed to sop up every sound in the room.

Ted was the first to step up onto the dais. Everyone else in the room was silent as he bent over Harvey and said quietly: "Did you write that book, Harvey?"

Harvey seemed to drift slowly back from the black pit inside; as he looked up at Ted, life started to come back into his eyes.

"Yes," Harvey said.

"Are you okay now?" Ted asked, with almost a lover's tenderness.

Harvey retrieved his glasses, put them on, sat up straighter in his chair. "Yes, I'm all right," he said. Tone was coming back into his voice but there was still a certain dull flatness to it. He fished his cigarettes out of his shirt pocket, stuck one in his mouth, lit it, exhaled smoke.

"I . . . I'm sorry I flew off the handle like that," Harvey said. Slowly, his voice was reassuming its former cool power. He was projecting his voice out to all of them as he said: "I guess that proves I'm human too." He even managed a ghost of a laugh. "I sent my book to a literary agency knowing I was no writer, and knowing the whole thing would have to be rewritten and thinking it would be treated confidentially. I guess I have some ego left after all, because I *did* feel awfully foolish having my rough draft read back to me . . . "

Doris stepped up onto the dais beside Ted, looked me square in the eye across the sea of people and said very loudly: "Tom Hollander, that was a thoroughly rotten thing to do."

A semi-audible sound came off the crowd around the dais, like a thunderstorm gathering, like a crowd contemplating becoming a mob. Hackles went up on my neck. I smelled waves of ugliness coming off their bodies aimed at me. The imbeciles!

"Doris! For Chrissakes, weren't you *listening!*"

"We were listening," Ted said coldly. His blue eyes were hard and shiny—perhaps too hard and too shiny like a brittle pane of glass over unfaceable fear.

"Well goddammit, what's the matter with you people!" I shouted. "Harvey's crazy! He's stark raving nuts inside! A mongoloid idiot can see that!" I waved the book over my head like the proverbial bloody shirt. "This thing is a classic example of a crank book! Harvey's a crank!"

Suddenly I noticed that Rich Rossi had been pushing his way through the mob towards me, his face red, his hands balled into fists. "Why don't you shut your fucking—"

"Stop!" Harvey shouted. "No violence, Rich." Rich obeyed his master's voice. Way we both were feeling, Harvey had probably saved *someone's* life.

"Look, look!" Ted shouted for attention. "Tom has read us a lot of stuff from Harvey's book. Some of it sounded pretty good and some of it sounded pretty bad. So what does all that prove . . . ?"

Harvey got to his feet. "It proves something pretty important," he said. He smiled wanly. "First of all, I'm afraid it proves I'm not much of a writer. But *that* should remind all of you that I'm only human; when I set out to express myself in a book, I can fail. No doubt when I express myself at these meetings or even in therapy sessions, I fail to an extent too. Total Consciousness is beyond verbal formulas. And I too have faults, perhaps I haven't achieved complete Total Consciousness yet myself. But Harvey Brustein is not what counts—"

Hog-grunts and whines of denial. Old Humble Harv! He had managed to turn humility into the highest form of arrogance—Old Humble Harv, simple human prophet of the Total Truth.

"No!" Harvey said. "I'm *not* what's important—the *Foundation* is what counts. And the Foundation is all of us, not just me. We're all imperfect, but the Foundation is our means for striving for the perfection of Total Consciousness. The whole is greater than the sum of its parts. That's what I was trying to say in my book. We must *all* merge our neurotic selves into the total community of the Foundation. As individuals, we can never be Totally Conscious—and that includes me, I need the Foundation as much as any of you. I've always insisted that I *wasn't* a therapist and you *weren't* my patients. We're all equal *members* of the Foundation. We must put ourselves behind us. I'm an individual; don't expect me to be perfect, you're sure to be disappointed. But through the Foundation, we can all taste perfection. The deaths of our egos is not an end but a beginning—the beginning of a community consciousness greater and purer than our own!"

"We came here to vote on going to San Francisco," Ted said. He turned his hot blue eyes on the crowd, challenged them with his size and his stance and his blind commitment. "I say let's do what we came here to do! I say let's vote *now!*"

"Yeah!"

"Yeah!"

"Vote!"

"Come on, vote!"

Harvey held up his hand for silence: it descended like a curtain. "All right," he said. "And before we vote, I want to thank you, all of you . . . "

As he said it, he stared across the room, and our eyes met. The thing in his eyes was neither hate nor triumph. It was as if Harvey was acknowledging a level of reality that only the two of us shared. On that level, he was my devil and I his. He had won and I had lost. But because we had fought on a plane above the reality of those we had fought over, there was a strange communion between us. We hated each other, each knew the other was mad, but in a strange curious way Harvey and I seemed to share the feeling that we were the only two real people in the room. The others were already shadows who had sold pieces of their souls. And how could the Smoker of Souls feel equality with his Dope?

"All in favor of moving the Foundation to San Francisco . . . ?"

A forest of hands.

"Against?"

Only a pitiful few.

And Arlene's was not among them.

■ ■ ■ ■ ■ ■ ■ ■ ■ ■ ■

The stairwell was warm and empty; down at the bottom was a door that led out into the cold. I stood alone on the landing at the top of the stairs. Behind me was light and warmth and the sounds of excited planning. I felt empty and drained and defeated. And alone.

I took one step down the stairs—

"Tom!"

I stopped, turned, saw Arlene framed in the doorway. I went back to her.

"You've changed your mind?"

Behind the armor of her glasses, her eyes were misty, forlorn, somehow terrified. But her jaw was a tight line of resolution.

"No," she said. "I was hoping you would . . . It's not too late . . . Harvey would understand . . . He's beyond vindictiveness . . . "

"He's beyond *anything* human," I said bitterly. Then, more savagely: "What the fuck's the matter with you, girl? You're not stupid! You're not crazy! You know what he is. How can you still go through with it?"

"I know what I am too," she said wanly. "Yes, I know what Harvey is . . . but I also know what I need him to be. What we all need him to be. And he's willing to try being that. Don't you need something greater than yourself to believe in?"

"Maybe I do . . . sure I do! But I'll be damned if I build me an idol out of shit and worship it for lack of anything better. And so will you, baby, so will you . . . "

"Maybe you're right," she whispered. "But I don't have any choice . . . "

I reached into my pocket and fished out my apartment key. I held it front of her face silently, like a priest thrusting his crucifix at a vampire.

And like a vampire confronted with that image of its own unfaceable, Arlene gasped, sobbed, began to cry, hid her face in her hands, and fled back into her cave.

I didn't follow her.

Instead, I descended the stairs, opened the door, and stopped outside. As I closed the door behind me, bitter cold hit me like a solid wall of chill—a chill that went through my coat, my clothes, my flesh, a chill in the center of my being, the marrow of my bones.

It had started to snow lightly. Though in a matter of hours the snow would be transmuted by New York's fetid alchemy into a filthy black sludge, at this moment the flakes drifting down were white and clean and cold and pure.

24
Hadj

The midafternoon thaw had turned the snow covering the city into a morass of thick black sludge. Now, as the sun began to go down, the slush was starting to freeze into a turgid gray jelly; in a few hours it would be a treacherous sheen of gun-metal colored ice. I remembered the clean white snow that had fallen nearly a month ago, on the night I had put the Foundation behind me forever. Even then, I had known it would come to this—the clean white promise of new-falling snow always fated to become gray sludge, frozen into deadly city-ice, thawed, refrozen, thawed again, like a junkie's dreams; and spring a lifetime away.

I stood shivering in my coat outside Ted and Doris' place—or the gray-brown tenement that *had been* Ted and Doris' place—watching Ted load the last of their stuff into the old VW bus he had bought for the trek to San Francisco, waiting to say goodbye.

Ted stuffed one last cardboard box into the bus, closed the big side door. Arlene and Doris, huddled in the building's doorway against the cold, stepped out onto the sludgy sidewalk and stood by Ted at the front door to the bus.

The three of them stared awkwardly at me; I stared at them. They were already ghosts out of my past; I was certain I would never see any of them again. Our world-lines were diverging forever. And I knew they were thinking the same thoughts about me. I knew they knew and they knew I knew.

A long, terribly long, moment of silence.

"I . . . I wish you were coming along," Ted finally said, his breath a plume of cold smoke from the heat-death of a universe.

"And I wish you were staying," I said.

"I wish I *could* stay . . . " Arlene said.

"You—" I started to give her the same old argument I had given her the half-dozen times I had seen her since the Foundation vote. I gave up before I had started. It was all so pointless, so fucking pointless.

"Well . . . goodbye . . . " I said. "And . . . good luck. I hope . . . I hope you all wake up someday . . . "

"Don't make it sound like a funeral," Doris said, trying to force a ghost of the old Earth-mother smile and not making it.

I tried to smile too, but I didn't do any better. From where I stood, it *was* a funeral; they were already dead. All that had made them human had been devoured by a Thing. Corpses. Zombies. Shadows. Perhaps they were thinking the same thing about me.

Maybe they were right.

Worst of all, maybe we were all right.

"Well . . . "

"Well . . . "

There was everything to say and no way to say it. There was nothing to say and a million ways to say it.

Ted opened the curb-side front door of the bus. Arlene climbed aboard, Doris after her. Ted walked around to the street-side of the bus, got in.

The motor whirred, coughed twice, and caught. Ted edged the bus away from the curb. He waved. Doris waved.

And then the bus pulled away from the curb and started off down the street, down the long street into the west. As the bus drove down the street and began to dwindle in the distance, I saw Arlene's face staring back at me. She was too far away for me to guess at her expression; she was like a little lost doll.

Then the bus turned the corner and they were gone from sight forever.

And I was left behind. I was free. I grovelled at the feet of nothing greater than myself. I was free. I was alone.

Was it worth it?

As I stood there with the city's filthy sludge freezing to obscene ice around me while Ted and Doris and Arlene drove off into the Foundation sunset, I felt as if everything I had ever been had been reduced to a single pinpoint of me-ness, the essence of Tom Hollander and nothing more, no past, no future, no excess baggage, no illusions. There was me and there was the universe. That was all. I owned nothing and nothing owned me.

It was cold solace.

But as I stood there feeling sorry for myself, I saw myself feeling sorry for myself, and it pissed me off. Asshole that you are to think you get something like freedom without paying dues!

Yeah, maybe I had something after all: I was free. Free to take the real trip, the real leap, without a parachute, the leap from the prison of the past into the unknown future--the real way, maybe the only

way to break on through to the other side. You gotta die to be born
again . . . ?

Well, maybe the old Tom Hollander *had* died and the new Tom
Hollander still waited in the womb of time to be born.

And quite suddenly, but with no surprise at the revelation, I knew
what I had to do.

All I had to do was make the Big Leap. And now there was no rationalization to hold me back.

Nothing at all . . .

■ ■ ■ ■ ■ ■ ■ ■ ■ ■ ■

Walking down the futuristic white-walled corridor—crowded
with pink-scrubbed cats in suits, expensive chicks in expensive
clothes, college students from Harvard and Vassar, Army officers,
who knows, rock stars, politicians, star surgeons, nuclear physicists,
novelists, minor movie stars, spies, diplomats—I felt myself melting
into the airport scene and really grooving behind it.

I felt almost stoned—Kennedy Airport was like another reality, or
maybe a kind of anteroom between realities, a place where all the
world-lines converged and then spread out again.

I had never flown before, but now, as I entered the huge, high-
ceilinged embarkation room and saw the 707 waiting outside the
glass wall of the terminal to whisk me off to LA, dug the people waiting to board the plane—Alabama hicks, Hollywood directors, senators, sausage salesmen, whores, Californians on the way home, emi-
grants, con-men, important dope-pushers—I understood why all
airports have futuristic architecture.

Because for me (and for how may of the others?) Kennedy was the
nexus-point between the known present and the unknown future,
was therefore part of the future already. The unknown future . . . Unknown?

Yeah, unknown. I mean, I knew I was on my way to Los Angeles
to take the slush-pile job at *Slick,* but that was just a reason to get on a
plane in New York and get off in Los Angeles instead of San Francisco or Timbuktu. As a matter of fact, for all the reality LA had for me,
it might as well be Timbuktu. And Timbuktu might as well be LA.
They were both nothing more than cities of the mind and I knew
dead-certain that LA would be a reality as different from New York
and everything I had ever known as Timbuktu or the dark side of the

moon. On the way to the airport, I had picked up the *Times* and seen that yesterday's high temperature in New York had been 30°. Yesterday's *low* in LA had been 52°. High had been 73°. 73° in December! Palm trees! Hollywood! Sunset Strip! Movie stars!

I checked in at the ticket desk, got a seat number written on my ticket, went and looked out the huge window at my 707. From this close, it seemed much smaller than I had imagined it, and the aluminum skin was dull and gray and grainy, as ordinary as a subway car. Somehow only now, looking at the weathered old plane, did the whole thing become really real.

But tell me it wasn't all a magic carpet ride! Within five hours, I'd be somewhere where the sun was shining and the temperature was forty degrees warmer, palm trees, movie studios, and yours truly met at the airport by a flunky (no doubt a very low-level flunky) from *Slick,* and off to play a new game which could end up with me as editor of a crotch-mag, and after that, who knows, there are lots of other airports around . . .

Yeah, airports *had* to have futuristic architecture. The future passes through them every minute of every day.

■ ■ ■ ■ ■ ■ ■ ■ ■ ■ ■

The tourist-class section of the plane was jammed. Three seats to each side of the aisle and a lot smaller inside than those TV commercials would have you believe. Not much different from being on a bus. I had lucked into a window seat. Beside me was some old bat who looked like an Iowa farmwife and beside her a cat who looked like an aging brassiere salesman. I had no urge to say one word to either of them. Yeah, a lot like a bus, or the subway.

Even the endless hurry-up-and-wait. Ticket desk. Wait. Board the plane. Wait. Plastic blond stewardess does her seat-belts and oxygen number. Wait. Ramp pulls back into the terminal like a hard-on wilting. Wait. Feeling of excitement as the plane as last starts to move. Building and building as the plane taxis further and further. Then stops. And I look out the little scratchy window and see that there are five other jets ahead of us, like a line waiting to take off. So we wait. Whoosh! The lead jet suddenly roars down the runway from a dead stop and I get a thrill and a chill as it belches gray smoke and bolts into the air. We move up a slot. And wait. Another plane takes off. Another short taxi. Wait . . .

I feel almost as if I'm watching a stripper do her thing. As each plane ahead of us takes off and we move one step closer to the Big Moment, the tension building in me is almost sexual, almost like waiting for acid to hit, like holding a spike above your vein, like sticking it in and feeling that little pain, and your finger on the plunger anticipating the Surge . . .

And then finally, FINALLY, we're on the line. The engines rev up to a tremendous roar and the whole plane is vibrating and I feel as if I'm inside some huge beast chomping at the bit, as if the power of the universe is being held back by a halter . . .

Then suddenly, the plane is moving, moving, faster and faster, a huge metal beast charging down the runway, faster and faster, the world flashing by, faster and faster and faster—

And then—the Big Surge! Something groovy seems to kick me in the base of the spine, like smack suddenly hitting, like an orgasm, like breaking on through to the other side, and like a great bird the plane leaps into the air like a thing alive, and there's nothing to see but the wild blue yonder, the pure blue blankness of the sky unfolding.

THE END